Faith

JUL 1 9

Faith

Michelle Larks

Urban Books, LLC
78 East Industry Court
Deer Park, NY 11729

Faith ©copyright 2010 Michelle Larks

ISBN 13: 978-1-60162-878-7
ISBN 10: 1-60162-878-1

First Printing May 2010
Printed in the United States of America

10 9 8 7 6 5 4 3 2 1

This is a work of fiction. Any references or similarities to actual events, real people, living, or dead, or to real locales are intended to give the novel a sense of reality. Any similarity in other names, characters, places, and incidents is entirely coincidental.

Distributed by Kensington Corp.
Submit Wholesale Orders to:
Kensington Publishing Corp.
C/O Penguin Group (USA) Inc.
Attention: Order Processing
405 Murray Hill Parkway
East Rutherford, NJ 07073-2316
Phone: 1-800-526-0275
Fax: 1-800-227-9604

Dedication

This book is dedicated to
Every man, woman, or child who
has been a victim of a sexual assault

Acknowledgments

As always, Praises Be To God. I firmly believe the scripture that says, "*In all ways acknowledge him and he will direct thy path.*" Father, thank you for showing me the way.

I would like to say to my mothers. Mary, Jean, Bertha, my father, I.H., and my father-in-law, George, thank you for encouraging and loving me.

My daughters, Mikeisha and Genesse, I love you more than you'll ever know.

Sisters: Patrice, Sabrina, Adrienne, Donna, Catherine, and Rolanda, and brothers: Jackie, Marc, Darryl, Wayne, Michael, and Rodney; my sisters and brothers-in-law, along with my nieces and nephews, thank you for keeping me grounded. I love you, family!

Patrice; my sister, thank you for stepping in as my VP of Marketing. Your help is invaluable. Kelley thanks for your help with my innumerable emails.

Raw Sistaz Book Club, APOOO Book Club (Yasmin), ARC Book Club (Locksie), OOSA Book Club, Delta Reviewer (Monique), Apex Reviews (Genevieve), Urban Reviews (Radiah), Shades of Romance Magazine (LaShaunda), Words of Inspiration Book Club (Sharon), The Literary World (Lauretta). Eve-

Acknowledgments

line, Nikki, Keisha, Angie, Rolanda, and Tavares for reading and reviewing for me before my books hit the shelves. I greatly appreciate your feedback.

Brooks, thank you for hooking up my newsletter. I love it, and so do my subscribers. And Tyora, thank you for setting up my blog tour and for your many emails full of pertinent information.

Shquestra, I'd like to send special thanks your way for sharing with me. Your information was very useful.

A special shout-out to all of the book clubs who have read and posted reviews for me, especially The Renaissance Men's Book Club of Memphis, TN. I had an enjoyable telephone meeting with your club. Oops, I can't forget the Women Of Excellence Book Club of Joliet, IL. You really know how to hook a sista up when it comes to a meal. I'd like to thank the many bookstores who have invited me multiple times to sign at your stores. I'd like to give a shout-out to my MySpace friends. You are the best. You leave such wonderful comments on my page, which uplifts my spirit.

Kudos to Constance Shabazz of Books Ink, and Glenn Murray of 220 Communications. It seems like you've provided me with an opportunity to promote my books every step of the way, starting with my first one.

Tee, Joylynn, and Kathleen, you all are the best! I thank God for allowing our paths to cross. It was fate.

My sista/girlfriends; Kelley, Cynthia D., Amania, Mina, and Fran Y., thank you for always calling or e-mailing me with encouragement, especially when I need it. Pat, a friend from the past, I'm glad we've reconnected.

Acknowledgments

To the libraries in and around the Chicago land area and afar, thank you for inviting me to participate in your Author Fairs.

My co-workers, neighbors, and friends, especially in the Bolingbrook area, thank you for supporting a sister, book-by-book.

I'd like to thank every reader who has purchased any of my books over the years. I don't know where I'd be without you. If I've forgotten anyone, please forgive me.

Fred, what can I say except we make an excellent team! Please continue to love and support me.

Michelle

Prologue

Monet Caldwell inhaled loudly, held her breath, exhaled, then drew a deep cleansing breath. She smiled as she remembered her Lamaze exercises, and felt she was doing fine, even without her coach. Then her pretty smile faded abruptly because her situation at home, merely co-existing with her husband, Marcus, was not what she envisioned as a new bride twenty years ago when she imagined giving birth to their first child.

The gorgeous, petite, five feet two, formerly size five, olive skin woman, with a mop of reddish blond curly hair, was upstairs in her bedroom sitting on the chaise lounge timing her contractions, while her dog, Mitzi, stood loyally at her feet. The only sound in the room was the ticking of a clock sitting on an oval table next to the chaise.

Monet's overnight suitcase sat upright next to the closet door. As she waited for the next contraction, her eyes roamed around the burgundy and gold striped bedroom. Matching borders were at the top of the walls inside the attached bathroom. Monet missed Marcus so much that her eyes became flooded with tears. She knew if she called him, he would come to her aid. But their marriage had been in a state of flux during her entire pregnancy, and somewhere deep within her soul, Monet wanted Marcus to come to her of his own volition.

A contraction poked Monet so hard that she moaned. She put one hand around her abdomen and massaged her temple with the other one. Mitzi stood at attention, her tongue waging as she cocked her head to the side, watching her mistress.

Monet picked up her mother's Bible, which was lying next to her on the chaise. She pressed the book next to her heart and prayed silently. *You told us that life wouldn't be easy, Lord, but I never imagined anything like this happening in my life.* She sighed. "Lord, keep me and my baby in your kind, loving arms. I know through your grace that we will both be fine. And when my labor of love has passed, I'll shout out your glory for bringing me through another valley along my journey of life. Because only you and Marcus know how long and hard I've prayed for a baby," she said aloud.

The contraction passed, and Monet couldn't keep a tiny grin off her face at the thought of her burly, chocolate colored bear of a husband. At six feet in height, his closely shorn hair was graying distinguishably at the temples. Much to Monet's delight, her handsome husband's face still took her breath away. Marcus was employed as a police detective. Where he'd begun serving as a member of Chicago's finest shortly after the couple migrated to Chicago from a small town in Alabama over twenty years ago as newlyweds.

Forty-two-year-old Monet had two brothers, and forty-five-year-old Marcus had an older sister who lived in Texas. His parents were deceased. Monet's mother died instantly in a freak bus accident. The driver lost control of the vehicle and plowed into pedestrians crossing the street in the crosswalk. The accident occurred five years ago. After her mother's death, Monet's unmarried twin brothers, Derek and Duane, three years her junior, moved to Chicago, from Alabama to be closer to their sibling. Monet's father had deserted the family when she was four years old. She had only fuzzy memories of the man she called Daddy.

Monet and Marcus met in middle school and became high school sweethearts. After Monet's graduation, she attended a small private college in Alabama and obtained a nursing degree. Her specialty was that of a neonatal nurse. The staff often said

she had the *touch*. The Neonatal Care Unit boasted a high sur-
vival rate for its newborns. Many a night, if a parent wasn't at the
hospital to see their child, Monet could be found providing the
infant with a dose of TLC.

After graduating high school, Marcus joined the army where
he served as a military police officer. His stint in the army ended
when Monet graduated from college.

Monet glanced at the clock on the nightstand; her contractions were close to twenty minutes apart. Her obstetrician, Dr.
Armstrong, had instructed her to come to the hospital when
the contractions were ten to fifteen minutes apart. For the most
part, Monet had enjoyed an uneventful pregnancy, even though
she had been categorized as a high risk patient due to her age.

Mitzi barked sharply as Monet stood up, waddled over and
picked up her overnight bag. She clutched the suitcase in her
hand and dropped her cell phone into the pocket of her maternity jeans. She clutched the banister tightly as she walked slowly
down the stairs. Mitzi trotted beside her.

Then a contraction hit her so hard that she felt like someone had punched her in the back. She momentarily let go of the
banister, dropped the suitcase, and fell forward. Like a ballerina,
she managed to turn sideways. She tried to regain her balance
as she slid down four stairs. Mitzi began barking loudly. Monet
moaned as her water broke. She managed to pull her cell phone
out of her pocket and dial 911.

Monet mumbled, "I need help. I'm in labor, and I fell down
the stairs. Please send someone to help me." Then she passed
out.

Chapter 1

Monet looked up and across the counter of the nurse's station desk as the sound of cracking bubblegum assaulted her eardrums.

"Ma'am, where is the maternity ward?" A stout, middle-aged woman with short twisties in her head stood on the other side of the desk. She held a potted fern in one hand and several pink and purple balloons proclaiming, *It's a Girl* in her other one.

"Down the hall," Monet pointed the way with her ink pen, "and around the corner."

The woman shyly said, "Thank you." She walked down the hallway per Monet's directions.

Monet continued to make notations in the folders when the telephone rang. "St. Bernard's Hospital, this is Nurse Cald-well. How may I direct your call?" she answered.

"Hi, Nay-Nay." Nay-Nay was Marcus's pet name for his wife. "I know you're tired after pulling that double today. I wanted to know if you want me to pick you up from work?"

They lived in the community of Auburn on the southwest side of Chicago on the 3800 block of West Eighty-fifthStreet. Monet and Marcus worked in the community of Englewood, one of the most economically challenged areas on the south side of Chicago. When the pair moved from Alabama to the Windy City, they were young and idealistic and decided to work in communities where they could make the biggest impact in the lives of African Americans.

Marcus worked at the Seventh District Police Station on Sixty-third Street, and the hospital was located on Sixty-fourth Street, so they worked less than five miles apart from each other.

"No, that's okay, honey; I'm good. I'm just about done here. This place has been like Union Station during Christmas travel all night," Monet joked, as she laid the folder in the to-be-filed pile.

"Hmm, that bad? I guess you're tired then. By the time you leave the hospital, it will be close to midnight. I can swing by and pick you up; that's no problem. You don't need to drive if you're that tired. We can come back to the hospital tomorrow to get your car," Marcus offered.

"Well, I am tired, but I can make it home," Monet replied. A smile crossed her face as she thought about her and Marcus's tryst between the sheets earlier that morning. Monet looked down at her stomach and thought, *maybe God has blessed us, and we made a baby this morning.*

"Okay, don't say I didn't offer to come get you. I'll call you later. Love you, babe. Be careful," he said.

"I love you too, Marcus. I promise I'll be careful. You take care of yourself," she responded before ending the call.

After she had finished adding notation to the files, Monet stood up, stretched her body, and rubbed the lower portion of her back. As she smoothed down the top of her now wrinkled green scrubs that she'd worn to work that morning, Monet prayed that she had gotten pregnant and envisioned smoothing the top over a baby bump. She sat back down in the ergonomic chair and was putting the remaining folders in the tray to-be-filed when Dr. Edwards walked over to the desk.

"I realize that it's time for you to get off work, Nurse Caldwell, but I have an emergency." He glanced down at his still beeping pager. "Would you make sure this prescription gets filled for the patient in room 110?" Without waiting for Monet to reply, Dr.

Edwards handed her a thick manila folder. "The prescription's inside the folder on top."

"Sure, Dr. Edwards." Monet stifled a yawn as she took the folder from him and laid it on the counter. She had just pulled a double, working the first and second shifts, and was tired. She knew that traffic would be lighter than normal at that time of the night on the Dan Ryan Expressway, and barring any accidents, she should be home in twenty minutes.

Monet asked a nurse's aide to take the prescription to the pharmacy ASAP and to wait for it to be filled. After the young man departed, she removed her black leather purse from her bottom desk drawer and walked to the locker area. Several minutes later, she had put on her hooded spring jacket, locked her locker, and was headed home.

No matter how busy her day was, or how tired she felt, Monet always stopped by the neonatal ICU to look at the babies and would say a prayer for the newborns before leaving the hospital. Since she and Marcus had been unable to have children, she considered the babies in the nursery her own.

A smile slid across her face as she watched the different shades of babies. Some of the tiny faces were screwed up and crying, while others slept peacefully. Monet's tiredness was forgotten.

She bowed her head, closed her eyes, and said softly, "Lord, thank you for helping me to complete another day of work at St. Bernard's Hospital. Thank you for keeping me in my right mind as I cared for your children. Father, I beg you to take care of the innocent babies here in this hospital today, and all over the world in every hospital right now. Help their parents to do the best they can to love and take care of your precious children. God above, if it's in your will, please bless Marcus and me with children. These blessings I ask in your Son's name. Amen." Monet smiled at the babies and turned to walk to the elevator, which delivered her down to the first floor.

The temperature was mild for the fall season in Chicago in October. Halloween was next week, and paper ghosts, goblins, and witches adorned the pediatric ward and other areas of the hospital.

When Monet reached the hospital entrance, David, the security guard, was seated at his post at the main entrance. He asked Monet if she wanted him to walk her to her car since it was close to midnight.

"No." Monet shook her head. "I should be all right."

"Well, I'll see you tomorrow, Mrs. Caldwell. Be careful." He doffed his navy blue and white striped brimmed hat at her.

"I'm off work tomorrow; I'll see you on Monday," Monet corrected David. "Have a nice weekend."

She walked out the door and traveled half a block to the corner and turned left toward the parking lot. She was filled with a buoyancy of hopefulness. Monet had taken her temperature that morning and discovered that she was ovulating. She and Marcus had made tender love before she'd left for work that morning. Memories of the couple's coming together caused merriment to tug at the corners of her mouth.

When Monet entered the parking lot, she noticed the area was somewhat dim around her car due to the nonfunctioning overhead light. She frowned at the security camera which didn't appear to be functioning either. She hesitated, debating if she should go back to the hospital and take Dave up on his invitation to escort her to her car. *Stop being silly*, she chided herself. *You've walked in this lot millions of times.* She then decided to chance it since her car was no more than a few feet away. Her hand shook slightly as she removed her key remote from her parka pocket.

Suddenly the hairs on the back of Monet's neck stood at attention. She sensed someone behind her. But before she could react, she was pushed from behind. She fell hard, and became sprawled face down on the ground, weight pinning down her body. Monet was frozen, as a cloud of foul breath invaded the back of her head.

Terror filled her soul. "Please let me go," she moaned. "You can have my purse."

A sinister chuckle followed her pronouncement. Then a male voice growled, "Did I say I wanted your money? Now shut up!"

Monet felt her body being dragged into a clump of tall bushes outside the parking lot area. *Please, Lord, don't forsake me*, she prayed. She tried to grab hold of the gold cross that always hung around her neck, but her shaking fingers couldn't grasp the chain.

Her attacker flipped her over like they were gymnasts performing in a tournament, and pinned her arms behind her back. Monet groaned and squeezed her eyes shut. She had no desire to see his face.

Her lips moved as she began silently reciting the Twenty-Third Psalm. *The Lord is my shepherd; I shall not want. He maketh me to lie down in green pastures; He leadeth me beside the still waters. He restoreth my soul; He leadeth me in the path of righteous for His namesake. Yea, though I walk through the valley of death, I will fear no evil; for thou art with me; they rod and staff they comfort me. Thou preparest a table before me in the presence of my enemies; thou anointest my head with oil; my cup runneth over. Surely goodness and mercy shall follow me all the days of my life; and I will dwell in the house of the Lord forever.*

She could feel the material from her scrub pants scrapping across her skin like sandpaper, as her attacker tore the garment from her body. After he had his way with her, his fist smashed into the side of Monet's head, rendering her unconscious. Then the deranged man hit her in the face over and over again.

Chapter 2

Marcus was sitting at his desk in the police station, going over his notes for tonight's assignment. He paused and laid the pen on the desk. He hated doing what he considered a housekeeping chore . . . adding notes to a couple of his other case files. He worked in the Bureau of Investigative Services Division. He had about one hour or so before he and the squad would leave the station for a surveillance assignment.

He glanced at the clock. It was nearly one o'clock in the morning, and Marcus assumed Monet was home by now. He picked up the telephone to call her, and then put it back inside the cradle. He knew his wife had to be tired. She had been putting in a lot of overtime hours since last month, due to one of the nurses retiring. The Human Resources Department of the hospital wasn't having much luck finding a replacement.

Marcus ran his hand over his head, rubbed his eyes, and resumed writing. He would rather be on the streets protecting the citizens of Chicago.

He weighed two hundred thirty pounds, and his body was all muscle, like cut marble. His tall height, along with an inch long scar on his left cheek, remnant of a burglary call gone awry, put fear in most lawbreakers when they came face-to-face with Detective Caldwell. Being a police officer for over twenty years, he'd seen the *good, bad and ugly* in people. His demeanor was one of seriousness, except when he was around Monet. Then he let his guard down. He loved God first, and then his wife more than life itself.

Bruce, one of Marcus's fellow officers strolled over to his desk and asked him, "Hey, man, did you hear there was some trouble at St. Bernard's Hospital awhile ago? The call came in about half an hour ago. One of the nurses was hurt. Isn't that where your wife works?"

Marcus's breathing became labored. He felt as though he was experiencing an anxiety attack. "Uh, yeah, that's where Monet works. But she got off over an hour ago, so I'm sure she's okay." He tried to ignore the SOS signs that somersaulted across his mind.

Bruce held up his hands. "I was just checking to see if you'd heard the news. We have a preparation meeting in fifteen minutes. I'll see you there."

"Yeah, I'll see you later." Marcus was disturbed by the news Bruce had given him. He picked up the telephone and called his house. The phone rang and rang until the answering machine came on. "Nay-Nay, if you're there, pick up." He waited for his wife to pick up. He glanced at his watch, noting that it was almost time for him to go into the meeting. He hung up and dialed his wife's cell phone number. The call was connected, and he could hear breathing on the line. "Nay-Nay, are you there?" he asked as his hands began trembling uncontrollably.

A threatening snicker greeted Marcus's ear. He held the phone away from his ear, and then put it back. "Who is this? Where is my wife?" he asked frantically, rising from the chair so abruptly it nearly toppled over.

The man on the telephone laughed aloud, and then disconnected the call.

Marcus sprinted rapidly out of the room to the area that logged incoming calls. He looked almost unbalanced as he shouted at the clerk, "Louise, did you receive a call from St. Bernard Hospital?"

Louise looked at Marcus and was so taken aback by his expression that her mouth drooped fearfully. She barely recognized him; he had a scowl on his face and held his body rigidly. "Yeah, a call came in," she looked down and typed on her PC, "about forty-five minutes ago. Why? How come you got a bee in your bonnet?"

"What else did the hospital say, Louise? My wife works there, and I can't reach her." Marcus made an effort not to yell at the older woman. The vein in his head throbbed uncontrollably.

Louise's heart palpitated rapidly. "Oh Lord. They said a woman was assaulted. Smitty went over to investigate the call and take a report. I'm sorry, Marc. I hope your wife is okay. Maybe she got tied up in traffic or something." Her voice trailed off sympathetically.

"Did the hospital say anything about the woman's condition? Was she conscious when they brought her in?" Marcus asked fearfully. He felt lightheaded, like he was hyperventilating. He tried to take a couple of deep breaths.

"No, they didn't say. I'm sorry, I didn't ask." Louise prayed silently, *Lord, please don't let the victim be Monet Caldwell. I think Marcus would go crazy.*

"Okay, Lou, I'm going over to St. Bernard's Hospital to see what's up." Marcus rushed back to his desk, picked up his briefcase from the floor, and locked his desk.

The chief of police stood in front of Marcus's desk. "Where are you going?" Chief Walter Davis asked with a concerned look on his face.

"I don't have time to explain everything now, but I need to get over to St. Bernard's Hospital. I think the woman who was assaulted was Monet." Marcus's deep bass voice trembled.

"What makes you think the woman is Monet?" Walter asked.

"Because I called her cell phone and a man answered. I can't stop and talk right now, sir." Marcus snapped shut the two locks on his briefcase. The sound was abrupt, and the noise caused

Marcus to flinch. He began walking rapidly, almost running toward the door. "I'll call you later and fill you in."

"Okay, Marc, be careful. I hope things work out for the best for you and Monet," Walter said.

"Thank you." A grimace marred Marcus's face. He exhaled loudly, "I hope so too."

He practically ran down the hallway, his stride was so brisk. He heard his partner, Wade, call his name and turned to look down the hallway.

Wade jogged over to him. "The chief thought I should come with you just in case the victim is Monet," he said.

"Let's go then," Marcus replied, and the men battled the wind as they walked to the parking lot. They got inside an older model brown Crown Victoria and sped away.

During the short drive to the hospital, Marcus's heart shied away from the possibility that Monet could be the victim at St. Bernard's. But his logical, orderly mind knew the woman in the hospital was probably Monet.

Wade was fifty years old, five years Marcus's senior. He was an inch taller than his wife, Liz, and his cinnamon colored face projected a kindly demeanor. He was medium in build and put God first in his life, followed by Liz, his children, family and friends. Wade could be depended on to be level headed in a crisis, which is why he drove himself and Marcus to the hospital. He kept glancing worriedly at his partner.

"You okay, man?" he asked.

"I don't know. I can't imagine anything happening to Monet. She's my life, man," Marcus replied.

"I know what you mean. Shoot, I feel the same way about Liz and my kids. The kids drive me crazy sometimes, but I'd still lay down my life for them. But you know, man, if the victim is Monet, you two will get through this situation. You know the Lord doesn't put more on us than we can bear."

Marcus shook his head from side to side sadly. "In my head, I know you're right. But why would a loving God allow this to happen to Monet? You know my baby; she wouldn't hurt a fly. She'd try to shoo one out the door or window before she'd kill it. I don't know if I can take it if Monet is hurt badly."

"You'll be okay, Marc. Just trust in God. Plus, we don't know that Monet was hurt yet, so we could be jumping the gun." Wade tried to calm his partner.

"Wade, I called Nay-Nay's cell phone," Marcus looked troubled, and his voice dropped, "and a man answered. He actually laughed and hung up. If I had any hopes about Monet not being the victim, they were thwarted when I heard that voice. Man, that voice is in my head. It's like he's laughing and pleased about what he did."

"Don't let him get to you, Marc. You know how those types are. The good thing is the cell phone has a GPS system, so maybe we can get a handle on him. Let's just hope he keeps her cell phone a little longer." Secretly Wade agreed with Marcus's assessment of the situation, but thought he needed to encourage his friend for what lay ahead when they arrived at the hospital.

"If he hurt Monet, then I want to hurt him back," Marcus confessed as he peered out the window. "I want him to suffer like she's suffering."

"Naw, man, you can't do that. Vengeance is mine, said the Lord. Let God and the courts take care of this matter, and everything will work out. You'll need your strength to take care of Monet if she's hurt. As soon as we get to the hospital, I'm going to go see Smitty and tell him about Monet's cell phone; it could be a promising lead. Don't be foolish, Marc; let the people best equipped for these situations do what they have to do," Wade said.

When they arrived at the hospital, Wade pulled the car in front of the emergency room entrance and said to Marcus, "I know you're eager to see what's going on, but before we go in, I want to say a quick prayer."

"Go ahead, make it quick," Marcus replied tight lipped.

Wade turned off the car and bowed his head. "Father, we come to you, asking that you take care of Monet and Marcus. If Monet is hurt, Lord, heal her body like I know you can. Give Marcus wisdom to do the right thing, and leave the legalities to the proper authorities. We know that your way isn't easy at times, but we can take comfort in knowing that you promised never to leave us. And I know that you won't. I ask this blessing in Jesus' name. Amen."

He glanced over at Marcus, who sat in the car brushing tears away from his eyes. "Aw, come on, Marc, everything's going to be all right. We've been with each other through some tough times, and if Monet is hurt, then no doubt it's going to be one of the toughest experiences you've ever faced. But I got your back, and you know Liz is with me. We'll help both of you get through this; I promise," Wade said sincerely.

Marcus tried to stifle a sob. "I don't know if I can take it if something has happened to Monet. You and I know what women who've been assaulted look like and the mental anguish they go through afterward. It's one thing when it happens to a stranger, but another thing when it's your wife." He dropped his head in his hands, and his shoulders shook as he cried.

Wade just sat in the car and waited for his friend and partner to compose himself. He couldn't argue with Marcus. If Liz were in the hospital bloody and bruised, he didn't know how he would react. But he hoped that Marcus would turn his burden over to God. After all, He was the only one who could sustain them during this crisis.

A few minutes elapsed then Marcus wiped his eyes and put his stoic, police business expression back on his face. He turned to Wade and said, "I'm ready, and I hope, like you said, God will see us through this."

The two men got out of the car and walked to the entrance of the hospital, uncertain as to what they might find inside. When they walked into the building, Smitty was waiting for them at the front security desk with a grim look on his face.Marcus knew then that Monet had been assaulted.

Smitty told Marcus the words he'd never hoped to hear, "Marc, I'm sorry. The victim is Monet. Why don't you go up to see about her while I talk to Wade about what we know and what we've done so far?"

Marcus nodded. He felt desolate and so alone. Just knowing that Monet was hurt made him feel like a vital part of his body was missing.

"Do you want me to come up with you?" Wade asked Marcus.

"No, we all know how important it is to process all the information while it's still fresh in everyone's minds. I'll go see Nay-Nay and come back and talk to you later. I take it you're the lead detective on the case, Smitty?" Marcus said.

"Yes, that's correct. I promise to do whatever I can to find out who's responsible for hurting your wife, and bring the perp to justice," Smitty said.

Marcus nodded, thinking, *If you don't find him, you better believe that I will.* "I'll be back later," he said to Smitty. He turned and walked to the nurse's station in the emergency room. *Lord, let her be okay, and I will make it all right myself. Take care of my wife,* he prayed.

Chapter 3

Monet coughed and opened a swollen, blackened eye. Then she opened her other eye and looked around at the unfamiliar surroundings. Suddenly her memory kicked in about what had happened, and she screamed through puffy lips as she tried to sit upright in the bed. Marcus burst into the room from the hallway and ran to her side. He attempted to take his bruised and battered wife into his arms, but she cowered and pushed Marcus away from her body with failing arms. Then she collapsed back onto the bed from pain. Marcus stood helplessly, with his arms dangling by his sides. He reached out to touch Monet again, his hand brushing the top of her head.

His voice cracked as he said, "Babe, it's me, Marcus. You've been hurt, and you're in the hospital. They're going to take care of you."

Monet looked over at Marcus with deadened eyes. She tried to moisten her cracked lips, but cringed from the pain. She raised a hand and felt her lips. "My God, what happened to me?" Her eyes traveled over her body.

Monet's primary care physician, Dr. Washington, who worked at St. Bernard, walked in the room, and Jean, a nurse, followed her. The women went over to the bed. Dr. Washington bent over Monet and said, "I'm glad to see that you've regained consciousness. We know you suffered a mild concussion. The good news is that you came to on your own."

Monet looked at the doctor blankly, like she didn't have a

clue as to what she was talking about. Then she turned over in the bed and faced the wall.

Dr. Washington, a tall, regal looking African American woman said to Marcus, "Can I talk to you outside for a minute?" Marcus glanced over at Monet and nodded. The nurse checked Monet while Marcus and the doctor left the room and stood in the hallway. "I know how distressful this must be to you, Mr. Caldwell. Trust me when I say we'll do our best to help Monet. She's one of our own," Dr. Washington stated.

"I know she was beaten, that's obvious. Please tell me that my wife wasn't violated," Marcus begged. His heart felt like it was breaking. It was one thing to see people injured; that was normal for him in his line of work. But it was excruciating to see the aftermath of a crime perpetrated against a loved one. He wasn't handling the situation well from an emotional standpoint.

His wife had been beaten and God knows what else, and life just seemed to go on as usual. He could hear the buzz from other patients in cubicles waiting to see a doctor. How could God allow life to just go on? Marcus had a hard time dealing with that.

"Mr. Caldwell, I'm sorry, but from our preliminary exam, it appears Monet was sexually assaulted," Dr. Washington said sorrowfully.

"How could that happen?" Marcus's voice rose. "I know the hospital isn't in the best area in the city, but you have security guards and cameras. Did anyone see anything?"

Dr. Washington shook her head. "The security camera in the parking lot was malfunctioning, so we don't have anything on tape. Dave, the security guard, is beside himself with grief. He offered to escort Monet to her car, but she refused."

"My God, can't you guys do anything right? You mean all of this could've been prevented if the security guard had done his job? I have a mind to sue this hospital." Marcus voice rained thunder on the doctor.

"Mr. Caldwell, I am so sorry. Maybe Monet got a good look at the man, and she'll be able to help the police identify him. Everyone loves Monet here at the hospital. She's one of the best nurses in the maternity ward. Believe me, we'll do anything we can to help her." Dr. Washington's hand tugged nervously on the stethoscope hanging around her neck.

"Did you at least run tests for STDs and AIDS?" Marcus asked, as his stomach somersaulted inside his body.

"Yes we did, and we've put a rush on them so we can get the results ASAP. We should have them today by noon," Dr. Washington answered. Her heart went out to Marcus. She could only imagine what he must be feeling.

"Monet looked so banged up. Does she have any internal injuries?" Marcus asked.

Dr. Washington shook her head. "We know that she suffered a concussion. One of her arms was wretched out of the socket, and we had to reset it. Her body is bruised, but most of the assault was to her face, and the swelling should subside as the week goes on."

"Okay, I'm going back to stay with Monet." Marcus turned away from the doctor, His hollowed checks seemed pinched with anguish as he returned to the room.

Dr. Washington walked to the nurses' station. She instructed one of the nurse's aides to stay on the laboratory until Monet's test results were available, and to bring them to her immediately. She shook her head sadly as she peered toward Monet's cubicle.

"Also, call central registration and make sure a room is ready for Monet. We need to move her to a regular room since she's conscious," Dr. Washington said.

"Will do," the nurse stated. "It's a shame what happened to Monet. No one is safe anywhere, even at work."

"Just make the calls," Dr. Washington instructed. She picked up a chart and walked to the next cubicle to handle the next emergency.

***

Marcus sat in the chair next to Monet's bed. He took her hand and she tried to resist, but he kept holding it until she stopped struggling. She turned and looked at Marcus. Her swollen eyes spilled tears.

"Marcus, I'm so sorry," she choked out.

"Babe, you have nothing to be sorry about. What happened isn't your fault," he reassured her gently.

"Dave offered to walk me to my car, and I said no." Monet's voice crumbled with agony.

"You had no way of knowing that a degenerate was lurking outside, just waiting for someone to prey upon." Marcus tried to console his wife.

Monet began sobbing loudly. The sounds were raspy and ugly. Marcus hopped out of the chair and sat on the bed next to her. He pulled her into his arms, and they cried together. After they had released some of the horror they were feeling, the couple looked up to see an orderly walking into the cubicle pushing a wheelchair.

"Hello, Miss Monet," Ramon said. "Dr. Washington told me to come and get you and take you the fifth floor. They have a room waiting for you. Miss Monet, I just want to say I'm so sorry about what happened."

Monet dropped her eyes and nodded her head.

Jean returned to the cubicle. "Ramon, give us a moment before you take Nurse Caldwell upstairs." She held a dressing gown. "Let me help her put this on, and I'll call you when she's ready."

"Okay. Just holler when you're ready," the young man replied, and walked out of the cubicle.

"Can you stand up?" Jean asked Monet.

When Monet stood up, her legs wobbled like Jell-O. She immediately grabbed her head. Marcus caught his wife before she fell back onto the bed.

"Sit on the bed, and I'll help you get the gown on. Then your husband and I will help you into the chair," Jean instructed Monet compassionately.

Monet followed Jean's instruction, and before long, the gown enclosed her body. Marcus picked up his wife, cradled her like she was a baby, and gently deposited her into the wheelchair.

"Are you ready?" Jean questioned. She couldn't help but notice the unhappy look on her fellow nurse's face.

"I don't know . . . I don't want anyone to see me like this." Monet lightly touched her face and shivered. "I haven't seen my face, but I bruise easily, so I know I must look a wreck."

"Why don't I get another gown and you can use that to shield your face?" Jean suggested, wringing her hands.

"Thanks, I guess that will have to do," Monet replied miserably.

The nurse left and returned a few minutes later with a dressing gown and a white bath towel. She held them out to Monet. "Take your pick." Monet chose the towel.

Jean hesitated. "Um, I think I should warn you that some of the media have converged upon the hospital. Not a lot, but enough to disrupt the flow of business around here a bit. We've done our best to keep them at bay. Monet, getting you healed is our number one priority. So Ramon is going to wheel you through a back entrance and up to the fifth floor," she said.

"Thanks, Jean. I don't think I'm quite ready to face anyone at this point." Monet looked down at the floor.

"If you're ready, I'll get Ramon and we can get you settled in your room. Dr. Washington wants you to stay overnight for observation," Jean said.

"I'm not really ready," Monet gulped, "but now is as good a time as any." She reached for Marcus's hand and clutched it tightly.

Jean nodded and went to get Ramon. Then the four of them

headed for the freight elevator, up to a private room on the fifth floor. Before long, Monet was in bed and had taken a sedative and painkiller that Dr. Washington had prescribed.

Marcus sat on the bed beside his wife and held her gently in his arms until she fell asleep. It pained him like a toothache to see her beautiful face battered. Monet was light skinned, and he knew it was going to take some time before the bruises completely faded.

Vines of wrath wrapped around his heart. Every time Monet moaned, or her body quivered, he felt so angry that he wanted to kill the man who had harmed his wife. What galled Marcus the most was how the man had the nerve to laugh in his face. Marcus realized that what he was thinking was wrong, but he couldn't help himself. After all, that was his wife lying in the hospital bed looking like someone had used her face for a punching bag.

Marcus gently pulled his arms from around Monet's body and laid her back on the bed. He stood up and rubbed his face hurriedly, trying to erase the tracks of tears that he knew were showing. He decided to call Monet's brothers, and hoped that Wade had called Liz to come to the hospital. He was surprised to see that only a few hours had elapsed because it seemed like a lifetime had gone by since he'd left the police station.

He took once last look at Monet. "Lord, I know you said vengeance is yours. But that philosophy doesn't sit too well with me. I would be less than a man if I didn't protect what's mine. And that lady lying over there on that bed is my everything. Thank you, God, for sparing her life. I know it could have been worse. But if it takes every breath in my body and the rest of the days of my life, I will find the man that did this to Monet and . . ." Marcus ceased speaking; he hadn't thought beyond that.

When he walked out of the room, his shoulders were set, and he was determined to find out exactly what Smitty and Wade had learned so far. He also made a mental note to stop at the gift shop and have flowers delivered to Monet's room. He wasn't looking where he was going and almost ran over Liz.

"Sorry," he said, reaching out to steady Liz.

Liz opened her arms, stood on her toes and hugged Marcus, who hugged her back. The medium tall, plus sized, caramel colored woman, who always had a cheerful smile, sniffled. "How is she?" she asked, after she stepped away from Marcus's embrace. Liz had a pretty dimpled face, a heart and smile as large as her curvy hips, and she was anxious about her friend's mental and physical state. She had a light sprinkling of freckles across the bridge of her nose, and she wore her hair cut short and gelled.

"Nay-Nay is awake and responsive, so I guess she's doing as well as can be expected under the circumstances. But she hasn't talked about what happened," Marcus answered.

"I'm so sorry, Marc. Monet didn't deserve what happened to her. No one should have to go through that. There are some sick people in the world," Liz commiserated. She was employed in the Human Resources Department at the hospital. She also had a master's degree in Psychology, and was Monet's best friend. "Do the police have any leads yet? I looked for Wade when I got here, but Smitty told me he was out doing some investigating."

"That's just what I was about to do myself. If you could sit with Monet until I get back from checking in with the guys and running a few errands, I would really appreciate it," Marcus said.

"Boy, you know you don't have to ask me that," Liz scolded. "That's my best friend in there. Monet's like a sister to me. I'll stay as long as you need me."

"Thanks, Liz. Monet's asleep. When she wakes up, call me."

"No problem. Marc, I think I know you pretty well, and I'm asking you not to be hasty. Let the investigation run its course. Please don't try to take matters into your own hands," Liz implored, and pulled on his jacket for emphasis.

"I guess you do know me, and I'll wait for the department to do their job. But if I feel like they aren't being effective, then I can't promise that I won't get involved," Marcus said.

"I had a feeling you were going to say that." Liz sighed. "I know you're focused on the department right now, but I implore you to remain prayerful. This is a prime situation for Satan to cast doubts in your mind. We both know the Father above is in charge, and He will take care of this situation as He does everything in life," she said.

"I know what you're saying." Marcus folded his arms across his chest. "Still, I took vows with Monet, and I promised to love, cherish, and take care of her. And that's what I'm going to do," he said, in a chilling tone of voice.

"Turn this matter over to the Lord," Liz urged, holding her arms out.

"You know that I will, but I plan to still be actively involved in finding out who did this to my wife. Look, Liz, I've got to go; I need to call Monet's brothers. I just hope they haven't seen anything on television and think I'm ignoring them," he said.

"I can call them while Monet is asleep, and anything else you want me to do," she said.

"No, I'll call them myself. I just need you to stay with my baby. I'll be back whenever you call me, or within an hour or so."

The two of them turned toward the sound of a cart being pushed down the hall. The cart was full of flowers, and was being maneuvered by a young, gangling man. He peered carefully at each room number and finally stopped outside of Monet's room.

"Oh, what beautiful flowers," Liz said, admiring the floral displays. "This will help cheer up Monet."

"Do you have ID?" Marcus asked the young man, looking him up and down.

The young man looked nervous and held up a badge around his neck. Marcus walked over and looked at the ID. "Okay, Liz, I'm out of here," he said, satisfied the aide was just delivering flowers.

"Marcus, if you see or talk to Wade, would you tell him that I'm here?" she asked. He nodded. She squeezed his arm and walked inside Monet's room.

Marcus was walking toward the elevator when he spied Dr. Washington. She beckoned for him to come join her at the nurse's station.

"I wanted you to know the STD screenings came back negative, so Monet is fine from that standpoint. We should have the results of the HIV/AIDS tests by the middle of next week," Dr. Washington stated.

"Thank you, Dr. Washington." Marcus' lips formed a pained smile. He looked upward, and then back at the physician. "Thank God for that. I know Monet will be relieved when she hears the news."

"I will be checking on her, and I'll talk to you later, Mr. Caldwell." Dr. Washington walked to another patient's room.

Marcus headed toward the elevator. He was visibly calmed by Dr. Washington's news. He knew firsthand the results in Monet's case were sometimes not as positive, and his brain couldn't wrap itself around the possibility of a positive HIV test. He literally itched to do anything he could to bring Monet's attacker to justice, along with dispensing his own brand of irate husband revenge. He felt like he could relate to the sayings about an eye for an eye, and people reaping what they sow.

He picked up his stride and pulled out his cell phone to call Wade, hoping desperately that his partner or Smitty had some good news for him. Monet's assailant had made her attack personal, and Marcus didn't intend to take what happened to his wife lightly.

Chapter 4

Marcus closed his cell phone after talking to Smitty, who told him to meet the team in the security area on the first floor. After he stepped out of the elevator on the first floor, he did a double take, shocked at the media fest that was taking place.

A public relations person from the hospital was holding a press conference. Several reporters broke away from the discussion when they saw Marcus and swarmed around him, asking if he had any comments. Marcus said that he didn't, and that he had confidence the police would be able to solve the case soon. He stopped and asked the security guard for directions to the security room.

When Marcus arrived in the room, he found Wade, Smitty, and a couple of other police officers sitting at a table, having a meeting. They greeted him solemnly.

"I'm going around the corner to call Monet's brothers, then I'll come back, and you can tell me what you have," Marcus informed his brother officers.

The police officers nodded and resumed their conversation. Marcus walked outside the door and took his cell phone out of his jacket pocket and called Monet's brother, Duane. He quickly explained what had happened. Duane told Marcus he would call his brother, Derek, and they would be at the hospital within an hour.

Marcus closed his cell phone and it sounded again. He peered at the caller ID and saw Reverend Ruth Wilcox's name. He quickly opened the phone. "Hello, Reverend Wilcox. How are you doing?" he said.

"I'm blessed, Marcus. Liz called to tell me about Monet. I wanted to know if there is anything I or the church can do to help? And if it would be okay for me to come to the hospital today to see Monet?" the minister asked.

"We're holding up as well as can be expected. I can't think of anything we need right at this moment. And by all means come by. It wouldn't hurt for you to see Monet. She isn't saying much right now, but I guess that's normal," he said.

"God will heal Monet," Reverend Wilcox said consolingly. "I will visit her later today. She glanced down at her watch. "It's almost two o'clock in the afternoon now. And if there's anything I can do, please feel free to call me. You are not alone."

"Thank you, and we'll see you later today." Marcus closed his phone and returned to the security office. After he sat in a hard blue plastic seat, he looked around table. "So what do you have? Any good leads?" he asked.

Smitty cleared his throat and looked down at a piece of paper in front of him. "Marcus, let me start out by saying the chief doesn't want you involved in the case, and I agree with him. You're too close to the vic, sorry, I mean Monet. We'll keep you abreast of all the information we collect, but we ask that you let us do our jobs."

Marcus's chin jutted up aggressively. He wanted to argue, but knew that in the long run it wouldn't do him any good. He reluctantly nodded his head. "Okay, I can do that." Though his lips said those words, he knew that he would be doing some investigating of his own. "What do you know so far?"

"The hospital created a rape kit. We're hoping there's a sample of the perp's DNA. We've sent the sample to the lab, and they're running a match as we speak. So maybe we'll get lucky there," Smitty reported.

"I checked the scene, and the perp made off with Monet's car, and her purse is also gone. So we have an APB out describing the car, and hopefully we'll hear something from that soon. The canine squad has scoured the area, and we found cigarette butts near the bushes where the attack took place. So all in all, I would say things look promising," Wade added, then he closed his case book.

"What about people in the neighborhood? Has anyone canvassed door-to-door?" Marcus asked, shifting in his seat because he felt antsy.

"On it," Smitty said. "We know the drill. So far no one has reported seeing and/or hearing anything. But we'll continue checking people within a twenty mile radius of the hospital. I'm encouraged by the DNA evidence because that means we can nail him once we get a match."

"That's assuming we get a match," Marcus interjected. "We don't in all cases."

"We're going to remain positive until we hear otherwise," Smitty informed Marcus. "I know you're eager for us to catch this guy, and we're with you on that, buddy. But let us do our job," he urged, knowing that his request was futile.

"That's it?" Marcus asked, strumming his fingers on the table top, as if he thought the squad should be doing more.

"We still need to talk to Monet to see if she saw anything or got a good look at the perp's face," Smitty added, in a hushed tone of voice. "How soon do you think she'll be up to it?"

"My wife was beaten pretty badly," Marcus said, looking down at the table. "If you can hold off until tomorrow before you question her, I would appreciate it." He looked back up. "Did Wade tell you that the attacker has Monet's cell phone too? Has anyone tried calling her number?" he asked.

"I did," Wade nodded, "but the phone just rang. I have a court order pending to get Monet's phone records released." He pushed his silver wire-framed glasses up on his nose. "We have an appointment with your cell phone provider to see if they'll cooperate with us without the order. If Sprint is amen-able, maybe we can track down where Monet's phone is now."

"It sounds like you all have your bases covered," Marcus admitted.

"Just to set your mind at ease, I'll question Monet myself," Wade told his partner. "I think it will help her if someone she knows and is sensitive to the situation talks to her."

"Good idea," Marcus said grudgingly.

"So that's where we are. If we get any new leads, we'll see where they take us," Smitty summarized. "The hospital is going to offer a reward for information leading to the perpetrator's arrest. That's why they're holding a press conference. So that should help. They aren't going to mention the sexual assault, just the attack. Now, why don't you go upstairs and be a supportive husband to your wife?"

Wade looked at Marcus and nodded approvingly at Smitty's suggestion.

"First I'm going to run home to shower and change, and bring Monet some clothes," Marcus said as he stood up. "I'll check with you later. I assume you're going to run the investigation from this room?"

"Yeah, we'll be here. But keep in mind what I said about your involvement in the investigation," Smitty warned Marcus, pointing at him with an outstretched finger.

"I heard you, man. I'll see you later." Marcus departed from the room. When he arrived at the entrance he saw his brothers-in-law, Duane and Derek, entering the hospital.

"How is Monet?" they asked breathlessly at the same time, after exchanging greetings with Marcus.

"She's pretty banged up, and emotionally, she's a wreck as you would expect her to be under the circumstances. The doctor said she'll heal, but that will take time," Marcus said.

Derek, who was a no-nonsense blustery type, asked Marcus point blank, "Have they found the pervert who did this to my sister?" His face showed how upset he was by the situation.

"We're working on it. There are some promising leads, which the guys are looking into," he replied.

"I have to warn you, the media is here. For the sake of the investigation, if they ask you any questions, just reply no comment," Marcus instructed.

"I disagree," Duane interjected. Marcus was surprised. Of the two brothers, Duane was the passive one, usually content to go with the flow.

"Why do you say that?" Marcus turned and peered curiously at Duane.

"I think you or someone in the family should make an appeal to the people of Chicago and ask for anyone who has any information to step forward. You could even offer a reward. Why don't you talk to the Fraternal Order of Police about it?" Duane suggested. He worked as a network analyst at Kennedy King College, which wasn't located too far from the hospital. He and Monet often had lunch together. Derek worked as a manager for a clothing store.

Marcus rubbed the stubble on his chin. "The hospital is offering a reward. I'll have Wade talk to the union and see if we can up the ante," he said.

"You need to stop thinking like a policeman and think like a husband!" Duane shouted. "How do we know the person who did this to my sister wasn't some crazy that you helped put away?"

Marcus felt like he'd taken a hit to the gut. That same thought had been haunting him all morning. "Don't you think I've thought of that myself?" His voice was barely above a whisper. "It's tearing me apart to see Monet lying in the hospital bed beaten and battered. I'm doing the best I can to help the police and be there for my wife. Try to keep those types of comments to a minimum, please." There was a hint of a tremble in Marcus's voice.

Duane realized his brother-in-law was holding on to his emotions by a tenacious thread. He walked over to Marcus and patted his arm. "I'm sorry, man. I didn't mean to come off sounding so harsh. You're Monet's husband and a police officer, and I know that you'll do anything to find who did this terrible thing to our sister and bring him to justice," he said apologetically.

The brothers were identical twins. They shared the same light complexion as their sister and had hazel colored eyes, courtesy of their father, who was of Creole lineage from New Orleans. They were average in height, five feet ten inches, and that's where the resemblance ended. Derek was muscular in build, with heavy facial hair covering his face, and he favored hip hop clothing. Derek was slim like Monet, clean shaven, and was more conservative in dress. Derek wore his curly hair clipped low on the top and sides and slightly longer in the back, while Duane made sure he went to the barbershop every Saturday to keep his waves immaculate. The brothers refused to settle down and marry, much to Monet's consternation. She said the family wasn't procreating, and that her brothers needed to remedy the situation.

Derek nodded at his brother's rant appreciatively. "Who would have thought little brother had it in him? That's usually my role. But we're all family, and we've got to stick together, and make sure big sister comes through this ordeal in one piece. Marc, we got your back, and we'll go by all the decisions you make," he said.

"I agree," Duane said quickly. "But if Derek and I have suggestions, I hope you'll at least listen to us."

"Definitely, and I promise to keep you in the loop about the investigation," Marcus said. "I'm heading home to shower and change clothes and bring some stuff back to the hospital for Monet. I'll see you later."

"Duane looked at his brother, and said, "What do you say about us getting some flowers for Monet? You know how she loves plants; maybe that will cheer her up."

"Good thinking, bro, I second that motion," Derek replied. "We'll go to a florist, and then come back here. There's one not too far from here. The flowers here at the hospital are too expensive."

"Monet is probably still asleep anyway. By the time you get back, she should be awake," Marcus said.

The three men left the hospital together, each equally concerned about their loved one on the fifth floor.

Upstairs in Monet's room, Liz continued to sit vigil in a chair next to her bed, reading the Daily Word pamphlet. She read the entry for the day and the scripture accompanying the message in her Bible, which she always kept in her oversized tote bag. Liz looked up when she heard Monet stirring.

"Hey sister, how are you feeling?" Liz asked.

Monet's eyes filled with tears. "I hurt all over, and I know I look like I was hit by a truck. Liz, I've never been more afraid in my life."

Liz quickly stood up and sat on the bed. "Will it hurt if I give you a hug?" she asked Monet, patting her arm.

"Probably. Just be gentle," Monet murmured as Liz chan-ged her mind and patted Monet's hand.

"Go ahead and cry and get it out of your system. Monet, do you realize how blessed you are?" Liz asked.

"I don't know what you mean?" Monet's eyes widened and she looked at Liz like her friend was crazy. "I was beaten up and sexually assaulted. How could you consider that as being blessed?" She leaned back in the bed.

"Because you weren't killed, nor were any of your bones broken. All your injuries are temporary ones that will heal. I know what happened was horrendous, and it proves how many sick people are out there roaming the streets. But God had your back, Monet. And for that you have to be grateful."

"I am," Monet said in a teeny voice. "I really am. Before I blacked out, I remember reciting the Twenty-Third Psalm, and I prayed the Lord would see me through the attack. But every time I close my eyes, I see and feel him on me. I feel so dirty."

Liz rubbed Monet's arm. "Trust me, it wasn't your fault. Don't try to put that guilt on yourself."

"I know Marcus must hate me. If only I had let Dave walk me to my car, none of this would have happened. And Marcus called and asked me if I wanted a ride home, and I turned him down." Tears trickled down Monet's face.

"Marcus doesn't hate you, so get that thought out of your mind. Everything happens for a reason. We don't understand why sometimes, and we may never, but I know this incident could be a test of your faith. Monet, when you think about the positives, they far outweigh the negatives. You may need counseling with Reverend Wilcox to get past the trauma. But trust me when I say you're lucky, no, not lucky, it's God's will that you're still here and that I'm in this room talking to you."

"I guess so." Monet's voice trailed off. She turned away from Liz.

"I have something I want to read to you, and I want you to listen to the words. Will you promise me that?" Liz looked over at Monet and could see her head bobbing up and down.

Liz opened her Bible to Hebrews 13:5 and 6 and read, "*Let your conversation be without covetousness and be content with such things as ye have; for he hath said, I will never leave thee, nor forsake thee. So that we may boldly say, the Lord is my helper, and I will not fear what any man shall do unto me.* Do you know right now, lying in that bed, that you are a witness to that scripture? We know the Lord didn't forsake you, you are so blessed, and I want you to repeat with me, 'I will not fear what any man shall do unto me.'"

Monet turned over in the bed, cautiously favoring her sore arm. Then she said the words with Liz.

Liz sat back on the bed, and asked, "Can I pray for you?"

Monet nodded, and Liz took her hand. The women clo-sed their eyes and bowed their heads as Liz proceeded to pray. "Gracious Father, my savior and redeemer. I give thanks today that you spared my sister's life last night, and as you promised, you didn't forsake her. Lord, give Monet the wisdom to know that the things that happen in life are temporary, and we are just on a journey to attain your grace so that we might reside in heaven with you and our loved ones who have gone on before us. Lord, I know Monet is hurt and she'll weep tonight, but I know with your mercy, joy will come in the morning, and that in time this crisis, too, shall pass. Lord, give Monet and Marcus strength. It's not an easy road they are going to walk, but let them feel a sense of comfort knowing that you will be right there with them when they falter. In the midst of this ordeal, I praise your name, Lord. Father, these blessings I ask in your Son's name. Amen."

Liz continued holding Monet's hand as she cried silently. She whispered to Monet, "I promise if you lean on the Lord, better days are ahead for you and Marcus."

There was a knock at the closed door. A nurse walked into the room carrying a tray of medicine. A volunteer followed behind him with a cart full of flowers.

He asked Monet, "Where should I put these?"

"How about on the shelf on the other side of the room," Liz said.

"They are beautiful, but where did all these flowers come from?" Monet asked.

"I'll let you know when the nurse is done dispensing your meds," Liz said.

"How are you feeling, Nurse Caldwell?" the male nurse asked Monet.

"I'm still sore, and my head is still hurting a little bit, but not as bad as before," she responded.

"I guess I'm on time then since it's time for your next dose of medicine." He handed Monet two pills, and while Liz poured her a cup of water, he said, "I want you to know the nurses are keeping you in our prayers."

"Thanks, Morton, I appreciate it," Monet said, after she had ingested the pills and washed them down with water. She felt overwhelmed by the showing of love. "One can never have enough prayers." She turned to the volunteer, and said, "If I get any more flowers, would you take them to some of the elderly patients on the floor?"

The volunteer said to Liz and Morton, "And she wonders why she's loved?" Not waiting for an answer, she turned to Monet and said, "Nurse Caldwell, it's because of gestures like that . . . giving flowers to the elderly. Who else but you, in the midst of your pain, would do something like that?"

"You're right," Liz replied, "and that's why God was with you today, my sister."

After the nurse informed Monet to let her know if she needed anything else, he and the volunteer left her room.

Liz walked over to the shelf and removed the cards from the floral displays. Then she walked back and sat in the chair and read the cards to Monet. Most of them were from various departments in the hospital. Everyone who knew Monet knew she was special. She always had a kind word and a bright cheery smile for her co-workers. She counseled many of them, and loaned a good number of them money when times were tight. She was active in the church, and in addition to singing in the choir, she also volunteered to keep the food pantry stocked. On her days off work, she could be found at church feeding the homeless. She had no major worries in the world, other than her inability to conceive a child.

Liz glanced over at Monet. She had fallen asleep again. This time Liz noted that Monet's face looked a little more relaxed. Liz hoped she had been able to bring some solace to her friend. She also wondered what, if any, news Wade had been able to discover about the attack. She wasn't worried because like Marcus, Wade was a skilled detective. Liz knew that her husband wouldn't leave any stone unturned.

Chapter 5

Marcus arrived at his and Monet's tan, Colonial style, two story brick house. He unlocked the door and walked inside. Mitzi ran up to greet him. He picked her up and petted Monet's baby, as he called the small brown and beige Pomeranian-bred dog.

"Yeah, girl, I bet you're hungry. Let me get you something to eat." Marcus set the dog on the floor, reached inside the cabinet over the sink, and removed a can of dog food. He then placed it on the gold and white veined marble counter top. He bent down and picked up Mitzi's water and food bowls from the floor. He washed and rinsed them, filled them with food and water, and set them back on the floor. Mitzi nails scratched the white and navy blue ceramic tile floor as she ran to her corner of the kitchen and began devouring her food.

Marcus checked the messages on the answering machine and wasn't surprised that it was full. There were many calls from members of The Temple, and some from Marcus's co-workers. He saved some of the messages, then he went into the olive green living room where many beautiful varieties of potted plants were placed near the large beveled windows. He dropped down heavily on the cream-colored leather sectional couch. He closed his eyes and laid his head along the edge of the sofa. He couldn't believe that his life had executed a 360 degree turn so quickly. Marcus likened his life to driving in an automobile, sliding on ice, and spinning until he stopped, facing the opposite direction.

He stood and walked back into the kitchen and took the *Yellow Pages* out of the pantry. He quickly thumbed through the book until he found listings for locksmiths. He chided himself for not remembering to have the locks changed sooner. Mitzi walked into the living room and sat at his feet. She looked up and stared at him as if to say, *where's my mistress?*

The second locksmith Marcus called was available. After he explained who he was and what he wanted, the gentleman said that he'd seen the story about Monet's attack on the news. He promised to be at the Caldwell house within an hour. Marcus then called his neighbor, Mr. Jamison, who had a key to the house, and asked him if he could let the locksmith in the house while he went back to the hospital. Mr. Jamison was more than happy to assist his neighbor. Like everyone else in the Caldwells's neighborhood Mr. Jamison was appalled and saddened by Monet's attack. Marcus called the locksmith back and gave him Mr. Jamison's telephone number. He instructed the locksmith to call Mr. Jamison when he arrived at the house, alerting that his neighbor would allow him access inside.

Marcus's mind tried to process how, not even twenty-four hours ago, he and Monet had made love in hopes of conceiving a child. Afterward Marcus had departed for work, feeling satisfied and looking forward to dinner and a movie with his wife over the weekend. Instead, Monet was now lying in a hospital bed, and he was at home trying to put back together the shattered pieces of their lives.

He had a bone to pick with his Heavenly Father. He was angry that God had allowed his wife to be harmed. The Caldwells lived what Marcus considered a quiet Christian life. The Sundays they didn't have to work, he and Monet attended church faithfully. They gave money freely and did whatever tasks the church asked of them.

Marcus sighed. Then he stood and walked into the kitchen

to get a bottle of cranberry juice out of the refrigerator. He un-screwed the top, drank greedily, and then set the bottle on the table. He wiped his mouth with the back of his hand and went upstairs to the bathroom. He turned on the water to warm it up for his shower, then stripped off his clothing.

Half an hour later, Marcus was dressed in a pair of jeans and a pullover shirt. He picked up the cordless phone from the night-stand and called the hospital to check on Monet. Duane an-swered the telephone.

"How is Monet doing?" Marcus asked. He walked to his dress-er, took out a pair of socks, and sat on the bed.

"She can't eat yet because of the hairline fracture of her jaw-bone, so they're feeding her through an IV for lunch. The nurse gave her medicine for the pain, and now she's asleep. Do you want us to stay here until you get back?" Duane asked, as he glanced at his sister.

"Is Liz still there?" Marcus asked.

"No, she left a little while after we got here. She said she'd be back later." The nurse's aide brought more flowers to Mon-et's room. Duane pointed to the counter near the closet for the nurse to put them there.

"Okay, I'll be there in about forty-five minutes. I'm going to pack a bag for Monet, and then I'll be on my way."

"We'll see you when you get here," Duane replied.

"Later, man," Marcus said, then clicked off the telephone and finished putting on his socks and shoes.

He went inside their walk-in closet, took out Monet's beige and green floral overnight bag, and laid it on the bed. Then he opened her dresser drawer and removed some nightgowns with matching robes and put them in the suitcase. Marcus was debat-ing what else he should pack when the doorbell chimed. He walked downstairs to the front door and opened it to find Liz.

"Well, come on in. Talk about perfect timing." He stepped aside so she could enter.

"I thought I'd come over and help you pack some things to take to the hospital for Monet. I know you need my help, don't you?" Liz pecked him on his cheek.

"Yeah," Marcus said, holding up his hands as if in surrender. "I knew about the nightgowns, but I wasn't sure what else she needed."

"See, that's where a best friend comes in handy. Let me help you pack. I know you're itching to get back to the hospital," Liz said.

"You're right. Follow me." She trailed Marcus to the master bedroom. He scratched his head, then pointed to the bed. Liz took off her jacket and laid it on the bed next to the suitcase. "Most of her stuff is in the armoire, and the stuff for her hair is on the vanity over there." He nodded toward a brass and glass vanity on the south wall of the bedroom.

Liz had always admired the bridge oak bedroom set, complemented by rust colored carpeting. A large screen television sat on a brass stand opposite the bed. Liz pulled open a drawer and removed underwear and put them inside the suitcase. The drawer was scented by a jasmine sachet.

Fifteen minutes later, Liz had completed her task. Marcus turned off the light in the bedroom, and they went downstairs to the kitchen.

"Would you like something to drink?" Marcus asked, looking around the room, trying to recall if he may have forgotten something.

"No, I'm fine and ready to go. I know you're ready to return to the hospital, and I'm sure if Monet is awake, she's probably wondering where you are. How are you holding up, Marcus?" Liz stood near the sink and took her car keys out of her pants pocket.

"Still a little angry, but I'm trying to come to terms with all that's happened." Marcus opened the refrigerator and put the juice back inside of it.

"You've got to let the anger go," Liz scolded lightly.

"I will do the best I can," Marcus conceded. "But I've made a vow to find the guy that did that to Monet, even if it takes my last breath."

"You really don't have to do anything but let God handle this. You know that, don't you?" Liz could sympathize with what happened, but knew that Marcus could be hot tempered at times.

"Yeah, yeah, I know. But it's my job to bring the bad guys to justice, and I would be less than a man if I didn't do the same for my wife," Marcus answered definitively, his expression resolute.

"I'm not saying don't do anything. You're a policeman like Wade, so it's your nature to correct the world of all the ills. I'm just saying don't become obsessed. Leave justice to God. We all reap what we sow, and Monet's attacker is no different. God will tend to him," Liz replied unwaveringly.

Marcus looked at his watch impatiently. "I hear you, Liz. Now, if you're ready, I need to get back to the hospital."

"I've said my peace, and I hope you heed my words. It wouldn't hurt for both of you to get counseling, whether it's with a psychologist or with Reverend Wilcox. You and Monet have been through a terrible ordeal. Don't be too proud to ask for help," Liz implored.

"Gotcha. Can we go?" Marcus asked, stepping toward the door.

"Sure. I think I left my jacket in the bedroom. I'll go upstairs and grab it, and then I'll be ready to go." Liz rushed upstairs to the bedroom and returned to the kitchen. "Oh, do you want me to take Mitzi home with me? I know you'll be in and out of the hospital over the next few days."

"I hadn't thought about her," Marcus admitted. "Let me get her things together and I'll bring her out to the car." He took a plastic bag out of the pantry and filled it with a couple cans of dog food and treats. Then he picked up Mitzi and put her jeweled leash around her neck. After he was done, Marcus took his keys out of his pocket and locked the back door. He and Liz walked to Liz's car, and when she unlocked the door, Marcus put Mitzi in the backseat.

Liz got in her car and said, "I'll drop Mitzi off at my house and meet you at the hospital." The Harrisons lived a few miles from Marcus and Monet's house.

Marcus entered his SUV and started it up. When he arrived at the hospital, he was surprised to see Liz pulling in the hospital parking lot behind him. After he parked his vehicle, he waited for Liz, and they walked inside the hospital.

Liz went directly to Monet's room, while Marcus made a detour to the security area. Smitty had gone back to the precinct, and Wade and the team were wrapping up for the day.

Wade looked at Marcus, shook his head, and said, "Why am I not surprised you're here and not upstairs where you should be?" He picked up some notes off the table.

"'Cause you know me, and you know I won't rest until there's some resolution to the case," Marcus said intensely. "I take it there's nothing new, or you would've called me."

"Correct. There haven't been any new developments. And yes, I know you won't give up finding Monet's attacker. I'm done for the day after I talk to the policemen that Smitty assigned here. They're en route, and will stay here all night, just in case the perp is foolish enough to come back, which I doubt." Wade stood up and slipped on his jacket. "They should be here any minute."

Five minutes later, the door opened, and two plain clothes policemen walked into the room. They exchanged greetings and sat down, while Wade brought them up-to-date on the latest finding. Monet's purse had been found, minus her keys and wallet, which had been found in a garbage can fifteen miles south of the hospital. Her car hadn't been located yet. Wade concluded the meeting after asking if there were any questions, and there were not. He and Marcus left the room and headed to the elevator to see Monet.

As they rode to the fifth floor, Wade said, "So far we're making fair progress. We'll follow the evidence, and eventually get our man. I don't want you to do anything to compromise the case."

Marcus's eyes seemed to focus on a far off place as Wade continued to speak. He just wished the odds the squad had provided had been more favorable than fair. To his way of thinking, good would have been better.

"In addition to the officers staying here at the hospital tonight, the chief has approved two plain clothes officers to stay at your house tonight as a precaution. You can't be sure what the perp might be thinking. Did you remember to change the locks in your house?" Wade asked. "We also pulled the records of Monet's cell phone to see what satellite towers they hit."

Marcus nodded to indicate that he was in agreement with the steps taken to solve the case. Wade and Marcus exited the elevator and walked down the hallway to Monet's room. As they passed the nurse's station, a couple of hospital employees expressed wishes for Monet to have a speedy recovery.

"Well, we can tell your wife is loved at her workplace," Wade observed.

"I figured that she was. Still, it's another thing to actually see and hear it." Marcus nodded. He rapped lightly on the door, and then pushed it open.

Derek, Duane, Liz, and Reverend Wilcox were visiting Monet, who was asleep.

"Hello, Marcus and Wade," Reverend Wilcox said. She gave them a light hug. "I wanted to stop by and see if there was anything I could do."

Marcus and Wade were stunned by the number of floral arrangements in the room. After checking a few of the cards on the vases, Marcus put the overnight case in the closet.

Liz pointed to the floral arrangements and said, "The flowers just seem to keep coming. Monet told the nursing staff to give some of them to the elderly patients. This is what's left."

"That sounds like something Monet would do," Marcus said, continuing to check the cards.

"I'll see if I can get a couple of extra chairs," Wade said, and then left the room.

Marcus walked over to Monet and kissed her forehead carefully. Her face seemed more swollen to him than it did earlier.

Liz noticed his reaction. "The swelling should start to subside shortly. They've been giving her antibiotics and icepacks for the swelling."

Wade returned with a couple of chairs. He placed them on the wall near the end of the bed and sat down.

Reverend Wilcox asked Marcus, "Did Monet's doctor say when she'll be released?"

"Earlier she said if all continues to go well, she'll be released maybe Sunday or Monday," he responded.

"That's good news. I will make sure we mention her at church on Sunday, and of course say a prayer for her."

"Thank you, Reverend Wilcox," Marcus said. He looked over at Monet, who stirred in the bed but didn't wake up.

"Doctor Washington says it's good that she's sleeping because it will help her body to mend. Did you guys have a chance to talk to her?" Marcus asked Derek and Duane.

"For a few minutes. We didn't want to tire her out, and she was pretty groggy," Duane answered, looking away from the bed, which seemed to dominate the room.

"Well, I didn't plan on staying long. I have a few more members to visit while I'm here at the hospital." Reverend Wilcox stood up and removed her coat from the back of the chair. "If you don't mind, Marcus, I'd like to read a scripture and say a prayer for Monet."

"That will be fine," Marcus responded.

Reverend Wilcox took her Bible out of her black leather tote bag and asked everyone to stand near the edge of the bed and hold hands. She opened her Bible to the book of Psalms. "I will read from Psalm 86:6 and 7. *'Give ear, Oh Lord, unto my prayer, and attend to the voice of my supplications. In the days of my trouble I will call upon thee, for thou wilt answer me.'* Father above, I thank you. For even in the midst of heartache and pain, I can and will say thank you. Thank you for sparing Sister Monet's life, and because the injuries she has suffered are temporary. Weeping may endure for a night, but joy will come for Monet and Marcus in the morning. It might not feel like it right now at this minute, but I know my sister was blessed today, Lord, by your grace and mercy. And Father, as Monet begins to heal, let her know that she is not alone, that she only has to lean on your everlasting arms.

"Let not hate or revenge fester in Monet and Marcus's hearts, Father. Give them the wisdom to know that you will fix any ordeal they endure. Maybe not as soon as they would want or like, but let them know that you will fix it, that you will do it in your own time. Lord, I claim these blessings and the victory in your name. Amen."

"Amen," everyone echoed.

Monet stirred, and tried to sit up. She clutched her arm. "Reverend Wilcox, I didn't know you were here," she said, pushing back her hair off her brow. "Somebody should have awakened me." She looked at everyone in the room with swollen, accusing eyes.

"I'm sure they just wanted you to get your rest," Reverend Wilcox said, putting her Bible back in her bag. She walked over to Monet and talked to her quietly for a few minutes. When she finished, everyone decided to leave so that Monet could rest.

"I'll be back to see you tomorrow," Liz said. She rubbed Monet's arm. Wade did the same.

Derek and Duane asked Monet if there was anything she needed. She said no. Her brothers hugged her and told her they, too, would see her tomorrow. Everyone departed.

"I'm going to take the chairs back to the nurse's station," Marcus told his wife. "I brought some of your nightgowns. Do you want to change into one?"

"No, I'll do that tomorrow," she said. She lay back in the bed.

Marcus picked up the chairs and left the room. He returned a few minutes later. He sat in a chaise seat where a nurse had thoughtfully put a sheet, pillow, and light blanket for him.

"Did you eat?" Monet asked him as she moved gingerly in the bed.

"No, I'm not hungry. I'll get something later," Marcus answered, as he watched his wife with an eagle eye. "Are you feeling okay? Do you want me to call the nurse?"

"No, I'm okay. If I go back to sleep, have the nurse bring you a dinner menu; that way, you can dine with me while I have my meal intravenously."

"I will," Marcus assured his wife.

The nurse came into the room and checked Monet's vital signs. Monet mentioned bringing in a menu for Marcus. The nurse said she'd return with one shortly.

"You didn't have to do that," Marcus said. "I could've gotten something to eat from the vending machine. I think the cafeteria is open twenty-four hours."

"I want you to stay with me." Monet yawned and flin-ched because it was painful to open her mouth wide.

Marcus jumped up from his seat. "Are you sure that you don't want me to call the nurse? You look like you're in terrible pain."

Monet tried to smile, and that hurt too. "I'll make it. You

know I don't like to take medicine unnecessarily. If the pain becomes unbearable, I'll let the nurse know. You can dim the lights over my bed." She knew that Marcus was feeling helpless, and figured that would give him something to do. "And adjust my bed and fix my pillows."

Marcus did as she asked. Then he sat back down and held Monet's hand in his own. "You know I'm not going to rest until I find out who did this to you, don't you?" he said, his voice choking up.

"Oh, Marcus," Monet shook her head sadly, "I really wish you would leave it alone. Let Wade and the guys handle the case. I'm going to need you to lean on. I felt better after talking to Liz and Reverend Wilcox. Still, every time I close my eyes the attack happens over and over." She began sniffling.

"I know, babe, and that's why I want the guy found immediately," Marcus growled.

"Can you just let it go for me? I don't want to have to worry about you and what you're doing. Please?" Monet begged.

Marcus nodded, although he knew he wasn't being tru-thful. There were some things a man had to do for his wife, and protection was high on his list. How dare someone attack his wife, and he was a policeman. *I don't think so,* Marcus thought.

"Marcus Caldwell, I want you to promise me that you won't actively take a role in the investigation," Monet said firmly. Her eyes bore holes into her husband's.

"Monet, I can't promise that. I would be less than a man if I did. I will just offer my input to the team and nothing else. Can you accept that?" He brushed a curl away from Monet's face.

She nodded her head. "I guess that will do for now. We'll talk about this later. You know Reverend Wilcox is right. Even in the midst of heartache, we can still thank the Lord that I wasn't killed. Let's take comfort from that."

"Oh, I'm grateful, Monet, from the bottom of my heart." Marcus put his hand over his chest.

The nurse returned to the room with a fresh ice pack for Monet to put on her face. Then she handed Marcus a menu. "I'll come back later to get it," she said, before departing the room.

Monet held the bag to her face for a while, then put it on the table next to her bed. She lay down and drifted off to sleep. Marcus stood up and pulled the sheet up around the upper part of her body. He kissed her forehead, sat down, picked up the remote for the television, and remained by his wife's side until he, too, fell asleep.

Chapter 6

A few months after the attack, Monet was home still recuperating. The memory of the attack was fresh in her mind, and she was still somewhat fearful about returning to scene of the crime. Marcus suggested she take a leave of absence from work, and Monet followed his advice. She would be off work for sixty days.

The police hadn't had any luck in finding Monet's attacker. Wade and Smitty vowed the case would remain active until the crime was solved. Several officers volunteered their free time to help in the search. Even though a reward was offered, the few leads the team received hadn't panned out.

Monet sat at the kitchen table, stirring a cup of decaffeinated coffee with a splash of milk. She hummed along with Mary Mary, one of Monet's favorite gospel groups, as they sang "Yesterday." The song had become her mantra.

Suddenly she jumped up from her seat and ran to the powder room near the back of the house by the den. Her stomach had been squeamish for some time now. She suffered a bout of dry heaves and returned to the kitchen. *I'll have to remember to mention how lousy I've been feeling to Dr. Washington. It's probably just nerves*, she absently thought.

Of all the rooms in the house, the kitchen was Monet's pride and joy. She and Marcus had it remodeled two years ago. The large room boasted a blond wooden table framed by six chairs that sat in a breakfast nook. She loved to cook, so the couple had installed an island, complete with copper pots and pans hanging over it. The appliances were bone colored. The kitchen was a cozy room, the heart of the house.

Monet rinsed her cup and put it inside the dishwasher. Then she went upstairs to dress for her doctor's appointment. She was grateful that she would see Dr. Washington at her office in Hyde Park instead of the hospital.

She walked inside the closet and removed a pair of stonewashed jeans and a white cable-knit sweater. Monet went into the bathroom, showered, and then dressed. She sat down at her vanity and finger combed her corkscrew, naturally curly hair. Her facial swelling had subsided, but her face still bore faint traces of black and blue marks. She put a little eye shadow on the lids above her hazel colored eyes. She grabbed her purse and started down the stairs.

Before she went inside the garage, Monet set the security alarm. The couple didn't have an alarm installed before the attack, and when Monet asked if they could get one, Marcus was more than happy to comply.

Monet's eyes zoomed around the garage before she got into her new midnight blue Toyota Solaris. After her car was recovered three weeks after it was stolen and processed by the police department for evidence, Marcus sold the car. Monet turned on the ignition and pressed the remote control to open the garage door.

Thirty minutes later, she pulled into a space in the parking garage in Hyde Park. When she got to the doctor's office, she signed the appointment sheet, took a seat, and picked up the latest copy of O *Magazine*.

After a short time, a nurse walked into the waiting area and said, "Monet Caldwell."

Monet stood up and followed the nurse to examination room number three. The nurse took her blood pressure reading and temperature. After that, she told Monet to remove her clothing and gave her a gown to change into. After she entered notations into the computer, the nurse announced the doctor would be with her shortly, and then she left.

Monet removed her clothing and sat in the chilly, sterile room reading the magazine she'd brought into the room with her. Ten minutes later, Dr. Washington walked into the examination room.

"How are you feeling, Monet?" she asked, smiling. Her white coat looked pristine, like she'd just started her day. Her reading glasses dangled from a chain around her neck.

"Not bad," Monet replied as she nervously folded her hands on her lap.

Dr. Washington listened to Monet's heart rate and examined her face. "The bruises are fading; that's good." She sat at the small table in the room and keyed data into the tablet PC. "How have you been feeling from an emotional standpoint? Have the dreams abated?"

"Somewhat." Monet averted her eyes from the doctor.

"Would you like me to prescribe medication to help you sleep?"

"No, not really. I hate taking medicine," Monet said airily.

"We'll see how you're doing a month from now. If you aren't sleeping any better by then, I'll prescribe something for you, maybe Ambien CR, okay?"

"Yes," Monet said. She felt cold and briskly rubbed her forearms.

"Have you given any further thought to counseling?" Dr. Washington pressed save on the keyboard and returned her attention to Monet.

"Actually, my minister suggested I do a few sessions with her, and I'm going to start that on Friday," Monet informed the doctor.

"That's good. It probably wouldn't hurt to participate in a rape crisis group too. I can recommend a few in the area affiliated with the University of Chicago Hospital."

"I don't know if I can talk about what happened to me with strangers. It's too personal." Monet shook her head.

"That's exactly who you should talk about it to, other women who have been in the same predicament as you. They will understand where you're coming from. I certainly can't force you to do so, but I've conducted some of the sessions myself, and I know first-hand that they do help," Dr. Washington told Monet kindly.

"I can't make any promises, but I'll think about it," she said evasively.

"How are you and Marcus doing, from an intimacy standpoint?" Dr. Washington probed.

"I . . . I . . . I . . . not yet," Monet confessed. "I feel so bad about not being able to be intimate with Marcus. I know he didn't rape me, but I freeze up when he tries to touch me." She dropped her head and rubbed her eyes.

"That, my dear, is why you need counseling. In most cases, women can't come to terms with the ordeal alone. They need help to work through the issue," Dr. Washington said comfortingly.

"Marcus is patient with me, and that helps. I'm just not ready to participate in the physical act, but I don't mind him holding me. It took me a couple of weeks before I could stand for him to do that," Monet explained candidly.

"That's good, and I consider that progress. I just want you to think about the support group, and by all means talk to you minister. It doesn't hurt to have guidance from a spiritual perspective. The quicker you talk to someone, the sooner your life will be back on track," Dr. Washington said, as she jotted down a name and number on a pad. She tore off the paper and handed it to Monet. "This is Sheila Winston's number. She facilitates the crisis group at the University of Chicago Hospital. If you decide to try it, then give her a call. Is there anything else going on with you?" Dr. Washington looked at Monet casually. Her large dark brown eyes seemed magnified behind the glass lenses, and were filled with compassion. She thought Monet looked a little tired or rundown.

"Well, I have been feeling nauseated for the past few weeks. I'm sure it's nothing, just nerves." Monet's voice trailed off.

"Hmmm. When was the last time you had your period?" Dr. Washington folded her hands together. She had an inkling of what was happening with Monet. She suggested Monet take the "morning after pill" following the assault, but Monet declined the offer.

"Let me think." Monet closed and opened her eyes. "You know I'm irregular, I think about a few weeks before the attack."

"Are you experiencing any other symptoms?" Dr. Washington probed gently.

"My breasts have been tender and odors bother me." Monet gasped and said cautiously, "Dr. Washington, you don't think I'm pregnant, do you?"

"It won't take us long to find out. I'm going to order a pregnancy test and send you next door to the lab to take a blood test," Dr. Washington advised. She stood up. "Why don't you get dressed, come back to the nurse's area, and Erica will give you a cup for a urine sample. While we wait for the results, you can go across the hall for the blood test. I'll write up the order now."

"So you do think I'm pregnant?" Monet asked, in a shaky voice. "I just assumed it was nerves."

"It could be nerves, but we can't rule that possibility out. Still that's easy enough for us to find out." Dr. Washington looked at her watch and said, "I'll see you in my office in about twenty to thirty minutes."

Monet nodded, feeling shell shocked. She sat on the examination table for a few minutes. When she rose, her body was shaking so badly that she could barely get dressed. She put her sweater on backward and her socks on inside out.

"Lord, could it be true? Am I really pregnant?" She laughed aloud giddily, then became somber. "Is the child Marcus's or my attacker's? God, forgive me. What am I saying? I know this baby is Marcus's. You told me Marcus and I would have a child." Her breathing became shallow, and she felt lightheaded.

The couple had been trying to get pregnant since year three of their marriage. They had been examined what seemed like a million times by various doctors, and there wasn't a medical reason for why they couldn't conceive. Monet had wanted to try in-vitro, but Marcus vetoed the idea. Years ago she had broached the subject of adoption, but Marcus didn't want to, citing that he wanted their biological child or none at all.

Monet prayed daily, a prayer she called the baby's prayer. She was both elated and apprehensive by the possibility of being with child. What if the baby wasn't Marcus's? Then she pushed those musings to the back of her mind because God had told her otherwise, and she always trusted God.

Monet dressed and berated herself for jumping the gun. Her legs were shaking as she walked to the nurse's station and got the cup from Erica. Then she went into the restroom. When she was done, she placed the cup on the side of the sink, washed her hands, and then returned it the nurse, who gave Monet a work order for the lab. Thoughts swirled in and out of her mind as the lab technician took a vial of blood.

The technician put a bandage on Monet's arm and said, "You won't have long to wait for the results. Your doctor put a rush on the test."

Monet tried to smile. Then she returned to the physician's waiting room.

Minutes later, Erica escorted Monet to Dr. Washington's office. As she waited for the doctor, her stomach felt like fish were darting inside of it. She looked up at the door, mentally willing Dr. Washington to hurry back and tell her what the test revealed.

Chapter 7

"What have you got there, Marcus?" Wade asked. He'd just returned from the kitchen area after pouring himself a cup of coffee.

"Travel brochures." Marcus held them up. "I was thinking about taking Monet on a Hawaiian cruise for the holidays. So I've been checking around, doing some research online, and calling travel agencies."

"That sounds like a good plan," Wade answered. "If it weren't for the kids, me and Liz would go with you." He sat down at his desk and began eating a donut.

"I know." Marcus nodded. "If we don't go to Hawaii, then we'll be at your house for Christmas, and you'll come to ours for New Year's."

Wade picked up his coffee and sipped. "That tastes good. Nothing is better than a good cup of coffee in the morning. And yeah, I figured you and Monet would be at the house for Christmas like always."

The couples, along with Liz and Wade's children, usually spent major holidays together. The friends rotated, meeting at each other's houses on the last Friday of each month for a fish fry.

Marcus nodded and left the room to refresh his own cup of coffee. When he returned to his desk, Wade asked, "Did you mention your idea to Monet?" He began moving files on his desk.

"Not yet, I wanted to check the prices first. The Hawaiian cruise is for ten days, departing the day before Christmas Eve, so that would cover both holidays. I checked with the chief, and he approved the time off," Marcus said.

"Are you sure Monet would want to go? Christmas is her favorite time of the year," Wade queried. He put a file on the bottom of his three tier tray.

"I thought about that, but I still think it would be good for us to get away. Monet still hasn't fully recovered from the attack. Some nights she wakes up screaming and can't go back to sleep. So I think a change of pace would be good medicine for both of us."

Wade nodded. "Great. I imagine Monet's symptoms are normal considering what she's gone through. What does her doctor say? What's her name?" He snapped his fingers. "Wallace?"

"No," Marcus corrected. "It's Dr. Washington. Monet has an appointment with her today. Doc mentioned giving her a sleep aid the last time she was there, but Nay-Nay fought that suggestion. She doesn't like doing the pill thing."

Wade paused with his filing and complimented his friend. "I want to say that you've stepped up to the plate for Monet, just like I knew you would."

"I couldn't do any less, and I know if something happened to me, Nay-Nay would do the same." Marcus's telephone rang. "Excuse me," he said, picking up the phone. He listened intently for a few minutes and wrote notes on the pad next to his phone.

Wade looked at his partner, who seemed to be involved in an intense conversation. Marcus had knocked over his cup of coffee and made no effort to clean up the mess. Wade sprung up out of his seat and took napkins off his desk and handed them to Marcus, who ignored him. Wade sopped up the spilled liquid and waited for Marcus to get off the telephone. Marcus hung up the telephone, stroked his beard, and looked at Wade with an astounded expression on his face.

Wade raised his eyebrows inquiringly, and asked, "What's up, man? What was that about?"

"I never would've believed that call if I hadn't heard it with my own ears," Marcus replied, staring at Wade with amazed filled eyes.

"Believed what? What are you talking about?" Wade asked impatiently.

"I talked to a man on the phone who said he was Monet's father. He wants to meet her and the twins." Marcus shook his head in disbelief.

"I thought Monet's father was dead?" Wade cocked his head to the side and peered at Marcus.

"The truth is Monet's old man deserted his family when she was a kid. He just up and left Birmingham, and hasn't been heard from since," Marcus said.

"That's remarkable," Wade muttered, shaking his head. "What are you going to do? Do you think Monet wants to meet him? What about your brothers-in-law? What will their reaction be?"

"I really don't know. Monet has expressed sadness over the years from not knowing her father. But she never tried to actively seek him. I don't remember Derek or Duane saying anything one way or the other." Marcus shrugged his shoulders, and then held up damp pieces of paper and waved them in the air.

"So, what are you going to do? How did you respond to his request? What's his name?" Wade asked. His arm was propped on the desk, and his face rested on his hand.

"His name is Aron Reynolds. I told him I'd think about what he wanted and call him back in a few days," Marcus replied.

"How did he track you down?" Wade went into investigation mode, drilling his partner.

"He said he saw one of the newspaper articles about Monet's attack." Marcus frowned. "He also said that Monet's mother gave him our information." He set the papers back on his desk, wiped his hands on a napkin, and leaned back in his chair.

"I wonder what he's been doing all of these years," Wade mused, shaking his head.

"The call came from a prison in Illinois, and I plan on finding out what he's in for before I say anything to Monet or the twins."

"I don't know that you're approaching this correctly. I think you should at least tell Monet's brothers. I can understand your wanting to protect Monet in the long run," Wade advised.

"I hear what you're saying, but I still want to check Aron out myself, and then I'll take things from there, depending on what I find out. I think they'll trust my intuition on this. I won't let too much time elapse before I tell them," Marcus promised. "Too bad you and Liz can't go with us on the cruise. I know the girls would enjoy the trip together," he said, changing the subject.

"I hear you, but all the kids will be home this year, and this is Samera's first Christmas." Wade picked up a picture of his nine-month-old granddaughter from his desk and grinned like the proud grandfather he was. "She's our first grandbaby, and Liz is driving me crazy. She's been shopping like there's no tomorrow. I keep reminding her that Samera is a baby and won't remember a thing about the holiday."

"I imagine if Nay-Nay and I were in the same position, she would be doing the same thing." Marcus felt a twinge of longing for the children they would never have.

"I didn't mean anything by bringing up Samera." Wade looked away as if he'd committed a faux-pas.

"Hey, dude, it ain't nothing. I can live the rest of my life without little ones; it's Monet I feel for. I don't think she'll ever give up her desire to have children. We've seen so many doctors over the years, and remember we went to Jerusalem to the Wailing Wall, and to Hot Springs Arkansas to bathe in the spas. We've had more ministers pray over us than terminally ill patients in a hospital. And at the end of the day, all the doctors could tell us was that there aren't any medical issues with me or Nay-Nay that would stop us from having a baby," Marcus reminisced.

"I remember those times." Wade nodded. "I'm surprised you two didn't go the in-vitro route."

"Trust me, we almost did. When Monet's mother passed, she had an insurance policy, and the amount doubled due to her being in an accident. Monet wanted to use the money for in-vitro. It took me months to talk her out of the idea."

Wade cleared his throat. "Well, me and Liz, and WJ and Genesse consider you two to be honorary grandparents to Samera."

"I know, and trust me, Monet has been spending money on Samera too," Marcus said. The men shared a laugh, and then he said, "I guess we should get back to work."

Marcus was grateful that he had a friend that he could talk to about his most intimate issues, and it was a bonus that Monet and Liz were best friends. The men had worked together since they were rookies on the police squad, and had lived in the same apartment building before they bought their homes in Auburn.

Wade was like the brother Marcus didn't have, and Liz more than filled the void as a sister for Monet. They were godparents to all of Liz and Wade's children; WJ (for Wade Junior), Shavon, and their youngest daughter, Erin. Liz was an only child, and Wade had one brother.

When WJ and Genesse got married, Monet and Marcus con-tributed to the pair's wedding costs, and were escorted to their seats along with the couple's parents and grandparents.

The department clerk walked over to Marcus and Wade. "This just came in." She handed an assignment sheet to Marcus. "The chief wants you to get on it right away."

Marcus scanned the paper. "There was a murder on Seventy-first Street and Eggleston." He told the clerk, "Tell the chief we're on it. I guess I'll call Monet later and see how her doctor visit went," he said to Wade, as they stood up and prepared to leave. They placed their weapons in their shoulder holsters and left the room.

Marcus's thoughts strayed to Monet once again, and he hoped her visit with Dr. Washington had gone well. He didn't have a clue that their lives were about to career out of control again.

Chapter 8

More time elapsed, and Monet was fidgeting in her chair, still waiting for Dr. Washington to return. She almost couldn't believe there was even a remote possibility that she was pregnant. She shifted into denial mode and decided, until she heard otherwise, that she was just suffering after effects from the attack. Her heart rate accelerated when she thought about being raped. She pulled a book out of her bag and began to read it to pass the time.

Dr. Washington walked into the room with a subdued look on her face and sat heavily down in the chair next to Monet.

Monet swallowed a couple of times and thought, *Dear Lord, she looks so serious, I hope I'm not dying.* "Well?" She guffawed nervously. "What are the test results? You look so grim. I hope I'm not dying or anything."

"Monet, in all my years of practicing medicine, I've never encountered a situation like this. You are definitely pregnant, this is December and I'd say you're about two months along," Dr. Washington stated.

At first, Monet sat in stunned silence. Then she smiled to herself and chortled with glee. She said softly, then louder and raised her hands in the air. "Thank you, Jesus. Father, you answered my prayers." She pressed her hands together, as if in prayer.

Dr. Washington watched Monet for a few minutes. Then she moistened her lips and said, "I would usually congratulate my patient at this point in the conversation, if the circumstances were different. But with the timing of the pregnancy, coinciding with the time of the rape and your conception issue, I'm truly at a loss for words."

"Why?" Monet asked, as her left eyebrow rose quizzically. "I beg to differ. I believe congratulations *are* in order."

Dr. Washington said as gently as she could, "I think there's a great possibility that the baby you're carrying might be your attacker's and not your husband's child."

"You're wrong," Monet replied vehemently. "I know this is Marcus's baby. I had been ovulating that morning and for a few days before that. Oh, Lord," she moaned, "it couldn't be *his* baby. God wouldn't be so cruel to me." She composed herself and said, "I know this baby is a girl, and that it's me and Marcus's child. There's nothing you can say to convince me otherwise."

"I know this news is totally unexpected, but I think you should at least consider the possibility that the child might not be Marcus's. I know this is a lot for you to comprehend. One option available to you is to terminate the pregnancy. Trust me, no one would fault you under the circumstances." Dr. Washington spoke in a kindly tone of voice while she reached for Monet's hand.

Monet snatched her hand away from the doctor. "No, you're wrong, Dr. Washington. I'm a Christian, and I would never have an abortion under any circumstances. I knew one day I would become pregnant because God told me that I would."

Dr. Washington was worried that Monet might be having a breakdown. So keeping her expression neutral, she asked, "When did He tell you that?"

Monet waved her hand dismissively. "He has told me that many times. Sometimes in my dreams, and other times I could feel Him speaking to me in my heart."

The doctor looked at Monet pityingly. "I believe you if you say so, but what will Marcus say? I'm sure your ordeal has been as difficult for him as it has been for you."

For the first time since Dr. Washington had given Monet the news that she was pregnant, Monet felt doubtful. "I don't know how Marcus will feel. But we've been married for a long time, and I know he'll come around."

"What if he doesn't? Are you willing to sacrifice your marriage over a child that more than likely is not your husband's?" Dr. Washington probed.

"I respect you as my doctor, but I think you're out of line. If you continue talking to me in that vein, then it's best that I leave before I say something I might later regret. Is there anything else?" Monet said distantly. She picked her purse up off the floor and stood up.

Dr. Washington walked around the desk and sat in her chair. "I'm sorry if I offended you. That wasn't my intention. But I would be remiss if I didn't mention the possibility of the baby's paternity." She touched her chest. "If you think you want to continue the pregnancy, then I can give you a referral for a good obstetrician." The doctor felt like she'd handled the situation incorrectly and wanted to make amends. Monet had been her patient for years.

"No, I can find one on my own. Thank you, Dr. Washington," Monet said frostily. She put on her jacket. "I'm a nurse, I know doctors too." She lifted her chin up defiantly.

"I'm sorry if I was out of line," Dr. Washington apologized. "I just wanted you to be aware of all your options, and to keep an open mind where you husband is concerned. Men are proud, and though there are a many who would accept children by other men, I'm just not sure how your husband would react under the circumstances."

"Your apology is accepted, and I understand what you're saying, Dr. Washington. But I know what God told me, and I have never given up hope that one day I would have Marcus's son or daughter," Monet said fervently. She put the strap of her purse on her shoulder.

"Okay then. On your way out, I'd like you to make an appointment with me for a month from now, and we'll see how you're doing and feeling. Monet, don't hesitate to call me if you need anything. I have to respect your feelings, so accept my congratulations." Dr. Washington tried to interject some gaiety into her voice and smile at Monet, but her efforts weren't quite successful.

"Thank you. I'll make the appointment, and believe me, I'll be fine," Monet said even as butterflies darted inside her stomach. Though she spoke with an air of bravado, she wasn't sure what Marcus would think. She prayed he would be as excited and joyful as she was, but knew there was a chance he might accept the news like Dr. Washington predicted.

Monet and Dr. Washington said good-bye, and Monet left the doctor's office. She went to the nurse's station and made an appointment for the second week in January. There was a bounce in her step as she walked to the elevator, and then to the parking lot to her car. Monet sat in her car for a moment, trying to rein in her thoughts. The couple had always planned to name their child Faith, if the Lord saw fit to bless their union with a daughter.

She bowed her head, and said aloud, "Lord, thank you for giving me my daughter, Faith. It seems like a lifetime ago when Marcus and I said we'd name our first daughter Faith Imani. I couldn't tell Dr. Washington that when Marcus rejected my idea to adopt, you told me that I would have a daughter and that I had to be patient. I suffered from what I call the Sarah Syndrome, and I believe with you, God, all things are possible. Father, I don't know how Marcus is going to react to the news, but I pray he will trust and believe in you. God, again, thank you for my miracle, Faith Imani Caldwell." She closed her eyes and listened to God tell her to be strong for the times that lay ahead, and how she would be blessed. Peace inundated Monet's being. And she knew in that instant that her belief and instincts were correct . . . Marcus was Faith's father; she had no reason to doubt that.

As she turned on the car, a satisfied grin split her face. When she stopped at the booth to pay her parking fee, the attendant looked at her and said, "You must have gotten some good news. You are positively glowing."

"Yes, the best news in the world. I'm going to be a mother," Monet said, preening prettily. She handed the woman her parking ticket and a five dollar bill.

"Well, congratulations. I wish you the best. What do you want, a girl or boy?" The attendant handed Monet the change.

"I'm having a girl," Monet said, and put the two dollar bills into her wallet.

"Well good for you. I wish you the best."

"Thanks, I'll see you next time." Monet drove out of the lot and headed south to her home.

She had to concentrate hard on driving because her mind kept wandering to the long awaited news Dr. Washington had given her. She was going to be a mother.

She parked her car in the garage. When she opened the backdoor, Mitzi greeted her at the door, wagging her tail rapidly. Monet picked up her pet and hugged her. "How's Momma's baby?" She fussed over her baby, while Mitzi licked her face. She put Mitzi down on the floor.

Monet walked to the foyer and took out a hanger and hung up her coat. Then she returned to the kitchen and put water in Mitzi's dish. Satisfied that her pet was taken care of, she walked into her office located near the kitchen area. The den had been made into an office for Monet, and the basement was Marcus's domain. The walls in the room were painted a soft beige hue, and Monet collected fabric African murals in earth tone colors, which covered two walls. In addition to the murals, many African and Native American statues were situated on wood shelves, along with a top of the line computer on a glass desk. A flat screen television was mounted on another wall. Beige carpeting complemented a burnt orange sofa with a matching wingback chair. An antique table was positioned in front of the sofa, and there was a wood burning fireplace on another wall.

Monet sat on the sofa, kicked off her shoes, and curled her legs underneath her body. She stroked her tummy. "Hello, Faith," she whispered, "this is your mommy speaking. I'm so glad that God gave you to me. I can hardly wait to see your beautiful face. We have a lot to talk about, and we don't have to wait until you make your arrival. I have a lot to tell you."

She bit her fingernails. Though she had put on a brave face for Dr. Washington, reality had set in, and doubts about the baby's paternity, due to her fear of Marcus's reaction, clouded Monet's mind.

What if Marcus doesn't believe that Faith is his baby and leaves me? There is no way he'd raise the child of a rapist. Oh Lord, I wish my momma was here. She would hold me in her arms and tell me that everything is going to be okay. Lord, give me strength to face Marcus, and help me to convince him that Faith is his baby. Show me the way, Lord.

Monet picked up her Bible from the table. She could hear her mother's voice in her mind saying, "Baby, take your burdens to the Lord, and He'll work them out." She opened the Bible to a random page, intent on seeing where the Spirit would lead her. As she read, she felt fortified in her belief. The scripture was just what she needed, like a dose of medicine.

She had opened the Bible to Philippians 4:4. Her fingers traced the words as she silently read, *Rejoice in the Lord always; and again I say, Rejoice. Let your moderation be known unto all men. The Lord is at hand. Be careful for nothing, but in everything by prayer and supplication with thanksgiving let your requests be made known unto God. And the peace of God, which passeth understanding, shall keep your hearts and minds through Christ Jesus. Finally, brethren whatsoever things are true, whatsoever things are honest, whatsoever things are just, whatsoever things are pure, whatsoever things are lovely, whatsoever things are of good report; if there be any virtue, and if there be any praise think on these things. Those things which ye have both learned, and received, and heard, and seen in me, do; and the God of peace shall be with you.*

When Monet finished reading the scripture, she held her hands over her face and began sobbing, a cleansing cry, and she read the passage over and over because it brought peace to her very being. She curled up on the sofa with her hands cradled protectively over her abdomen, and within minutes she fell asleep; dreaming about a caramel colored baby girl with her mother's eyes and her father's dark hair.

Mitzi licked Monet's hand, which had fallen off the couch and dangled near the floor. When Monet sat up, her stomach felt queasy. She rushed to the bathroom just in time to avoid making a mess on the floor that she would have hated to clean up. She returned to the kitchen, with Mitzi trotting behind her.

"Thank you for waking me up," she told the dog. "Now I can prepare Daddy's favorite meal and share the good news with him."

The dog sashayed across the floor and laid on her doggy bed, playing with a rubber toy, while Monet opened the refrigerator and cabinets in search of the perfect food for the soul. She had cooked a full course meal nearly every day since she'd been off work. Marcus loved her being home. She decided to prepare broiled steaks, and a steamed broccoli and cauliflower blend, along with twice baked potatoes and a Caesar salad. She thought a strawberry cheesecake for dessert would cap off the meal. She set the ingredients on the countertop, and then walked down to the basement.

Marcus and Monet were not heavy drinkers, but enjoyed a

glass of champagne on New Year's Eve and wine to celebrate their birthdays. In the summer, Marcus indulged in a few beers. Monet walked over to the wine rack and removed a bottle of sparkling cider. She thought her news called for a celebration. When she returned upstairs, Monet put the cider in the refrigerator to chill.

Before long, appetizing aromas filled the kitchen as Monet completed her chore. She glanced at the apple shaped clock on the wall above the microwave. Marcus would be home in about twenty minutes. She hurriedly put the dishes and utensils she had used in the dishwasher. While the cheesecake was chilling in the refrigerator, and the steaks were set low in the oven, Monet rushed upstairs to take a shower.

She had just finished dressing in a gold lounging outfit, and was pulling at her hair when she heard the garage door closing, signaling Marcus had arrived home from work. Monet hurriedly put the back of a gold stud on the back of her earlobe, and then she sprayed Tresor over her body. She lined her lips with chocolate colored lipstick and dashed downstairs.

She paused on the stairway, watching Marcus stand in the foyer, sorting through the mail. *Lord, please make it all right. I beg that you put understanding in Marcus's heart. Father, I don't want to have to choose between him and our baby,* Monet silently prayed.

Marcus looked up and saw Monet staring at him. He smiled and then winked at his wife and said, "What's up, pretty lady? How was your day? You look beautiful."

Monet wiped her perspiring hands on the side of her pants and tried to keep her body from trembling. She returned Marcus's smile and blew him a kiss. "Thank you, honey. I had a fantastic day. I can hardly wait to tell you about it."

Chapter 9

Monet walked down the few remaining stairs and into the foyer. Marcus held out his arms, and she walked into them and stood on her toes. Marcus kissed her passionately. The couple shared their first real kiss in months.

Then she pulled away from him breathlessly, looked up at him and asked, "How are you doing, handsome?"

"Not bad." He inhaled the scent of her hair, and the strands tickled his nose. "Um, you smell good. How did your doctor's appointment go?" He leaned away from her and peered down. "Is everything okay?"

"Just fine." Monet burrowed into Marcus's body. Then she looked up at him. "I've fixed your favorite meal, along with my favorite vegetables. Darn it, I need to check on the steaks." She scurried into the kitchen.

Marcus took off his jacket and hung it in the closet. Then he walked into the dining room. Monet had set out their best China and crystal glassware. Two chocolate colored tapers burned brightly in the eggshell white room.

"Aw sukey now, we're having a candlelight dinner. This must be a special occasion." Marcus's nose twitched as he rubbed his hands together. "I smell steaks. Thank you, babe."

Monet walked over to Marcus. "I have some wonderful news that I'd like to share with you at dinner."

He pulled her into his arms, and for once, she didn't flinch from his touch. "I love you, Nay-Nay. I don't know what I'd do

without you. Now give me a few minutes to shower. You're looking fine and smelling good; I don't want to be half-stepping. I've
got to keep up with my baby."

Monet nodded. "Make it quick. By the time you finish, I
should have dinner on the table. Now go." She shooed him away
with love in her eyes. Marcus looked at her, and his eyes reflected the depth of his feelings for her.

"I'll be back before you can say abracadabra," Marcus joked,
and jogged up the stairs.

Monet went back into the kitchen and put the vegetables inside a bowl. She removed a silver platter from the bottom cabinet, and forked the steaks, topped with onions and mushrooms,
into it.

Then she took the food and walked into the dining room
and set everything on the mahogany table built for twelve. Monet
smoothed down a corner of the manila lace tablecloth that had
belonged to her mother, Gayvelle. She put the ice bucket with
the bottle of sparkling cider on the matching buffet. She had
purchased a bunch of lilies on her way home from her doctor's
appointment, and they added a beautiful touch to the table.

It didn't take Marcus long to return to the dining room. He
sat across the table from Monet, looking handsome in a pair of
dark slacks and a pumpkin colored pullover sweater. She had
dimmed the overhead lights and lit the candles. She picked up
the remote in front of her plate and turned on the portable
stereo, which was tuned to Marcus's favorite jazz station. She
turned the volume down low.

She looked at Marcus and asked, "Would you bless the food?"

"It would be my pleasure. Though I don't know why you're
sitting all the way down there. Why don't you come sit next to
me?" He patted the empty chair next to him. Intense love radi-
ated from his eyes.

Monet picked up her plate and relocated to the chair next
to her husband.

Marcus took Monet's right hand in his own, kissed it, and then the couple bowed their heads. "Father, bless the food we are about to receive for the nourishment of our bodies, and double bless the cook. Lord, we've faced some tough times recently, and you've brought us intact from the storm. Continue to bless me and Monet. Amen."

"Amen," Monet echoed, and then put her napkin in her lap.

Marcus put a steak on his plate and then the other one on Monet's. They passed the bowls back and forth until their plates were full of food. Marcus dominated the conversation about his workday, but didn't mention that Monet's father had called. He had put out some feelers before he left work and was waiting on some responses.

"I'll be doing some surveillance work next week. There have been reports of a chop shop operating on the southwest side of the city, so the chief assigned me and Wade to the case. He believes in the detectives being cross-trained and rotates the personnel monthly. How did your doctor's appointment go?" Marcus asked.

She averted her eyes and asked evasively, "Do you want coffee? I forgot to bring it in here. I'll go to the kitchen and get it." Monet started to stand up.

Marcus stopped her. "No, I'm good. I've been dominating the conversation. Tell me about your day." He cut a piece of cheesecake with his fork, and was chewing it as he watched Monet. He sensed she was being elusive about something.

"Well, my visit with Dr. Washington went well for the most part. She was a little concerned that I haven't been sleeping well. She wanted to give me a prescription for Ambien, but I passed for now. She also suggested I join a rape support group."

"Hmmm." Marcus continued eating his cheesecake while Monet's sat uneaten on her plate. After he finished swallowing, he asked, "How do you feel about doing that?"

"I told her I would think about it, and I will." She cut her cheesecake into tiny squares.

"So what gives with the elaborate dinner?" Marcus's hand swept over the food. "Don't get me wrong, you usually cook a great meal for dinner, but this time you've gone all out. Are we celebrating something?" He looked up into the air. "I know I didn't miss our anniversary, and it's not your birthday or mine."

"Yes, you could say we're celebrating," Monet tittered nervously. She clasped her trembling hands together.

"Well, what is it?" Marcus lifted his eyebrow. "Don't keep me waiting."

Monet took her husband's hand. "Marcus, our dreams have come true. What have we prayed for more than anything else in the world?"

"I don't know about you, but I prayed that the fool that attacked you didn't have AIDS. And we already got back your test results for that, and it was negative." Marcus looked at Monet searchingly.

She took a deep breath and moistened her lips. Unconsciously her hand strayed to her abdomen. "Marcus," she said, with a smile bright as a hundred watt bulb, "we're going to be parents. I'm pregnant."

Marcus sagged in the chair for a moment and a smile flitted across his face. Then reality set in, and he held his hand up. "Hold on. I know you didn't say what I thought you said."

"I said that I'm pregnant. My due date is July fifteenth," she informed him proudly. She smiled at her husband tentatively. She could tell from Marcus's expression that he wasn't taking the news well.

He stared at her with his mouth wide open, and his body quaked with rage. He was struck silent. He covered his face with this hands and thought, *God, why did you have to do this to us? What did we do to deserve this? No, Monet, can't have this baby. She's obviously mentally ill from the rape. She knows there's no way in the world I can be this baby's father.*

Monet was horrified by Marcus's reaction. Mitzi stood in the doorway barking loudly. Monet stood so abruptly that her glass of cider tilted to the side before it straightened. She fell back into her chair and dropped her head, while Marcus's breathing became labored. Mitzi scampered into the room and ran between Marcus and Monet, barking furiously. Finally she was spent and lay down by her mistress's feet. Marcus looked like all the blood had been drained from his body. His mind desperately desired to dive into denial. He wished they had never had the conversation they'd just shared.

With his face devoid of color, Marcus stared at Monet, who sat huddled in her seat. Her shoulders shook as she wept silently. Reality jump started Marcus's mind, and he pondered how his wife could look so attractive when she greeted him, prepare an appetizing meal, and then wound him so deeply. His mind clicked to the conclusion that he had to try and reason with Monet about terminating the pregnancy. The conversation had to happen immediately before more time elapsed, and she balked at his suggestion.

His legs felt weak as he stood up and sat in the empty chair next to Monet. He moistened his lips and carefully considered his next words. "Nay-Nay, I'm sorry for the way I reacted to your news. But my God, woman, how did you expect me to react? There's no way you're pregnant with my child. Have you forgotten we can't have children?"

Monet held up her head and looked at Marcus with dewy eyes. "Have you forgotten there was no medical reason why we couldn't have children?" she asked him. "Did it ever occur to you that God picked now for us to have a child?"

Marcus withdrew from his wife like she'd stabbed him. He spoke in a careful, soothing tone of voice. "I may not be a doctor or anything, but I know that we've been married for twenty years, and we've never had a baby." He lifted his hands and bent his fingers in the air to emphasize his point. "Then you got raped, Monet. That's what happened; you were raped. Then you make me a special dinner to announce that you're pregnant, and expect me to believe it's our baby?" He looked at her like she had taken leave of her senses.

Monet, in turn, looked at him with widened, teary eyes. Her feelings were equally hurt, as if Marcus had told her he wanted a divorce.

"What did Dr. Washington say?" He folded his arms across his chest. "She's the expert."

"Well," Monet's voice faltered, "she kind of thought like you do, that there's a possibility the baby might not be yours."

Marcus pounded the wooden table with all his might. "Well, dang, Monet, what more do you need to convince you that this baby isn't mine? Even your own doctor has doubts." The annoyance in his voice bounced off the walls.

Monet jumped when his fist hit the table. "Marcus, it's doesn't matter to me one whit what Dr. Washington believes, I know what I believe in my heart. This baby," she pointed to her abdomen, "is yours and mine, and I know that's true because God told me we were going to have a baby."

"Well, when did He tell you that?" coldly spewed from Marcus's lips. His eyes were tight as slits. "Before or after you were raped?"

"I can't believe you said that." Monet put her hand over her mouth, jumped up from the table, and rushed out of the room and down the hall to the washroom. She kneeled on the cool tiled floor and heaved into the toilet. She prayed Marcus would come and see about her, but he didn't.

When she returned to the table, Marcus was sitting in the same spot, his face swollen with righteous indignation. He refused to look at her.

"Honey," Monet stood beside Marcus, then she reached over and touched him lightly on the shoulder, "I don't care what Dr. Washington says, I'm one hundred percent sure that you're Faith's father."

Marcus shrank away from Monet's touch, as if she were a poisonous snake. "You have sunk so heavily into denial that you don't realize what you're saying. That child you're carrying is not mine, and I want you to have an abortion now," he demanded, glaring at her fiercely.

"Now, I think you've lost your mind," Monet whispered. She inhaled deeply, and sat back down in the chair. "There is no way I'm having an abortion. Do you realize how long it took for the Lord to bless us with a child?"

"What if the baby is the rapist's child, Monet?" Marcus fired back at her. "What will you do then? I think you need to take the blinders off your eyes and face reality. The plain ugly truth is that you've been impregnated by a rapist." He snapped his lips tightly together.

"No," Monet spit out as she hopped up from the chair. "I may have been raped, but I haven't lost my mind. And you know what, Marcus? God has my back if no one else does. He promised never to leave me, and even if you walk out that door, I know that He won't ever leave me alone. In the book of Isaiah, the scripture says, *Fear thou not; for I am with thee; be ye not dismayed; for I am your God; I will strengthen thee; yea, I will help thee; yea, I will uphold thee with the right hand of my righteousness.* That means, Marcus, I will never lose hope or sight of what I know to be true, because God has got me." Her body trembled like a wind blown leaf. She crossed her arms across her chest and said, "I am having this baby whether you like it or not."

"If you do, then I am out of here. I'm gone, Monet," he retorted in a bone chilling tone of voice. "Here's an ultimatum to you since you want to throw out your own. Be careful what you do because I know you don't want to trash our love, or our twenty years of marriage. I can tolerate many things in life, but I will not, and I'm going to repeat this to you so there is no misunderstanding, I will not raise the child of a rapist under any circumstances. You got that?" Marcus's eyes shot fiery blazes at his wife.

"There's something you forgot in your tidy equation, Marcus," Monet said, in a low undertone. "This baby is a part of me too. How could you ask me to destroy a part of myself?" Tears poured down her face, and she folded her head inside her arms and bawled like a baby.

Marcus turned and stumbled away from her, as if he were blind. He stomped from the dining room to the foyer. Monet could hear him fumbling as he looked for his keys. He jerked the door open, stormed out of it, and slammed it so loudly that it seemed like the hinges moaned.

Monet looked at the doorway wearily. *Well, that didn't go well at all.* She rose from the chair, walked to her office, picked up the Bible off the cocktail table, and held it in her arms. She sat down on the couch and rocked back and forward, sobbing as if she had been handed a fatal medical prognosis. She could hear Mitzi moaning in the kitchen, making a noise that sounded like crying.

"Come here, baby," Monet said in a hoarse sounding voice. Mitzi trotted into the office and she picked her up and cradled the dog's body next to her own. "He'll be back," she crooned to herself and Mitzi. "And when the baby is born, Marcus will be very sorry about the way he acted toward me tonight."

Monet experienced sorrow as she thought about what had just transpired between her and Marcus. "Lord, I know sometimes our way is difficult, but what just happened with me and Marcus has hurt me almost as much as when Momma died. I remember how lovingly and kind Marcus treated me when my

mother died, and afterward when I mourned her passing. He
has been so patient with me since the rape." Her voice seemed
to close up, and her breathing became shallow. She took deeps
breaths until she calmed down. "But why did he have to hurt me
like that? I had a premonition that Marcus might have a hard
time believing me about the baby. I just never imagined it would
disintegrate into a full-fledged debacle. And if my own husband
doesn't believe me, then who will?" She bit the insides of her
cheeks, trying to stifle a sob.

Her hand tightened on the Bible, and Mitzi's warm body nuzz-
led against her comfortingly. "I guess this is how Jesus felt when
He came to the end of His earthly road. I must have faith that
everything will work out the way you planned in the end. And
Lord, even if this baby is the child of a rapist, I will love her
because she's mine too." A smile flickered on her face, then
died. "I will not let the devil dominate my mind with negative
thoughts. This is me and Marcus's baby, and that's all there is
to it. Lord, keep me strong for the days ahead because I'm going
to need you and will have to lean on you more than ever before.
And Lord, take care of Marcus. I know he will eventually see the
light, even if I have to wait nine months."

Monet sighed and put the Bible on the table and sat in her
office, silently waiting for her husband to return home. Mitzi,
ever loyal to her mistress, never left Monet's side. As the hour
drew later, Monet stood and went to the kitchen to let Mitzi out
the back door. Then she returned to her office and lay on the
sofa. Her mind was overwhelmed with thoughts of how Marcus
was doing at that moment. She said a prayer, asking for the Lord
to keep her husband safe as she let Mitzi back inside the house.
Mitzi toenails made a click-clacking noise as she followed Monet
to her office to wait for Marcus.

Chapter 10

Around three o'clock in the morning, the shrill tone of the telephone rang and broke the silence in the Harrisons' house. Wade, who was closer to the phone, didn't answer it right away.

Liz turned over in the bed and poked her husband in the side. "Wade," she said, "the phone's ringing."

"Okay," he replied and burrowed further under the warm cozy eider down comforter.

"Wade, get the phone," Liz repeated as she poked her husband again.

He rolled over and fumbled for his glasses, and then clicked on the black cordless phone. He cleared his throat and said, "Hello."

Liz was completely awake by then, and she sat upright on her side of the bed.

"You have who, where? Yes, I know him. Just keep him there, and I'll be there in thirty minutes." Wade clicked the phone off and put it back in the base. Then he rose from the bed and began shedding his pajamas.

"What's wrong?" Liz asked, swinging her legs over the side of the bed, poised to get up if necessary. "Who was on the telephone?"

Wade exhaled heavily. He really didn't want to tell Liz who the call was about, but knew if he didn't that she would hound him mercilessly.

"That was the owner of a bar near the job. Uh, there's a problem. They want me to come down there." Wade opened the closet door, took out a dark woolen shirt and pulled it over his head. He put on a pair of blue jeans and zipped them up. He took his wallet from the nightstand drawer and stuffed it in his pocket.

Liz rolled her eyes, then asked Wade, "What kind of problem, and involving who? Is it your brother, Chester, again?"

Wade buckled his black leather belt around his waist. Then he sat on his side of the bed and put on his socks and shoes. Tension rose in the air like a vapor. A call from a bar in the wee hours of the morning had occurred too many times for Liz. He glanced behind him and saw his wife sitting rigidly on her side of the bed, scowling at him.

"It's Chester, isn't it? It's too early in the morning for this. Doesn't he realize we have to go to work in the morning?" Liz yawned and covered her mouth.

"Uh, no it isn't Chet this time. Apparently Marcus is drunk and has gotten into a fight at a bar." Wade bent over and tied his shoes. Then he sat up and opened the top nightstand drawer and removed his keys.

"Good Lord, what's gotten into Marcus? I've never known him to do anything that rash before." Liz rose from the bed, looking fearful. "I wonder if something happened to Monet." Her knees went weak and her body sagged as she put her hand out on the bed to break her fall.

Wade walked around the side of the bed and sat down next to Liz. "Now Lizzie, don't jump to conclusions. If something happened to Monet, then Marcus would have called us."

Liz grabbed Wade's arm and clutched it firmly. "I guess so. But my gut feeling is telling me that something is terribly wrong with Marcus and Monet. Wade, this is just so not like Marcus."

He gently disengaged Liz's arm from his own. "Let me go see what's going on. I'll call you as soon as I can." He kissed the top of her head and squeezed her arm. Then he stood up and said, "I'll call you later."

Liz tugged on the sleeve of his shirt. "I want to go with you." She pulled the yellow and black scarf off her head. "It will only take me a minute to get dressed. Please let me go, Wade," she begged.

"No, Liz, this is man's business. Marcus is my best friend, and I'm going to see about him like he would for me." With that said, Wade turned and walked out of the room.

Liz heard the back door open then close and Wade locking it. She held her breath until she heard the garage door rise and shut, and finally the purr of the engine of Wade's beige Jeep Laredo SUV as he drove down the alley. She felt edgy, felt the need to do something, anything. So Liz smoothed out the melon and black comforter that was bunched in the middle of the black lacquered king sized bed that she and Wade shared. She walked around the bed and picked up the cordless telephone. She punched in the number to Monet and Marcus's house. The telephone rang and rang, and when Liz heard the generic voice mail greeting, she clicked off the phone. She turned on the phone again and tried Monet's cell phone number. She still didn't receive an answer.

Liz became agitated. She stood up, walked out of the bedroom and down the hall to the kitchen. She turned on the burner under a silver tea kettle, which she had filled with water the previous night. Then Liz opened the pantry and removed a tea bag from a nearly empty box. When the orange tea was ready for consumption, she poured herself a cup and sat at her glass table. She blew on the tea to cool it off before taking a few sips. Then she set the cup on the table, walked over to her desk in the corner of the kitchen, and picked up the cordless phone. She quickly entered Monet's telephone number, and still there was no answer.

After an hour had elapsed, Liz became very concerned. She decided to get dressed and call Monet again. If she still didn't get an answer, she would go to the Caldwells' house. She began mentally composing a letter in her mind to leave on the kitchen table to explain her absence to Wade. She stood, left the half empty cup sitting on the table, and walked rapidly to her bedroom to get dressed.

Monet, where are you? Liz thought as she got dressed.

Wade turned up the collar of his leather jacket as he walked toward the bar on West Sixty-third Street. The red and blue neon sign simply read Otis's Longue. The bar wasn't more than a hole in the wall. He was relieved there wasn't any sign of Chicago's finest around and about. The bar owner had informed Wade when he called him, that he had found Wade's telephone number in Marcus's wallet as an emergency contact. The owner explained how Monet's name was listed on the card too, but he figured what happened at the bar was, as he called it, *"Men's bidness."* The owner went on to explain that he could see from Marcus's work ID card that he was a policeman. The older man assured Wade that if he could get Marcus out of the bar without further incident, then he wouldn't press charges against Marcus.

Wade pushed the door open and saw Marcus sitting at one of the few tables that still stood upright. His hands were covering his face. The place was empty. The mirror behind the bar was cracked, and many bottles of liquor and glasses were broken and leaking onto the floor. Bowls of peanuts were upended. It was obvious that some type of brawl had taken place.

A short, thin, dark skinned man with tufts of gray hair shooting out of his head, wearing dark jeans and a sweat shirt that overflowed his body sat on a barstool. He introduced himself as Lee Otis Fowler, the owner. Wade noticed a sawed off shotgun lying against the side of the bar.

The man looked Wade up and down with beady eyes and asked, "You must be Harrison?"

"Yes," Wade replied, as he walked toward his friend.

"Look, man, I gots to have my money. Do you see what yo' boy done?" Lee Otis pointed toward Marcus. "I done lost a whole lotta money up in tonight, and somebody gots to pay for this." His hand swept an arc in the air.

"Give me a minute to talk to him. You'll get your money," Wade said disgustedly.

He walked over to where Marcus was sitting, picked up a chair off the floor and sat it upright across the table from Marcus.

He waited for Marcus to say something, and when he didn't, he said, "What's up, man?" Marcus didn't respond for a minute, so Wade tried another tactic. "Come on, Marc, tell me what's going on? This isn't like you, fighting in public. You're lucky the owner is looking for money and didn't call the police. You'd be written up so fast at work that your head would spin. I heard that Liz called Monet a few times earlier tonight for their nightly prayer session, and no one answered. What's going on?"

When Wade said Monet's name, Marcus looked up and Wade gasped. His partner's bloodshot eyes reflected unadulterated pain. Wade had never seen Marcus look as he did tonight, despite all the situations they'd encountered while working. Wade thought that maybe Liz was right, and something had happened to Monet.

Marcus whispered, "Monet," in a strangled voice. Then he put his head on the table and cried.

"Man, I think he's crazy or something. That's all he's been doing since I closed the place down . . . moaning 'bout his woman." The bar owner made a circle with his fingers around the side of his head.

"Did something happen to Monet?" Wade asked Marcus tentatively. His stomach felt like someone was dribbling a basketball inside of it.

"Nay-Nay, she's . . ." Marcus broke down, put his head on the table and began crying.

Wade surmised correctly that he wouldn't get any useful information out of Marcus until he sobered up. He decided to talk to the owner and get Marcus out of the bar as soon as he could. He stood up and walked back over to the bar and asked Lee Otis, "What happened here tonight?"

"Shoot, yo' boy walked in here with a chip on his shoulda. When he got here, he was quiet. He jist sat at the bar down at the end, and he kept drinking and drinking. He minded his bidness. Then later some young cats came in heah and they wuz talking. One of 'em said something 'bout how that nurse at St. Bernard that got beat up looked good, and he wouldn't mind hitting that." Lee Otis's rheumy eyes got wide. "The next thing I knowed, yo' boy snapped, and it was own. Dah cats tried to put up a fight, but they weren't no match for dude. Shoot, he was lucky they ain't had no pieces on 'em. Course they knows I don't allow that up in heah."

"Okay, I get your point," Wade said impatiently. "How much you looking for as far as damages?"

"Shoot, he musta caused at least 5 G's wortha damage up in here," Lee Otis blustered.

"I don't want your estimate. I know you've probably had fights in here before. So call your clean-up guy, and then call me tomorrow morning with an estimate. You got a piece of paper?"

The owner took a slip of paper and a pen from the side of the cash register and handed them to Wade. Wade wrote down his name and telephone number, and he gave the paper back to the owner.

"Fair enough," Lee Otis replied. He folded the paper and put it inside his shirt pocket. "Jist get him outta here. I knowed he was the law." Lee Otis's voice dropped to a whisper. "Ain't he the one whose missus was raped? I thought I seen him on TV I feels sorry for 'em, that's why I ain't called the po-po. We don't need one of us in the paper with this kind of foolishness." Lee Otis nodded his head.

"I appreciate that," Wade agreed. "We're good for the repairs. I'm going to get him out of here. I'll talk to you tomorrow."

Lee Otis nodded and resumed cleaning up as Wade walked back to where Marcus was sitting. He pulled at Marcus's arm. "Come on, big guy, let's get out of here," he cajoled and begged, but Marcus wouldn't budge. "Hey, Lee Otis, come give me a hand getting him up!" Wade yelled, after his futile attempt to get Marcus to stand up. Lee Otis sauntered over to the table. "You take one side and I'll take the other," Wade instructed.

It took some time and effort before they managed to get Marcus out of the chair. Once he was somewhat upright, he leaned against Wade as he stood between the two men. With a lot of exertion, Wade and Lee Otis got Marcus outside and into Wade's SUV. Lee Otis closed the passenger door. Then he walked to the driver's side and exhaled exaggeratedly. He blew on his gnarled hands.

"Ya sho you don't wanna break a brotha off a li'l sumin' sumin'? It ain't like it was easy carrying a dude this size outta heah," Lee Otis said.

Wade reached in his pocket, took out his wallet and pulled out twenty dollars. "This money will go toward Marcus's repair bill," he informed the wiry man, as he handed the folded bill to Lee Otis.

"'Preciate it, man. Dat man got a hurtin' on him. I hope you can help him fo' he start tangling with the wrong crowd. He was lucky it wasn't gang bangers he was tussling with." Lee Otis blew on his cold hands. "I gots to go. Later."

While the car was warming up, Wade debated where to take his friend. Marcus was slumped against the window, and his head lolled back against the back of the seat. Wade put the key in the ignition, started the car, and pulled into traffic. There really wasn't any place to go except to his house. He sighed, knowing it was going to be a long night. Wade fought back tears because, like Liz, he assumed that something terrible happened to Monet. With the way his friend was acting, she might have even been dead.

At the same moment Wade was heading home with Marcus, Liz was ringing the doorbell to the Caldwells' house. When no one answered the door, she returned to her car, and rummaged through the glove compartment for the spare key she always kept to their home. She exited the car and walked inside the silver chain link gates.

"Lord, please let everything be all right," Liz mumbled, suddenly feeling frightened. Her hand wobbled as she put the key in the lock, turned it to the right, and walked inside the darkened house.

Chapter 11

Wade slowly backed his Laredo into the left side of the attached two-car garage of his and Liz's dark brick split level home. Marcus had slept; actually he'd snored during the ride to the Harrisons' home. Wade noticed that his wife's black Nissan Maxima was missing from the garage, and surmised that she had gone to the Caldwells' house. He turned off the engine and nudged Marcus.

Marcus opened his bleary eyes. He looked at Wade and said, "What?" He tried to sit erect, and his body toppled to his left. The scent of alcohol seemed to infuse the inside of the SUV.

Wade cracked open the window and waved his hand in the air. "We're at my house. I couldn't think of anyplace else to take you, considering what's happened to Monet," he said in a hushed tone of voice.

When Wade said Monet, Marcus slumped back into the seat. "Oh, you know what happened? Liz must have told you." He rubbed his eyes.

"No, I mean, isn't Monet . . . didn't she pass?" Wade looked at Marcus with a confused expression on his face.

"Pass for what?" Marcus said, holding his aching head in his hands. "I don't feel so good. My head is killing me. Can we have this discussion in the morning?"

"Marcus, where is Monet?" Wade raised his voice in exasperation.

"I don't know, I guess she's at home." He scratched his head.

Then his expression became frigid, and his tone of voice confrontational. "I don't want to talk about Monet." He turned and looked out the window.

"Why aren't you home with her, instead of out at a bar brawling like you're a teenager again?"

"Wade, you're my best friend, and all I can say is I'm tired. I'm so tired . . . can I stay at your house tonight?" All the air seemed to deflate from Marcus's body.

"Look, man, I can take you home; that's no problem." Wade was taken aback by the venomous expression that appeared on his friend's face.

"No, I don't want to go home. I don't have a home," Marcus mumbled. He rubbed his head again. "Wade, I know you have questions, but my body aches, my knuckles are sore, and my jaw is swollen." He cautiously stroked the side of his face. "Today has been the worst day of my life. I just want to go somewhere and sleep. If my life were a story that could be rewritten, then I'd wake up tomorrow and find out everything that has happened today was a dream." He laughed harshly. "But I know it isn't a dream. Instead it's become a nightmare."

"Okay, you're scaring me now." Wade held up his hands worriedly. "Sure, you can stay the rest of the night or what's left of it. But you know at some point you're going to have to go home and face the music, or do what you can to undo the nightmare." He unlocked the car doors and looked at Marcus. "I hope you can walk under your own steam because, buddy, I can't help you by myself."

After five minutes, Marcus had managed to get his body out of the SUV. He walked a little unsteadily to the back door, but managed to get there without harming himself, and without Wade's assistance. When they walked in the house, Marcus scuttled as fast as he could to the bathroom. Wade went up the short flight of five stairs and took a set of towels out of the linen closet.

He went back downstairs and put them on the floor outside the bathroom. "Marcus, I put some towels on the floor," he said.

"Thanks," he replied dolefully. His voice sounded strangled, like he was crying.

Wade shook his head at the idea. *My partner crying? No, I don't think so. I must have imagined that.* He went into the kitchen and put a filter into the coffeemaker. Then he saw Liz's note and read it. By the time the coffee had finished brewing, Marcus was walking into the kitchen.

Wade pointed to a chair and said, "Sit." He removed a black ceramic mug with the word, Dad, in large red letters emblazed on it and poured coffee into it. Then he handed the cup to Marcus.

Marcus looked at the mug, and his first thought was to knock the cup out of Wade's hand. He shook his head and gestured with his hand that he didn't want the cup.

"I think you need to drink this and sober up," Wade advised. He placed the mug on the table and sat in the seat across from Marcus. Wade shrugged his shoulders. "Are you ready to talk about what's going on with you and Monet? The owner of the bar told me you went off after some thugs made remarks about her. That's not like you, Marcus. I know something else had to be going on. Do you want to talk about it?"

Marcus rubbed his aching jaw and winced. "Not really. Not tonight anyway. I really just want some aspirin and to go to bed. I assume I can sleep on the sofa bed in the basement?" He tilted his head questioningly.

"I guess so. You're like a brother to me. Heck, you're closer to me than my own brother, and you know if you need someone to talk to, I'm your guy. We've been partners for a long time, and friends even longer. I won't judge you. But I do caution you to take your problems to the Lord."

Marcus's expression changed from boredom to chagrin. He

was upset with Wade's clumsy attempt to counsel him, and Wade didn't miss the look on his partner's face.

"Wade," Marcus said through clenched teeth and curled fists, "I said that I don't want to talk about it now. I know you have my best interest at heart, but now isn't the time. I have some things I need to sort out for myself. If you want to play junior minister, that's fine, but I don't want to listen to you wax philosophical regarding issues you know nothing about. If you don't want me here, I can call a cab and stay in a hotel."

Wade put his hands in the air. "Whoa, buddy, you don't have to get defensive with me. I was only trying to help you." He stood up. "Do what you have to do, but remember you may think that you're in control, but God is."

Marcus stood up abruptly and walked to the basement door outside the kitchen. "I'll talk to you in the morning." He opened and closed the door.

Wade could hear Marcus's heavy footsteps trampling down the stairs. He sat at the table, his mind going a mile a minute, genuinely worried about the state of Marcus's mind. He knew something was eating at the heart of his friend. And the fact that he didn't go home to Monet spoke volumes about the issue. He sipped the rest of his coffee.

When he finished, he put the cup in the sink and went to his and Liz's bedroom. He took off his clothes, put on his pajamas and sat on the side of the bed, bowed his head, and prayed.

"Lord, I don't know what's happening with Marcus and Monet tonight. You know Liz and I affectionately call them M&M. I know whatever is eating at my buddy has to be serious, Lord, or he wouldn't be at my house tonight. Father, I pray that you bring comfort to them and give them strength. Keep your arms around them, Father, and don't let go. I know that Marcus will talk to me tomorrow, and I ask, Lord, that you help me to say the right words to ease my friend's burden. Lord, thank you for putting it on Lee Otis's heart to call me tonight. There is no doubt in my mind that you were at work, taking care of your child. Help Monet and Marcus in their time of trouble. Amen."

He lay in bed for a time, hoping Liz was having more luck with Monet than he'd had with Marcus.

Chapter 12

Liz tiptoed into the Caldwells' darkened house. She could hear the stereo playing in Monet's office, though the volume was low. A medley of gospel songs was playing. She recognized the CD because she had given it to Monet as a gift a few months ago. A dim light that Monet had left on for Marcus shined in the living room.

Liz turned on the light in the foyer and softly called out Monet's name. When she didn't get an answer, she walked into the kitchen, and then into Monet's office. She found Monet stretched out on the sofa with a blanket covering her body and Mitzi nestled by her side.

The dog barked and jumped off the sofa and ran up to Liz. Monet turned over and saw Liz. She pushed her hair out of her eyes, sat up, and tried to smile, but instead a grimace converged on her face.

"Oh, Liz," she wailed, "Marcus is gone. He's left me. I've been calling him and he won't answer his cell phone."

Liz stood frozen to the spot as waves of shock ran through her body. She never expected to hear those dire words pass from either Marcus or Monet's lips. She walked rapidly to the sofa and sat down beside her friend. "Oh no," she said as her face crumpled into tears. She took Monet in her arms and they wept together.

When the crying frenzy had passed, Liz reached for a tissue in the box that sat on the bottom of the cocktail table and wiped her eyes. She handed one to Monet. "Can I make you a cup of coffee or tea?" she asked.

Monet answered despondently. "Tea will be fine."

Liz stood up, took off her coat, and laid it on the back of the computer chair. She walked into the kitchen, turned on the light, and reached in the cabinet for the teakettle. She put water in the teakettle, set it on the stove, and turned on a burner.

Monet had gone to the bathroom to wash her face. She was startled when she saw her face in the mirror. Her eyes were swollen and her lips chapped. She knew that she looked like death warmed over. Her eyes strayed down to her belly and back up to her face.

After she hung the towel on the rack, she went into the kitchen where Liz stood by the stove waiting on the water to finish heating. She had taken two cups from the cabinet and sat them on the table, along with two teabags.

"Do you want to sit in here or back in the office?" she asked Monet

Monet looked at her friend listlessly. "The office will be fine."

"I'll bring the tea in there when it's ready," Liz murmured.

Monet walked back to the office and sat hunched over on the sofa, wringing her hands together helplessly until Liz returned. Finally, Liz came back to the den carrying a tray with two cups on it. She set the tray on the table, gave Monet a cup, then sat on the sofa and took a cup for herself. The women sat in silence. The only sound in the room was the slurping of tea as they drank.

When Monet put her cup back on the tray, Liz said, "What's going on, Nay-Nay?"

Monet's face flashed happiness, then became clouded. "Remember how we used to listen to Frankie Beverly and Maze?" Liz nodded tentatively, not sure where the conversation was headed. Monet sighed audibly. "My favorite song by them was "Joy and

Pain." And right now I can relate to that song more than you could ever imagine." She took a deep breath and dropped her eyes to the floor. "My greatest wish in the world has come true, but it has also caused a serious rift in my marriage."

Since Liz had a degree in psychology, she knew exactly what Monet was telling her in a round about way. She stared at Monet for a second, then smiled at her sister/friend and said, "Congratulations, Nay-Nay." Her mind processed her earlier conversation with Wade, and the mystery was solved as to why Marcus had been out drinking.

Monet looked up, surprised to hear the word *congratulations* from Liz's lips. "You're the second person to tell me congratulations today and meant it," she said.

"I take it Marcus wasn't pleased by the news," Liz said, venturing a guess.

"Humph, that's an understatement." Monet shrugged her shoulders and wiped at her dampening eyes.

"He doesn't think the baby is his, right?" Liz prodded her friend as gently as she could, while shifting her body on the sofa.

"Yes, you hit it on the head." Monet sighed. "He doesn't think the baby is his, and wants me to have an abortion. When I disagreed with him and told him abortion wasn't an option, he stormed out of here like a hive of bees was on his tail. I haven't seen him since."

Liz debated whether she should tell Monet what Marcus had been up to, and debated with herself if she should hold her peace or speak now. She put her arm around Monet's shoulder. "What if the baby isn't Marcus's?"

Monet's eyes grew wide as an old vinyl record, and she put her hand on her abdomen. "I know the baby is Marcus's. The paternity of our child is the least of my worries." She furrowed her brow, as if in deep thought.

"If that's what you say and believe, then I believe you." Liz nodded, wishing that she could say more to comfort her friend. She knew Monet's life with Marcus during her pregnancy wasn't going to be easy.

Monet moaned. "Dr. Washington's reaction was the same as Marcus's. Neither one of them believes the baby could be Marcus's because of the rape." She looked away from Liz, feeling edgy.

"I can see Marcus's point, and unfortunately his is a normal reaction, especially under the circumstances. The ordeal was very difficult for him and you," Liz said, moistening her lips as she took Monet's hand in her own.

"I know how what happened to me really threw him for a loop, Liz. But I can't abort our child, and Marcus was wrong to ask me to do so," Monet cried almost hysterically.

"Maybe he just needs some time to adjust to the idea," Liz suggested supportively.

"I know, and I'm going to give him all the time he needs." Monet nodded her head. "But he walked out on me, Liz," she sobbed. "Even after I told him that God had told me I was going to have a daughter."

Liz nodded sensitively. She wasn't surprised to hear that proclamation. "You know I told you years ago that you should have told Marcus about God talking to you, along with your gifts of clairvoyance and healing. If he knew of your gift to predestine, perhaps he wouldn't be reacting so badly about the news." When Monet had initially revealed the scope of her gift to her, Liz was skeptical. But as more time went by, and Monet had confided in her about some events that had come to pass, Liz realized she was telling the truth.

Monet answered, "I tried to tell him so many times over the years, but he wouldn't hear of it. He said that he equates that stuff with hocus pocus, and asked me if my parents came from Louisiana or someplace like that. You and Reverend Wilcox are the only people, other than my mother, who I have discussed my talks with God to. And as you know, my mother had the same gift. God, I wish she were here with me right now." She picked up a sodden tissue off the table and dabbed at her eyes.

"Monet, I'll be here for you as much as I can. And with Marcus, you'll just have to give him time to adjust to the idea."

"What if he leaves me for good?" Monet swallowed hard. "He's acting like he wants me to choose between him and our child."

"You've just got to hold on to your faith as tight as you can." Liz made a fist. "And know that God will see you through this." She rubbed Monet's arm.

"I know what you're saying is true. But not being with Marcus is like not having an arm or leg. I don't know that I can get through this pregnancy without him." Monet's body slumped while her face drooped.

"You may have to go it solo, and you can. And Nay-Nay, you know why you can get through this?" Liz reminded her friend encouragingly.

"Yes," Monet nodded her head. "Because I'm a child of God," she said, with Liz saying it with her. Liz clasped Monet's hands tightly in her own.

"It's been a long day. Why don't we go upstairs and get ready for bed? I need to call Wade and tell him I'm going to spend the night here. I'll call work tomorrow to take the day off and spend it with you," Liz said.

"Okay." Monet stood up and reached over to pick up the tray from off the table.

"No, I'll get that." Liz stood and scooped up the tray and cups. "Let's turn in, I'm beat. I'll fix breakfast for you in the morning, and we'll talk some more."

Monet turned to Liz and hugged her. "Thank you. I don't know what I'd do without you. Follow me to the guest bedroom where you and Wade usually sleep when you stay over. I think you two still have some nightclothes on the shelf in the closet."

"Okay," Liz replied. "And I think you're right. I remember leaving a set of pajamas here for us. It's not like I can fit into your clothes as tiny as you are. But we'll see what your weight is in about eight months."

Monet turned off the light in her office while Liz took the tray into the kitchen, put the cups in the sink, and rinsed them. She turned off the light and joined Monet in the hallway.

With her head turned to the side, Mitzi looked at her mistress and wagged her tail hopefully, as if asking Monet if she could sleep upstairs in the master bedroom with her.

Monet snapped her fingers and said, "In there, Mitzi." She pointed toward the kitchen.

The dog stood up promptly and tried to follow Monet upstairs. Liz laughed and walked over to the dog, scooped her up, and walked toward the kitchen. Liz turned on the light, put the dog in her doggie bed, and then turned off the light.

The women walked up the stairs together. Monet went toward the master bedroom, while Liz went to the guest bedroom across the hall. They said goodnight. Monet changed into a nightgown and fell asleep as soon as her head hit the pillow.

Liz sat on the side of the pine antique bed complemented by a matching dresser and tall chest of drawers. A television stood on the middle shelf of a pine entertainment center. A full length mirror stood in one corner of the room. The room was painted in earth tones, green and a cinnamon brown, which added a nice touch to the dark furniture. The bedroom set had belonged to Monet's mother, and had been shipped to Chicago after Gayvelle's affairs were settled.

Liz hated to lie on the lacy, ecru colored comforter. She felt like it was too delicate to use for sleeping and that it was more like window dressing. She walked across the room to the closet and removed a brown cotton comforter. Then she removed the lacy bedspread from the bed, and replaced it with the comforter.

When she was done with that, she nodded with satisfaction, sat on the edge of the bed, and removed her shoes and socks. She padded over to the closet, removed her gown, then quickly stripped off her clothes and donned the gown.

Liz had laid her cell phone on the nightstand next to the bed, and it suddenly vibrated, startling her. She looked at caller ID and saw her home number.

"Hi, hon," she answered.

"Lizzie, why didn't you call me back?" Wade sounded aggravated. "I was starting to worry about you." He was lying on his back, wearing red and white striped pajamas, and his feet were crossed at the ankles.

"This is the first opportunity I've had to call you since I got here. Monet and I have been talking, and we just turned in," Liz whispered, as she stretched her body on the bed.

"I guess we were wrong, huh?" Wade said. "Monet is obviously all right, or we wouldn't be having this conversation."

"Yes, we were way off the mark. Where's Marcus?" Liz asked.

"He's in the basement asleep on the sofa bed. I went downstairs and checked on him before I called it a night. He's knocked out."

"I'm getting ready to crawl into the bed." Liz covered her mouth as she yawned and ran her hand over her head.

"Do you want to tell me what sent my buddy over the edge and then some?" Wade asked.

"It's too long of a story to get into tonight. I'm hoping Marcus will talk to you himself, and maybe you can try to talk some sense into him," Liz replied as she snuggled deep down in the bed.

"He definitely wasn't in a talking mood tonight." Wade gave his wife a recap of what had happened tonight.

"That's a shame," Liz said when he finished speaking. "Look, I'm tired, we're both emotionally drained. I'm going to take a vacation day tomorrow and spend the day with Monet. Maybe you should see if you can get the day off too. I know with the help of the Lord, maybe we can get our friends back on track."

"Humph, don't count on it," Wade snorted. "Marcus has really flipped the script. Are you sure you don't want to tell me what happened? I hate to be in suspense until tomorrow. Plus, if I knew what I was up against, then I'd know how to approach Marcus."

"No, hon, it would take too long. What helps is that you're a good listener, so I know you'll be fine."

"Man, a brother can't get anything out of you," Wade said to his wife grumpily. "I guess I'll have to talk to Marcus in the morning and go at it cold turkey."

"Uh-huh, you got that right. I'm going to turn in. Are you going to miss me tonight?" Liz asked in a semi-serious tone of voice as she pulled down the sleeve of her gown. She felt grateful that her and Wade's marriage had never been tested to the degree that Monet and Marcus's had.

"Like a thirsty man stranded in the desert," he quipped. "Seriously, yes, I miss you already. Shoot, I missed you when I left to go get Marcus and pulled into the garage and saw your car gone."

"You're laying it on a bit thick." Liz laughed. "I love you, Wade, and I'll see you tomorrow."

"Love you too, Miss Lizzie," he said. "Sleep tight. I know God will put the right words in our mouths to help our friends. Goodnight."

"Goodnight, Wadie poo," Liz said. Then she clicked her phone off and shifted in the bed to get comfortable.

With a smile on his face that matched the one on his wife's, Wade turned off the light on the nightstand.

Marcus groaned as he turned over on the sofa and rea-ched

for Monet. Though he was still asleep, he stretched out his arm and patted the empty space next to him.

While at the Caldwell residence, a sob escaped Monet's lips. She sighed and said, "Marcus." Then she folded her arms around her waist.

It was going to be a long night for both couples, each separated from the one they loved.

Chapter 13

Wade awoke at six A.M., the same time he rose for work every morning. He opened his eyes, almost expecting to see Liz lying next to him snoring. He picked up the cordless phone from his nightstand and called the precinct. When the department clerk answered his call, Wade asked to be transferred to the chief.

He quickly explained to the man in charge that he and Marcus needed to take the day off, that a family emergency had arisen. Chief Davis asked Wade if everything was all right, as if he sensed there was more to the request than he was being told. Wade reassured him that he had everything under control, and that they would report for work the following morning as scheduled.

Wade then got out of the bed, showered, and dressed. Then he went to the kitchen to put on a pot of coffee. While the java brewed, he strolled into the living room and returned to the kitchen with his Bible, the current issue of the *Daily Word* pamphlet, and The *Chicago Sun Times* newspaper. Usually he and Liz shared a spiritual meal before they headed for work if their schedules coincided.

The theme for the day in the pamphlet was overcoming fear, and the scripture was taken from the Twenty-third Psalm. Wade felt encouraged when he reached the end of the page and read the prayer, which thanked God for His promise to be with him always. The author bade Christians to faithfully trust in God, and to walk courageously with their Heavenly Father all the days of their life. Wade meditated on the lessons and the scripture. He felt how apropos the reading was, and how it seemed tailor made for his and Liz's situation. The scripture encouraged Wade.

He stood and walked to the counter to pour himself a cup of coffee. He took the cream out of the refrigerator and sat back down on the cane back chair. He was thumbing through the sports section of the newspaper when he heard the basement door open. Marcus walked into the kitchen looking glum, like he'd lost his way and reason in life. He flexed his hand as if it pained him.

Marcus sat at the table while Wade rose from his seat to prepare a cup of coffee for his friend. When he was done, he handed the cup to Marcus, who added a couple spoonfuls of sugar, and then gratefully sipped the coffee.

Wade sat back down in the chair and said, "Good morning. Let me be the first to tell you that you look like death warmed over. Do you need an aspirin? Your face is swollen."

"What I need to do is call work to take the day off, and an aspirin wouldn't hurt," Marcus said tiredly, as he massaged his temples.

"I already got that covered," Wade told him. "I spoke to Chief Davis this morning." He stood up, went to the bathroom, and returned to the kitchen with a bottle of aspirin. He tossed the bottle to Marcus, who poured two pills into his hand, and then sipped some coffee to wash them down.

Wade pulled Lee Otis's telephone number out of his shirt pocket and handed it to Marcus. "You need to call this guy this morning and settle up your bar bill."

"What is this for?" Marcus asked as he held the scrap of paper away from his face, trying to read the writing.

"Not only did you overindulge last night, you also caused a ruckus. You were brawling. Don't tell me you don't remember anything about last night?" Wade asked skeptically as he lifted his left eyebrow. He stood and went to the stove and poured himself another cup of coffee.

"Actually, I don't remember too much about last night; just parts of it," Marcus admitted, looking abashed. He dropped his head toward the floor.

"Do you remember the part that led you to the bar to begin with?" Wade asked.

"Unfortunately I do. I wish I could forget it and everything else that happened over the past couple of months," Marcus sputtered. "Monet is pregnant."

Wade coughed from choking on his coffee. He hadn't seen that one coming. "Okay, I admit that's big. From your reaction, I guess you don't think the baby is yours?"

"You got that right. Monet's in super denial mode. I think she needs to see a shrink. I told her there's no way the baby she's carrying is mine." Marcus snapped his lips shut.

"I agree with you that the timing might not be right, but if you made love to her around the same time, then there is a possibility the child could be yours. At least that's what I think," Wade interjected.

"Monet hasn't gotten pregnant in almost twenty years of marriage, and our anniversary is on Valentine Day. It was bad enough that she was battered and every little detail was reported in the newspaper and on the local news, and now she's pregnant." Marcus's eyebrows shot up.

"I'm not going to lie; that's heavy, but only because you're looking at the situation through the eyes of someone who's not saved." Wade held out his hand toward Marcus. "I know that you're saved and what you're experiencing is a test of faith," Wade said.

"Being saved or not doesn't change the facts, Wade," Marcus said crankily. He wished Wade would just leave him alone until he could figure out what to do.

"Let me see; your wife of almost twenty years, who you profess to love more than anyone in the world, is assaulted, and now she's pregnant. Both of you have taken every test under the sun, which have shown there isn't any reason why she can't conceive. And you're one hundred percent sure the child isn't yours? Did I leave out anything?" Wade asked patiently.

"All that you said is true, except you left out the part where I told Monet she had to choose between me and that baby." Marcus swallowed so hard that his throat hurt. "And you know what, Wade, I meant what I said. I want her to have an abortion right now. I have no desire at this stage in my life to become the laughing stock in our community or our jobs."

"Oh," Wade nodded, "so now you're concerned with how people will perceive you, but not about your wife's feelings or God's? Remember Him? He's the head of our life."

"What would you do if you were in my situation, Wade?" Marcus asked unenthusiastically, although he already knew the answer to that question.

"I would accept the child as my own. Didn't Joseph do the same for Mary and Jesus?" he said.

"Mary wasn't raped." Marcus's voice rose slightly.

"I know, but that wasn't the point I was making. As Christians, we're responsible for one another, and you know that I don't approve of abortion. Sometimes we have to come out of our comfort zone and do things we normally wouldn't do."

"That's your theory, but my feelings are different. I see nothing wrong with Monet having an abortion under the circumstances. Rape is a valid reason for legally terminating a pregnancy," Marcus stated.

"What about from a moral standpoint? And how would you feel about Monet terminating the pregnancy, knowing there's a possibility that the child could be yours? Wouldn't that be the same as killing your own child?" Wade asked.

"Morals have nothing to do with rape," Marcus said loftily.

"What about half of that baby is a part of Monet?" Wade asked huskily. "The woman you say you love more than life itself."

"I admit that's where I struggle," Marcus conceded begrudgingly. "But I can't do it . . . and I won't."

"Sure you can. Turn it over to Jesus, and let Him guide you," Wade suggested. He was trying very hard not to be judgmental.

"I know you disagree with me, but I can't help the way I feel," Marcus said. "My wife was attacked, and there is nothing I could do about that. And if she goes through with this pregnancy, I'll have to look at the offspring of the animal that did that to her every day. It ain't happening, dude. Monet will have to get rid of it," he stated adamantly.

"You're not thinking about this clearly," Wade replied, trying to keep an even tone in his voice.

Marcus's body bristled, and then he dropped his eyes. "If Monet had gotten pregnant by me one time during our marriage, then I would probably look at the situation differently. But she hasn't, and miracles don't happen, at least they haven't in my lifetime."

Wade shook his head sorrowfully and held up his hands. "You're wrong, man. Monet wasn't killed during the attack, and that was a miracle. She can see, walk. and think. Sometimes our Heavenly Father sends us gifts when He thinks we're ready to cope with the situation. But don't fool yourself, Marcus. God doesn't make mistakes. Whatever happens is an event that He has orchestrated. I suggest you go home and talk to Monet. Have you forgotten how badly she wants a baby?"

"That's what tears me apart about the entire situation." Marcus opened and closed his jaw and flinched from the pain. "I *do* know how badly she wants a child. I've heard her go on about that our entire marriage. But I think her blindness about the conception runs so deep that she'll accept that the baby is the rapist's seed," Marcus spat.

"You've got some issues you really need to work out," Wade said, with a feeling of dismay building in his chest. "We all thought that Monet needed counseling, but maybe you're the one who needs counseling."

"There isn't anything wrong with me that my wife can't fix by doing what's right for both of us, and not just for herself." Marcus pushed the chair back from the table and stood up. "I've had enough of this conversation, and frankly, I think it's time for me to go."

"Where are you going? Your car isn't here for you to go any-where. Did you forget I had to drive you here from the bar?" Wade sipped his coffee.

"I can always take public transportation," Marcus said stub-bornly.

"I'll take you to your car. I was really hoping we could come to a meeting of the minds regarding this issue," Wade said. "But I see that isn't going to happen, at least not today. You need to pray and allow God to direct you." He drank the remainder of his coffee and went to his bedroom to get his car keys and wallet.

When Wade returned to the kitchen, he found Marcus stand-ing in front of the back door looking out the window. He looked like he wanted to bolt the premises immediately. He opened the door and went outside.

Wade made sure the front door was locked before he went back into the kitchen and outside. He unlocked the door to the garage, then he and Marcus went and got into the car. Wade drove out of the garage and headed north to the bar. The two men rode in silence for a few miles.

"Marcus, I don't want you to think I'm choosing sides," Wade finally spoke. "I intend to support you and Monet. You're both in a tough predicament, but I know in the long run, you'll both weather the storm. I would suggest you stay prayerful and listen to God as He guides you."

Marcus shook his head and complained, "Can't you just be a friend, and leave God out of this for once?"

Wade laughed. "You wish, but no I can't. God is involved in every facet of our lives, so if you can't trust Him to guide you right now, I'll keep the prayers going out to Him to help you and Monet."

"I appreciate you being here for me, Wade, and know if the situation was reversed, I'd do the same."

"Fair enough for now," Wade said graciously. "But know at some point, you're going to have to take your burden to the Lord, and allow Him to work it out to His satisfaction, not yours or Monet's. Since we both attend church, the same one I might add, you know what the Father wants you to do."

"I know," Marcus threw his hands in the air, "but sometimes turning the other cheek is easier said than done. It was bad enough Monet was raped, she was also beaten, and that's not something I take lightly. And she's pregnant on top of that. It's too much, Wade. You know I'm right."

"There is no right or wrong sometimes, Marc. At times it's about acceptance of a situation, and I have a strong feeling that's what you're going to have to do, whether you want to or not."

"We'll see about that," Marcus said grudgingly. Then he turned to the window and looked out of it. He didn't talk to Wade the remainder of the ride to the bar.

Liz had tossed and turned most of the night. A few times during the night, she'd heard Monet sobbing, and Mitzi had crept upstairs and made mournful noises outside Monet's bedroom door. Liz didn't want to intrude, because she knew if Monet wanted comforting that she would've come to the guest bedroom. Liz bathed, dressed, tidied the room, called her job, and scheduled the day off work.

She was half sitting and lying in the middle of the bed, checking her palm pilot, when she heard a scratching noise at the door. She knew it was Mitzi, and that it was probably time for her to go outside. She rose from the bed and opened the door. Liz went downstairs, and Mitzi trotted behind her. She opened the backdoor to allow the dog to go outside to handle her business. While Mitzi was outside, Liz found a can of dog food in the pantry, which she emptied in Mitzi's food bowl, and filled the other dish with water.

A few minutes later, she opened the door to let Mitzi back inside, and she ran to her bowls. Liz opened the curtains over the sink, and then washed her hands. After drying them, she checked the refrigerator to make sure Monet had the ingredients for Denver omelets, which she did. Liz filled the coffeemaker, took the chopping board out of the pantry, and then removed food from the refrigerator and began preparing the morning meal.

Monet came downstairs when Liz was putting the ingredients in a skillet. "You put on coffee, bless you," she said. She had on a pair of sea blue pajamas, with matching bedroom slippers on her feet. She took a cup out of the cabinet, poured herself a cup of coffee, and sat at the kitchen table.

"Did Marcus call you?" Liz asked as she put a skillet on the stove.

"No. I called his cell phone, but he didn't answer. When he's ready to talk, he'll call me," Monet said wearily.

Liz turned the burner under the skillet to low. The aroma of the diced potatoes wrecked havoc in both Liz and Monet's stomachs.

"That smells good." Monet inhaled. "I wasn't really that hungry, but I am now. I'll put plates on the table while you finish cooking."

Minutes later the women were eating at the table. Monet blessed the food, and they began digging into their breakfast.

Liz wiped her mouth with a napkin. "Girl, I'm stuffed, I can't eat another bite."

Monet pushed her seat back from the table and giggled. "Me either. I haven't had an omelet in a long time."

"Wade loves my omelets. We have them at least twice a month," Liz boasted.

"As well he should. I remember my momma telling me the way to a man's heart is through his stomach. She would make me stay in the kitchen until I perfected the dishes she taught me to cook." Monet had a faraway look in her eyes as she reflected on the past.

"I think I told you I had one of those mothers who couldn't cook. My dad was the cook in the family," Liz said after she sipped some orange juice. "I'm glad to see a little bit more life in your face. You had me worried last night."

"I guess I'm settling down a little." Monet nervously twisted a curl around her finger. Her eyes were clear and focused, although she appeared a little tired, no doubt due to the stress of the situation.

"Good. You know I'm here for you, and I think I can speak for Wade too. You have a difficult road to travel, but I know in my heart," Liz put her hand over her chest, "that you're going to be fine. Marcus may take a different leg of the journey, but I believe the two of you are going to meet at a juncture in the road, and then travel together again."

"Thanks, Liz; you always seem to know the right thing to say. That's what I love about you as a sister/friend." Monet smiled a bit.

"Girl, I got your back, right behind the Lord. You and my goddaughter are going to be fine. I know you're missing your mother too."

Monet nodded. "This breech with Marcus would be easier to endure had she been around. I know she's up there in heaven being my biggest cheerleader." Her voice broke abruptly. She put a hand over her damp eyes, and then cleared her throat.

"It'll be okay," Liz said forcefully, as she grabbed Monet's hand. "Father in heaven, I thank you for allowing us to see another day. You woke us up clothed in our right mind, ready to do your will. We ask, Lord, that you guide us, and keep my sister-girl safe in your loving arms. Father, some burdens we have to turn over to you because it's beyond our scope of understanding, so we leave Marcus's burdens in your hands. Lord, help Monet to realize she's not alone. Wade and I are here for her, and most of all, you are. Father, give us strength and keep us safe as we go about the day."

"Amen," Monet said. "I guess the Lord knew what He was doing when He made us prayer partners this year. We haven't been prayer partners," Monet counted on her fingers, "for five years."

"That's true. We were so upset when Reverend Wilcox instructed us to switch partners on an annual basis back then. Her reasoning was that we could best serve others more effectively if we rotated. Then this year when she assigned us to each other, I was ecstatic. Who would have thought how much we'd need each other now?" Liz didn't wait for Monet to answer, she continued speaking. "One thing I can say about the Lord, He always steps in right on time," Liz sat back down in her chair. "Everything in life happens for a reason."

"You know, you might be onto something there. You know who I really miss having in my life outside of my momma, Liz?" Monet said to her friend.

"Who's that?" Liz queried.

"My daddy. You know I never knew my father." Monet looked away from Liz. "I never told you this. Instead I told you my father was dead. I guess I was a little ashamed to tell anyone the truth. Still, I knew the day would come when I'd have to tell you the truth. I just didn't imagine it would be today." Monet sighed, then she looked at Liz's face. "Daddy left my momma when I was five years old and the twins were two. I have vague memories of him, and I sense that we weren't close. I wasn't a daddy's girl; my heart always belonged to Momma. I think he had an issue with me because of my gift.

"When the twins and me became older, we heard rumors in town that Daddy had gotten himself into some kind of trouble, and Mama never really explained what happened. When the boys hit their teen years, they missed having a father figure, and Derek became somewhat rebellious. I don't think he ever recovered from not having a dad to raise him. I wish I knew why Daddy left home. Although he was never very affectionate with me, I remember him always staring at me with a baffled look on his face. When I was in college, I became obsessive about trying to analyze our relationship, but then eventually let it go."

Liz nodded. She knew there had to be a mystery regarding Monet father's departure. Her friend would talk endlessly about her mother, but never about her father.

Monet had a haunted look on her face as she nibbled her lower lip. "At one time I thought maybe my mother had an affair and had me outside the marriage. But when I look at pictures of my father, I see my own face. So I knew that wasn't it. Then one day I got my courage up and asked my mother what had happened? Why didn't my father like me?"

"Oh, Nay-Nay, I'm so sorry you had to go through that. But you know the events we experience in life make us stronger," Liz commiserated soothingly.

"I know that now, but I couldn't accept it years ago." Monet shook her head and wrinkled her nose. "I had to grow spiritually before I could understand my parents' unique relationship. It was different from everyone else's I knew."

"You know most of us don't know what goes on behind clo-sed doors. Sometimes we only see what people want us to see," Liz added.

"Then I got it in my mind that maybe Momma wasn't my mother, and I was my father's outside child. Boy did I struggle with that one." Monet shrugged her shoulders. "Especially since I didn't look like her. My mother was very dark in complexion, and I used to say, how could someone her color have a child my color? It was too confusing."

"Well, that wasn't true, was it?" Liz asked. When Monet did-n't respond, Liz repeated the question.

Chapter 14

"No, it wasn't true." Monet shook her head from side to side. "I think I was almost eighteen years old before I got up enough courage to ask my mother why my father didn't care for me. Can you guess what she said?"

"Well, don't keep me in suspense," Liz said, her head resting on her hand.

"One of the reasons my father left was because I was a spooky child. I overheard him telling my mother that. I sensed his distaste. He went on to say that he thought I was possessed or something. I remember him saying that like it was yesterday. On some level I know it was because of my struggle trying to learn to cope with the gift. My mother said that I was a moody child because of the voices in my head. It wasn't until I was older and saved that I was able to discern voices of people in my head from God's voice. Momma told me that would eventually happen, and it did.

"I didn't talk until I was almost three years old. It seemed, at an early age, I would sense or dream about events that happened, and it must have frightened me. My mother explained what was happening to me when I was around seven years old. My father and my mother were having their own issues too, as I later found out."

"If you got the gift from your mother, and it was passed down from mother to daughter for generations, how did your dad deal with your mother's gift?" Liz asked, perplexed.

"Momma told me that he didn't really know about it when they got married. He knew there was something a little different about her, but as long as she cooked and kept the house clean, he didn't probe too deeply. Momma told me that she would just keep to herself until the voices stopped talking in her head. I think that's why I haven't made a big deal out of Marcus not supporting me. This gift can put a terrible strain on a marriage," Monet said.

"And you didn't want the same thing that happened to your mother to happen to you, and you did what you were taught by your mother." Liz nodded, as she filled in the blanks.

"You got it," Monet said. "Because I didn't talk until I was older, my cousins later told me that my daddy thought I was deaf and dumb. That made me more determined not to allow my gift to interfere with my marriage, or that's what I thought at first, until I realized that God is in control and not me. I've tried to talk to Marcus about the voices I get from people and God's voice speaking to me, but he wasn't hearing me."

"That's too bad. I imagine experiencing those feelings and sensations can take a toll on you," Liz said.

"I look at the gift as a family inherited ministry from God. Most of the women in my family view it that way. My mother used her gift as a mid-wife, and like her, I chose to work with newborn babies. Some of my relatives healed through herbs they grew that helped people recover from injuries. Others have worked in the medical field as nurses like me, and a few have gone on to become doctors. Once I had a full understanding of what the gift entails, I've done my best to use it in a way that would please God. No one knows this, and I know Marcus would be furious if he knew that sometimes on my days off, I work with the police in the smaller suburbs and towns, trying to help them solve crimes by using my voice and sensory perception," Monet said.

"Do you ever sense bad feelings about yourself or Marcus?" Liz asked nosily.

"No, not about myself, but I've had feelings about Marcus. I'll call him at work and ask him about situations to be aware of when he's working undercover. Like where someone was hiding in a building, and even where a bomb was located. Most of the time, I'm on target, and I know that somewhere in the back of his mind he realizes that, but he just refuses to deal with it. And before you ask, if I sensed something about you and Wade, I'd let you know in a subtle way, like I do with Marcus." Monet smiled.

"So other than voices or feelings, do you experience any other signs?" Liz was fascinated by the conversation.

"No, that's it. I know it sounds weird, but that's my life." Monet smiled. "When I've shared my information with a select few friends in the past, they couldn't accept it. Later, after I accepted Christ as my personal Savior, I learned better how to use my gift. I was close to a cousin when I was growing up, she had the gift too. But we lost contact after college. She lives in Seattle, and she's a doctor. It would have been easier to stay in Alabama because my family is there, and they're like me. But I wanted to move beyond Alabama and see the world."

"I think being able to help mankind at that level is an anointing from God. Now what about the lottery or things like that?" Liz asked, trying to lighten the mood. "You have any numbers for me to play today in the pick-four game?"

"Don't even go there," Monet quipped back with laughter. "Honestly, I've never tried it."

Liz felt honored that Monet had shared so much information with her. Liz, like the nurses in Monet's unit, knew there was something special about Nurse Caldwell. Liz had met Monet's mother many times before her death, and she just seemed like a quiet, attractive, older woman, who seemed at peace with herself and her lot in life. Serenity came to mind when Liz thought of Monet's mother. The only time Gayvelle really became animated was when she talked about Monet or her sons. It was apparent to anyone who saw them together, that mother and daughter shared a close relationship.

"What about your mother and the bus accident. Did you sense she was going to pass away?" Liz asked.

"I had a dream about her the night before, and it seemed like Momma was far away from me. We were in a field, and she was walking ahead of me, and I was running, trying to catch up with her. But no matter how hard I tried, I couldn't. I could literally feel my legs pumping in the dream. At the end of the dream, she turned and blew me a kiss, and then she was gone.

"I called her the next morning after I awakened, but we never talked. She had already left for work. I felt out of sorts and I couldn't seem to stop crying, and the details of the dream stayed in my head. Looking back in retrospect, I realize that she was trying to prepare me for what lay ahead," Monet admitted. Her eyes clouded with tears as she clasped and unclasped her hands. "A few minutes before Duane called to tell me what had happened to Momma, I had a premonition of doves soaring upward in the air. I knew that Duane was calling me with bad news. I believe that's when Momma's soul left her body.

"I looked at a clock, and I noted the time I saw the doves on a piece of paper, and the time matched the time of death on my mother's death certificate," Monet added.

"I take my hat off to you and all the women in your family. God gave you all a gift which you all have used wisely."

"I don't know about all of us." Monet smiled. "My cousin, Sharla, worked as a psychic, like Miss Cleo, for a while for monetary gain. But after a few months, her gift was gone just like that." She snapped her fingers.

"Wow, that's amazing," Liz exclaimed as she folded her arms

across her chest. "I want you to know that you have my total support, and I understand why you won't have an abortion. All I can say is based on what you told me, I believe the baby is Marcus's. Keep your head up, and hold on to God's unchanging hand. I'll be there for you in any capacity you want me to be."

"Thank you, Liz." Monet sniffled. She took a napkin out of the napkin holder and blew her nose. "God will surely bless you. Maybe I should have pushed Marcus harder and made him listen to my story."

"Maybe this is a test that Marcus has to face himself," Liz interjected. "Did you ever think of that?"

"I hadn't," Monet admitted as she shook her head. "Sometimes I don't know how I'm going to endure being pregnant and not having him with me to share the joy."

"Keep the faith, and you'll be all right. In Matthew 17:19 and 20, the Bible says if we have the faith the size of a mustard seed, then we can move mountains. Marcus is a piece of cake compared to a mountain. He'll come around. Just believe that he will." Liz took Monet's hand and held it tightly.

Though Monet nodded, she wished she knew where her husband was and why he hadn't returned her phone call. *Marcus, where are you?* kept drifting through her mind.

Chapter 15

Around eleven A.M., Marcus and Wade returned to the bar, or the scene of the crime, as Wade solemnly informed his friend. Marcus talked to Lee Otis, who gave him two estimates he'd gotten to clean up and fix the place.

Marcus was shaken when he realized how out of control he had been the previous night and vowed to leave liquor alone. Lee Otis reassured him that he wouldn't have any problems with the punks he'd tangled with trying to file charges against him or anything because they all had criminal records.

"Lee Otis, I'll have your money this afternoon," Marcus told the older man.

Lee Otis replied crustily, "That will be fine. I'll jist close down the joint for a couple of days. Ya need to lay off the sauce, man, cuz ya get crazy." He continued sweeping debris like he'd been doing when Marcus and Wade arrived.

Marcus and Wade walked outside and two blocks down the street to Marcus's silver Chevy Blazer. Marcus was about to get into the vehicle when Wade asked him, "Where are you going?"

"I don't know. I was thinking about staying at the Extended Stay in Alsip, or in Blue Island for a few days until I can get my head together. Or maybe I'll stay permanently," Marcus said. Alsip and Blue Island were suburbs located on the outskirts of Chicago.

"The quickest way for you to get things together is to go back to Monet and work things out with her," Wade advised.

"Monet has made it clear that she plans on continuing the pregnancy, so there's nothing for us to work out. My position is that I'm not going to stand by and watch her body swell with another man's seed." Marcus had a tinge of anger in his voice, clearly peeved with his friend, who he perceived as taking Monet's side. "I appreciate your concern," he said through clenched teeth, "but this is my dilemma, and I will deal with it as I see fit."

Wade threw up his hands in surrender. "You're right, it's your dilemma, and it's up to you to work it out. You and Monet have been married a long time. You can't just drop out of her life and not talk to her about it. I know you love her, and that you will work this out. We've always been able to talk to each other about anything before. I guess this topic is out of bounds.".

"It is for now. Don't get me wrong, I appreciate your support and you taking the day off of work today for me, but I need to figure this out on my own." Marcus waved his hand and unlocked his car door. "I've got to go. I'm pretty sure that I'll see you at work tomorrow." He got in his vehicle and drove off.

Wade nodded and walked back to his jeep. After he entered his car, he nodded his head and said, "Humph. Marcus is going to learn the hard way. But that's okay, Lord, Liz and I will be there for him and Monet, just like you'd have us be."

While he was sitting at a red light, Marcus watched Wade activate his right turn signal. Seconds later, Wade pulled into traffic and drove in the opposite direction. Marcus followed his progress until he could no longer see the jeep. His light turned green, and he pulled into a parking space, turned off the Blazer and punched the steering wheel until he cringed from the pain.

He whispered, "Why did this have to happen to us? Nay-Nay used to always say she was going to have a baby, but she failed to mention it would be with another man. I can endure a lot, I'm a strong black man, but I refuse to be a father to another man's baby, especially a rapist."

Marcus rubbed his head, and then reached into his glove compartment and pulled out a pair of dark sunglasses to put on his face. He drove to the bank to get a cashier's check for Lee Otis. After taking the check to Lee Otis, he drove out to Alsip and checked into the Extended Stay.

He took the elevator to the second floor to Room 208. He paid for the room for a week. He realized he didn't have any clothing with him and walked over to the bed and lay down across it. A longing for Monet stung his soul. He sat up and turned on the radio. When he heard Luther Vandross singing, "A House Is Not A Home," a frown marred his face, and he quickly turned the radio off. *That is definitely not a song I want to hear right now.*

One part of his brain realized Wade was right, that he did need to talk to Monet. The other side of him didn't want to see her at all because he knew she hadn't changed her position any more than he had. Marcus decided to take a nap. His head still wasn't straight from the drinking binge the night before, and he decided after his nap that he'd go out to get some clothing, food, and a replacement cell phone. His had been damaged during the melee at the bar.

He fell asleep thinking about Monet with a swollen belly, and groaned even while he was asleep.

At the Caldwells' house, Monet and Liz were sitting at the kitchen table. They had just finished eating lunch, soup and tuna sandwiches, when Monet told Liz, "You can go home if you like. I'll be fine."

Liz had errands that she needed to tend to and a meeting at the church that evening. "Are you sure?" she asked. "I can stay another night if you want me to." The doorbell sounded. "I'll get it," she said. She walked to the front door and looked out the peephole to see Wade. A smile spread across her face as she opened the door. "Hi, honey," she chirped, after she closed and locked the door.

"Hi, Lizzie," Wade greeted his wife, and then kissed her on the lips.

"Is that Marcus?" Monet called out. She wrung her hands together anxiously. She looked up at the doorway to see Liz and Wade enter the room.

Wade walked over to Monet and bent down and hugged her. Then he sat on the chair across from her. He didn't miss the look of disappointment on her face.

"I guess you couldn't talk Marcus into coming home," she said sadly.

"I tried, Monet, with all my might, but he's hurting right now and not thinking straight. Give him time, he'll come around," Wade said as upbeat as he could manage.

"I understand," Monet said, although she really didn't. She looked down at the floor. "Why hasn't he called me?"

"He misplaced his cell phone last night. He said something about going to get a replacement one today, so I'm sure he'll call you later," Wade said.

"Did he say when he was coming home?" she asked hopefully.

Wade struggled as he decided whether he should give Monet hope, or just tell her the truth. "He really didn't say when he was coming home, Monet. He mentioned staying in a hotel tonight. But I know once he has time to think about things sensibly that he'll be back."

"You think so?" She chewed on her nail.

"Yes, I know he'll come back. We just need to give him time to get himself together."

"I agree with Wade; he'll be back." Liz stood up, walked over to Monet and rubbed her back.

"Did he tell you where he was going?" Monet asked. She wanted Liz and Wade to go home so she could go upstairs and cry. And when she was done crying, then go find her man and bring him home where he belonged.

"He said something about staying at an Extended Stay in Alsip or Blue Island," Wade answered.

"Okay." Monet nodded as wheels began turning in her mind. "Why don't you two go home? I'll be fine." She crossed her ankles to keep from jumping up, grabbing her keys and running out of the house.

Liz assumed incorrectly that Monet was devastated by the news Wade had told them, and she said loyally, "I can stay with you another night, or you could stay with me and Wade. We'd love to have you."

"That's okay," Monet protested. "Wade, take your wife home, and I'll talk to you two later." She stood up and tried to discretely shoo them out of the house.

Monet quickly ushered the couple to the front door and opened it. Instead of making small talk like she usually did, Monet, to all intents and purposes, kicked the couple out, albeit graciously. As Liz was buttoning her coat, she finally figured out where Monet was going. It wasn't like her friend to rush her and Wade unless she was plotting something. Based on her unusual actions, both Wade and Liz figured out Monet's plot to visit Marcus.

Liz was thrilled at her friend's initiative, and she was sure Marcus wouldn't be able to resist Monet's pleading with him to come home. Wade, on the other hand, knew how obstinate Marcus could be.

He stood up and said clumsily, "Monet, I'm not sure if it's a good idea for you to go see Marcus. He really is in a bad state." Wade tried to advise his friend.

"I didn't say anything about going to see Marcus," she said innocently. She nervously ran her fingers through her hair.

"Don't say I didn't warn you." Wade shook his head in capitulation. "Well, I guess I'll head home. Don't hesitate to call us if you need anything," he said. "I'll see myself out." He hugged Monet and departed.

Liz looked at Monet, who was still standing by the end of the sofa. "You're going to see him, aren't you?"

Monet nodded. "I know Marcus is hurting, but I'm going to do what I can to bring him home."

"Just be prepared for the possibility that he might not come with you," Liz cautioned her friend. "I'll call you later." She squeezed Monet's arm, and like Wade, departed.

Monet walked to the door and locked it. Then she rushed upstairs to her bathroom and quickly showered. She put on a pair of jeans and a teal colored sweater. Monet scurried back downstairs to her office. She powered on her PC and did a Google search on Extended Stay locations. She called the hotel in Blue Island, and was told that Marcus Caldwell wasn't registered there. Then when she called the Extended Stay in Alsip and hit the jack pot. The reservationist asked her if she wanted to be connected to Marcus's room.

"No, that's okay, I'll call back later," Monet answered, with a smile and purpose on her face. Mitzi trotted into the room. Monet looked at her and said, "I forgot to give you your treats. I'm sorry, baby." She went into the kitchen and put a handful of cinnamon and honey treats into Mitzi's bowl and filled the water bowl. "Mommy's going to bring Daddy home," she informed the dog.

Mitzi barked and wagged her tail and resumed lapping the water, while Monet went back upstairs and got her purse. She came downstairs to the hall closet and took out her brown leather jacket and put it on. She walked back into the kitchen, blew Mitzi a kiss, and went out the back door, on a mission to bring her man home.

Chapter 16

A loud knock on the door awakened Marcus. He turned over in the bed and banged his head against the headboard. He groaned and put his hands over his eyes and stood up. Rat-a-tat sounded at the door. He walked over to it, and peered out the peephole before opening the door. His heart skipped a beat when he saw Monet standing there looking forlorn. It took all the will-power that he possessed not to pull his wife into his arms. He took a few steps backward, and Monet walked into the room.

She stopped and stood on her toes and touched Marcus's puffy cheek. "I don't have to ask you how you feel. You look terrible. What happened to your face?" Monet walked to a chair and sat down. Her eyes roamed over Marcus like she hadn't seen him in years.

Marcus sat on the bed. He moistened his dry lips. "I've had better days. My face is fine," he said in a low voice. He looked out the window, and then back at Monet. "Why are you here?"

"Because you're my husband, I love you, and you should be home with me," she said fervently, leaning forward in the chair.

Marcus sighed heavily. "I can't come home with you, Nay-Nay. We talked about it, and I'm not changing my position."

"I can't believe you're being this way." She looked at him, and disbelief screamed from her eyes.

"You have no idea how cruel people can be. Your pregnancy will fuel the gossip mill, and I want no part of that. And I can't pretend to love that baby. I think it's best we go our separate ways." Marcus tried to defend his position.

"Since when have we cared about what the world thinks?" Monet asked as her heart plunged down to her feet.

"Since you were raped and your beating was on page two of the local newspapers, and the lead story on the local television stations," he answered brutally.

"I don't believe you." Her hand drifted to her abdomen.

"Believe me." He snapped his lips shut.

"What can I do to convince you that it's your baby I'm carrying?" Monet cried.

"There's nothing you can do or say." Marcus presented a tough exterior, but inside, he was hurting just as badly as Monet.

Monet sat upright in her seat. "You're just going to throw away twenty years of marriage like that?" She snapped her fingers.

"Actually, as far as I'm concerned, you're the one throwing away our marriage for that kid inside you. You chose the rapist's baby over me," Marcus announced tersely.

Monet stood up and walked over to the bed and sat next to Marcus. "Is that what you think?"

"If you aren't having an abortion, then I guess that says it all," he proclaimed. He folded his arms across his chest.

"Marcus, there's something I probably should have told you twenty years ago. I've tried over the years, but now I have to be firm and make sure you understand just what I'm saying."

Marcus didn't reply. He just watched Monet with a stony face.

"Remember me telling you how I sense things?" He nodded reluctantly. "I wasn't totally honest with you. I'm intuitive, and I have dreams about events and people."

Marcus laughed harshly, and the sound echoed off the thin walls. "I think you've been watching too much Psychic Detectives on Tru TV," he mocked.

"Don't make fun of me," she said testily. "It's a gift that's been passed down from mother to daughter. I sort of have psychic abilities." Monet's voice trailed off.

Marcus tuned her out and thought, *Poor baby; she's worse off than I thought. The shock of the attack has obviously scrambled her brain. Psychic, yeah right.* He shook his head skeptically.

Monet stamped her foot on the carpeted floor to get her husband's attention. "Marcus, are you listening to me? Have you heard a word I've said?" she yelled.

Yeah, you think that you're psychic. Nice try, Nay-Nay," he said.

She squared her shoulders, clearly exasperated. "You're not funny, Marcus. I'm serious. My mother had the gift, she passed it down to me, and I'm going to pass it down to Faith." She patted her tummy.

"Did you sense you were going to be attacked that night, Monet?" he asked frostily. He walked over to the desk to the ice bucket and dropped a few cubes inside a glass. He went into the bathroom and filled the glass with water. Then he returned to the room and sat on the bed.

"Ouch, that hurt. But the answer to your question is no. I rarely sense anything bad happening to myself, only to other people. God told me that one day, I was going to have your child, and I believe Him. Still, I've had feelings about you, and I've warned you over the years to be careful," she shot back.

"I have no recollection as to what you're talking about." Marcus scratched his head. "All of the men's wives tell them to be careful. Are they psychic too?"

"Sure you do, if you'd stop to think about what I'm saying. Remember when I called and asked you to check your gun, and later you told me how it had misfired. You are being ultra stubborn, Marcus Ezekiel Caldwell." Monet pointed her finger at her husband and tightened her lips.

"It doesn't have to be this way," he whispered softly. "All you have to do is take care of the problem. Then our lives will be back on track after I find your attacker and the sperm donor." He looked down pointedly at Monet's midsection.

"Lord, forgive him for he knows not what he says." Monet put her hands in front of her as if in prayer. She felt like her husband was ripping her heart apart bit by bit. She moved close to Marcus, slid her arms around his waist and laid her head on his shoulder. "Marcus, I love you dearly. You are my soul mate, the man God sent me to spend my life with, but I'm not having an abortion."

He took her trembling hands in his own. He eased her back onto the bed and lay down next to her. He pulled her tenderly into his arms. Marcus inhaled strawberry bath gel from her neck and held her tightly.

Monet spoke tenderly. "Darling, can't you just put your trust in Jesus? He won't fail us. Marcus, I can't do this without you. Please just come home with me. I'm scared to stay in the house alone. What if the attacker comes to our house? I'm begging you to stay with me until paternity tests can be run. If she isn't your baby, then I'll move back to Alabama. Would you do that for me? Just stay with me until after the baby is born. Please, I'm begging you," she pleaded.

His grip around her waist drew tighter. "Yes, I'll do that, Monet," he whispered. "I vowed on our wedding day to protect you, and I will. I won't rest until I find the man that did that to you. I will stay in the house in the basement until you've had the ba . . . ba . . . kid." Marcus's mouth didn't want to say baby. His throat seemed to tighten up saying that word.

Monet snuggled closer to him. She always felt at peace and protected in his strong arms. Marcus's light breath on her neck felt so familiar. She closed her eyes.

Lord, I know that life is hard sometimes, and this is one of those times for me and Marcus. Her eyelids fluttered, and then her expression became serious. *A lot of times people talk about couples being unequally yoked, and I want to say that our yoke is a bit tilted right now. I know that life comes at us that way sometimes. It can be because of illness, financial strain, or an addiction. And sometimes a partner has to shoulder the load, emotionally or financially, for the other. That's what happening with me and Marcus. I know that I'll have to bear the brunt of our burdens right now. But you know what, Lord? It's all right. We all have to play that role a time or two if we keep living. Lord, you answered my prayer, Marcus is coming home. I know I just have to have faith, keep leaning on your everlasting arms, praying for your help, and you will deliver us from this dilemma. Father, keep me strong as I go through this journey, and I ask you to walk with us. I can do all things through God, who strengthens me. Amen.* Monet sighed and pulled Marcus's arm tighter around her waist.

For a long time Marcus and Monet lay entwined in each other's arms. Then they came together with a rhythmic urgency that seemed to inflame both of them. Monet fell asleep with Marcus's arm around her waist.

An hour later, Marcus awakened, and he gazed at Monet, who was still asleep. She had a look of peace on her face that had been missing for a long time. He caressed her face and closed his eyes, wondering how could something that felt so good hurt so bad at the same time. Then he fell back asleep.

Chapter 17

When Marcus awakened later, Monet was standing at the hotel window. She turned toward the bed when she heard him moving. He glanced at his watch. It was late, close to nine P.M. Monet walked to the chair and took her jacket off of it.

"We need to get out of here. I need to get back and check on Mitzi," she said.

"Why don't you go on ahead, and I'll be back there later tonight or in the morning," Marcus said elusively, not meeting her inquisitive eyes.

"Okay, that will be fine. I'll see you when I see you." She picked up her purse from the kitchenette counter and walked to the door. She waved to Marcus and walked out the door, to the parking lot and drove home.

Marcus didn't return home for a week, and Monet just bided her time. There was no doubt in her mind that her husband would eventually come back. She was in her office painting, one of her pastimes to ease stress, when she heard the kitchen door open and close. She held her breath until she heard him call her name. She wiped her hands on a rag and willed herself not to run to the kitchen.

"I'm here, in the office. I'm coming," she answered. She walked out the room to the kitchen.

Marcus had dropped an oversized gym bag on the floor, and was cradling Mitzi in his arms. The tiny dog kept licking Marcus's hairy face. The makings of a gray beard were woven into the bottom of his face. Monet stared at him for a minute, and the affection she felt for him shone on her face.

Marcus awkwardly put Mitzi down. "How are you doing?" he asked. His eyes looked tired.

"I'm good." Her arms hung at her sides.

"Well, I'm going to go downstairs and set up my living quarters," he said, picking up the gym bag. The dark sweat suit molded to his body. "I'll probably bring some of my clothes and things down there."

"You don't have to do that," she protested. "You know it doesn't have to be this way."

"I know," he conceded, "but it's just the best way for now." He walked to the basement door, which was off the kitchen, and went downstairs.

Monet returned to her office, feeling joy and pain. Her husband was home, but in a sense he wasn't. She walked over to the easel and resumed painting.

Later she fixed dinner and asked Marcus if he wanted to join her. She knew the aromas from the kitchen were mouthwatering, just the way she planned. But he informed her he didn't plan on sharing dinner with her that night, or any other night. He would eat out or bring food home with him. Monet, of course, was disappointed. Later that evening she prayed for strength.

When Marcus was home from work, or needed to relieve stress, he'd play his saxophone, which he did that evening. And likewise, Wade played the guitar. The partners were music aficionados. Between the two men, they had amassed an impressive collection of music going back to the vinyl era.

The melodies Marcus played the evening he returned home were so poignant that they brought tears to Monet's eyes. She painted and he played the saxophone. And an uneasy truce had been reached between the couple. Separate living quarters became a way of life in the Caldwells' household.

She and Liz prayed nightly, asking God to change the situation, though they were well aware that God operated on His own time. After their prayer sessions, Monet would talk to Faith, or read her stories and play gospel music. She also began explaining to her daughter about their special gift from God.

Three months had elapsed, and Monet was sporting a baby bump. She selected a doctor on staff at Northwestern Memorial Hospital, Dr. Armstrong, as her obstetrician. Morning sickness had nearly passed, and Monet was feeling good. She had just returned home from a doctor's appointment. Though she was considered a high risk patient because of her age, by and large she was doing well.

She hadn't informed her brothers about the pregnancy, so she decided to invite them to dinner to share her news with them. Because Chicago was in the throes of a harsh winter, Monet and her brothers hadn't seen each other since before Christmas. Marcus and Monet had stayed home for the holidays in their neutral corners.

Monet's attendance at church had become sporadic as her body swelled with child. She wasn't sure how her church would respond to her pregnancy in light of the attack. Monet was ashamed of her feelings. She longed to call Reverend Wilcox and explain what was happening. Every day she said that she would call her, but she didn't. She knew Marcus wanted to keep the pregnancy a secret as long as possible, and Monet acquiesced with his wishes since they were merely co-existing.

"Hey, twin," Monet said into Duane's cell phone voice mail, "I'm fixing a pot of stew for dinner tonight. Why don't you two come by? Give me a call later." She thoughtfully clicked off the phone.

Duane called back to say that he and Derek would come for

dinner. A couple of hours later, Monet had just taken the corn-bread out of the oven when the doorbell rang. She set the pan on top of the oven and went to open the front door. Her broth-ers walked in. They exchanged greetings, hung their coats in the hall closet, and then the siblings walked to the kitchen.

The brothers sat down at the kitchen table, and then Derek stood up and walked to the refrigerator and took out two bottles of cranberry juice. He tossed one bottle to Duane, who caught it easily. A dusty rose sweat suit clung to Monet's body as she brushed butter over the top of the warm, golden brown corn-bread.

"Looks like you put on some weigh there," Derek observed as his eyes scanned Monet's body. Then he turned up the bottle and drank.

"Hmmm," she murmured, "I have. That's why I invited you over for dinner, to share my news with you . . . that I'm preg-nant." She sat at the table.

Derek sputtered and quickly grabbed a napkin and pre-ssed it to his mouth.

Duane's mouth dropped open, and he said, "Say what?"

Monet smiled smugly. "Come this summer, I'm having a little girl. You guys are going to be uncles."

The brothers glanced at each other. There was a period of silence, then Duane asked her in a quiet tone of voice, "When did you find out you were pregnant?

"Back in December, I'm nearly five months along," she an-swered evenly.

"Just whose baby are you having?" Derek asked.

"I'm hurt that you would ask me that question. But if you must know, it's Marcus's baby," she answered.

"Isn't that around the same time you were attacked?" Derek asked. He leaned forward in his seat and stared into his sister's face.

"Yes, it's around the same time. But regardless of the timing, I know that Marcus is the baby's father," Monet said with quiet dignity. She folded her hands on the table.

"What does Marcus think?" Duane and Derek exchanged concerned looks.

"Well, he isn't as convinced as I am that this is his child. He'll see the light when the baby is born." She waved her hand airily.

"Nay-Nay, I love you, but are you sure you're doing the right thing? You and Marcus haven't ever been able to have a child, and now you're pregnant. I just find the timing a little iffy," Duane commented.

"So does Marcus, and it's caused a strain in our marriage. We're both living in the house, but we're still kind of estranged. Marcus is staying in the basement. But hey, at least he's here with me." She tried to sound upbeat.

"Let's see, a man brutally attacked you, you've never been pregnant before, and then you expect your husband to take your word that he's the father. That makes no sense to me. No wonder Marcus has distanced himself from you, and he's moved downstairs. I don't blame him," Derek said judgmentally.

"I know the timing is off, but I know this baby is Marcus's child." Monet's face was serene, and her tone of voice was steady.

"More like you wish," Derek muttered. He leaned back in the chair and rubbed his hand over his head, a habit that surfaced whenever he was nervous. "I have to say I agree with Marcus. And it's not even a matter of timing. You've never even conceived with him."

Duane, who was closer to his sister than Derek said, "Derek, I don't think that comment was called for. If Monet says the baby is Marcus's, then we have to believe her. She's our sister, and we should give her our support."

"Well, I can't, and I won't. That baby is probably the attacker's, so we already know it has deviant genes just because of how it was conceived. Who knows what else is in the monster's background. I think you should get rid of it. You've been with your husband for twenty years and nothing has happened," Derek said impassionedly.

"There will be no abortion; it's morally wrong in God's eyes. And I know that this is Marcus's baby because God told me so," Monet announced calmly, though her insides were churning. She knew the discussion with her brothers was going to be difficult, but she never imagined Derek not supporting her.

"So now you're hearing voices like Momma did." Derek shook his head pityingly. "And you're going to end up like her . . . without a husband."

"Dude, there was no need for you to go there." Duane objected to his brother's choice of words. "Monet is the only relative we have outside of each other, so we should support and respect her decision. It's what Momma would want us to do. And Derek, you know Momma had the gift, and you're well aware it's passed down from mother to daughter."

"I never believed in that gibberish," Derek confessed, turning up his nose like he smelled a bad odor. "People don't have those kinds of gifts. That's just nonsense. And that superstition cost us a father. Momma should've thought about our feelings, and how hard it was for us growing up without a father."

"I think Momma did the best she could under the circumstances," Duane said, trying to lighten the mood between his siblings. He could sense a storm brewing and didn't miss the look of consternation on his sister's face. "We may not have had much money growing up, but we made do, and our house was filled with love. You're the one in heavy denial, brother. Dig deep within yourself and draw on our childhood memories."

Derek waved his hand. "Monet has enjoyed a happy marriage for years. Why should she jeopardize it because of the actions of a pervert?"

The brothers began arguing, and Monet sat in her chair with tears streaming down her face. "Stop," she said, but Derek and Duane ignored her. She put her hands over her face.

The back door opened and Marcus walked in. He stomped his feet on the doormat, took off his coat and hung it on the coat hook. Then he asked nonchalantly, "What's going on?" He looked at his wife, and then at his brothers-in-law.

"How come one of y'all didn't tell us what was going on over here?" Derek stood up and pointed at Monet, and then at Marcus. "I thought we were closer than that," he snarled at his brother-in-law.

"Well, truthfully, it's not my news to share. I've been leaving that up to Monet. I had no say-so in this pregnancy. So pardon me; the new arrival is your sister's news." Marcus waited to see how his wife would deal with the situation. The twins were her family. If they didn't support her, maybe that would open her eyes and force her to do the right thing.

Monet stood up and said somberly, "I'm so disappointed in you, Derek. I'm your sister, why can't you support me?"

"What do you mean by support you? I'm trying to get you to see the light. You having a rapist's baby is just plain sick. This whole situation is a mess." Derek sat down and drummed his fingers on the kitchen table.

Marcus felt a rush of elation. "Finally, someone sees things my way." He nodded to Derek as Monet shot him a defiant look.

"When will you realize this situation is not about you, Marcus Caldwell," she retorted. She stood up and planted her hands on her hips.

"Well, it was before you got yourself knocked up. I tell you, that kid hasn't even been born yet, and it's disrupting our lives. Before you got pregnant, we could sit down and discuss issues as a family without everyone arguing," he added smugly. He looked to Derek for support, and his brother-in-law didn't disappoint him.

"He's right, Monet. There's is only so much a man can take," Derek said chauvinistically.

"You are wrong, my brother," Duane said to his twin. "You know Momma always told us to look out for each other. Why are you acting like this and taking Marcus's side?"

"Because I want to save Monet from the heartbreak that was Momma's fate. She suffered her whole life. And Monet is wrong. She shouldn't force Marcus to be a father to a child that obviously isn't his, considering the way that child was conceived," Derek replied brusquely. He pounded the top of the wooden table with his fist to emphasize his point.

The brothers began going at it again. Marcus monetarily felt ashamed for the division he'd caused the family. Then he shrugged off the feeling. He had manipulated Derek and his tactic worked. Monet needed to see what she was up against. He watched her trying to keep the peace between her brothers when the doorbell rang.

"I'll get it," he said to unhearing ears. He walked out of the kitchen to the front door. When he opened the door, Reverend Wilcox stood outside the door clutching her handbag and stomping snow off her boots.

"Hello, Marcus," she greeted him. "Is this a bad time?"

Marcus was aware for the first time how loud Monet and her brothers sounded. The level of their voices had reached a high decibel level.

"Uh, no, Reverend Wilcox, come on in," he said. He stepped aside to allow her to enter.

"I haven't talked to or seen Monet in church for a while, and I was beginning to become concerned about her," she said.

"Well," Marcus dropped his hands to his side, "we've had some issues, but we're working them out."

"If the sounds from the kitchen are any indication, then I'd say you have your work cut out for you." Reverend Wilcox smiled. She took off her black leather gloves and stuck them in her pockets. Then she took off her boots and sat them on the welcome mat near the door.

"I just got home from work and was getting ready to change clothes. Oh, I'm sorry, let me take your coat," Marcus said.

She unbuttoned her black wool coat, took it off, and handed it to Marcus. He opened the closet and hung it up.

"Why don't you have a seat in the living room, and I'll send Monet in," he said graciously. He turned on the light in the living room and walked toward the kitchen.

"Thank you," Reverend Wilcox replied. She walked into the living room and sat on the couch. She put her bag beside her feet on the floor.

Marcus said to Monet and her brothers, "You all need to keep it down. Monet, Reverend Wilcox is in the living room. She wants to see you."

Monet swiped her hands over her face and said to Marcus and her brothers, "We aren't done talking yet."

Marcus said, "I need you guys to hang around if you can. I had a phone call awhile back and again today that I'd like to share with you."

"No can do today. I have a date as soon as I leave here. What's it about?" Derek asked. He walked over to the stove and removed the top off the simmering stew. "This smells good. Is it done yet, Monet?"

Monet looked at her brother disgustedly. "Yes, the stew is done. I'm going to talk to Reverend Wilcox. Save some for me." She walked out of the kitchen.

When she arrived in the living room, Reverend Wilcox was standing at the mantle looking at a silver framed 8x10 picture of Monet's mother and a portrait of Marcus and Monet on their wedding day. She turned when Monet came in the room. The women hugged and sat on the couch.

"How are you doing, dear? I probably should have called before I came over. But I was in the neighborhood visiting Sister Williams, and thought I'd drop by. I'd see you in the back of the church sometimes, but you'd leave before I had a chance to speak to you." Reverend Wilcox looked at Monet's face and body. "Oh my, you're with child."

"Yes, I am," she said shyly. She pushed a stray curl out of her face. "Before you ask, I'm about five months along."

"Well, then, congratulations are in order." Reverend Wilcox looked genuinely happy for Monet. She smoothed down the hem of her navy blue skirt. She wore a matching jacket with an ivory colored blouse. A strand of pearls encircled her neck, and pearl earrings adorned her ears.

They chatted, and Monet brought Reverend Wilcox up to speed with what had been going on in her life.

"This has to be a difficult time for you," Reverend Wilcox said sympathetically. She smoothed back her silver close cropped hair. "You should have called me. I hate to think of you suffering alone."

"Well, as you know, Liz and I are prayer partners again, and we pray every night. I know I haven't been coming to church like I should, but between morning sickness and the weather, I've been taking it easy." Monet caressed her stomach. "And Marcus has me almost paranoid about leaving the house, about what people will think when they see that I'm pregnant."

"You haven't returned to work yet?" Reverend Wilcox asked, as she took her turquoise cashmere scarf from around her neck, folded it, and laid it on her lap.

"No, I don't plan on going back until after I have the baby. My doctor has diagnosed me as a high risk case, and I've waited so long to conceive that I just don't want anything to go wrong," Monet explained.

"I can understand that." Reverend Wilcox bobbed her head

up and down. "But you don't want to seclude yourself away from life. I hope you're participating in some activities. I've missed you at church. Perhaps you can do some volunteering?" she suggested.

"I'll think about it." Monet nodded. "I always said I suffered from the Sarah's Syndrome. And God has blessed me like He blessed her."

"Yes, and I remember how we prayed together many a times that you would conceive. Whenever I called altar prayer at church, you were the first person to come out of the choir stand."

"I always believed and knew that I would have a baby. I just didn't envision these circumstances." Monet leaned comfortably against the back of the couch.

"I know dear, and many a night I've included you in my prayers," Reverend Wilcox remarked calmly. She patted Monet's hand.

"I need all the prayers I can get. I'm sleeping upstairs in the bedroom, and he's in the basement." Monet lips tightened in a grimace. She had left out that part and a few other facts when she told Reverend Wilcox her latest happenings. Monet felt ashamed for not being totally honest with her minister.

"You can take some comfort in knowing that he's still here. He hasn't deserted you completely," Reverend Wilcox said soothingly.

"That's true, and I do, but it's still a complex situation. I don't know what I'd do without Liz and Wade in my life. Liz is going to be my Lamaze coach."

"That's a blessing and a testament to God's intervention. Where one door is closed, another one is opened. I wouldn't expect less from Liz and Wade."

"Sometimes I feel so selfish and wonder if I'm handling the situation with Marcus correctly. I feel so conflicted about this situation. What do you think?" Monet asked. She held her breath, waiting for the Reverend's response.

"Life can get so difficult sometimes, and no one is aware of that better than me. In the long run you'll have to be patient, do what you feel is right in your heart, and everything will work out as God has ordained. From what I can see, Marcus is a pure alpha male, and he feels that he let you down by not being able to protect you when you needed it most. But he knows in the back of his mind that there was nothing he could do to stop the attack from happening. Keep praying, and know that God will resolve the situation. You can't be concerned about what people will say; everyone has their own opinion about how things should be done. But at the end of the day, you have to do what God guides you to do, and keep your head up. I really wish you'd come back to church and return to your rightful place in the choir stand. "

Monet nodded. "I miss church. It was the high point of my week. You know what, Reverend Wilcox?"

"What's that?" she asked.

Monet explained about her conversations with God, and how He assured her to be patient and that everything would be all right. Monet went on to say how she had been leaning on the Lord more heavily than before. They continued talking, and she felt comforted. One-on-one time with Reverend Wilcox, to Monet, was a treat, on the scale of talking to her mother.

Reverend Wilcox looked at her watch. "It's later than I realized. It's time for me to head home." She and Monet stood up. "Monet, I want you to remember this simple verse when life gets overwhelming, and I believe it will comfort you. It's from the book of Second Corinthians 5:7: *For we walk by faith, not sight.*"

Then she took Monet's hands in her own and bowed her head. "Heavenly Father, we know that you can make a way out of no way. No matter how bleak our lives may look, we only have to come to you with a meek and humble heart, because only you, Father, know what is really in our hearts. Lord, take care of Marcus and Monet. Help Marcus to understand that even in this uncertain time, you are still watching over his family, and that you never put more on us than we can bear. Father, I ask that you protect the new life that Monet is carrying. And when that baby makes her appearance, we'll claim the victory for the miracle that you have bestowed upon your daughter, Monet. These blessings I ask in Jesus' name. Amen."

"Amen," Monet said in a strong voice. Then she and Reverend Wilcox walked hand in hand to the foyer. Monet took Reverend Wilcox's coat out of the closet and handed it to her. When Reverend Wilcox put on her coat, she hugged Monet.

"Keep the faith, Monet, and I promise you that everything will proceed according to God's will," Reverend Wilcox said.

"I will," she said, choking up.

"Come back to church soon. We miss you." Reverend Wilcox reached out and pressed Monet's hands together.

Monet nodded her head and said, "I'll be there on Sunday."

After the women exchanged good-byes and Reverend Wilcox left, Monet locked the door. Then she headed to the kitchen. Duane and Derek had gone home after coming to the living room to speak to Reverend Wilcox and telling Monet that they were heading home. Marcus had long since retired to the basement. She wondered what the important news was that Marcus had wanted to share with them. Then she thought, *Whatever it is, it can wait for another day.* Monet fixed herself a bowl of stew and sat at the table and ate dinner alone, except for Mitzi. With so much tension in the air, the little dog had become more protective of her mistress.

Chapter 18

Monet returned to the Temple the Sunday after Reverend Wilcox's visit as she promised she would. With strong impassioned cajoling from Monet, Liz, and Wade, Marcus agreed to attend the morning service with his wife. She called her brothers Saturday morning and asked them to join her for moral support. Duane promised he would be there, and Derek said he'd try to attend, but that it would depend on the outcome of his date the night before.

Monet had awakened early Sunday morning around six, feeling jittery as if angst had soaked into her soul. She knew it was due to a combination of Marcus's attitude, and their going out in public for the first time together during her pregnancy. She tried deep breathing exercises and praying, but afterward she was still left with a feeling of uneasiness.

Finally, after praying to God, asking Him to give her strength for the day ahead, Monet picked up her Bible and turned to Romans 8:26 and read, "*Likewise the Spirit also helpeth our infirmities; for we know not what we should pray as we ought; but the Spirit itself can make intercession for us with groaning that cannot be uttered.*" She read the verse again, this time silently, using her finger to underline the words as she read them.

After reading the scripture, Monet's spirit buoyed. She lay down on the bed for a few more minutes. Then she got up, made up the bed, walked to the closet, removed a black pantsuit since the temperature had dropped below zero, along with a butter colored blouse, and set them on the bed.

After she showered, she spread Victoria's Secret pear body lotion over her body and donned her undergarments and hosiery, then put on a fluffy pink chenille robe. Then Monet went downstairs to the kitchen to prepare breakfast. She cooked enough eggs, bacon, grits, biscuits, and coffee for both of them, and then called Marcus, but he didn't answer. She heard him stirring around in the basement. Monet sat down at the kitchen table, and once again, ate breakfast alone. She drained a glass of milk and placed it in the sink, along with her plate and utensils.

Twenty minutes later, Monet was dressed and sitting on her vanity stool applying her makeup. She pressed her lips together after putting on a coat of red lipstick. She then slid her feet into a pair of black leather boots. She put a gold bangle watch on her wrist, a gold chain that belonged to her mother around her neck, and gold hoop earrings in her pierced ears. She sprayed Lancome's perfume, Hypnose, over her suit jacket, and then put it on.

Monet looked at her face in the mirror and tried to smile, though her lips trembled. "I don't know why I feel so uneasy. Lord, grant me peace," she said aloud.

She walked downstairs and found Marcus sitting in the living room watching *Sports Center* on the plasma television. He caught sight of his wife and his breath seemed to catch in his throat. He thought, *She is still as fine as the first time I saw her in study hall when I was in tenth grade.*

He wanted to gather her in his arms and never let go. Instead, he asked Monet brusquely, "Are you ready to go?" He walked to the foyer and removed their coats from the closet.

When he held up Monet's coat and she put her arms into the bell shaped sleeves, the scent of Hypnose wafting from her body tantalized his sense of smell. Anyone looking at Monet would think she was thirty years old instead of forty. Her curly hair was piled high on her head, and Marcus thought she looked elegant.

Monet wanted to reach out and hug Marcus. He looked so handsome in his black suit and white shirt, accessorized with a yellow tie. But his stoic expression kept her urge at bay. She waited for him to put on his black wool coat, and then they walked to the kitchen and out the back door.

"Did you—" she began saying.

"Yes, I gave Mitzi her food this morning," Marcus replied, cutting her off.

A few minutes later, they were in traffic headed to the Temple. Monet turned the radio to WVAZ and listened to Effie Roth host the gospel brunch during the drive. When they arrived at church, the parking lot was starting to fill with automobiles. They walked inside to find Liz and Wade chatting with other members. When they spied their friends, they ended the conversation and sped toward Monet and Marcus.

The women gabbed, while Wade thumped Marcus on the back. "I'm glad you came today," he said. "I think you'll feel better when you leave. Church will fill your soul with peace, and cure all your ills."

Marcus sucked his breath loudly and stopped himself from rolling his eyes.

"I wonder if my brothers will join us today," Monet commented to Liz as she looked around the area.

"I haven't seen them yet. Let's go to the ladies room before service starts," Liz said.

Monet looked at her watch. "Okay, but let's hurry up. I don't want to be late for the start of service." She unbuttoned her coat and took off her hat.

The women told the men they would return in a few minutes. The restroom was empty. Liz went into a stall and emerged seconds later. Monet took off her coat and draped it over her arm. She took a long tailed comb out of her purse and picked at her hair. Liz washed her hands and re-applied her lipstick.

"I like that suit," Monet told Liz as she looked at her friend from head to toe. "Where did you get those matching shoes from? They look new."

"Girl, you know me, I'm the DSW queen. I was browsing the mall and saw them and thought they would go perfect with my royal blue suit."

"Nice." Monet nodded. "I think it's time for us to go. The parking lot was beginning to get crowded. I hope we can all sit together."

"Don't worry about it, we'll be fine," Liz replied.

They left the ladies room and walked to the sanctuary. The doors were still closed. The choir had marched into the auditorium before Monet and Marcus's arrival, and the combined choirs were now singing "The Lord's Prayer." Monet was pleased to see Duane standing with Marcus and Wade. The siblings embraced and exchanged greetings. When the usher opened the middle door, Marcus stood on one side of Monet and Duane on the other, while Liz and Wade walked behind them.

When they entered the sanctuary, the congregation rose and began clapping. Monet was taken aback and her steps faltered. She was confused for a moment, until she realized they were clapping for her.

Her eyes filled with tears and she said, "Thank you, Father." The usher walked them to the third row of the middle pew.

Reverend Wilcox came down from the pulpit and embraced Monet and told her, "Welcome home."

Marcus sat next to his wife, and Liz slid on the other side. "You knew about this, didn't you?" Monet asked Liz.

"Of course I did," she replied smugly. "I knew you were feeling a little shaky about coming out in public and returning to church, so Reverend Wilcox and I put our heads together and came up with this, so you could get it over with in one fell swoop."

"Elizabeth Anne Harrison, I'm going to get you later," Monet promised.

The church clerk read the announcements. Before the choir sang their A selection, Avis, the choir director, walked up to the pulpit. "Giving honor to God and Reverend Wilcox, I'd like to just say how happy I am to see our sister and choir member, Monet Caldwell, at church today. Our prayers were with you for a speedy recovery, and God didn't fail us. Church, doesn't she look good?" The congregation clapped fervently as the organist played a jazzy riff. "We've missed you, Monet," Avis continued. "And we await your return to your rightful place in the choir. The choir would like to dedicate our A and B selections to our sister, Monet."

Monet initially felt abashed when Avis began talking, then her heart filled with joy that spilled over from her eyes as the choir began singing "Jesus Can Work It Out." Her head swayed to the beat of the music, and peace flooded her heart when the choir began singing their B selection, "Long As I Got Jesus, I Don't Need Nobody Else."

After tithes and offerings were collected, Reverend Wilcox walked to the pulpit and said in a cherry voice, "Isn't God good, church?" Replies of *Amen* and *Hallelujah* and thunderous clapping rented the air. "I don't know what you came to do, but I came to praise His name." She raised her hands. "I was talking to a new church member the other day. Her walk with God is a new one, and she said to me, Reverend Wilcox, I just don't understand why God allows bad things to happen to good people."

Marcus felt like she was talking to him, and he squirmed in his seat, while Monet's eye brimmed with tears.

"We go to church, we spread the news about Jesus, and yes, we tithe. Some people feel like that means they have a first class ticket to heaven, along with immunity from the trials and tribulations of life," Reverend Wilcox said. Then she took a sip of water. "But church, that's not what life is about. We suffer through all types of ordeals, and along the way we learn to trust in God and know that He will never leave or forsake us." The church clapped, signaling their approval. "For those of you that have your Bibles with you today, I'd like you to open it to Isaiah 26:3 and 4, and Proverbs 3:5 and 6. Please read along with me," she instructed the church.

The congregation's voices sounded strong as they read, "*Thou will keep him in perfect peace, whose mind stayed is stayed on thee: because he trusteth in thee. Trust ye in the Lord for ever; for in the Lord Jehovah is everlasting strength.*" There was a rustle of pages as the members turned to the book of Proverbs. Then they continued reading. "*Trust in the Lord with all your heart and lean not unto thine own understanding. In all thy ways acknowledge him and he will direct thy path.*"

"Trusting in the Lord is what helps Christians accept the bad things in life that happen to good people, and help us realize that we're not alone." Reverend Wilcox eyes roamed around the sanctuary.

"We live in a busy world, a digital society with statistics that tell us how quickly someone is killed, or how many children are born a minute, how many people will die from cancer or AIDS in a year. All you have to do is log on to a computer, do a Google search, and you'll be privy to all kinds of information. But despite the bad news that seems to overwhelm us at times, the earthquakes and hurricanes, rising unemployment, and hard times, there is one constant in life that's never mentioned in the newspapers and that's the love of Christ. He's our redeemer, our Savior, our bright and morning star, and He will never leave us alone. He will bring us comfort and peace when we need it most." Reverend Wilcox continued her sermon on trusting in the Lord and having faith that He would provide deliverance in any situation.

Marcus half-listened and wore a bored expression on his face. He felt like Reverend Wilcox was singling him out, while Monet was totally intent on listening to the Word. Wade glanced at Marcus a couple of times, and could see by the set of his friend's rigid jaw that he didn't comprehend what Reverend Wilcox was saying. Wade closed his eyes and said a prayer for his friend.

By the time Reverend Wilcox had finished her sermon, the church was on their feet rocking. Monet, Liz, and Wade were along with them, while Marcus and Duane sat in their seats. The doors to the church were opened to prospective new members, and several people walked down the aisle to the front row, where they were welcomed by the deacon board and ministry staff. The choir sang, "God Be With You Until We Meet Again," and re-cited the benediction.

Monet's spirit was overflowing, and she berated herself for not coming to church sooner. Reverend Wilcox stood in the back of the church at the conclusion of the service to speak with her members. Liz whispered to Monet that Reverend Wilcox wanted Monet to join her.

Monet's eyes widened. "Me?"

"Yes you. The members have been inquiring about you ever since the attack, so Reverend Wilcox and I thought it would encourage you to know that you're not alone. The church loves you and stands behind you one hundred percent," Liz stated.

Monet turned to look at Marcus. He quickly said, "I'll pass. I'll see you in the parking lot when you're done." He put on his coat and black fedora hat and went outside.

Liz was disappointed in Marcus's response. Quietly, she just took Monet's hand and they walked to the rear of the church to join Reverend Wilcox.

"It would've been nice if you had joined your wife," Wade said, walking out of the sanctuary behind Marcus.

"She'll be fine without me," he replied brusquely as he turned to watch a good portion of the membership swarm around Monet.

"Yes, she will," Wade agreed," but she still needs your love and support."

"I know, Wade, and I'm doing the best I can. Look, I'll talk to you later." Marcus turned and left the church.

Monet was in church for over an hour. The outpouring of love was overwhelming to her at times, and tears streamed from her eyes. Liz handed her a tissue to dab at her eyes.

When the last member had departed from the line, Monet turned and said, "Thank you so much, Reverend Wilcox. Talking to everyone was just what I needed. My heart is so full." Her voice broke.

Reverend Wilcox embraced her. "I'm glad. I thought you needed to see how precious you are in our eyes and in God's."

Liz cleared her throat and held her hand out to Reverend Wilcox. "Your sermon was just beautiful. I'm going to find my husband and head home. Again, thank you."

"Bless you, Liz. I'll see you back here at church on Wednesday for the mission committee meeting," Reverend Wilcox said.

Liz squeezed Monet's arm. "I'll call you later." Then she left.

"Reverend Wilcox, I still feel like I can't get through to Marcus. I was hoping he would lighten up a bit, but that doesn't seem to be the case." Monet shook her head sadly.

"Everyone reacts to adversity differently, dear. We'll continue to pray for Marcus. I know in time he'll come around," she said sagely. "Now, I'm going to let you get out of here. I know Marcus is waiting for you, and I'm going to visit my mother. Hopefully, I'll see you at church next week," she said.

"Oh, you will, no doubt." Monet nodded her head. "Thank you for everything, Reverend Wilcox."

The women hugged one last time, then Reverend Wilcox

walked to her office, and Monet walked out of the church to find Marcus. Her heart was light and her step purposeful. Her belief was reinforced that whatever lay ahead, she wasn't alone. God would be by her side. And she prayed for patience to deal with Marcus better. Sometimes one partner has to step up for the other, and Monet knew she was going to have to climb a lot of stairs.

Chapter 19

Hours later, Monet walked into her kitchen after changing out of her church outfit. She took a ceramic bowl from the cabinet, walked to the stove, and ladled spoonfuls of the leftover stew into the bowl. Though she had cooked a traditional Sunday dinner, she had a craving for stew that wouldn't be denied. She set the bowl on the counter and cut herself a piece of cornbread, put it in the microwave and warmed it. Then she sat at the table, said a prayer, and began eating.

Duane had come over after church, and Derek joined them afterward. Duane, Derek, and Marcus walked upstairs from the basement and sat in chairs around the kitchen table. They talked about the NBA while waiting for Monet to finish eating.

"I have tickets to the Bulls game on Sunday," Derek informed Marcus. "You're welcome to join me."

"Let me check my schedule at work and see what the assignment chart looks like. With Monet not working, I've been putting in some overtime," he told his brother-in-law.

"Fine, just give me a call," Derek said.

The brothers lived in a three-flat apartment they owned on the southeast side of the city. They were confirmed bachelors. Both men claimed they hadn't found the right woman they wanted to settle down with. Duane had been dating a woman named Elise for the past ten years. He said they were content with their relationship just the way it was. Derek, on the other hand, went through women like the seasons. He was every bit the player he claimed to be.

"Is there anything new with Monet's case?" Duane asked. He stood up, went to the refrigerator freezer, and took out a gallon of French vanilla ice cream. "Anybody want some?" he asked.

"I'll take a bowl," Derek replied.

"None for me," Marcus said. "Well, you know we found Monet's purse not too far from the hospital. Her wallet and keys were taken out of the purse. The locks have been changed on the house, and we put in an alarm system. We've dusted Monet's car for fingerprints, but our culprit's prints weren't in the AFIS database, nor was his DNA in CODIS. So we're kind of at an impasse for now."

"That's too bad," Derek said. "Don't let me find that guy before y'all do. I swear it'll be on. It's too bad that he's walking the streets waiting to prey on other women." Derek scraped the bottom of the bowl, eating the last of his ice cream.

"Do you want more?" Monet asked. "There's more in the freezer downstairs." The brothers shook their heads.

"So Marcus, what did you want to talk to us about the other day?" Derek asked as he pushed his chair away from the table.

He burped, and Monet frowned and said, "Eww, I know Momma trained you better than that."

"Excuse me," he mumbled.

"Anyway," Marcus interjected, "I received a call from a prisoner at the Dwight Correctional Facility. Aron Reynolds will be released from the facility shortly, and he's looking for a sponsor on the outside."

Monet asked in a strangled tone of voice, "Our father?" Her eyes grew as round as salad plates as she looked at her brothers.

"The one and only," Marcus answered. He looked around the table to gauge everyone's reaction. "He's paid his debt to society."

Derek looked uninterested; he wore a bored expression on his face. Duane, on the other hand, was just as flabbergasted as Monet.

"Now, that's what I call news. Why did he call you?" Duane asked.

"He doesn't have anywhere to stay, and he needs someone to vouch for him, for lack of a better term," Marcus stated.

"How do you know it's really him?" Derek asked. His foot tapped rhythmically on the tile floor.

"Well, I'm a detective, so of course I checked out his story," Marcus informed them.

"So that's where he's been for the past thirty plus years? And what was he in jail for?" The words slipped out of Monet's mouth like rapid fire.

"Your father is the type of man, if it weren't for bad luck, he wouldn't have any luck at all," Marcus said. Monet and her brothers hung onto his words. "He was imprisoned thirty-five years ago for murder in the first degree," he informed the trio succinctly.

"Mercy me," Monet whispered. "Do you know what happened?" She tried to wrap the words Marcus had just spoken around her brain, but was struggling.

"From what I was able to piece together, he was imprisoned about a year or so after he moved from Alabama," Marcus enlightened them.

Duane shook his head in doubt. His eyes were as round as Monet's. "I wonder if Momma knew what happened to him."

"She probably did," Monet said. "One way or the other, believe me, she knew."

"Well, I hope you told him no," Derek announced. "Our lives are set and established, and we have no room or place for him this late in the game."

"Speak for yourself," Monet advised Derek. "He's our father."

"Monet, is being pregnant rattling your brain or something? You heard Marcus say our father is a murderer." His voice rose when he said the word murderer.

"What did you tell him, Marcus?" Duane asked, reserving judgment.

"I told him that I had to talk to you all and see what you think. If it makes you feel any better, Derek, I've made contact with the prison officials and from all reports, your father has been a model prisoner for the past twenty-five years," he said.

"I say no, let the chips fall where they may for the old man. We don't owe him a darn anything," Derek announced.

"We owe him our lives, "Monet said. "Without Daddy, none of us would've been born. I think we should help him."

"You would think that," Derek snorted. He stood up, went to the refrigerator and removed a pitcher of ice tea.

"What do you think, Duane?" Monet ignored Derek. Whenever the siblings squared off against each other, usually Duane sided with Monet.

"I think we should proceed with caution, and have Marcus continue to check things out a bit more. He's already gotten the ball rolling, and now it's up to us to see how far we want to carry things." Duane's tone was grave.

"That's a good suggestion. I don't think Momma would want us to turn our backs on him. So we've got to do the right thing," Monet said.

"Who appointed you to decide what's right or wrong?" Derek asked Monet. "Your own house isn't in order, and I don't think you need to be bringing more drama into this house. And anyway, I didn't hear Marcus volunteering this house," he remarked with cruel candor. He looked down at his wrist to check the time.

Marcus opened his mouth to reply, and then closed it. He folded his arms across his chest. This wasn't his battle to fight. He looked across the table at Monet, whose face seemed to crumble with agony.

She bit her lower lip and said carefully, "The last time I

checked, the deed to this house had my name on it too, so I have some say so. And I didn't say I was bringing him here. If Daddy stays anywhere, it should be at you and Duane's place."

The argument was beginning to escalate. "Hey," Marcus said, whistling shrilly. Monet, Derek, and Duane stopped talking and looked at him. "Does anyone have a picture of your dad?" he asked. "I'm one hundred percent sure he's your father, but I want to make sure."

"I have a picture upstairs in the attic with Momma's stuff that I brought back with me from Alabama," Monet replied.

"I still think we should leave him be. He hasn't done anything for us in all these years, so he's not in any position to ask us for any favors," Derek stated.

"I'm curious," Duane stated. "I'd like to know his story; why he wasn't in our lives, and most of all, how he ended up killing someone?" He and Monet shivered. "I know you have his case file, why don't you share it with us?" he asked Marcus.

"I think he needs to tell you in his own words," Marcus said as he yawned. "Well then, my work here is done. Once Monet gives me the picture, then I can verify that he is your father. And then you three can decide where to go from there." He pushed his chair back from the table and stood up. Then he strolled to the basement door and went downstairs.

"Do you want to take anything home with you before I put up the food" Monet asked her brothers.

"I'll make myself a plate," Duane answered. He walked to the pantry and took out a box of aluminum foil and Tupperware bowls.

Monet put a plastic lid on top of the bowl of stew and removed other bowls from the cabinet to put the food in.

"I guess we'll get out of here," Duane remarked, after getting some food. Derek went to the foyer to get his and Duane's jackets. Duane walked over to Monet and said, "I'll work on Derek, and Dad will stay at our place."

Monet's expression brightened. "Thanks. I think that will be the best place for him. Of course, he'll stay here sometimes."

"I'll talk to you later," Derek said, coming back into the kitchen. He put an orange and navy blue Chicago Bears skullcap on his head, the matching jacket, and gloves on his hands. "Duane, I'm going to warm up the car." Then he left the kitchen, walked through the living room, and out the front door.

Duane looked at his sister, and compassion shone in his eyes. "Don't let Marcus and Derek work your nerves. They are two of the most stubborn men I've ever known. Call me if you need anything." He squeezed Monet's arm gently. Duane and Monet could hear Derek impatiently blowing the car horn, indicating he was ready to go.

Monet followed Duane to the door. After he left, she locked it, and then returned to the kitchen where she put the food in bowls and in the refrigerator. She wiped the kitchen table clean and checked on Mitzi, who was in her bed asleep. She filled Mitzi's water bowl, flipped off the light switch, and went upstairs to the master bedroom.

After she had showered and changed into her nightclothes, Monet got into bed and read her Bible for a little while. Her mind tried to process the fact that her father had actually contacted Marcus. And she wondered how her father knew how to get in touch with her husband. Monet wasn't privy to the fact that her mother had given her father her and Marcus's address and phone numbers years ago. As Monet continued to ponder the mystery, she closed her Bible and put it on the nightstand when the telephone rang.

"Hi, Liz," she said after she glanced at caller ID.

"Hey, Monet. How was dinner?" Liz asked. She picked up the remote and turned the channel to BET to watch Sunday Best. Wade was downstairs in the den watching the news.

"Today was a good day. I felt so uplifted after church. I think the nausea has finally passed. I fixed dinner and the boys came over. Marcus even joined us, sort of." Monet crinkled her nose daintily.

"When are you going to stop calling those old brothers of yours *boys?*" Liz teased. "I know they've got to be close to forty years old."

"Not yet, and they'll always be boys to me," Monet mused as she pulled the comforter over her waist.

"What do you want to do first?" Liz asked. "Pray or talk?"

"Let's talk first. You'll have to keep me in your prayers even more after I tell you about the bombshell Marcus dropped on me and my brothers at dinner," Monet commented.

"What was that?" Liz asked nosily. She waited for Monet to reply with bated breath.

"My father is alive," Monet blurted out. "And he contacted Marcus."

"You've got to be kidding." Liz's mouth formed a perfect O. "That's unbelievable. So where has he been all this time?"

"Would you believe right here in Illinois, in prison?" Monet's voice trembled.

"Oh wow," Liz exclaimed, as she sat upright in the bed. "That's too much. What is he in for?"

"Murder One." Monet's tongue tripped on the word murder.

"Hmmm. So what did he want to talk to Marcus about?" Liz relaxed her body against the pillows.

"Well, his request was two-fold. He wanted Marcus to sponsor him when he gets out of prison, and he'd like to meet with me, Duane, and Derek, of course," Monet explained.

"How do you feel about that, and how did your brothers take the news?" Liz asked.

"I'm still sorting it out," Monet murmured softly. "Duane was open to the possibility, as you know he would be. Derek was another story."

There was a moment of silence between the women. Then Liz asked, "Do you think your mother knew your father was incarcerated?"

"I've been asking myself that same question," Monet admitted as she shrugged her shoulders helplessly. "I really don't know. I always thought when he left her, that was the end of things for them. But now I'm not so sure."

"What did Marcus have to say about all of this?"

"You know Marcus. He was pretty much just the messenger. He said he'd continue to check my father out and keep us posted."

"Do you want to see your father?" Liz queried.

"A part of me does, but the other part is scared like a kid." Monet tittered nervously. "I feel like he rejected me, and that's a feeling I've carried with me all my life. Most of the time, I've pushed those feelings to the back of my heart, but tonight they came raging out like a thunderstorm."

"I can understand that," Liz said. "As children, we want to feel unconditional love from our parents. As adults, we understand that life doesn't always work that way. It doesn't lessen the feeling of rejection, but it helps knowing parents aren't infallible. Did your mom ever talk to you and your brothers about your father?"

"No, not much. I pray that things go well with my dad, me, and the boys," Monet commented.

"Speaking of prayer, shall we?" Liz asked.

"I think this would be a great time. Shall I go first?" Monet asked.

"By all means," Liz took her Bible off her nightstand and held it in her hand. They always liked to pray while holding onto the Word.

Monet bowed her head and closed her eyes. "Gracious Father, thank you for allowing me to see another day. All praises to you. Though I am going through some issues, I still have a house to live in, clothes on my back, and you provide my daily bread. Lord, I ask that you put love in Marcus's heart. Most of all, God, give me strength for what lies ahead, and I know if I can lean on you and trust your guidance, which I will, I know that everything is going to be all right. Amen."

"Amen," Liz echoed. Like Monet, she bowed her head and closed her eyes. "Father, thank you for waking us up this morning, clothed in our right minds as we went about doing your business, giving you the thanks and the praises. Lord, bless our biological families, along with our church family. Lord, take care of the sick and shut-in, heal their bodies and minds. Lord, keep your unchanging hand on my sister, Monet. Father, she is carrying a heavy burden. All she has to do is release her worries to you, and you'll take all her hurt and fears away. Father, continue to work with Marcus. Put love in his heart and help him trust in you and have faith, because you are the only one who can make a way out of no way. When we fall short, help us to see the error of our ways and do better. Amen."

"Thank you, Liz. That was a heartfelt prayer." Monet had nothing but good things to say about her friend's prayer.

"Thank you," Liz said modestly. "Your prayer wasn't shabby either. Well, I've got to get up in the morning, so I'll talk to you tomorrow. Get some sleep, and don't worry so much. We want a happy baby."

"You know me so well." Monet sighed. "I'll try, although I have a craving for ice cream now."

"Handle your business, sweetie. I'll talk to you later. Goodnight."

Monet told her the same, and the friends disconnected the call. Monet held the phone thoughtfully in her hand for a minute before placing it back in the base. She lay in the bed, debating if she should go downstairs for the ice cream that seemed to beckon her from the freezer.

Chapter 20

After tossing and turning in the bed for fifteen minutes, Monet rose and sat on Marcus's side of the bed. She badly wanted to talk to her husband about the emotions swirling around in her head regarding her father's request. But Marcus had made it clear by his actions over the past few months that he was just staying at their residence for her protection and nothing else.

He never asked about her doctor's appointments, and outright refused to discuss anything regarding the baby. If Monet was in the kitchen when he arrived home, he greeted her politely, and then headed for the basement, usually with a bag containing his dinner in hand.

Monet looked up at the ceiling, and an idea blossomed inside her head. She hadn't been in the attic in awhile, and maybe there might be a better picture of her father in her mother's possessions than the one she had. Monet and her brothers only had small Polaroid snapshots of their father, which were tattered and fading.

She rose from the bed and picked up her robe from the end of the bed. She walked out of the room and to the staircase leading to the attic. She walked carefully up the ten steps, and when she reached the top, she twisted the doorknob and flipped the light switch on. She walked the length of the room to boxes simply labeled MOMMA'S STUFF that were neatly stacked against a wall on the south side of the building. Monet felt closer to her mother among her possessions.

Her mother's antique rocking chair sat on a wall near the boxes, and Monet walked over to the chair and sat down. She removed the top from the first box and laid it on the floor next to the chair. Then she began burrowing through the items inside.

She found a copy of her father's birth certificate and her parents' marriage license. She hastily put some of the items, like report cards, diplomas, and old family photos of her mother's family back inside the box. She decided to check one more box before calling it a night. She would resume her search in the morning.

Monet gasped when she saw a large brown envelope with her name written on it in her mother's handwriting. Inside the envelope was a smaller envelope with her name written on it, which caused her to tremble with anticipation. She poured the pictures out of the larger envelope onto her lap. She quickly riffled through the photographs of her family at various stages of their lives.

Her eyes were drawn to a picture of her perched on her father's lap. Monet looked awkward; there wasn't a glimmer of a smile on her face in the black and white photograph. Aron, her father, looked uncomfortable; his arm was snaked around her waist. She was relieved to see pictures of her parents in happier times. The clothes they wore looked so old fashioned. There were pictures of her father and the twins. Aron looked pleased as punch holding the boys in his lap. As Monet continued to thumb through the portraits, she found an 8x10 picture of her father that she could give to Marcus.

Suddenly she felt tired. She put the pictures back inside the envelope, stood up and stretched, raising her arms over her head. Monet picked up the letter and put it in her robe pocket. Turning off the light, she walked downstairs, went into the kitchen, and left the picture of her father on the counter, where Marcus would see it when he left for work the next morning.

She went upstairs and to bed. When she fell asleep, visions of her father's face in the picture occupied her dreams.

At seven thirty the following morning, Marcus sat up in the sofa bed and his body ached. His joints told him that he was too old to sleep on the thin mattress of the sofa bed, but he had made his bed and now he had to lie in it. The bathroom in the basement had a shower, so Marcus went in there to bathe.

Thirty minutes later he had shaved and dressed. He converted the bed back to a sofa and then went upstairs to make coffee. Marcus went out the front door to get the newspaper, and went back into the kitchen. He sat at the table drinking his coffee and scanning the newspaper.

After he read the sports section, he closed the newspaper, stood up, and put his cup in the sink. He went back downstairs and picked up his wallet from off the cocktail table, stuffed it inside his pocket, and put on his watch. Then he returned to the kitchen, took his black leather jacket off the coat hook, along with his leather cap. He was walking out the door when he looked at the counter and saw the picture of Monet's dad. He picked it up and stared at it for a few minutes. Marcus thought, *Well, now, I know who Monet got that widow's peak from.* Then he put the picture inside his black leather briefcase and headed off to work.

Usually he and Wade rotated driving to work together. Their relationship had become strained as Monet's pregnancy advanced. Marcus sensed Wade's disapproval of how he was handling the situation. This would have been Marcus's week to pick up his partner and drive to work. After the two couldn't come to a meeting of the minds, they began traveling to work in separate cars.

Marcus clipped his Bluetooth device on the side of his ear

after he got in his car. He pressed the remote for the garage to open and started the car. As he was driving, his cell phone rang. His foot pressed the brakes as he stopped for a red light.

Marcus saw Reverend Wilcox's name on the caller ID unit. "Hello," he greeted her.

"Marcus, how are you feeling today?" she asked. She was at the Temple and had just finished her morning meditation.

"Good." Marcus fought hard to keep the annoyance out of his voice.

"That's great," Reverend Wilcox said cheerfully. "How is Monet feeling?"

"She's doing well," Marcus answered. His manners kicked in. "How are you doing, Reverend Wilcox?" He scowled out of his rearview mirror as a green Hyundai Elantra pulled up too close to his bumper.

"I'm doing just fine. I know you're wondering why I'm calling you," she ventured in a more serious tone of voice.

"A couple of topics come to mind," Marcus said evenly. He glanced back out his rearview mirror.

"Are you always this witty this early in the morning?" she joked. "I'd like to talk to you whenever you can make time for me."

Marcus kept his eyes on the traffic around him. "If you want to talk about Monet and her pregnancy, then I really don't have anything to say." His body tensed up.

Reverend Wilcox knew Marcus was going to be challenge. *At least he's honest*, she thought. "Actually, I wanted to talk about you, and see if there's anything I can do to help you cope with your home situation a little better."

"I appreciate you wanting to help, Reverend Wilcox, but there's really nothing you can say to make my life better. It's what it is, and I'm coping with it the best I can."

"Well, it's been my experience in these types of circumstances

that sometimes it helps to talk to someone, a minister or maybe
a therapist, when one is going through a dilemma. I sense that
you're not keen on talking to me, but would you make an excep-
tion this time? One talk, that's all I request."

"Did Monet, Wade, or Liz put you up to this?" Marcus was
suspicious. He put on his left turn signal and steered his Blazer
to the left turn lane.

"None of the above." Reverend Wilcox chortled merrily. She
tried desperately to break the ice with Marcus and put him at
ease. "Give me a little credit. Can you make a little time for your
minister one day this week? Whenever you're available, I'll make
myself available."

He knew she wouldn't relent until he gave in, so he said,
"How about Friday at five o'clock?"

Reverend Wilcox opened her date book, which lay open on
her Pledge-smelling, wooden desk. "That sounds good. If you're
agreeable, we can meet at the church."

"That's fine," Marcus answered tersely, as he turned onto
the street where his station was located. He parked in the parking lot of the gray two story building.

"Okay, I'll see you then. And Marcus, know that you're not
alone during what I know has to be a trying time for you and
Monet. You have a lot of good people in your corner who would
do anything to help you. Most of all, Jesus is there for you. All
you have to do is call on Him and release your burdens to Him."

"I know." He exhaled loudly before disconnecting the call.

From out the corner of his eye, Marcus noticed Wade parking his jeep. He debated whether or not he should wait on Wade
to join him, and decided not to. Marcus hurried out of his Blazer and opened the back door to remove his briefcase from the
backseat. Then he walked rapidly to the building entrance and
walked inside the station.

The noise level was minimal for a change. Marcus supposed

the natives had stayed inside last night since the temperature had fallen below freezing, which may have deterred some would be criminals.

Since Monet's attack, the mood in the detective's room had changed. In the past the atmosphere had been upbeat. As the detectives waited on the clerk to distribute the reports and assignments, they would shoot the breeze. The subjects would run the gamut, from current events, hot dates, husbands, wives, and children, to the state of Chicago's sport teams and politics. Lately, the vibes had been somber, like everyone was attending a funeral.

Marcus didn't make eye contact with his co-workers as he walked into the large room to his desk. He said a tepid good morning to several detectives, then pulled out his chair, took off his jacket, and draped it around the back of the chair. He laid his hat on the desk, sat in his leather swivel chair, opened the briefcase, and took out his notepad and wrote notes in it.

Ten minutes later, Wade walked into the room carrying a couple boxes of Dunkin Donuts. He sat them on the counter, went to the coffee pot. and poured himself a cup of dark brew.

A detective named William Abrams walked over to the counter and said, "See, that's what I'm talking about. Good going, Harrison."

"I figured we were due for a picker-upper." Wade grabbed two jelly donuts and walked to his desk. After he set the coffee mug and a doughnut on his desk, he handed Marcus the other doughnut and asked, "How are you doing?"

"I'm okay," he replied, not looking at Wade. He opened his desk drawer and removed the number for Aron's soon to be parole officer, and then turned on his PC.

The department clerk, Mona, walked into the room. She greeted the detectives and began passing out assignment sheets.

After Marcus's PC had finished booting, he logged on to

AFIS as he did every morning, to see if there had been any hits in the database of the fingerprints found on Monet's car. Sadly, like previous days, there were none. He looked up from the computer monitor to see Smitty standing in front of his desk.

"What can I do for you?" Marcus asked in a neutral tone of voice.

"I just wanted to say that me and the guys," Smitty gestured behind him, "haven't given up on finding Monet's attacker. We're still following up on leads, and however long it takes we will get him."

"And you felt compelled to make that statement for what reason?" Marcus asked Smitty with a deadpan expression on his face.

"Well, we feel like you think we aren't giving our best effort in finding Monet's attacker, and I just wanted to reassure you that we are. You're one of us, and anybody that hurts one of ours, hurts us too. The team has met off hours, even sometimes on the weekends, to follow up on leads. Marc, we just wanted you to know that we're never going to give up."

Wade nodded encouragingly at Smitty. Then he leaned back in his chair. He was at his wits end trying to think of something to do to bring Marcus out of his funk. He figured maybe Smitty talking to Marcus would let him know that he wasn't alone in his quest to find the attacker.

Marcus dropped his hands on the desk. His eyes stung, and he closed and re-opened them. All eyes in the room seemed to be riveted on him. Mona paused handing out the next assignment and even she stopped in her tracks to stare at Marcus and Smitty.

Marcus moistened his lips and said candidly, "Look, I'm sorry if I gave you the impression that you and the guys weren't doing your job. This whole ordeal has been trying for me and Monet. What I did think was that you guys kept me out of the loop and that bothered me."

"There was a good reason for that." Smitty held up his hands. "The chief told us that you're too close to the situation. We're sorry, but the chief is the one who signs off on our checks, so we have to follow his directions."

Marcus's eyes roamed the room. "That's all well and good, but what if it were your wife who was attacked? What would you all do? Would you just drop it?"

One of the other team members, Larry, stood up and said, "Marcus, we know how you feel, and we'd probably do the same thing if it happened to us. But we aren't in a position where we can jeopardize our jobs. We need our checks."

"You say that we're a family, but in reality, we're family with strings attached," Marcus sputtered. "Look, you've said your piece, and I appreciate all you do. But that's not going to stop me from doing what I have to do to solve the crime against me and my wife." He stood up and left the room.

Wade felt troubled. He stood up and left the room to search for Marcus. He went to the lounge area and found him standing at the window, staring out of it.

"Marc," he began saying, "the chief talked to me yesterday, and there have been some complaints about your attitude. Some of the guys find it disruptive." Wade was clearly uncomfortable.

"And," Marcus said belligerently. He flexed his hands and curled them into fists.

"Hey, buddy," Wade help up his hands, "I'm on your side. But you've got to lighten up some. God knows this situation is hard on you. You've got to find a way to get over it so your life isn't consumed by what happened."

"Excuse me," Marcus said through gritted teeth. "I can't help but feel a little pressure here. My wife was raped, and now every day I have to watch her belly swell with that animal's child. And to complicate matters, her old man, who she hasn't seen in years, is getting out of the joint after serving time for murder one. And my life, as I knew it, has been obliterated like an atomic bomb was dropped on it. Man, I've had it up to here." He ran his hand across his neck.

Wade could feel waves of hopelessness emanating from Marcus's body, and he prayed that God would help him find the words to say so Marcus would realize all he had to do was pray for God to ease his burdens. All Wade could think to say was, "Come on now, brother. I'm with you, and the Lord is with you. Marcus, you're not alone."

"Yeah, yeah," he said heatedly. "Where was God when Monet was being raped? How come He didn't protect her then? Where was your God then?" Marcus's shoulders were hunched up, and he moved toward Wade menacingly.

Wade put his hand on his chest and shook his head sadly. "He's not only my God, Marc, He's yours too. And you know as well as I do that the situation could've been worse. Monet could have been killed. Is that what you would have preferred, that she died? God was there, nobody but God protected her."

"How can you fix your mouth to ask me that?" Marcus had the grace to look ashamed for a moment. Then his face hardened. "The way I see it, Wade, is that God is the reason Monet is pregnant. That is what your God has done for me. Look, I've got things to do. I'll try to do better at work. Tell the chief that you've talked to me, and that the message was delivered." With that, he turned and walked out of the room.

Wade watched his friend walk out the door and thought, *Lord, work with my brother, hold him tight in your arms, and don't let him go. Show him the way, because Marcus is in need of your help today.*

A few minutes later, a troubled Wade left the room and decided to talk to Chief Davis. He walked to the chief's office and stood at the desk of Renee, the chief's secretary.

"Have a seat, Wade, I'll see if he's available," she said. Wade sat down while Renee buzzed the chief and informed him that

Wade was waiting to see him. Then she turned her attention back to her PC and continued entering data. Her telephone rang minutes later. "Okay, Chief Davis, I'll send him in," she replied. She told Wade, "You can go in now." She stood and ushered him into Chief Davis's office.

"Harrison." Chief Davis nodded at Wade. "Have a seat."

"Hello, sir." Wade felt uncomfortable as he sat in the chair in front of the chief's desk. He felt like a Judas, as if he was betraying his best friend.

The men talked about office business for a while. Then Chief Davis cut to the chase. "How is he doing?" He picked up a cherry wood pipe off his desk and stroked it.

"Sir, Marcus is under a lot of pressure. He's distraught because his wife's attacker hasn't been found, and he looks at the perp being loose as a personal attack on his manhood," Wade explained.

"Hmmm." Chief Davis bobbed his head up and down. "I can see that. Marcus has always been full of pride. I hope he can pull it together because if he can't, then I'm going to have to pull him off the streets, assign him to a desk job, and recommend that he undergo counseling."

Wade wiped his sweaty palms on the sides of his pants. "Could you just give him more time? It's really not my place to tell you this, but under the circumstances, I feel you should know that Marcus's wife is pregnant, and he's convinced the pregnancy is a result of the rape."

That news got the chief's attention. He'd been looking down at a paper in Marcus's folder. He looked up at Wade, down at the papers, then up at Wade again, his mouth slightly open.

"I promise I'll keep an eye on him. And if I feel as though he's slipping or unable to cope well, I'll bring it to your attention immediately. If Marcus is unable to or is suspended from work, I'm afraid he'll snap. He's got to feel useful somewhere, since he feels like he's failed at home."

Chief Davis stuck the pipe in his mouth. "The whole thing is a shame. I think you're taking a lot on your shoulders, Harrison. You know partners are like lifelines. A situation could jump off at any time, and you've got to make sure you can rely on your partner's actions."

"I hear you, sir, but I couldn't do any less. Marcus and I have been partners for fifteen years. He's more than a partner to me, he's like a brother. Pulling him off the job now would just further damage his psyche. If I feel like I can't handle the situation, I'll talk to you," Wade promised.

"See that you do. If your suggestion fails, then it's on you, Harrison," the chief growled. His telephone rang. He laid the pipe down on his desk and pressed a button on the telephone. "Yes, Renee?"

"Chief, you have a meeting in five minutes," the secretary reminded her boss.

"Okay, Renee, I'm coming. Harrison is leaving." He pressed the button again and the call was disconnected.

"Why don't you talk to Renee on your way out, and set up an appointment with me on a weekly basis to talk about Caldwell's progress, or the lack thereof?" Chief Davis instructed.

Wade stood up and pushed the chair closer to the desk. "Yes, sir. I mean I will, sir."

"I swear when I talk to you, Harrison, I feel like I'm in the military." He closed the file. "Keep me in the loop," he further instructed.

"I will." Wade flashed him a smile as he walked out of the office. He paused at Renee's desk and told her the chief's request.

Renee clicked on an icon on the PC monitor and che-cked Chief Davis's schedule. "He's free in the mornings at six thirty. I know your shift doesn't start until seven. Can you come in early on Fridays?

Wade nodded. Nobody said it would be easy, but he was willing to go the extra mile for Marcus.

Renee scheduled the meeting as a recurring one for three months. "I'll see you next Friday, Wade. Rose Woodson is one of my close friends, and she told me Marcus has been having a hard time. I just wanted to compliment you on hanging in there for your friend. God will bless you, and one day Marcus will realize what you've done and he'll be grateful."

"Thanks, Renee. I think so too." He smiled at her, then left the room and returned to the detective's area.

After he sat down at his desk, Wade turned and asked Marcus if anything had come in for them while he'd been gone. Marcus told him no. Wade opened his case book and before he began to transcribe notes into it, Wade looked over at Marcus. He was hunched over the PC keyboard typing with his hunt and peck method.

Wade hoped that Marcus would be able to get himself together, because if he didn't, Wade knew Chief Davis would make good on his threat to assign Marcus to a desk job. Wade prayed he was up to the task of keeping his friend in check because he didn't want Marcus's life to spiral even further out of control. Wade sighed and turned his attention back to his almost illegible scrawling handwriting and ordered his mind to stay on work, and as his grandmother used to admonish him as a child, to stop borrowing trouble.

Chapter 21

"Goodness gracious, I forgot I had a doctor's appointment this morning," Monet moaned when she awakened at ten o'clock. She sprang out of bed and rushed into the bathroom, showered and dressed. After she put food and water out for Mitzi, she left the house and drove to Dr. Armstrong's office in Chatham.

An hour later, she pulled her car into a parking space, got out of the car, and walked briskly to the two story building. The wind was high in Chicago, and seared her eyes. Monet walked inside the elevator and pushed the button for the second floor. The elevator seemed to take forever to climb one floor. She sighed and glanced at her watch. She was only running five minutes behind schedule. She exited the elevator and walked down the hallway to office 310. She pushed the door open and walked inside to the receptionist's desk.

"Dr. Armstrong is running a little behind schedule," Pat, the nurse/receptionist, notified Monet after instructing her to add her name to the sign-in sheet.

After she complied, she handed her insurance card to Pat, who made a copy of it and returned the card to her. As she took her seat, Monet noticed there were three patients ahead of her, in various stages of pregnancy.

She remembered when she saw the doctor for her yearly pap smear test, how envious she was of the doctor's pregnant patients. She looked down at her abdomen and smiled. Then Monet pulled a paperback book out of her purse and began reading.

She was so engrossed in the book that Pat had to repeat her name a couple of times. Monet looked up at the receptionist. "Did you call me?" she asked.

"Yes, I did. The doctor can see you now." Pat opened the door leading to the examination area. She walked beside Monet. "You're in room C. So how have you been feeling?"

"Not bad," Monet said, "The worst of the nausea seems to have passed."

"Good," Pat nodded her head. She weighed Monet and took her vitals. "You can put on the dressing gown. The doctor will be in to see you soon."

"Thank you." Monet quickly took off her clothing and put on the dressing gown. While she waited for the doctor, she resumed reading her book. She looked up when Dr. Armstrong walked into the room and quickly set the book on the chair where her clothing had been placed. "Hello, Dr. Armstrong," she said, as she climbed back on the examining table.

"Hello, Monet. How are you feeling?" Dr. Armstrong she sat in a chair next to the table and quickly scanned Monet's chart. "Your pressure is good, and you've gained fifteen pounds total; not bad." She stood up and walked to the table. She told Monet to lie down, and then began her examination. When she was done, Dr. Armstrong told her she could sit up. "Everything seems fine, and the baby's heartbeat is strong. Are you sleeping okay? What's new with you?" she asked, as she made notations on Monet's chart.

"Well, I think I felt the baby move yesterday," Monet said shyly. "The sensation was a fluttering one in the pit of my stomach. Could I hear her heartbeat?"

"Sure." Dr. Armstrong stood up and handed Monet her stethoscope. Then she sat back down. "You're a nurse, so I don't have to give you any instructions."

Monet fumbled slightly as she put the earpieces in her ears. Then she placed the circular metal portion of the instrument on her belly. She rolled it over her belly until she heard the baby's heartbeat. Her smile was as bright as a ray of sunlight. "Oh my, her heartbeat is so strong." She took the stethoscope from around her neck and handed it back to Dr. Armstrong.

The doctor said, "I'd say you're doing well. Are you drinking plenty of milk, taking your prenatal pills, and resting?" Monet nodded yes. Dr. Armstrong closed Monet's file and looked at her. "When you finish dressing I'd like to talk to you in my office." She stood up and closed the door behind her.

Monet felt apprehensive for a few minutes as her mind raced to figure out what the doctor might want to talk to her about. She rose from the examination table and got dressed. Ten minutes later, she sat in the brown chair in front of Dr. Armstrong's desk, twisting the strap of her purse nervously.

The doctor leaned back away from her desk. "Let me put your mind at ease, I only want to schedule you for tests at the hospital. A blood workup, ultrasound test, and I'd like you to consider taking an amniocentesis."

Monet looked upward, and then back at the doctor. "I have no problem with the blood workup or taking an ultrasound test. But are you scheduling the amniocentesis because you think something is wrong, or as a precaution?"

"Monet," Dr. Armstrong said gently, "you're forty-two years old. Granted, we haven't had any issues, but because of your age, we still have to be proactive with your care. I just don't want any surprises when it's time for you to deliver."

"I understand what you're saying." Monet nodded her head. "But I know the baby is fine. If there are any birth defects, and I know there aren't, then I'll deal with it when the time comes."

"Actually new studies show that an amniocentesis can be administered in a mother's third trimester of pregnancy at the discretion of a patient's physician. I thought if we do the amniocentesis now, then we can run a DNA test at the same time. That might help put your husband's mind at ease regarding the paternity of the child. Raising a child with birth defects isn't easy." Dr. Armstrong sat up erect in her chair.

"Regardless of the results of an amniocentesis or an ultrasound test, I'll welcome my child into the world. I am not interested in learning the sex of the baby, I already know I'm having a girl," Monet said imploringly, as she leaned forward in her chair.

"I understand," Dr. Armstrong said soothingly. "I just wanted you to be aware of your options and what you might be facing."

"You know what? My life might be in shambles right now. But as long as I have Jesus to lean on, and I do, then I'll be fine. Is that it?"

"Yes, but I'd still like you to consider taking the amniocentesis." Dr. Armstrong was aware that she had upset her patient. "How are things with you and Marcus? Any better?"

"No, not really. But hey, I'm making it." Monet shrugged her shoulders.

"I'm not asking to get in your business or anything. Your mental state is just as important as your physical one. That's all I'm getting at," Dr. Armstrong said apologetically.

"No harm done. Since I'm a nurse, I understand what you're saying. Actually, God has seen fit to bless me with a pair of wonderful friends and my brothers, which I consider my support system. They all make it their business to make sure I stay as upbeat as I can during the pregnancy. Liz, my best girlfriend, will attend Lamaze classes with me, so when the time comes I'll be fine, whether Marcus comes around or not."

"Great," Dr. Armstrong said. "A support system is quite important at this time. My grandmother, bless her heart, had an old saying: *A sad mother makes for a sad baby*, so I try to do what I can to keep my mothers' moods upbeat and positive."

"I appreciate your efforts," Monet said meekly. "I just get a little cranky sometimes. It must be my hormones." She and the doctor shared a laugh.

"Well, I've written a prescription for vitamins, and I've also given you paperwork for the amniocentesis test, ultrasound procedure, and the lab workup. Do whatever you feel is best." Dr. Armstrong handed Monet three pieces of paper.

She stood up and said, "Okay, I'll see you when? In three weeks?"

Dr. Armstrong looked up. "Make your next appointment with Pat for three weeks, and by that time I should have all the lab results back. It's time for me to see my next patient."

Monet nodded as she put the papers inside her purse. She waved good-bye and said, "I'll see you next time." She stopped at the reception desk and made her next appointment. As she was walking to her car, Monet decided to have lunch at a neighborhood café before returning home.

When Monet arrived at her house, she let Mitzi out in the backyard so she could get some exercise. She hung up her coat in the hall closet, and then returned to the kitchen, picked up the cordless phone, and made an appointment for her lab work at the hospital. She turned the paperwork for the amniocentesis over and over in her hand. Then she stuffed it back into her purse. She felt the test was a waste of time, and she wasn't going to have it done.

She let Mitzi back in the house, and the tiny dog followed Monet upstairs to the bedroom. Monet removed her shoes, pulled back the comforter, and lay in the bed. Within minutes, she was asleep with a Mona Lisa smile on her face.

The ringing telephone interrupted her nap. Liz called to see how her doctor's appointment had gone. Monet told her, and then explained about her misgivings with taking an amniocentesis. Liz agreed with her decision, since it didn't affect her pregnancy one way or the other. Liz told Monet she had a meeting and would call her back later.

Just as Monet hung up the cordless phone and laid her head on the pillow, the telephone rang again. Her manager at the hospital, Angela Sullivan, usually called her Monday afternoons to see how she was feeling. So far Monet hadn't told anyone at work about her pregnancy, and decided to test the waters and see what Angie's reaction would be.

When Monet requested an extension of her leave of absence, she told St. Bernard that she still hadn't fully recovered from the attack. Upper management approved the extension and told Monet to come back when she felt ready. Angie had assured Monet that there would always be a place for her at the maternity ward.

She removed the cordless phone from the base, peered at caller ID and clicked it on. "Hello, Angie," she greeted her manager.

"Hi, Monet. How are you doing?" Angela asked.

"I'm good. How is everyone there doing?" Monet missed working at the hospital.

"We're all doing well. Everyone told me to tell you hello and that they're thinking about you."

"Tell everyone I said hello. How are the babies?" Monet asked.

"We had six births since I last talked to you. One is a very tiny preemie. She weighs a little over a pound, so she'll be with us for a while. And Cydney Mitchell brought little Ashley in to see us last week. She has gained a lot of weight. Ashley is a pretty little thing and feisty." Angela laughed.

"I remember how her tiny arms would flail, and she'd kick her legs when we had to insert an IV into her." Monet joined in Angela's laughter. "Well, I'm glad to hear that she's doing well."

"Successes are always good. Cydney sends her love and gratefulness to you," Angela informed.

"I was only doing my job," Monet replied modestly. She

looked across the room at Mitzi. The dog stood up, arched her back, and shook her body as if she were stretching. Then she laid back down in her corner of the room.

"So when do you think you'll come back to work?" Angela asked, as she did every week.

"Not for at least another four plus months," Monet answered. She couldn't keep a smile from her face.

"Hmmm, four months? That's a nice round number. Is there anything significant about six months?"

"Angie, I'm pregnant," Monet answered shyly." Her tongue seemed to glide over the word pregnant. Her eyes fell to her midsection, and she patted it.

"Wow." Angela's mouth dropped open. She, like most of the staff in the department, was aware of how much Monet wanted a baby. "Congratulations, Monet," she said awkwardly. She did the math in her head and deduced her employee's baby was conceived around the time of the rape.

"Thank you, Angie," Monet said quietly. She had almost gotten used to the lack of enthusiastic responses when she announced that she was pregnant.

"How are you feeling? I guess since you've passed the first trimester you must be sighing with relief," Angie added to the stagnant conversation.

"Yes, I am, as well as being grateful to God," Monet commented.

"Marcus was here a couple of weeks ago investigating a case, and he never said a word. So how is he taking the news?" Angela asked curiously.

"He was surprised to say the least," Monet replied casually. "I think he'd given up hope that we'd ever have a child."

"So which do you prefer, a girl or boy?" Angela queried. She sensed no more information would be forthcoming about Marcus.

"Like most mothers, I want a healthy baby. But I already know our baby is a girl," Monet answered succinctly.

"Well, Monet, I'm happy for you. I know you've always want-ed a baby. You'll have to come by and see us when you feel up to it. I'll be sure to share the news with the staff. That's okay with you, isn't it?"

"That's fine." Monet nodded. Then she speculated how Mar-cus would feel about her telling people her news. She dismissed the thought, rationalizing she couldn't keep the secret forever. After all, her pregnancy was becoming more evident every day.

The two women conversed a few more minutes before hang-ing up, after promising to talk to each other the upcoming week.

Monet stretched her arms over her head. Since sleep wasn't on her agenda any longer, she went downstairs to get a glass of milk. She walked into the kitchen, took a carton of milk from the refrigerator and poured herself a full glass. She drank the milk, put the glass in the sink, and walked into the den. She sat on the sofa and mulled over her conversation with Angela.

She thought the conversation overall had gone fair, and prayed aloud to her Heavenly Father. "Lord, I guess not every-one is going to see things the way I do, and I have to accept their opinion. I know that Faith is my and Marcus's child. Thank you for bringing Liz and Wade into our lives years ago. They have been the angels you sent to help us along the way. Lord, I will lean on you, my rock of Gibraltar."

Psalm 22 came to mind, and Monet shut her eyes tightly and recited the words. "*My soul waits only upon God; for my expectation is from him. He only is my rock and my salvation; He is my deference, I shall not be moved. In God is my salvation and my glory: the rock of my strength, and my refuge is in God.*" An old gospel song Monet's mother used to hum came to her mind: "Jesus Is A Rock In A Weary Land."

It was now close to four o'clock, and Monet was at odds as

to what to do with the remainder of her day. She picked the remote control off the table, turned on the television, and channel surfed for a few minutes. She turned to WLS and watched the news.

When the news went off, she stroked her chin, remembering the letter her mother had written to her. Monet left the den and went upstairs to her bedroom. She walked to her nightstand and pulled the letter out of the top drawer. She walked back to the attic, sat in her mother's rocking chair, and opened the letter.

Chapter 22

A little after one o'clock on the day of Monet's doctor appointment, Marcus and Wade were on their lunch break. While Wade went into a greasy spoon to get hot dogs, Marcus reached into the glove compartment and removed his cell phone and the slip of paper that had the telephone number to Dwight Prison, the facility where Aron Reynolds was incarcerated. He looked at the paper, opened his phone, and punched in the numbers. After being transferred a couple of times, Marcus finally spoke to the warden's secretary, Levi Smith.

"My name is Marcus Caldwell. I'm a detective with the Chicago Police Department, and I'd like to make an appointment with Warden Jones," he stated.

"What is this regarding?" Levi asked, in a bored tone of voice.

"It's about my father-in-law, Aron Reynolds," Marcus explained "He's due to be released from there soon, and he called and asked me if I'd help him wade through the red tape. I wanted to get a feel for Aron's personality and his behavior since he's been there."

Levi scrawled the name Aron Reynolds on a notepad in loping letters. "Give me your number, I'll make some inquiries and call you back," he said.

Marcus recited his cell number to Levi. By the time he ended the call, Wade had returned to the car. Marcus returned his cell phone to the glove compartment as Wade got in the vehicle.

"Did we get any calls from the station? Is anything happening?" Wade asked.

"No, not yet," Marcus said. He took his chili dog and fries out the brown bag that Wade had placed on the floor, and set it in front of him on the dashboard. Wade passed him a can of Coke.

Wade looked at Marcus disgustedly. "I know Monet's been cooking since she's not working. All this food is going to do is harden your arteries and send you to an early grave."

"I work out; I'm okay," Marcus said, pointedly looking at the pouch that circled Wade's stomach.

"Now, you're just plain wrong," Wade admonished as he took a ham and cheese sandwich out of the bag for himself. The men munched on their food, and for a time there was a sense of camaraderie between them like before Monet's assault.

Wade finished eating first and wiped his hands and mouth on a napkin. "So what's happening with you?" he asked.

Marcus explained about Monet's father's request, and Wade listened intently. When he finished talking, Wade's eyebrows rose skeptically.

"What does Monet and her brothers make of this?" he asked.

"I think Monet and Duane are curious, and Derek is being Derek. He doesn't want to have anything to do with his father. I'd like to check out their father, Aron Reynolds, myself. Who knows? Maybe there's a connection between him and Monet's assault."

"I don't think so," Wade replied dubiously. He put the napkin in the paper bag and swallowed more Coke.

"You know people can find out whatever information they want in the joint. Maybe Aron angered someone who had access to his records. Nothing is impossible when it comes to a criminal's mind. All I know is that I can't leave any stone unturned." Marcus said stubbornly. He put his last French fry in his mouth and chewed.

Wade held up his hands. "I understand. So where are you going from here?"

"Well, the warden's secretary is going to call me back. If things stay quiet at the precinct, which you truly can't predict in a city the size of Chicago, then I'd like to ride out to Dwight Correctional Facility this week or early next week. I'll run the request by the chief," Marcus said.

"That makes sense." Wade started the engine. "I guess it's time for us to get back to the station."

"Hey, Wade, what do you think about going to Dwight with me?" Marcus asked, as he looked out the car window.

"Sure, I'll go with you. Someone has to keep you out of trouble."

"Thanks, man; I appreciate it," Marcus said gratefully.

Before long the two had returned to headquarters, and it would be another couple hours before the workday ended. Marcus sat at his desk writing case notes. He and Wade were scheduled to look at surveillance tape from a robbery in twenty minutes.

Monet stared at her mother's neat printing for a long time. She had an intense longing for her mother that tugged at her heartstrings. Her hands shook as she used the tip of her pink fingernail to slit open the top of the brown envelope. She was so overcome by the longing for her mother that she laid the letter in her lap until she composed herself. Though her mother had been gone for five years, at times it felt like yesterday.

She took a tissue from her pocket and blew her nose. Then she picked up the letter again and quickly scanned it. She was stunned to learn that her mother knew her father was in prison, and even more taken aback that she had never shared the information with her children.

Her mother confessed how she was mistaken in allowing them to think their father had been gone all those years and never tried to contact them. She asked for forgiveness, citing she just wasn't sure how to tell them their father was in prison for murder. She didn't want to give them another reason to dislike him more, and it was her hope that her children would reconcile with him one day.

A sense of discomfort nibbled at Monet's heart. She had always felt her mother was perfect, but the contents of the letter proved her wrong. She shuddered at the thought of her brothers' reactions, especially Derek's. The letter went on to explain that her mother had corresponded with their father while he was in prison and that she had kept the missives for them to read and draw their own conclusions. The letters were in a safe deposit box at a bank located about twenty miles from their mother's home. The keys to the box were inside the brown envelope.

Their father, according to their mother, had battled demons his entire life, and hadn't been able to overcome them until his later years. Those demons affected her and Aron's marriage. She added that she felt he had changed for the better after he went to prison.

The second page of the letter went into detail about how he couldn't cope with Monet as a child. Her mother said that she believed her father loved her, and just as equally, he feared her. She revealed how she didn't tell him about the gift until they were married, and how that was a mistake. She basically took the blame for the breakdown of her marriage, and placed the responsibility for her children not having a relationship with their father squarely on her shoulders.

Monet's eyes filled with tears, and droplets of water trickled down her face as she read the rest of the letter. Then she put it in her pocket and went to her bedroom. She lay in the bed, turned on her side, and wondered if her fate would be akin to her mother's. The enormity of the gift that was passed down from mother to daughter and seemed to negatively affect marriages gnawed at her mind.

A sigh escaped Monet's lips as she realized that her work was cut out for her because her daughter would, too, share the gift. A light sensation flitted inside Monet's abdomen and she felt comforted, as if baby Faith knew what she was feeling. Monet felt desolate because she would have loved to share the baby's moving with Marcus. She imagined his big hand stroking her belly and smiled. Monet's hand stole down to her abdomen and she patted the mound gently, then she went to sleep.

Marcus arrived home at six o'clock that evening, and was surprised to find the house dark. He fumbled for the light switch in the kitchen, and set a brown bag of Chinese food on the table. After he hung his jacket on the hook behind the door, he looked at the stove and saw that Monet hadn't cooked. He wondered if she felt well. He walked upstairs to make sure she was okay.

He dimmed the light in the hallway when he reached the last step, and peeped into the master bedroom. Marcus saw the wrinkles on Monet's face, and wanted to smooth them away. She looked tired, and he wondered if he were the cause. He was about leave when he caught sight of her stomach. He was shocked to see how thick her waist had become. Grief traveled through his body. Marcus watched his wife a few more seconds before he turned and went downstairs.

He went to the foyer and looked at the mail that Monet had set atop the black and gold lacquered, scalloped edged console table. An oval mirror, with sconces on each side, was placed above the table. A burgundy wine colored Persian rug, intertwined with black and gold threads, greeted guests when they walked through the front door.

The mail was mostly bills and magazines for Monet. He stuffed the bills in his pocket and strolled to the kitchen, making sure Mitzi had food and water. Then he took his bag of food and headed to the basement. He turned on the light and walked down a flight of eight stairs. Marcus put the bag on the card table next to his pride and joy, a fifty-two inch high definition television with surround sound.

He had been in a quiet, but reasonably good mood. But after seeing Monet's baby bump, his good mood vanished like a puff of smoke. He looked longingly at the wooden wet bar on the other side of the paneled basement. He could use a drink, but after his brouhaha at Lee Otis's bar, he'd sworn off liquor and had made good on that promise. He picked up the TV remote off the cocktail table in front of the couch and channel surfed until he found a basketball game on *ESPN*.

Though the Chinese food had gotten cold, Marcus didn't have the energy to walk across the room to the microwave to warm it up. He decided to eat it cold. Twenty minutes had elapsed, and he had finished eating, but he still couldn't keep his mind from drifting to the picture of Monet's stomach.

He heard the doorbell ring, and figured Monet had awakened and that she would answer it. Marcus just sat inertly with his head against the back of the couch, when the doorbell rang again.

"Now who could that be?" He lifted his body off the couch and ran upstairs in time to see a UPS driver entering his brown truck. He pointed to the steps, where a box lay. Marcus picked it up and brought it inside the house. When he looked at the label, he saw that it was addressed to Monet and was from a dress store. She had ordered maternity clothes.

Monet walked down the stairs. "Hello," she said warily. "Would you take that box upstairs for me?"

Marcus nodded. When he returned downstairs, Monet was in the kitchen looking for something to eat in the refrigerator. She held the door open with one hand, and her other hand was rooted on the side of her hip.

"How was your day, Marcus?" She interrupted him before he could take refuge in the basement.

"Not bad, same ole, same ole. How was yours?"

"Not bad either. I talked to Angie, and I had a doctor's appointment today," she announced as she closed the refrigerator and took a pint of chocolate chip ice cream out of the freezer.

"Hmmm," Marcus grunted. He looked down at the floor.

Monet waited for him to ask her how the visit went, but he didn't. "I kept hoping you'd change your mind and go with me," she said.

Marcus threw up his hands and said, "Hey, that's your thing, not mine. I have nothing to do with your situation."

"It would be nice," she said, taking a spoon out of the cabinet, "if you would at least ask me how the visit went. Can't we be a little more civil to each other?"

"Nay-Nay, I'm really not interested in your doctor visits." Marcus looked at her stomach, and his knees sagged momentarily as his heart seemed to bounce to his feet. She was showing more than he thought. *Why couldn't that be my child she's carrying,* he thought.

"A lawyer called today. His name is Attorney Garner, and he wanted to know if we'd discussed suing the hospital for negligence," Monet announced after she swallowed a spoonful of ice cream. "I wonder where he got that idea from."

That was another bone of contention between the couple. Marcus was in favor of suing the hospital. He felt someone needed to pay for Monet's injuries and the state of disarray their marriage had dissolved into.

"I talked to him a couple weeks ago, and asked him to let me know if we had a case. He shouldn't have called you about that anyway. He was supposed to call me." Marcus was clearly annoyed. "What did he say?"

"He said we had a case because the camera was out in the

parking lot. I thanked him for his time and services, and asked him to send us a bill," Monet said placidly.

"Why did you do that?" Marcus exploded. In the past they would have discussed the issue together, but now the two were on different wavelengths.

"Marcus, I know you didn't really think I was going to sue the hospital. It wasn't their fault what happened. I was in the wrong place at the wrong time. True enough I was hurt, and I realize I could have been killed. But my wounds have healed, and God spared my life."

"It would have been nice if you had talked to me before you pulled Mike off the case," he said, with a tinge of venom in his voice. His eyes narrowed as he rubbed his chin and shook his head.

"I could say the same thing of you about talking to him in the first place, but I won't. I'm not under any circumstances going to sue St. Bernard's. They couldn't afford it, and the people in the community need that hospital to remain open more then we need the money to appease your ego," Monet said. She put the half eaten carton of ice cream back in the freezer.

"My ego has nothing to do with this," Marcus retorted. "I just think someone needs to pay."

"We both are, because you can't see what's right in front of your face."

"Oh, I see all right," Marcus said in a nasty tone. "I see my wife, who doesn't seem to give a crap about my opinion and does what she wants."

"Let me tell you something, Marcus Caldwell." Monet pointed her finger at him. "The bottom line is you're wrong. You barely talk to me. Shoot, you act like I don't exist, and you're the one who initiated the dialogue with the attorney, not me. I fix dinner for you, which you refuse to eat. I hate this gulf between us, but I'm not changing my position. I'm having our child, and you need to get with the program." She turned on her heels and marched out of the kitchen and upstairs to the bedroom.

Marcus stood in the kitchen fuming; his lips were twisted in fury. Mitzi stood up and howled mournfully, then lay back down in her basket and covered her eyes with her paws, as if she couldn't bear the strain in the Caldwell household.

A coil of hot anger wrapped around Marcus's heart, and he ran up the stairs to their bedroom. "Why can't you see how this situation is tearing us apart?" He tried to keep the bitterness he felt out of his voice.

Monet was sitting on the bed, and her expression was as miserable as her husband's. "Marc, I see just as clearly as you do what has happened to us. And I also see somewhere along the way you lost your faith in God."

Marcus shook his head. "I don't know, perhaps you're right. I don't understand why God would allow you to be beaten and raped. Why would a God who promises never to leave us alone let something like that happen to you?"

"Oh, sweetie," Monet murmured. She wanted to go to Marcus and wrap her arms around his body. She wished he'd sit on the bed next to her. "God never said that our way would be easy. We'll always have trials and tribulations to endure. He spared my life," she whispered. "Imagine how you would've felt if the hospital called to tell you that I had died."

"I feel like our marriage is dying, and I don't understand why it has to be this way." Marcus sighed heavily.

"No matter what we endure here on this earth, imagine how God felt knowing Jesus was going to die on the cross? He sent His only begotten son here to teach the world about His father's goodness and mercy, and then His son is crucified. If God could do that for mankind, surely we can trust in Him." Monet looked at Marcus, hoping she was getting through to him. But she wasn't.

Marcus's face was stony as he said, "All I know is that you've put your feelings before mine. I don't agree with any of the choices you've made. You know what, Monet? Forget it. Just continue to do things your way." He stormed out of the room.

She sat on the bed feeling like she'd been slapped. Then she fell to her knees. She closed her eyes as tears seeped down her cheeks, bowed her head and clasped her hands tightly together. "Father, forgive him for he knows not what he is doing or saying." Monet prayed fervently like she'd never prayed before. Her lips moved quickly. When she was done making pleas to God for intercession, she stretched across the bed, unable to sleep for the longest time. In the basement, Marcus's saxophone keened and moaned.

Chapter 23

Although Marcus assumed he would visit Aron the same week he reached out to him, it actually took a month and was the end of April before he'd been cleared to visit Dwight Correctional Facility and meet with the warden and prison officials.

Wade accompanied Marcus to Dwight, Illinois. The ride from the south side of Chicago to downstate Illinois took close to four hours. The partners talked about their cases and sports and their annual fishing trip.

Half an hour upon arriving at the prison, Marcus and Wade were sitting on a sofa outside Warden Jones's office waiting to see him.

Levi apologized for the warden's unavailability for the umpteenth time. "He's been very busy lately working on the budget. I'm sure he'll be available any minute." The phone on Levi's desk buzzed. He snatched up the receiver. When he disconnected the call, he told Marcus and Wade, "He can see you now." He stood up and escorted them into the office.

Warden Jones stood up. "Hello, I'm Warden Jones. I apologize for the delay." He sat down in his massive swivel chair after the men shook hands. Wade and Marcus made themselves comfortable in chairs in front of the warden's desk. "Detectives, what can I do for you?" the warden asked.

"We're here regarding Aron Reynolds," Marcus explained. "He's my father-in-law. We recently found out that he's been incarcerated here for thirty years, and that he's nearly done serving his time."

Warden Jones nodded. "Okay, I remember now." He put on a pair of thick wire framed glasses and opened a file on his desk. "Let's see what we have here. Aron Reynolds has been a prisoner here since nineteen seventy-one. He was transferred here from the Joliet Correctional Facility two years into his sentence due to overcrowding. We had problems with his behavior after he was transferred here. He got into fights, we knew he was dealing drugs, and he had a belligerent attitude. The prisoner spent a lot of time in the hole. Then about twenty years ago a woman began visiting him once or twice a year and he settled down. And we haven't had any trouble from him since then. He finished high school while he's been here and received a college degree. He has also participated in religious services. He could have gotten out on parole earlier, but he chose to serve out his time. He has reached out to his victim's family. Aron turned sixty-seven years old last September. That's his story in a nutshell. Are you aware of the circumstances that brought him here?" the warden asked. He leaned back in his chair and his phone buzzed. "Excuse me," he said. "Yes, Levi, what is it? I thought I asked you to hold my calls." He listened for a few minutes, and then said, "Okay, send him in." Warden Jones turned his attention back to Wade and Marcus. "The guard who works on Aron's cellblock is available to join us."

The door opened, and another man walked into the office and took the last vacant chair in front of the warden's desk.

"This is Charles Little." Warden Jones introduced the guard to the two detectives. Charles was a portly man, with a receding hairline, who looked like he hadn't exercised in years. "I was just giving Detectives Caldwell and Harrison background information about prisoner 17703256. Detective Caldwell is the prisoner's son-in-law."

"Pleased to meet you." Charles nodded to Marcus and Wade. "I interact with the prisoners on a daily basis, so I can answer any questions you have about old Aron."

"I'd like to thank both of you for taking the time out to see us," Marcus said. "I also wanted to know if it would be possible for us to see Aron Reynolds today."

The two prison officials looked at each other. Charles deferred to his boss.

"I don't see why not. Charlie, what would be the best time to set up the meeting?" asked Warden Jones.

"After lunch would be a good time," he answered.

"I was giving the detectives the prisoner's background information. Aron will be released next month, so he's taken all the psychological evaluations, and everyone feels he's ready to re-enter society. Because of his age, we don't anticipate him returning to a life of crime," the warden said.

"Does he seem sincere about his religious learning?" Wade asked.

The guard nodded. "He's been attending church here for about fifteen years. We know a lot of men do that so it can look good when they have parole hearings, but that situation didn't apply to Aron."

"That's unusual, isn't it?" Marcus asked.

"I guess it's not if a person had truly undergone a religious conversion. Aron wasn't one of them up-in-your-face born again Christians though. He just seemed to enjoy the services. We can give you the pastor's name who volunteers here, if you need to talk to him for more information," Charles replied.

"Thanks," Marcus said, "but I don't think that will be necessary." He took out a notepad and began writing notes on it. "In the beginning, did Aron deny killing the victim?"

Warden Jones shook his head. "Most of the men here would sell their mother if they could get out of here, Aron wasn't that type. After he stopped fighting the other inmates, he settled down for the long haul. He works in the horticultural area. He seems to really have an affinity for growing plants."

"I don't know how well that trait will serve him in Chicago," the guard snorted. "We try to encourage the men to learn more marketable skills when they have the opportunity, but not old Aron. He said he was from the south, where dirt and growing plants was in his blood since he grew up on a farm."

"You never can tell about that. Some people do hire people to tend to their lawns and gardens," Wade said quietly. Something about the guard put him off.

"So you don't think he'll fall back on his old ways?" Marcus asked.

"Son, all we do is test them and factor in their behavioral patterns. It's not a perfect science. Aron hasn't done anything for us to assume that he would go back to his criminal ways," the warden said.

"Only time will tell," the guard added.

"Well, I have a wife and we live in a decent community, so we don't want to introduce an undesirable person to the neighborhood," Marcus said.

"What were the circumstances that led to him being incarcerated?" Wade asked the warden.

He looked down and flipped the pages in the file. "He was stealing a car and got caught by the owner. Aron said the owner pulled his gun on him first, so the shooting was self-defense. He said he hadn't actually taken the car at that point, so he was a victim of circumstances. That didn't fly of course. He went to trial and was found guilty and sent to Joliet. You were aware that the crime happened on the south side of Chicago, weren't you?"

"Yes, I was able to find some information about the case in the archives," Marcus replied. He was still writing notes.

"All felons say they are innocent. If I had a dime for every time I heard that lame excuse, I wouldn't have to work another day of my life," the guard interjected complacently into the conversation.

"And some of them are telling the truth," Wade said quietly. "Look how new DNA testing has cleared thousands of men."

"You sound like you side with prisoners. You're one of us, and as a detective, I would think your outlook on them would be different." Charles looked at Wade with a slight sneer on his face.

"I'm for justice period." Wade's tone of voice brooked no argument. "We have enough black men in jail; surely the innocent ones deserve a fair shake. If a man has been found guilty of a crime, then of course, he should do the time. We all know back in the fifties, and even now, how racial prejudice exists, and a lot of men get a bum deal. So I keep an open mind, that's all."

"Did anyone visit Aron when he was in Joliet?" Marcus asked.

"Not a soul for the longest time, and then a woman started visiting him from time to time about twenty years ago. We thought he was a single man without any family, so I was quite surprised when I got your call," the warden answered.

"What about letters, mail? Did he receive anything from anyone?"

"Yes, he did, but that was years ago," Charlie answered. "They were mostly from a small town in Louisiana. We thought he might go back to Louisiana after he gets released. According to our records, Aron was born and raised in New Orleans, and later he migrated to Alabama. He received letters from Alabama too."

"The letters from Louisiana stopped about ten years ago. We were able to surmise they were from a relative, maybe a sister or aunt. The letters from Alabama stopped five years ago. They were from a woman, and they shared the same surname," the warden announced, after checking the file once again. "I'm sorry, I should've asked you when you arrived if you'd like something to drink; coffee or tea, maybe?"

Wade and Marcus declined the offer and asked the warden

and guard several more questions. When they were done talking a half an hour later, the guard said to give him twenty minutes, and then they could visit Aron. He left the office and returned to the cellblock.

Warden Jones stood up. "Gentlemen, it's been a pleasure. I hope we were able to help you somewhat. I have a lunch appointment, and then a meeting afterward. Feel free to contact me if you have any further questions. You can wait for Charlie in the waiting area, and he will escort you to Aron's cellblock."

Marcus and Wade rose from their chairs. "Thank you, Warden Jones. You've been very helpful. I guess all that's left to do is meet the man himself," Marcus said. The men shook the warden's hand and walked back out to the waiting area to await Charlie's return.

Back in Chicago at the Caldwells' residence, Monet was on pins and needles, anticipating Marcus's return. She kept looking at the grandfather clock in the living room, like doing so would make time go faster, even though she had no idea when he would be back.

Monet, with Duane's help a week ago, had returned to the attic and brought down all the memorabilia their mother had amassed over the years. Monet must have looked at the pictures of her father a million times, until the corners of the snapshots were dog-eared. Duane flew to Alabama long enough to retrieve documents from their mother's secret safe-deposit box and return to Chicago. Luckily, she had granted access to the box to all her children. In the box were Aron's unopened letters to his children over the years. Duane and Monet poured through the letters like they were reading a novel. Even now, weeks later, Monet was in the process of re-reading the letters.

The decision as to where Aron would reside once he was released from prison was still up in the air. Derek maintained his stance that he wanted no part of his father, while Monet and Duane, being more opened minded, were willing to hear his side of the story.

Monet picked up a picture of Aron when he must have been around thirty years old. She said, "Daddy," but didn't feel any connection to the stern looking, handsome man in the sepia print. She opened the last letter Aron had written to them dated 2004 and read it again.

To my children,

I'm sorry I ain't been around you or tried to contact you most of your life before now. I did you all and your momma wrong. I know now that I should have stayed with Gay and helped her raise our family.

I was a young man with a lot of anger in me. I think it was 'cause I didn't have nobody to encourage me in life, and my Pops always told me that I wouldn't amount to nothing. He was right. Gayvelle was the only person who encouraged me, but I was too proud to listen to and believe in what she was telling me.

The way my Pops treated me filled me with anger that I didn't know how to let go of my rage. Don't be upset with your momma for not telling you about me. I told her to tell you when she thought the time was right.

Despite all that has happened, Gay has been kind to me. She could have divorced me a long time ago. So some love for me must have remained in her heart because otherwise, she never would have written to me all those years ago. I hope one day you'll find forgiveness in your heart and let me try to make it up to you.

Your father,

Aron Reynolds

Monet just shook her head. *Why can't I feel any love in my heart for this man? Is it because he left Momma and us? I just can't figure it out.* She rubbed her finger along her father's face. *A murderer, that sounds so horrible. My father is a killer. God, I hope he didn't kill any children.* She had run a Google search on her father's name, but didn't get any hits.

The baby kicked vigorously, and Monet smiled and rub-bed her now noticeable, rotund belly. "Okay, little girl, are you trying to tell me that you're hungry, or are you just trying to get my attention?" She set the picture on the table and slowly rose off the couch.

Her blood workup from the lab had come back within normal readings, and the ultra sound procedure didn't disclose any abnormalities. But she declined taking the amniocentesis test. She knew that Faith was just fine, and didn't want to subject her baby to any intrusive test. Monet was the picture of health and wore that pregnant woman glow. She was nearing the end of her second trimester.

She had asked Liz and Wade to be Faith's godparents, and they accepted proudly. Reverend Wilcox was a source of comfort to Monet, and made herself available whenever she needed someone to talk to if Liz wasn't available. All in all, life was good. The only blot on the horizon was Marcus's attitude. The police hadn't found any new leads regarding her attacker, so her case remained opened, but cold.

Monet was headed to the kitchen for milk when the door-bell rang. She walked to the front door and squinted out the peephole. Liz was standing on the top step holding a bag of food. Monet unlocked the door, and Liz stepped inside the house.

"How are you and my goddaughter doing?" Liz asked, after setting the bag on the table in the foyer and taking off her coat, which she hung in the closet.

"I'm doing fine, but baby girl has been kicking up a storm. I think she's hungry." Monet laughed as she rubbed her abdomen.

"Then my timing was perfect. I brought you some turnip

greens, cornbread, and a jar of ice tea. I know you're probably worried about what's going on in Dwight, so I left work early to spend the afternoon with you."

"Thank you, and yes, your timing is impeccable. I've had a craving for greens since last weekend. My momma used to make the best greens in the world." Monet looked away from Liz.

"Sweetie, I know you're longing for your mother right about now. My mother was a lot of help to me when I was pregnant and after my babies were born. Let's go to the kitchen and warm up the food."

"Let's do just that," Monet said gaily, as she put her arm through Liz's arm, and they walked to the kitchen.

She removed two glasses from the counter, and then sat in a kitchen chair while Liz put the bowl of greens in the microwave to heat them. She opened the freezer, took out a tray of ice, put a couple of cubes in their glasses, and then poured the tea into the glasses.

"Have you heard from Wade?" Monet couldn't prevent the question from coming out of her mouth.

"He called to say they had made it to Dwight safely and that was it," Liz answered. The microwave beeped, signaling the food was warm. "You haven't heard from Marcus?"

"No. Not that I expected to, but I was hoping he would call me since he was going to see my father." Monet's voice trembled. She stood up and took two plates out of the cabinet and forks and knives out of the drawer. She placed them on the table and put napkins next to the plates.

"Why don't you sit down and relax? Worrying isn't going to change the situation. We'll know the answers to your questions in due time," Liz advised.

Monet sighed. "You're right. I might as well enjoy some of the perks of being pregnant and getting spoiled while I can."

"Now you're getting it." Liz smiled. "That was one of the

things I really loved about being pregnant. That and the mostly wrong predictions from family and friends as to what sex my babies were going to be. Come to think of it, all your predications were always right."

"Yes I was, wasn't I?" Monet dipped her head. "Sometimes I get so caught up in the situation with Marcus that I forget to enjoy life and just be happy."

"Well, that's what I'm here for," Liz said, after she had placed a helping of greens and a piece of cornbread on their plates. She wiped her hands on a paper towel and sat down across from Monet. They grabbed each other's hands and Monet said grace.

Afterward, Liz looked at Monet and asked, "Are you good? Do you need anything?"

A tomato would go great with the greens. Would you get me one out of the vegetable bin?" Monet threw a dash of pepper on her greens and then sipped her tea. "Um, that's good."

Liz handed Monet a tomato. She diced the red vegetable and mixed them into her greens. Liz had prepared the greens with smoked turkey wings, giving the dish a mouth-watering taste. Monet put a forkful of food in her mouth, and quickly followed that up with several more forkfuls.

"Liz, these greens taste almost as good as my momma's did." Monet held two fingers close together.

"Well, thank you. I brought enough to last you a few days."

"I thank you, and Faith thanks you. She has settled down for now." Monet set her glass of tea on the table after taking a few sips.

"Monet, Wade and I have been talking, and we'd like to buy a bedroom set for the baby. What do you think about that?"

"I'm touched, Liz, but you and Wade don't have to do that," she said.

"We want and would love to. You and Marcus have been so generous to us over the years. Like when Wade and I were a little short when it came to WJ's tuition money his first semester of college, you and Marcus made up the difference. You also helped us with the down payment on our house. Your love and support over the years has been immeasurable, and we want to do something in return since you and Marcus wouldn't accept repayment from us."

Monet could see from her friend's pleading eyes that she and Wade had their hearts set on buying the bedroom set. "Of course you can. I'm flattered, and all of us, me, Marcus, and Faith, appreciate your generosity."

Liz had finished eating. She stood up and put her plate in the sink. When she sat back down in the chair, she reached into her purse and pulled out some furniture catalogs. She placed them on the table in front of Monet's plate. "I saw some bedroom sets that I like and put a check mark beside them. After you finish eating, we can look at them and see what you like."

"That sounds like fun. I've been debating if I want to go the traditional pink route, or have white walls with a rainbow motif." Monet had just eaten the last of her greens and tomatoes. She burped softly and caressed her tummy. "Oops, I'm sorry, excuse me. I guess I'd better slow down." Her face reddened with embarrassment.

"Girl, don't start getting funny on me. With babies pressing on your internal organs, you've got to get some relief. Now I was the one who stayed humiliated. I had gas like I was a shareholder in People's Gas," Liz said unashamed.

"Now that you mentioned that, it seemed like there was always a faint odor about you when you were carrying your babies," Monet teased.

The women cracked up. Monet picked up a catalog and opened it. Her eyes alit on a white lacquered crib, dressing table, and changer. She also liked a dark pine set. She had an affinity for wood, which showed all over her house.

Monet and Liz looked at pictures of nursery sets and made a date to go visit the mall the following day to look at furniture. Monet was insistent that she wanted to wait until her ninth month before she bought baby furniture.

Liz had managed to successfully distract Monet from worrying about what was going on in Dwight. Every now and then, Monet would try to picture Marcus and her father in the same room, but the picture was always blurred.

Chapter 24

Marcus and Wade had just passed through the prison's last security checkpoint before they arrived in Aron's cellblock. A guard armed with a rifle escorted them to a small meeting room. After they removed their jackets and put them on the backs of their chairs in the tiny 5x5 cinder blocked room, the door opened.

Two different guards escorted into the room a white haired, elderly, heavily bearded man with a slight limp, wearing an orange correctional jumpsuit. The man rubbed his wrists and flexed his hands after one of the guards removed the manacles. Aron sat down in a metal chair across the table from Marcus. Wade had positioned his chair to Marcus's left side.

Marcus stared at his father-in-law. It was obvious which parent Monet had inherited her eye coloring from. The twins had their father's nose and mouth. Marcus noted that Monet and her brothers bore a stronger resemblance to their father than their mother.

Likewise, Aron peered intently at the man sitting in front of him. He saw a man whose curiosity and intelligence shone in his eyes. Aron also saw pain etched in the hollows of Marcus's face. It was an expression that Aron was familiar with. He knew the pain in his son-in-law's face mirrored his own at times.

"You must be Marcus," he said with just a touch of a southern accent.

"I am." Marcus studied the man sitting before him with his arms folded across his chest.

"I'm Aron Reynolds." He extended a withered hand.

Marcus debated whether to shake his hand or not, but finally he grudgingly held out his hand. Wade watched the interaction between the men in silent curiosity.

"How are my daughter and sons doing? Do they know you've come to see me?" The older man's voice was feeble and shook slightly.

"That's a shame that you have to ask me, not even a blood relative, how your family is doing?" Marcus said coldly.

"You're right. It isn't right, but it is what it is. I have tried to get in touch with them, but my wife decided the time wasn't right, and I honored to her wishes." Aron lifted his chin a notch, and his voice gained strength.

"Sure you did," Marcus sneered. "Obviously you didn't try hard enough."

"I did the best I could at the time. One thing I've learned from all these years of being locked up is that life doesn't always go the way you planned, and if you're lucky, you get another chance to make it right. That's all I ask of my children, an opportunity to make it right," Aron stated.

"What do you want from us, old man?" Marcus asked. He propped up his arm on the table and looked at Aron with a cynical glint in his eye.

"I would like to stay with you and my daughter until I can get on my feet. I want to try to get to know my girl and my boys," he countered.

"Did it ever occur to you that she and your sons might not want to see you?" Marcus shot back.

"I know my wife, and I have a pretty good idea of how she raised our children. She wrote me to say that she would ask them to see me, and I'm hoping they will at least grant an old man that one request."

"I hate to break it to you, Aron. You're not the most popular

person in the family right now. Just consider me here to do the
pre-screening, and if I approve, you may be in like Flynn. But
don't count on it." Marcus shifted his body in the uncomfortable chair.

He continued to interrogate Aron with the masterful skills
of the highly successful police detective that he was, and Aron
volleyed answers right back at his son-in-law. An hour later, Marcus seemed to lose steam. He looked Aron dead in the eyes and
asked him, "Can you give me one good reason why I should
convince your family that you've learned the error of your ways,
and why it would be a good idea for you to meet and stay with
them?" He leaned forward in his seat, anticipating the older
man's answer.

"Because I'm their father," he answered with quiet dignity.
"And every child should know his father." He bobbed his head
and added, "And that's what Gay would have wanted."

Acidic bile rose from Marcus's stomach to his throat. He
stood up abruptly. "Guard, would you let me out!" he yelled,
grabbing his jacket and rushing to the door.

Aron uneasily looked at Marcus retreating, trying to figure
what he'd done wrong. Then he shrugged his shoulders helplessly. Wade rose from his seat to follow his friend, but before he
could turn from the table, Aron grabbed his shirt sleeve. "What
did I do? Was it something I said? I didn't mean any harm."

Wade shook his head, sympathy evident in his demeanor.
"This scenario will play out just the way God intends it to. I
hope you don't wish my sister, Monet, any harm."

"Sir, I swear I don't. I just want to make up for years lost."
The guard walked over to Aron and asked him to stand up.
Then he snapped the handcuffs around his wrists and led him
out of the room.

Wade kept his eyes honed on Aron, who had turned toward
him. He looked at Wade, and whispered just loud enough for

him to hear, "Tell my son-in-law that the man who hurt Monet may be here in the prison."

Wade's complexion turned ashen, and he was thrown for a loop by the words Aron had uttered. He hurried out of the room to find Marcus. When he returned to the check-in-points, Marcus was nowhere to be found. Wade's personal possessions were returned to him, along with his gun. He looked for Marcus as he walked toward the exit. Wade sighed with relief once he was on the outside of the huge complex. He inhaled and exhaled deeply as he thought what a small blessing it was to enjoy the sunlight at one's own leisure.

He walked toward the car and found Marcus leaning against the SUV with a sickly look on his face. Marcus clicked the keyless remote control unit, unlocked the car, and both men got in the vehicle. There was silence until Marcus got on the ramp to enter the expressway.

He pursed his lips pensively, then glanced at Wade and commented, "I'd say he's a real piece of work. What do you think?"

"I think he's a man who's entered the elderly phase of his life. Time has run out for him. Perhaps, as he said, he's looking for peace and to right some wrongs in life. This world would be a better place if more people did that. 'I'm sorry' would go a long way toward making amends," Wade answered bluntly. "I didn't feel that he had any ulterior motives. And I know for a fact from Liz, because Monet told her, that he has tried to contact his children. I guess with you still not talking to Monet, she didn't tell you about the letters your mother-in-law left Monet and her brothers."

Marcus felt embarrassed. The gulf between him and Monet seemed to widen with each passing day. He knew that it was his fault, but he couldn't find it within himself to remedy the situation. "Hmmm, I didn't know that. But that doesn't change the fact that he's a man who took another person's life, was abusive toward his wife, and deserted his children."

"Whatever happened between Gayvelle and Aron has long since passed. It's not really our business or concern. I do know from the letters that Monet's mother left her and the twins that she asked for forgiveness from her children for not allowing Aron to reach out to them when he began straightening up his life. There are always two sides, maybe three, to a story. And if Monet and Duane, we'll leave Derek out of the equation for now, are willing to talk to their father, then who are we to stop them or pass judgment on Aron?"

"Well, I don't trust him," Marcus said mulishly. His jaw tightened, and the vein on the side of his head throbbed nonstop.

"Could it be that you're feeling a little guilt right now, and taking those feelings out on your father-in-law?" Wade prodded. "In Monet's mind, she may think you're not treating her correctly. That's why it's best not to judge another person harshly, because you may have to walk in their shoes one day. And we have all fallen short at some time or another and depended on God's mercy and forgiveness, and that includes Aron too."

The sunlight seemed to bounce off the gray asphalt road. Marcus reached in the cup holder and put his black Ray Ban wrap-around sunglasses on his face. When he was done, he said, "Okay, I get your point."

"Anyway, you left in such a hurry that you missed the surprise that Aron dropped," Wade said. He had debated with himself whether he should say anything to Marcus, but knew his friend would never forgive him if he didn't.

"What was that?" Marcus peered at Wade, puzzled. Then he looked back at the road ahead of him.

"Aron said he may know who assaulted Monet, and implied the person was inside the prison."

Marcus's mouth drooped open, then he frowned and snapped his lips together. He glanced at Wade, and the car swerved a bit before he gained control of it. "Come on, man, don't fall for that. You know what they say about cons; you can only trust half of what they say."

"This con happens to be your wife's father, and he had nothing to gain by revealing that information," Wade said mildly.

"I disagree with you, Wade. He could be just trying to get in good with the family. Score some brownie points," Marcus argued.

"Then again, he could be telling the truth. He didn't say that he verified the information. He just said that he heard the person who might have assaulted Monet was on the inside. What kind of man or father would he be if he didn't tell you that? I'm just saying it's something Smitty might want to check out," Wade suggested patiently.

"No, I'd like to check it out myself, so I'd have the pleasure of telling Aron how wrong he was," Marcus replied venomously.

"Well, I'm not going to sweat it because I know the chief isn't going to let you get involved. I just felt I should tell you what Aron said. Did you ever get around to talking to Reverend Wilcox? If you did, how did that go?" Wade changed the subject.

"It went as expected. The good Reverend gave me her spiel on life from a spiritual perspective, and how I should feel blessed, even though my wife is carrying the child of a rapist."

"I'm sure that's not what Reverend Wilcox said." Wade shook his head. "I know your talk with her was a little more detailed than that." He checked his cell phone for messages.

"Reverend Wilcox suggested I take a few counseling sessions with her or someone on the job. I informed her politely that I didn't need to talk to anyone, nor did I want to listen to someone telling me how I should react to a situation they know nothing about. Say, there's bottled water in a cooler in the back on the floor. Would you get me one?"

Wade unbuckled his seatbelt and reached in the backseat and removed a twelve ounce plastic bottle of spring water. He unloosened the cap and handed the bottle to Marcus, then said, "You know that you're making the ordeal tougher than it needs to be. When all you have to do is—"

"I know what I have to do according to you, Liz, Reverend Wilcox, and Monet . . . let go, and let God handle it. That seems to be the universal cure for whatever ails Christians," Marcus said.

"My granny used to say a hard head makes a soft behind," Wade said solemnly. "And she was correct. I just pray your words don't come back to haunt you one day, or you'll find yourself in the same predicament as your father-in-law."

"If I find out that I was wrong about anything regarding Monet's child, then I'll get down on my knees and beg her forgiveness. Heck, I'll apologize to the entire church. But I'm one hundred percent sure it won't come to that." Marcus threw back his head and laughed.

"You'd better start working on that speech then," Wade said soberly. "We all care for you, and hate to see you like this; sullen, moody, and distant from your wife. Liz and I will continue to pray for you as we always have."

"How about we agree to disagree about the way I'm handling my problems? I'm hungry, let's stop at the next exit and get something to eat?" Marcus suggested as he changed from the left exit to the right. Within minutes he pulled into a gas station/restaurant parking lot.

"You go ahead and get a table. I'll be there in a minute. I'm going to call Liz and tell her we're on our way back and what time she can expect us back in Chicago," Wade said, pulling his cell phone out of his jacket pocket.

"Sure, just lock up the car when you get out," Marcus said as he opened his door and went inside the restaurant.

Wade called Liz and relayed the information. She notified her husband that she was at Monet's house, and would stay there and they could ride home together since Marcus had picked Wade up from their house on the way to Dwight that morning. Liz didn't ask Wade any details about the visit.

Wade got out of the car and pressed the button to lock all the doors. Then he walked into the restaurant. Marcus was sitting at a table and waved Wade over.

Several hours later, the men were stuck in rush hour traffic a few miles from the Caldwells' residence. Finally, Marcus turned into the alley and parked the SUV inside the garage. Before he could put the key in the lock, Liz opened the door. Marcus and Wade walked into the house. Liz returned to her seat, and Monet was sitting at the table eating strawberries. The television was turned to *Judge Mathis*.

Wade walked over to Liz and kissed her on the cheek. Marcus and Monet looked at each other warily. Then Marcus nodded his head.

"Hello, Marcus," she said. "I called Duane and Derek and asked them to come over. They should be here any minute. There was no need in you going over what happened at the prison multiple times." Then she popped a strawberry inside her mouth.

"Something smells good in here," Wade observed. He looked at the stove and at the two women. "Who cooked?"

"Liz made oxtail stew and homemade biscuits. She's been here all afternoon spoiling me rotten. And I've loved every minute of it." Monet mugged.

"I enjoyed spending the day with Nay-Nay. She's spoiled me enough in the past; it was fun to give back to her." Liz smiled.

The doorbell chimed, the tones pealed throughout the house. "That's probably Duane and Derek. I'll let them in," Monet said, and started to rise from her seat.

"No, you stay there, I'll get it," Wade offered as he looked at Marcus, who was still standing next to the cabinet. Marcus shrugged his shoulders. Wade walked out of the room to the front door.

"Marcus, this is your house, why don't you have a seat?" Liz suggested. "I hope you don't plan on standing up during the entire time everyone is here."

"No, I don't. I'll be back in a minute. I need to run downstairs to the basement." He left the room, and when he returned, Duane and Derek were in the kitchen greeting everyone. Duane asked Marcus how he was doing, and he replied fine.

"Since this is a family matter, I think Wade and I should go home," Liz announced, and Wade nodded his agreement. Then the two of them left.

Derek sat at the table while Duane prepared bowls of the oxtail stew for him and Monet and heated the biscuits in the oven. Marcus informed his family that he would discuss his visit to prison after dinner. Marcus and Derek filled their bowls with steaming stew, and everyone's bowls were cleaned in no time while everybody chatted about inconsequential matters. Marcus, Derek, and Duane returned to the stove for second helpings.

After everyone had finished eating, Duane poured himself more lemonade. Then he took a deep breath and said to Marcus, "What happened in Dwight?"

"First off, Wade and I met with the warden and correctional officer, and then later we met your father." He looked at Duane, Derek, and then Monet, and then continued speaking. "I know you want to know my impression of him, and I can say that he seems to be contrite about how things went down in the past, and of course he wants to meet you. And he's also looking for someplace to stay after he leaves prison."

"Did he seem to be reformed to you?" Duane asked. "That's my biggest concern."

"I'm a little bit more cynical than Wade is, and I tend to take a wait and see attitude. Wade, on the other hand, thinks your father was sincere, and the guards who work closely with him think he's ready to enter society. The head warden mentioned there were problems when Aron initially came to the prison. He was somewhat unruly, fighting and that kind of stuff. He admitted Aron had settled down and become a model prisoner." Marcus got down to the nitty-gritty.

The siblings contemplated his observations. Then Monet asked her husband, "Do we look like him?" Her chin rested on her arm that was propped on the table. "From what I can tell from the pictures Momma saved of our father, it appears we favor him more than her."

Marcus nodded his head. "Yes, between your parents, his were the dominant genes, and he passed them to you three."

Derek rolled his eyes upward and muttered, "Just what I wished for when I was growing up, to look like a convicted murderer."

Monet and Duane frowned at their brother. Marcus made a decision not to mention Aron's comment about Monet's attacker being in jail until his tip could be checked out.

"I think this would be a good time to discuss Dad's living arrangements," Duane suggested. He turned toward his sister and asked, "Nay-Nay, do you have anything sweet to snack on?"

Monet nodded her head. "There's always ice cream in the freezer and fresh fruit."

"Well, he's not coming to stay with us," Derek announced. He looked at his brother challengingly, like he was spoiling for a fight.

"I don't see why not. He's our father," Duane protested.

"Why can't he stay with Monet and Marcus since they have more room than we do?" Derek looked at Monet, and then at his brother-in-law.

"I don't think that's a good idea, given the issues we have going on in this house," Marcus said, sharing his thoughts.

"If we won't take him in, then where will he go?" Monet asked.

"He'll have to stay someplace, like a half-way house," Marcus said. He stood up and began putting the bowls and utensils in the sink.

"Hmmm, I don't think we want that," Monet said thoughtfully. Faith began kicking again. She rubbed her abdomen in circular motions, and the baby stopped her movements.

"What do you suggest then?" Derek asked. He leaned back in his chair and folded his arms across his chest.

"I thought he could stay in your garden apartment," Monet said, as she wrung her hands together nervously. She looked at Derek to gauge his reaction to her suggestion.

"I don't think he should stay anywhere where he can come and go as he pleases. He needs to live somewhere where someone can keep an eye on him." Derek explained his rationale. "That's why he should stay here. At least we know he won't try anything shady, knowing that a policeman lives in the house." He put his hand on the back of his head.

"Actually, I agree with Monet. I think the garden apartment would be a good solution for all of us. We don't know what type of elements he'll associate with once he gets out, and whoever they are, they shouldn't be around Monet," Marcus stated.

"So, it's all right if me and Duane put our lives on the line?" Derek whined.

"Keep in mind we're talking about a sixty-seven-year-old man. He wasn't a mass murderer or anything. Outside of the murder conviction, your dad's previous record consists of petty crimes, nothing that sends up a red flag," Marcus said, trying to be fair. Plus, he didn't want to get stuck with Aron staying at their house.

"What do you think, Duane?" Monet asked. "You've been quiet." She rose and poured herself a glass of milk, then put a handful of strawberries in a napkin and sat back down at the table.

Duane had been following the conversation thoughtfully, and he spoke with candor. "I think Dad's staying with me and Derek would be the obvious choice. Between the two of us, we can keep an eye on him. Momma's letters didn't seem to indicate an impending danger, and we know that she would have known and said something to us in the letters."

"I swear I'm always outnumbered in this family," Derek groused with an unpleasant tone in his voice. "Okay, I guess he can stay with us. But any hint of trouble, he's out and on the street."

"Fair enough." Marcus nodded. "I'll get in touch with the proper authorities, and get the ball rolling."

"How soon will he be released?" Monet asked as she pulled the stem off a strawberry and dunked it in the milk. The men's eyes followed her actions, and they shook their heads.

"In a month," Marcus stated. "That's why we needed to have this discussion now."

Duane stood up and put the bowls and utensils in the dishwasher and wiped off the counter so his sister could relax.

Derek rose and pointed at Duane. "We need to get going as soon as Suzy Homemaker finishes his chores. I need to make a stop before we go home. So hurry up, bro."

Monet clumsily got out of her chair. Marcus did a double take when he saw how large her stomach had grown. He looked angry. "Goodnight everyone, I'm going to call it a day." He walked downstairs to the basement.

Duane shook his head sadly, then he, Monet, and Derek walked to the front door. Monet bade them goodnight, locked the door, and set the alarm. She turned off the lights in the living room and kitchen.

As she walked up the stairs to the master bedroom, Monet

thought, *Lord, I'm going to meet my father. After all these years, my father, Aron Reynolds, will be in my life. I don't know what to expect from him or what he will expect from me. What I do know is that you have never steered me in the wrong direction. So, thank you, Father. I can hardly wait to see my daddy.* Her spirit was filled with wonderment from the possibility of having her father in her life

Marcus, on the other hand, was more skeptical. His motto was cons were like leopards, they never changed their spots. He also said Monet was too kind-hearted, and she had been taken advantage of more than once. He snorted and shook his head. He picked the remote off the cocktail table in the basement and turned on the news.

Though he tried to banish the thought of Monet and her burgeoning belly out of his mind, he failed miserably. Monet looked beautiful to him, and he admitted she had never looked better in her life. It was obvious to Marcus that she was happy about her impending motherhood.

He couldn't find anything on television that he wanted to watch, so he removed his saxophone from its case and played through his aggressions. Later he got his clothing together for the following morning, and then pulled out the sofa bed and retired for the night, uncertain about his future with Monet, her baby, and now, her jailbird father.

Chapter 25

Contrary to Warden Jones's prediction that Aron would be released in a month, the process took close to six weeks. It was the middle of June on a Thursday before Marcus and Duane traveled to Dwight to pick him up from the correctional facility.

Monet had been ordered to stay off her feet and relax since she had now entered the beginning of her eighth month of Faith's conception. She was amazed at how quickly the time was elapsing during her pregnancy, and instead of the gentle fluttering that she had felt a few months ago, Faith was now kicking up a storm. On more than one occasion, Monet swore she felt the outline of a foot in her side. She continued to receive a clean bill of health from her doctor after her appointments.

Derek was supposed to come over and help Monet with chores around the house as she prepared a homecoming meal for Aron. Instead, he'd been a no-show. Monet guessed that he and Duane had had a disagreement of sorts. Liz and Wade had gone away for a couple's retreat weekend in Bloomingdale, Illinois.

Before Liz left for the trip, she'd baked Monet a red velvet cake and several sweet potato pies. Monet didn't have a clue as to her father's food choices, so since he was born in Louisiana, she decided to prepare a pot of gumbo jambalaya, along with shell fish, and a Caesar salad for dinner.

Her house was spotless. The wood floors shined, along with the tables and woodwork, thanks to Liz's help before her and Wade's weekend outing. Monet had lit vanilla scented candles throughout the house that morning, giving the house a pleasing scent. Sunlight peeped into every glistening window.

She took her cell phone out of the pocket of her blue and white striped smock top and tried calling Derek again, but was routed to voice mail. She closed the phone and slipped it back inside her pocket. She knew her brother would turn up when he was good and ready.

Last month, Wade had persuaded a kicking and screaming Marcus into helping him paint the baby's nursery. The men removed Gayvelle's old rocking chair from the attic and had taken it to a local upholstery shop. The new cushion matched the motif on the wall. And the chair now occupied a corner of the newly painted white walls with the rainbow motif. After they had finished their task, Monet couldn't stay out of the room.

The white lacquered furniture that Monet chose and Liz had ordered would be delivered within a couple of weeks. Lamaze classes had commenced at the hospital, and Liz accompanied Monet to class. If she couldn't make it, Wade gladly stood in. Monet should have been happy, except Marcus hadn't changed his position about the pregnancy. The couple's relationship had degenerated to that of strangers living in the same house.

Monet walked into the kitchen and peeped out the window to see if Marcus had returned from Dwight yet. There was no sign of her husband, brother, or father.

She decided to go upstairs and change into one of her favorite maternity outfits, and Mitzi followed her. Fifteen minutes later, Monet had finished dressing and returned downstairs. She went into the living room and plumped the pillows on the sofa when she heard Marcus's key in the backdoor.

Her heart was beating rapidly, her mouth felt dry as sandpaper, and her palms began sweating. She chided herself, *Calm down. It's only your father. You have nothing to fear.* Monet walked toward the kitchen as Duane called her name. Her legs felt as heavy as logs from the long awaited expectancy of finally seeing her Dad.

When she entered the kitchen, her eyes zoomed to her father, and she stared at him for the longest time. Her eyes took in her father's stooped shoulders, and the grey hair he'd combed back off his brow. Aron had shaved his unkempt beard, and bore little resemblance to the man Marcus and Wade had met in prison.

When Monet looked into her father's eyes, she saw a man humbled by his experiences and pain. All the memories she'd managed to suppress of him as a child, and the resentment she felt against him for deserting his family raced to the forefront of her mind, like a stallion running on an open range. She gulped audibly, and then smiled.

Aron, in turn, looked at eyes that duplicated his own. Although Monet and her brothers strongly favored him, he could see the little dimple in his daughter's left cheek, so like her mother's. The tremulous smile Monet bestowed upon her father looked so much like Gayvelle's grin that Aron's eyes filled with tears, which he blinked back. Regret for lost years showed in father and daughter's eyes. Aron held out his hand, and Monet walked toward him and put her own hand inside his deeply callused one.

"Hello, Daddy," she stammered. Aron continued holding her hand, and when she didn't resist, he pulled his daughter into a tight embrace.

When Aron released Monet's body, he said, "Hello, my daughter, it's been a long time. Too long. I hope in time you can find it in your heart to forgive a very foolish old man."

Monet nodded and managed to say, "All I can do is try."

Aron wore a solemn expression on his face, and then he smiled. "Look at you, all grown up and with child. Marcus and Duane didn't tell me that you're expecting a baby." He looked over at his son, who shrugged his shoulders helplessly.

"Yes, I am. I'm due next month." Monet nervously pushed a strand of hair off her face.

"Well, I'll leave you three alone. I'm sure you have a lot to talk about," Marcus announced, as he made his way to the basement.

"You're welcome to join us." With her eyes, Monet pleaded with Marcus to stay. "I made enough dinner for you."

"I'll pass for now. Maybe I'll get something later," he responded. He opened the basement door and walked down the stairs.

Aron looked around the kitchen. "You have a lovely house. I was just telling Marcus and Duane that I'd love to help you with your garden. You must have inherited your green thumb from Gay."

Monet felt a surreal sensation when she heard her father say her mother's name, considering how scant the time was when she saw them together. His tongue seemed to caress his late wife's name. Then Monet reminded herself they were young once upon a time and had dreams. It was unfortunate those dreams didn't reach fruition.

"Would you like something to eat?" she asked her father. "I know you must be hungry, Duane." She looked over at her brother.

Duane gave her a thumbs up sign. "Sure, that gumbo smells good." He walked to the sink and washed his hands. After he was done, Aron did the same.

Monet handed her father a paper towel and told him to have a seat. Aron would occupy the seat to Monet's left, with Duane on her right. Duane volunteered to put the food out on the table, and minutes later, Monet blessed the food, and the trio ate.

After Aron had eaten generous portions of the food, he pushed his chair back from the table and rubbed his stomach. "That's the best meal I've had in a long time. Thank you, Monet. Your mother taught you well. I can tell that you're a fine young woman."

"Would you like to see the house?" she asked as she stood

up. "Coffee is already in the coffeemaker. I thought we'd have some along with dessert. That is, if you drink coffee." Monet began babbling. She took a deep breath. "Give me a minute to start the coffee, then I'll give you the two dollar tour."

While she turned on the coffeemaker, Duane cleared the table. Monet then showed her father her house. She was proud of the place she and Marcus had called home for the past seventeen years. The fact that the mortgage was paid in full only added to the house's appeal.

They walked up to the second floor, and Aron was impressed. He couldn't imagine his daughter living in a place so fine. He reminisced about his and Gay's first home. It was a small four room shack in rural Alabama. Aron remembered the loving care Gay gave to the house, like it was a palace.

"I'm sure your brothers have also done well for themselves," Aron observed after peeping into the bedroom and bathrooms on the second floor. "So this is the little one's room," he said when they stopped in the nursery. "It's a very nice room. I grew plants in the joint and also did some carpentry work. Maybe you'll allow me to make something for the baby?" he asked hopefully.

"Sure," Monet bobbed her head up and down, "that would be great."

By the time they returned downstairs to the kitchen, the coffee was ready to be served. Monet noticed that Marcus had been in the pots and pans. The lid on one of the pots was slightly awry. She smiled at her father and Duane. "Why don't we eat in the dining room? I'll bring coffee and pie in there. Or would you prefer the red velvet cake?" she asked her father. "Duane, I know you want cake." Duane nodded that cake was his choice.

"Why don't you give me a little bit of both?" Aron grin-ned back at his daughter. He and Duane walked to the dining room table and sat down on cushioned chairs.

"Here we go," Monet said, after she brought the dessert and coffee into the room on a tray.

Aron cut a piece of the cake and put a forkful in his mouth. "This cake tastes wonderful. It melts in my mouth."

"I'm glad you enjoy it." Monet smiled. She ate a slice of potato pie.

"So how is it that none of you have any children, other than Monet, who has one in the making?" Aron asked, sipping his coffee.

"Well, Derek and I aren't married, and Monet is a late bloomer," Duane said quickly. He grinned at his sister.

"We're a small family, but we're close. Do you have any sisters or brothers?" Monet asked her father.

"Yes, I come from a large family. There were nine of us; four girls and five boys. We were dirt poor and I couldn't wait to leave the back roads of Louisiana. We lived in a parish not far from New Orleans. I've always been a restless soul, so after I turned eighteen, I moved away from my parents' house. I lived in The Big Easy and worked as a longshoreman, loading merchandise on the docks for a couple of years, and then I moved to Alabama. One of my cousins lived there. I met your mother not too long after moving to Alabama, and the rest, as they say, is history."

"Do you stay in touch with your people? I mean your sisters and brothers?" Monet asked.

Aron's eyes seemed to glaze over like he'd been transported to another time and place. "Yes and no. My parents are deceased. My brother, Paul, didn't want to have anything to do with me after I went to prison. But my little sister, Ernestine, used to write me. Then she stopped. I believe she's either very sick or dead. I would like to see her again. I'm sixty-seven years old, and I was the third youngest child, so many of my sisters and brothers have gone on before me."

"That's too bad," Monet murmured. She picked up her cup and sipped her coffee. When she set it back on the table, she said, "Momma made us promise that we would always remain close to each other."

"That's good and sounds like something Gay would do," Aron said respectfully. He cut a sliver of his cake with his fork and ate it

"I know we have a lot of catching up to do," Duane said, "but I'm curious as to why you left our mother and us."

"I knew one of you was going to ask me that question." Aron nodded his head. "And I figured it would be Derek. I practiced many times in my mind how I might answer that question. But the truth of the matter is I wasn't a good person back then, and all I was doing was poisoning my family. I knew I was making everyone unhappy and decided to cut my losses and leave."

"Your leaving didn't have anything to do with Momma's gift?" Duane asked point-blank. He looked down and used his fork to push cake crumbs around his plate.

Monet unconsciously held her breath, waiting for her father's answer.

Aron pushed his plate away from him and looked at his son, surprised. "I guess I'm going to have to come clean with you all, no matter how painful it may be to me. Yes, I had issues with the gift, as Gay called it. It's not easy living with someone who knows your every thought and can anticipate your every need. I was raised Catholic, and the gift went against my teachings," he said.

"So you're saying that you were religious?" Monet asked, puzzled. She had cloudy memories of her mother taking her and her brothers to a local Baptist church when they were small, but she couldn't remember her father ever attending services with them.

"Not as an adult," Aron admitted. "But I was raised in the church, and we went to Mass every Sunday. Your mother didn't talk too much about her gift when we were courting. She merely said she had strong feelings about things, situations, stuff like that. I didn't realize I was living with someone who could read thoughts and heal people. It reminded me of voodoo. I had an uncle that a woman put roots on, and he was never the same after that. I guess I looked at your mother as someone like that woman." He cleared his throat.

"She was so much more," Monet said, her eyes becoming moist.

"I know that now. Sometimes people don't realize what they have until it's gone, and that was the case with me. I had a precious jewel, and I didn't realize that until I sat in that prison all those years and had time to think about the hurts I had caused my family." Aron noticed Monet's glistening eyes, and he gently touched his daughter's shoulder. "I don't mean to upset you, Monet. We can talk about this at another time, if you find the conversation upsetting."

Monet wiped her eyes with the back of her hand and said, "I'm okay. This talk among us is long overdue."

"I also couldn't find a job worth a darn. There just wasn't anything available for a country boy in the south. I wanted to migrate to Chicago, but your mother didn't want to. She wanted to stay in Alabama to be close to her people. I was stubborn and felt like she was choosing them over me. I know now that she wanted to be with them because they could help her, and she was like all the women in her family; born with the gift. I tried working for her Uncle Will, but it just didn't work out. Then when you were born, Monet, you didn't talk, and you seemed to shun me, and that was almost the last straw. Your mother said your actions were normal and that you had the gift too, and you needed time to adjust."

Monet closed her eyes, and she could picture every incident that her father described. "So you couldn't deal with me, right?"

"Yes," Aron answered half-heartedly, "that's true. I was used to babies that talked all the time and got into trouble. But you didn't talk until you were nearly four years old. I didn't know what to make of you. If I tried to pick you up, you'd screech in a loud piercing voice. Do you know that you didn't say a word until the twins were born, and the first thing you said was 'Ooh babies.'" He chuckled at the memory.

"I'm speechless," Monet said. "I don't remember all of that. I just sensed that you didn't like me."

"And I felt you didn't like me," Aron responded in a gentle tone of voice.

"Well, I guess we had that in common," Monet commented.

The doorbell's chime resonated through the house, and Duane jumped up from his seat. "I'll get the door. It's probably Derek. You know he can't stand to be left out of the action." He left the room and walked to open the door.

Derek came in the house, dressed in denim jeans and a Bulls starter jersey. He removed a Bulls cap from his head and sat it on a table in the foyer. Then the brothers walked into the dining room.

Aron stood up. "Hello, son." He greeted Derek and held out his hand.

Derek refused to take it. "Well, if it isn't the prodigal father, returned home from the big house," he said sarcastically. He walked over to Monet, bent down and kissed the top of her head. "How are you feeling, Nay-Nay?"

"I'm good," she replied. "It would be nice if you greeted your father and acted like you were raised with some manners."

"Hello, Aron," Derek said, without looking at his father. "Did you cook, Monet?"

"Yes, there's plenty left in the kitchen. Help yourself," she said, staring first at her father, then her brother. Monet shook her head, acknowledging fireworks between the two men could erupt at any time. Derek had an evil expression on his face, like he was hoping for a fight.

Derek went into the kitchen, and Monet, Aron and Duane could hear the cabinet door opening and the clang of the pot top as he laid the lid on the counter. Several minutes later he returned to the dining room and sat in the chair across from Aron. He cut his eyes at his father a couple of times.

"You fixed shrimp, my favorite," Derek exclaimed. "And gumbo. I think I like you being at home." Quietness settled in the room like a heavy quilt as Derek ate.

"So Monet, I hear there's a test a woman can take to learn the sex of their baby. Have you taken that test? Do you know what you're having?" Aron asked his daughter.

"Yes, I've taken an ultrasound test, but I asked my doctor not to reveal the sex of the baby. It's not necessary, I already know that I'm having a girl," she said, as a big smile covered her face. Faith kicked her in the side.

"Great," Aron said. He looked over at Derek.

Derek looked at his father with a glower on this face. "Out of all the people in the world, how come you couldn't find any-body else to go live with?"

"I want to try and make amends with my children, and I like Chicago," Aron answered easily.

"Did it occur to you that it might be too late for you? That there's nothing you can say to us to make up for the way you left us and our mother?" Derek sneered.

"Maybe not," Aron folded his arms across his chest, "but I'd sure like to try."

"Humph, we'll see about that," Derek snorted. He laid his fork on his plate.

"So Derek, you must've been busy today. I thought you were going to come over earlier and help me out here in the house." Monet deftly changed the topic.

"I got busy, something came up. I got here when I could." He looked over at Aron again, who had an uncomfortable expression on his face. "Why did you put your hands on my mother?" he asked, seemingly out of the blue.

Duane looked alarmed and rolled his eyes. He suspected Derek had a hidden agenda. Monet sat in her chair feeling mortified.

"I didn't ever put my hands on your mother. I'm guilty of many things, but I wouldn't ever hit a woman," Aron said unwavering.

"That's not what Uncle Milton said." Derek shook his head. "He said that's the reason why you left, because you beat up on our mother."

"He's telling the truth," Duane said, with a hint of revulsion in his voice at his brother's behavior. "Momma put all the rumors to rest in the letters she left us. You should read them sometime."

"I guess I will one day." Derek curled his upper lip at Aron.

"Son, I'm not trying to cause any problems for any of you. I just want to try to get to know you before I leave this earth. Your mother forgave me, and in time, I hope you will."

"I guess you were lucky that Momma was a forgiving woman," Derek said, with a tinge of derision in his voice.

"Yes, that's the truth. She even came to visit me while I was in prison," Aron announced, picking up his cup and drinking the now lukewarm coffee.

"When?" Monet asked, sitting up erect in her chair and staring at her father.

"Usually she would visit me when she was here in Chicago visiting you and Marcus. She told me that she'd borrowed your car, and then she'd drive to Dwight. I was grateful that we were able to discuss our problems amicably. No matter how other people viewed our relationship, Gayvelle was the only woman I loved, and I know that she had feelings for me up until the end. It hurt me badly when she passed. Her lawyer sent me a letter that she was gone," Aron said.

Monet remembered her mother borrowing her car, and how she wouldn't divulge where she had been. She just said she was going to visit an old friend. Monet would wonder sometimes if Gayvelle had met a new man. Little did she know how far from the truth her suppositions were.

Aron continued speaking. "She told me to contact Marcus when my time was up, and that he would help me. Gayvelle thought very highly of him."

"Wow, Mom was busy as a bee, wasn't she?" Monet said. She could intuit that her father was telling the truth. "Did you think you and her would ever get back together again?"

"No, we didn't make up to that extent. I was just comforted knowing that she cared enough about me to visit and write. She could have gotten a divorce at any time, but she didn't."

"Enough of this mush." Derek banged his fist on the table, and the delicate china shimmied and clanged. "Tell us about you killing a man. I don't know how you live with yourself knowing that you took a human life. Discuss that, old man," he demanded of his father.

Marcus had been standing near the basement door, hidden from view, listening to the conversation between his wife, brothers-in-law, and his father-in-law, while Monet and Duane turned toward their father with bated breath. The tension in the room, like fog, thickened considerably.

Chapter 26

Aron's voice was low as he began talking, and then he sounded potent as he continued speaking. "When I first went to the joint, I was mad as all get out. Shoot, I was embarrassed at getting caught by what I thought was an easy mark. I gave myself more credit than that. I tried to justify my actions to the authorities and myself by saying I was in the wrong place at the wrong time, and that I shot the man in self-defense. Nobody could tell me nothing. I was the man. I knew it all, and I sure didn't want to hear that I was wrong about anything. Later, after much self-examination, I accepted responsibility for my actions." He explained the situation calmly, like he had made peace with himself and his lot in life.

"Obviously the judge or jury didn't believe you," Derek snorted. "Just cut to the chase and tell us what happened," he demanded arrogantly. He was on a mission to emphasize the worst side of his father to his siblings. He felt they were experiencing misplaced loyalty. Derek believed his Uncle Milton's tales about their father beating their mother, regardless of what story their mother decided to spin in her letters.

"I was young and foolish, running with the wrong crowd, drinking heavily, and hustling. I lived on Forty-seventh and South Park. I believe the street name was later changed to King Drive. All kind of activities happened in Bronzeville, especially at night. It was an exciting place for a young man from the backwoods of Louisiana and Alabama. New Orleans was hopping, but there was something about Chicago that held my interest. I sent money to Gay when I could, and she would send the money back to me and say it was tainted and that she couldn't accept it." With watery eyes, Aron bared his soul to his children.

Monet felt physically ill from hearing the story, and she buried her face in her hands. She knew her father's story was going to be unpleasant, but not this bad. She couldn't conceive this man being her mother's husband. Their beliefs were as different as night and day.

"You okay, Monet? Are you sure you want to hear this?" Aron asked caringly.

Monet nodded her head and uncovered her face. She resumed listening to her father's tale.

"I was on Thirty-fifth and Wabash breaking into a car when the owner came out of an apartment building and pulled a gun on me. I lied and tried to tell him I had a few drinks, and I thought the car belonged to one of my partners. But the man wasn't having it. He was irate and said I probably stole his brother's car that lived three blocks over from him. And you know what, he was probably right. I probably did, or one of the cats that I hung out with. The man wasn't buying my story, and I could see my life flashing in front of me. The situation changed quickly to kill or be killed, and I was fast on my feet. While I was talking to him, I had my gun out and I popped him, and got the heck out of dodge. I thought I was home free until an eyewitness stepped forward and nailed me. I knew my time had come to pay the piper."

Derek looked at his siblings disgustedly. "And this is the person you want to let back in our lives. I don't think so. What are you going to tell your child, Monet? That her granddaddy was a jailbird, probably like her father?"

Aron looked confused by the comment, and stole a look at Monet and Duane. Duane lifted his shoulders weakly and looked down at the floor. He opened then closed his mouth.

Monet leapt from her seat, and the white linen napkin on her lap fluttered to the floor. She looked pale as a ghost, and her voice trembled as she said, "That remark was uncalled for, Derek. I can't believe you said that to me. Excuse me, Duane and Daddy, I don't feel well. I will pray for you, Derek." She turned and went up the stairs.

"I don't care what you think of me; that was a terrible thing to say to your sister. I guess you got some of the devil in you, boy," Aron said to his son, bristling with annoyance. He didn't like Derek's comment one bit.

"He's right, Derek, you were out of line." Duane was mad. "I'm going to go see about Monet." He left the table and followed his sister upstairs.

"See, if you had just faded quietly and left us alone, none of this would have happened," Derek said icily, as he pointed his finger in Aron's face.

"Perhaps you're right," Aron said morosely. His face sagged, and he looked like a tired old man.

"Well, I'm out of here," Derek said arrogantly as he rose from his chair. "I proved my point. You're no good, and you're just trying to weasel your way back into our lives. Now if my brother and sister would come to their senses and not get sucked in by your sob story, then this family could return to normal."

"You're so angry with me being here that you would upset your sister like that. Maybe the apple didn't fall too far from the tree," Aron said pompously.

Derek walked around the table, grabbed Aron, and pulled him up by the collar of his shirt. Dishes clattered on the table. Marcus ran into the room and pulled Derek away from his father.

"You don't want to do this, man. Just walk away," Marcus urged his brother-in-law.

Derek let go of his father and rubbed his hands together. "I don't want him in my house. The deal is off. Let him find another place to stay." He stormed out of the room to the foyer. He snatched his cap off the table, then opened the front door and walked out, slamming the door behind him.

Aron sat down hard in the chair, almost falling. He dropped his head in his hands. "I didn't want our first meeting to be like this," he said over and over.

Duane rushed downstairs to the dining room. "What happened?" he asked Marcus, who pulled his brother-in-law into the kitchen.

"Derek, I don't know, man, he snapped or something, and was attacking your father. He said Aron can't stay with you guys. He's upset." Marcus's voice trailed off. "I guess he's going to have to stay here with me and Monet for the time being." He exhaled heavily.

"I'm sorry, Marc. You know Derek. Hopefully all of this will blow over soon, and he'll come to his senses. I mean I was bowled over by everything I heard tonight, but I never imagined Derek would turn on Monet or become physical with our father. That was a foul thing to do." Duane tugged on his bottom lip.

"I guess hearing the truth was too much for Derek to handle." Marcus wanted to ask Duane how Monet was doing, but couldn't bring himself to ask.

"I guess I'll finish cleaning up the kitchen and dining room, and then you can take me home. Since you picked me up this morning, I have no transportation. If you're living in the basement, where will Aron stay?' Duane asked.

"You know I've got a futon in my office in the basement. I guess he'll have to bunk there until Derek cools off, or we can come up with another plan."

"I'll work on Derek," Duane promised. "Who would have thought the evening would turn out like this? And it started off so promising." He shook his head incredulously. He went back into the dining room and talked to Aron, telling him about the change in living arrangements. Then Duane took the dishes off the dining room table and returned them to the kitchen. Marcus helped him tidy the kitchen and dining room, and when they were done, Marcus informed Aron that he was taking Duane home, and when he returned he would get him settled in for the night.

When the men left the house, Aron decided to go upstairs to see how Monet was faring. He hesitated at the closed door, and then finally rapped on it softly.

"Is that you, Marcus?" Monet asked in a raspy voice. She hoped against hope that her husband had come to her aid. Monet sounded like she'd been crying.

"No, it's me, your dad," Aron answered. "Can I come in?"

Monet really didn't want to be bothered with anyone. She wished Liz was at home so she could call her and talk about what had transpired. Monet bit her lip and sat up in the bed. "Yes, come in."

Aron walked into the room, and Monet noticed he had a slight limp. She gestured toward the chaise lounging chair. "Why don't you have a seat over there?"

"Thank you," he said with as much dignity as he could muster. He looked around the room. An étagère sat in a corner of the room, and several pictures of Gayvelle sat on one of the shelves. "May I?" he asked his daughter.

"Yes," Monet replied. She suddenly felt tired. She was aware that Derek had issues, but she never thought he would have aired them the way he did in front of their father.

Aron stood up and walked over to the étagère and removed the picture of Gayvelle. He stared at it for a time, and then returned it to its place. He did the same with other pictures of Monet and Marcus, Monet and her brothers, and Monet and Marcus posing with Liz and Wade when the couples vacationed together.

He held up the picture of the two couples and pointed to Wade. "This is the man who came to see me with Marcus, isn't it?"

"Yes, that's Wade and his wife, Liz. Wade and Marcus are best friends, as well as partners at work. Liz and I work at the same hospital. I'm on the nursing staff, and she's a manager in Human Resources. We've been friends for a long time."

"Hmmm." Aron put the picture back on the shelf. "I'm sorry about what happened tonight. I wanted to come clean with all of you about my past. Perhaps I should have waited before I said anything." He looked down at the floor.

"No, you were right." Monet sighed. "Marcus and I are having some issues, and Derek has taken Marcus's side. It's caused a strain between us. Derek was also very close to Momma. Kids used to call him a momma's boy when we were growing up. We tease him about never being married because he can't find a woman who could measure up to our mother. Though he pretends he disapproved of her. "

"I guess coming from me this might sound funny, but one should never side against a blood relative. It took me a long time to realize that. I just feel bad for being so stupid and wasting so much time." Aron exhaled heavily.

"You know what, all things happen in their time." Monet felt compelled to comfort her father. "I think of Ecclesiastes 3:1 especially when I need comforting. *To everything there is a season, and a time to every purpose under the heaven.* There is a reason God brought you to us. We may not know the reason yet, but it will be apparent in time."

"You know what, that sounds like something your mother would say," Aron exclaimed. "You're a very beautiful, kind, young woman. I'm proud to be your father, and I promise to do anything in my power to make things up to you."

"We can't go back and fix the past. But we can move forward

and hopefully create new wonderful memories," Monet said encouragingly. She sensed no evil in this man.

Aron nodded. "You're right. Derek has decreed that I can't stay in his and Duane's basement apartment as planned. So Marcus said I could stay here for the time being."

"That's good. We'll spend time getting to know each other, and I know Duane will come over as often as he can. He's been a good brother. Really they both have. I just feel closer to Duane."

"There's nothing wrong with that. When I was small, I looked up to my big brother, Paul. There was no wrong he could do in my eyes. I know he must've been ashamed of me and the life I chose to lead. He died fifteen years ago. I couldn't go to the funeral. My sister, Ernestine, wrote and sent me his obituary."

"That seems so weird to me, that we have relatives that we don't even know about," Monet mused. "I used to ask Momma about your family from time to time, and she would always say that she didn't know them very well."

"That was true. I was ashamed that I wasn't a better provider, so we didn't travel to New Orleans much to visit my family. Perhaps it would have helped if we had. I know you must be tired from preparing the meal for me. I'm going to go back downstairs and wait for Marcus to come back."

"I am a little tired," Monet admitted as she rubbed the space between her eyes. "Why don't you go downstairs and make yourself at home. There's a television in the living room, feel free to watch it if you like. Derek and Duane live fifteen miles away from here in the southeast part of the city, so Marcus will be gone at least half an hour."

"I'll do that and let you get your rest." Aron stood up. He held his hand out to Monet and she shook it. "Sweet dreams," he said.

"The same to you, Daddy." Monet smiled.

He closed the door behind him and walked down the stairs.

He turned off the light in the dining room and returned to the living room and sat on the sofa, waiting for Marcus to return.

Aron dozed off, and some time later, he felt someone shaking his shoulder to wake him up. He was disoriented for a minute. He shook his head, and saw Marcus standing over him.

"I guess you're going to have to bunk in the basement with me for a while," Marcus told him.

Aron stood up and stretched his body. "I'm bushed, lead the way."

Marcus stopped in the powder room on the way to the basement to get towels for Aron. The bag Aron had brought from the prison that held his meager possessions lay by the basement door. He picked it up and followed Marcus down the stairs.

It was obvious to Aron as he looked around the lower level of the house, from the clothing, messy table, and crumpled linen lying untidily upon the sofa, that his son-in-law lived in the basement and Monet upstairs. He wondered what could have happened to separate the couple. He hoped they could resolve their issues. It was clear as water to him that the two loved each other. Then he reflected on him and Gayvelle, and how the same could have been said of them.

Marcus led Aron to a small room off the main room of the basement. Aron noticed a pool table and large screen television. A table with a microwave was pushed against one wall, and the large wooden wet bar was on the other wall.

"This must be your hangout," Aron said.

"Yes, it is. Monet has her office upstairs, and that's where she hangs most of the time." Marcus adjusted the side of the futon and converted it to a bed. He left the room and went into the laundry room and returned with a couple of pillows, a sheet and blanket. On top of the bedding was a pair of his pajamas.

"Monet bought you some things for the basement apartment, including sleepwear, and they're over at the twins' house. If

Duane can't talk Derek into letting you stay there, then we'll go get them over the weekend. In the meantime, you'll have to make do with a pair of my pajamas. I know they're too big for you. Maybe you can roll the arms and legs or something."

"They will be fine," Aron said gratefully. "I want to thank you and Monet for opening your home to me, and for picking me up from prison today. I know you didn't have to do that."

"I did it for Monet," Marcus simply said. "I'm going to turn in myself. I have to work tomorrow. I'm warning you, Aron, don't do anything to disappoint or hurt Monet. She's a trusting soul, and I don't want you to do anything to break her heart."

"I won't," he said fervently, as he shook his head from side-to-side rapidly and held up his hand. "I swear, all I want to do is make up for lost time and get to know my children. I promised Gayvelle that I would."

"See that you do. Well, goodnight then." Marcus walked out of the room and made up his own bed for the night, while Aron was in the other room doing the same.

After he laid on the sofa bed, Marcus knew that he was going to have to talk to Aron about the statement he had made earlier regarding Monet's attacker, even if it were a false lead. He grudgingly admitted that Wade was right. And Marcus recalled how he had vowed not to leave any stone unturned.

He made a mental note to talk to his father-in-law over the weekend. *Who knows*, he thought, *maybe the old man might be on to something.*

Chapter 27

When Marcus returned home from work on Friday, Duane was at the Caldwells' house for the now resurrected monthly Friday night fish fry. The Caldwells' and Harrison's get-together had long since sputtered and died due to the strain in Monet and Marcus's marriage. Monet wanted to celebrate her father's homecoming and introduce her father to her and Marcus's best friends. So the fish fry gathering was resurrected at least one more time.

Monet fried fresh farm raised catfish and prepared a big pot of spaghetti. Liz made potato salad and coleslaw. Marcus found pictures that had been stored in the attic, along with Monet's and the twins' high school and college yearbooks, and placed them on the dining room table. Everyone had a good time, and only Derek was missing. The food was appetizing, and the conversation flowed. Liz gave Monet a thumbs-up sign, signaling her approval of Aron.

On Saturday, Derek still adamantly refused to allow Aron to stay in the garden apartment. So Marcus took Aron to the twins' apartment and collected the clothing and toiletries that Monet had purchased. On the way back home, Marcus took the older man on a tour of the city, and Aron was amazed at the changes that had taken place in Chicago since he'd been locked up. He was awed at how tall the Sears Tower was and the beauty of the Chicago skyline.

Sunday morning, Monet persuaded her father to attend

church with her. Monet had stopped driving due to her advancing pregnancy, so Marcus ended up taking father and daughter to church after Duane informed his sister that he wouldn't be attending church services.

Reverend Wilcox preached a rousing sermon. She took her text from the book of Colossians 3:13-17. Sometimes Monet marveled at how Reverend Wilcox always seemed to know when to preach about a situation that weighed heavily on her heart. Her spirit was lighter when Reverend Wilcox ended her sermon.

After the service had concluded, many members stop-ped by to greet Monet, to inquire about how she was doing, and to marvel at how big she'd gotten. She introduced the members and Reverend Wilcox to her father. Avis, the choir director, asked her to stop by the choir room before she left.

Fifteen minutes later, Monet with Marcus and her fat-her in tow, opened the door to the choir room and was touched and surprised to see the choir members had planned a baby shower for her. She gasped and put her hand over her mouth.

"You shouldn't have," is how she responded when she saw all the boxes wrapped in attractive shades of pink, yellow, and blue wrapping paper stacked on a table.

Avis put her hands on her hips and replied, "Miss Monet, I know you didn't think we were going to let your blessed event pass by and not acknowledge it. We're family, and family supports family." She took Monet by the hand and led her to a seat. "We know that you don't have time to open everything." Avis glanced at Marcus. "If you could open a few for now that would be great." Marcus nodded that he was okay with the suggestion.

Liz and Reverend Wilcox walked into the room and sat on both sides of Monet, smiling at her encouragingly. Reverend Wilcox brought a wrapped, ornate box with her for Monet.

Tears of happiness slipped down Monet's face. "I'm so overwhelmed. Thank you, everyone."

Avis handed her five boxes, and Monet quickly opened them. The first box contained a layette set, another contained crocheted blankets, and someone had given her a year's supply of cloth diapers. Reverend Wilcox and the ministry staff gave her a white, lacy christening outfit for the baby.

"I don't know what to say." Monet wiped the tears off her face. "This is so beautiful. I'm so grateful, and I love you all."

Twenty minutes later, Monet had opened the last of the five gifts. She talked to Avis and Reverend Wilcox, while Marcus and Wade transported all the boxes to Marcus's SUV.

"Thank you so much. I mean it from the bottom of my heart," Monet said, sniffling.

"You've gone through a lot of adversity this year and managed to hold fast to your faith," Reverend Wilcox said. "There are not many people who would have behaved as graciously as you have under the circumstances. I'm so proud of you, and I know your mother would be to. Just hold on, Monet, God is about to send blessings your way. There is no doubt in my heart that nothing but good times lie ahead for you."

More tears slid down Monet's wet face. She fanned herself. "I'm so emotional, it must be the hormones. I can't stop crying." She sniffled

"That's okay, Mommy," Avis teased her.

The women exchanged farewells, and Liz and Monet walked outside to the parking lot.

"I was going to have everyone over to my house for Sunday dinner, but I think your house might be more appropriate. As Faith's godmother, I'd like to help you open the rest of your gifts," Liz said.

"Are you sure?" Monet asked. "I didn't take anything out for dinner. I made a pound cake yesterday to bring to your house and that was it."

"Tell you what, Wade and I will swing by our house and

bring the food I prepared to your house. Wade had planned on grilling steaks and chicken, he can do that just as easily at your house. Then we can have fun in the nursery." Liz rubbed her hands together.

"That sounds like a plan. Can you believe next month this time I'll be a mother?" Monet said in awe as she peeped down at her abdomen

"Sure I can. It's been a long time coming, and I know you're going to be a great mother." Liz patted Monet's back.

"I hope so," Monet said gravely.

The women walked to their spouses' SUVs, which were parked next to each other, and informed the men of the change of plans. Liz climbed into Wade's vehicle, and Marcus helped Monet into his. They waved good-bye and said they'd see each other shortly.

By the time Liz and Wade arrived at the Caldwells' house, Marcus had already fired up the grill. In no time the steaks and chicken breasts were cooking and their appetizing aroma wafted in the air.

Though it was hot outdoors, a breeze from the huge oak trees on each side of the deck kept everyone cool. Monet was reclining in a chaise lounge; her belly looked like she had swallowed a watermelon. She had set a milkshake on the floor of the large wraparound wooden deck and was listening to a Kirk Franklin sing "Imagine Me" on the boom box that was playing from the kitchen window. Mitzi was in her element, running around the large emerald green, grassy backyard.

Monet wore a pink and white striped sundress, while Liz, Marcus, and Aron wore denim shorts with T-shirts. Monet felt content, and could feel Marcus staring at her from time to time through his dark sunshades. She tried to pretend she didn't notice. She had missed his touch and companionship during her pregnancy. She felt like she had lost her best friend, although he was still living in the house with her. Monet knew that she had to have the patience of Job, because when all was said and done, Marcus would see how wrong he had been. She held on to her faith like a lifeline.

Marcus couldn't stop his eyes from landing on his wife's face and body. And when he gazed at her stomach, his face would darken like thunder clouds and his lips would tighten. He put his feelings aside for the cookout and managed to be a genial host.

Marcus and Wade removed the glass picnic table with a matching striped umbrella and chairs from the garage and set them up on the deck. They drank ice cold sodas while they tended to the meat.

Liz was in the kitchen warming up baked beans and corn on the cob. She also prepared a fruit salad. She hummed along with the songs playing on the boom box as she worked.

Aron was in amazement of all the activity going on aro-und him. He had to give his wife credit; Gayvelle did a wonderful job of raising their children.

The cordless phone on the table next to Monet rang. She glanced at the caller ID and clicked it on. "Hi, Duane, how are you doing? We're outside enjoying the weather, and Marcus and Wade are cooking meat on the grill. Why don't you join us?" She listened for a minute and her face beamed. "Sure, bring Elise with you, we have plenty of food." She clicked off the telephone. "That was Duane," she informed everyone. "He and Elise are coming to dinner."

"In that case, I'll put more meat on the grill," Marcus said. He reached into the pan and put two more T-bone steaks on the Weber, along with a couple more pieces of chicken.

When Duane and Elise arrived, everyone was eating. The couple prepared heaping plates of food and joined the food fest. The mood was upbeat and jovial. Elise was in her early thirties, and was a pleasant looking woman who always retained a posi-tive outlook on life.

Following the meal, the women opted to go inside the house to the nursery to finish opening the baby gifts and put some of the items away. The men sat in companionable silence for a while.

Marcus stood up and put his and Wade's empty soda cans in the trash. He sat back down and said to Aron, "I've been mean-ing to ask you about the rumor that you heard in the correc-tional facility that Monet's attacker may be incarcerated there."

Aron moistened his lips. "There was a young cat there, not real young though. He looked to be around thirty years old or so, and he hadn't been in the joint too long, who was bragging that he was the one who messed up the policeman's wife. He said he didn't intend to hurt her that bad, but he was high on drugs and things just got out of control."

"Did you say anything to the officials at the prison?" Wade asked. He had felt drowsy from the food and sun, but now he was alert.

"No. Prison isn't the best place for snitches. I thought I could maybe help from out here," Aron answered.

"Do you know the man's name?" Marcus asked as his heart rate soared.

Aron said, "I don't know his given name, in the joint they called him Mad Dog. He was a big, tall, dark skinned menacing thing, with a large burn mark across the left side of his face. I didn't want to ask too many questions to call attention to my-self, so after I made a few inquiries, I dropped the subject."

Wade rubbed his chin thoughtfully. "I don't know why, but that name sounds familiar to me. It should be easy enough for us to get his legal name. We could talk to Smitty about pursuing this lead on Monday."

Marcus nodded. "I was thinking the same thing, except we could go to the chief ourselves."

Aron held out his hands, palms up. "I don't know if his story is true or not. We weren't even in the same cell block. I was what you'd call a hell raiser when I was imprisoned. It took a long time before I lost that fighting spirit. I didn't want to seem too interested in what happened to Monet, because I didn't want anyone to know she was my daughter. Had that stuff gone down before I decided to straighten up and fly right, there's no telling what I might have done. I wanted to put a hurting on him like he did my daughter, but I had to do the right thing and try to get the information to the right people," he remarked diffidently. He stole a glance at Marcus. Aron knew that his son-in-law didn't quite trust him yet, but he hoped in time that he would.

"You made the right decision. Had you acted on your impulses, it probably would have gotten you some additional time," Wade said astutely.

"He's right," Marcus added. "If we're lucky, he has a record as long as my arm. And if we can get a DNA match, then Mad Dog will be locked up for a long time."

"If he's already in prison, wouldn't his DNA already be in AFIS database?" Duane asked. He shrugged his shoulders. "Hey, I watch Forensic Files."

"It depends on if he's a repeat offender or not. This might be his first time getting caught, and Illinois, like a lot of states, is behind in updating their databases."

"Got you," Duane murmured. He leaned over the table, picked up a fork, reached into a platter, and put another chicken wing on his plate. "So do you think the warden would be willing to help you?"

"No doubt," Wade answered. "Or we may end up working with the sheriff's department. CPD has a good relationship with that group."

"Would Monet have to testify or anything?" Aron asked. "It seems like she's adjusted well after the attack, but she is pregnant." He lifted his eyebrows questioningly.

"She will probably be okay with it," Marcus said hesitantly. In reality, he didn't know what her reaction to the news would be since their relationship had deteriorated so badly.

Duane had finished eating and asked Aron to pass him a toothpick, which he stuck in the side of his mouth. "I think you two should check out this Mad Dog character. If he did the crime, then he has to pay the price and do more time."

"You won't get an argument from me," Marcus concurred. "I'm with you on that. Wade and I will talk to our chief on Monday, and get him to buy into us going back to Dwight. We'll see what we can find out."

"I don't think the chief is going to let you go to the prison, Marcus. He'll probably turn the information over to Smitty and let him run with it," Wade said. He pushed back his chair and stood up.

"We'll see about that," Marcus said in a portentous tone of voice, as if he knew something that everyone else didn't.

"I wouldn't count on it. The chief would never allow it," Wade warned his partner. "I'm going to the car to get my guitar. Liz suggested I bring it with us. She said something about her and Monet wanting us to play for them."

Aron turned to Marcus and asked with surprise, "What instrument do you play?"

"An alto saxophone," Marcus replied distractedly. His mind was consumed with thoughts of Mad Dog being someone from his past who might have held a grudge against him.

"Actually, he and Wade make pretty good music together," Duane told his father.

Inside the house, Monet, Liz, and Elise were still oohing and aahing over the baby gifts. The choir members had given Monet a variety of gifts; a car seat, stroller, high chair, and mountains of pink clothing.

Elise excused herself, saying she was going to check on Duane.

Monet peered at Liz as she was hanging a pink and white flow-ered short set in the closet.

Then Liz asked, "Have you heard from Derek? I thought he might join us today."

"He called a few days after putting his foot in his mouth and apologized," Monet replied, as she took the beautiful christening outfit out of a box. She handed it to Liz to hang up in the closet.

"Well, at least he said he was sorry." Liz picked up another box and put a pair of white satin booties in the dresser drawer.

"I have to admit that what he said to me sat the wrong way with me. At first I was mad, then sad because Derek really hurt my feelings. Then I had to pray over the situation. I didn't un-derstand how he could be so insensitive about my feelings and make those statements about Faith's paternity in front of our father. My father hasn't said anything about the state of siege at my house, but I'm sure he's put two and two together by now." Monet looked over at Liz, who was putting a small bag of *Huggies* on the changing table. "Liz, what do you think of my dad? I want your honest opinion."

There wasn't another chair in the room for Liz to sit on, so she leaned against the side of the baby bed. "You know I'm go-ing to keep it real. I think he's really trying to make amends. I'm sure his mortality has come into play, and my gut feeling tells me he's trying to do the right thing. It couldn't have been easy for him to ask if you or your brothers would take him in, but he did what he had to do."

"Do you think he came into our lives because that's what he wants, or because Momma asked him to?" The answer to that question had preoccupied Monet's mind for many days.

"I think a little bit of both. I don't sense any deception on his part. You're the person with the gift. What does your heart say to you?" Liz turned the question back on her friend.

"I think he's honest in his motives, but I hear Marcus saying

I feel that way because that's what I want to believe." Monet crinkled her nose.

"Then go with the flow, and be glad you have a parent in your life now with the baby coming. We know that God provides when we need it, and sister, it's your time."

"I believe you're right," Monet said thoughtfully as she tried to pick a box off the floor at the same time that Faith decided it was playtime. She rubbed her abdomen while the baby appeared to perform somersaults around her midsection.

"Let me get that for you," Liz offered. She walked over and handed Monet a couple more boxes.

Duane and Elise walked into the room. He walked over to his sister and gently tugged at a lock of her hair "Dinner was great as always. Elise and I are going downtown to Millennium Park for a concert, so we'll see you next time. I'll call you this week."

"Thanks for joining us, Elise. It was nice seeing you again; don't be a stranger. You don't have to wait for Duane to bring you over for a visit." Monet beamed a smile at the young woman.

"Thanks, Monet," Elise gushed. "The food was great like the company, and I love what you've done with the nursery. It's beautiful, just like your baby is going to be."

"Thank you," she said. "I'm not going to attempt to get up because it would take too long. We enjoyed your company too."

Duane and Elise departed and headed to downtown Chicago.

"She seems like a nice woman. Do you think your brother is finally going to settle down?" Liz asked as she opened another box and held up yellow pajamas.

"I don't know . . . I like her. All can say is that Duane has been with her longer than he has with any other woman in a long time. The twins are almost thirty-seven years old, and I keep telling them that it's time for them to settle down. Although I don't think Derek ever will."

"Then one out of two ain't bad," Liz quipped while Monet took a Black Ballerina lamp out of another box.

"Oh, isn't that beautiful?" Monet cooed enthusiastically. "I have to admit, the choir members have good taste. Sometimes we never know where our blessings are going to come from."

"You are so right." Liz nodded her head. "Let's finish a couple more boxes and head back downstairs. Maybe the guys will do us the honor of serenading us with some music."

"That would be nice," Monet said as Liz handed her three more boxes. "When Marcus returned home after his hotel stay, he began playing the saxophone even more than he usually does. And some nights the songs are so poignant they bring tears to my eyes. Later, I came to realize that's his way of coping with our situation."

"That's a healthy way to channel his aggression, and it's better than the alternative. Thank God he isn't drinking or, God forbid, using drugs."

"You're right. Even in the midst of this estrangement from Marcus, God is still blessing me. And that's what keeps me sane throughout this whole predicament, along with you being my prayer partner."

"Thank you," Liz said as she set a bottle of baby oil on top of the changing table and put a diaper genie on the floor next to the table. "Now hand me those outfits, and then we can go back downstairs and hopefully listen to some nice jazzy music."

Liz left boxes for Monet to open the following day. They returned to the backyard, where they found Marcus and Wade warming up their instruments. Aron was shooing a mosquito away from his bare arms.

"Give me a few minutes, and then let the music begin," Liz said. "I'm going to grab some fruit for me and Monet. Does anyone else want anything?"

Marcus and Wayne said they didn't, while Aron said he'd

like some fruit. When Liz returned, she handed Monet a bowl of strawberries and cream sprinkled with sugar on the top. She had slices of watermelon for herself and Aron.

After she sat down, she looked first at her husband, and then at Marcus. "What are you waiting for? Let the music begin," she said.

Monet rested the top of her arms on her stomach as Wade played the opening notes of "Never Can Say Good-bye" by The Jackson Five, and Marcus blew melodic notes as he joined Wade. As she watched her husband play his saxophone, Monet's eyes filled with tears. She, Liz, and Aron were treated to a beautiful mixture of jazz and R&B songs.

Half an hour later, sweat trickled down the sides of Marcus's face. With each heartrending note he played, Monet could feel the toll the past months had taken on her husband. Love for her husband seized and held onto Monet's heart, and she could feel Marcus's love for her in each note that he played. She sent him what she called a mental message that said I love you.

I think that I have loved you from the first moment you asked me if you could carry my books between classes back in high school. We have been through good times and not so good ones, and through it all, God has seen us through both. I know you're hurting, and there's something in you that just won't let you let go and let God handle it. But that's okay, because God knows you're hurting. Just hold on a little while longer, my love, and you will see the awesome power of God as He manifests Himself in our child. Hold on, Marcus, God loves you, and so do I.

Chapter 28

The gestation period for Monet's pregnancy had almost reached its culmination. She would reach forty weeks the following week. When she had gone to her appointment last week, Dr. Armstrong informed her that her wait was almost over, and that it wouldn't be long. The baby was making its descent into her womb to prepare for labor.

Liz and Monet had enjoyed attending Lamaze classes, and Liz made an extra effort to bolster her friend's spirits. She sensed Monet had the blues sometimes because Marcus wouldn't share the pregnancy experience with her.

The nursing department at St. Bernard's Hospital hosted a shower for Monet, and she had received so many items that she jokingly told her father they might have to build a wing onto the nursery.

Monet felt blissful and blessed. She and Aron talked more each day. They had formed a loving bond and gotten to know each other better. She saw glimpses of the man her mother had fallen in love with, and she knew that he, too, was enjoying their time together. Monet finally understood what Liz meant when she said she was a daddy's girl when she was growing up, and still was.

Marcus had gone to his superiors with the tip that Aron had provided, and surprisingly, it had panned out after a DNA sample was acquired from the felon. Mad Dog had no choice but to confess to the crime. Another twenty years was tacked onto the sentence he was currently serving.

As Wade had predicted, the chief denied Marcus's request to go with Smitty when he questioned Mad Dog, a.k.a., Jermaine Richardson. Only after a confession was obtained from Mad Dog did Chief Davis allow Marcus to go talk to the prisoner, but he set a stipulation that Wade go with him to the prison.

Wade complied with the edict, and the two men found themselves cooling their heels in a different cellblock. Just like before, two guards escorted the prisoner into the room and removed the cuffs from his hands, and then went to stand near the door. Mad Dog plopped down into his seat and stared sullenly at Marcus. Mad Dog's head was shaven. He seemed to leer at Marcus and Wade with thick lips. One side of his face was brown and pink as Aron had indicated. Marcus glared fiercely at the man sitting in front of him. Mad Dog could feel the aura of animosity that seemed to spring from Marcus, and it amused him.

He sneered at Marcus and asked, "Hey, dude, you got a square?"

Marcus shook his head, indicating that he didn't. His tongue snaked out of his mouth as he wet his lips. Mad Dog looked vaguely familiar to him. Marcus's voice was low and overflowed with hostility, as he asked Mad Dog in a flat tone of voice, "Why did you do it? Why my wife?"

"It wasn't nothing personal, brother. I needed money, and your wife was in the wrong place at the wrong time. Simple as that." Mad Dog looked away from Marcus with a bored look on his face.

"If it were as simple as that, then you could've just taken her purse. She probably would have given it to you. Why did you have to put your hands on her, and then rape her?" Marcus had to quell his inner demons to remain in control.

"Well, maybe I'll tell you if you can give me a square." Mad Dog leaned back in the chair. "What about you, partner number two, you got a square?" he asked Wade.

Wade pulled a pack of cigarettes out of his pocket and handed one to Mad Dog. Then he struck a match and lit it for him. Being a policeman and having visited prisons numerous times, Wade had enough foresight to bring a pack with him.

"That's more like it. Now, what did you say, partner number one?" Mad Dog wore a smirk on his face as he turned his attention back to Marcus.

"You heard what I said, and I'm not going to repeat myself," Marcus replied testily.

Mad Dog blew a smoke ring toward the ceiling. "Let's see, you asked me why I didn't just take her purse. I was high, and I ain't had none in awhile. Your lady was there, and hey, she looked good." He shrugged his shoulders.

Marcus shook his head and glared at the man sitting in front of him like he was pure evil. He cracked his knuckles to do something with his hands so that he wouldn't beat the fool in front of him to a pulp.

"Are you so hard up that you can't find someone on your own, instead of resorting to brutalizing women to suppress your urges?" Marcus asked the prisoner harshly.

"I can do whatever I want to when I choose to." Mad Dog flicked his ashes on the floor beside his chair.

"I think you mean that in the past tense because now you can't do a darn thing except what the guards allow you to do," Marcus said. It took all of his willpower not to reach across the table and grab Mad Dog by the neck and beat him senseless.

"Whatever," Mad Dog said. He inhaled the cigarette, and then exhaled a puff of smoke." Look, man, I done told you what you wanted to know. Your wife was just there, and I took her. Yeah, I may have roughed her up a bit. That's the way I roll; I like it rough. I'm a real man." He flexed his left arm mockingly at Marcus.

"You nearly broke her jaw, and her shoulder was wretched out of its socket. You beat her face so badly that she was lucky she didn't need plastic surgery when you were done, and all you can say is that you like it rough," Marcus growled. The vein in his forehead throbbed uncontrollably.

Mad Dog raised his hand. "Look here, man, you asked to see me, I didn't ask you to come here. I answered your questions. It ain't my fault you don't like what I said." He smirked.

One of the guards snarled sternly, "Keep your hands on the table and in sight."

"I guess I don't know my own strength," Mad Dog said sarcastically. He dropped the cigarette on the floor, stomped it out and asked Wade for another one. Wade complied with his request.

"I guess I was hoping to hear you say that you were sorry, but I guess there isn't a shred of decency in your body," Marcus spat.

"Marcus, why don't we go? You're not going to get what you came here for." Wade made a move to stand up, and when he did, Mad Dog jumped out of his seat, pulled a shank from the sleeve of his jumpsuit and lunged toward Marcus.

Marcus froze, and Wade pushed his partner out of Mad Dog's reach. The guards rushed the table. One of the guards wrestled the weapon away from Mad Dog, while the other pointed the rifle he held in his hand at their prisoner's head. The guard who gained possession of the shank, tossed it to the other guard, and then cuffed Mad Dog and pulled him roughly toward the door. The second guard apologized and said they'd come back to the room once they returned Mad Dog to his cell.

"I'm not through with you yet, partner number one. Don't you remember me? You tried to put me away ten years ago, and the charges didn't stick. I walked. Payback is a dog, a mad dog, ain't it?" He laughed evilly as the guards quickly escorted him through the door and out the room.

Marcus sat down hard in the chair and covered his face.

Wade walked over to him, leaned down, and said worriedly, "Are you all right?"

Marcus rubbed his face and said, "I think so. I think I saw my life flash before me when I saw that shank."

"I hear you, brother. I can't believe he had the audacity to try and harm you in front of me and the guards," Wade said as he stroked his chin.

"He's a psycho, just like we thought. I don't remember ever arresting him though. I went through my cases and so did Smitty, and the name Jermaine Richardson never surfaced as someone we needed to investigate," Marcus said.

"Ten years is a long time, maybe he used an alias back then. We've investigated so many cases over the years that we can't remember every single one of the perpetrators' names," Wade reminded Marcus.

"I guess you're right, but when I heard his birth name, it should have come back to me," Marcus remarked, mentally rebuking himself.

"You've had a lot on your mind. And I guess Smitty didn't see anything that threw up a red flag at him." Wade tried to console his friend.

"Thanks for having my back, Wade. I owe you," Marcus said, shuddering. He was still shaken at how close he had come to being injured or killed, depending on Mad Dog's aim.

"Hey, it's no big deal. You would have done the same for me," Wade replied, though his hands shook slightly.

The shorter guard returned to the room and informed Marcus, "Warden Jones wants to see you, and we need to take an incident report."

Marcus tried to stand up, but his legs were still shaky. "I thought I would have to. Where would this world be without red tape?" He looked upward.

The men followed the guard to his office, and within thirty minutes had completed the report and were on their way to the warden's office. Levi commiserated with Marcus before he led them into the warden's office.

"Detectives, I hear we had some excitement in the cellblock. I'm glad to see you're both okay. I take it you already filled out the incident report. Detective Caldwell, would you like to press charges against Jermaine? What he did was attempted assault," Warden Jones said.

"I'd prefer to just let it go," Marcus responded. "I think I've spent enough time here, and hopefully won't have to come back here for a while, even if I'm investigating a case. Plus, I don't want the prison to have a black mark on your watch."

"I hear you, and thank you. We'll handle the incident in our own way." Warden Jones sounded grateful. He held out his hand.

Marcus and Wade stood up, reached across the desk, thrust their hands out at the warden and took their leave. They entered their vehicle and proceeded to Interstate 55. Wade decided to drive and he kept glancing over at Marcus, who had become quiet.

"You sure you're all right?" Wade queried his partner.

"I am. I just wasn't expecting him to try to attack me. I swear I could see every mistake I've made in my life somersaulting before me, and man, it wasn't nothing good." Marcus felt tense. He adjusted the rearview mirror for lack of anything else to do.

"I guess you're referring to Monet?" Wade asked.

"That's part of it. I know I haven't been the best husband in the world to her over the past months, but I haven't deserted her. Under the circumstances, I've continued to support her as well as any man could be expected to. And now I learn this guy got revenge against me by hurting Monet." Marcus sighed half-heartedly. "The bad news just seems to keep coming."

"I know you feel that you've done the best you could do. But how would you feel, buddy, if you had been killed just now and never saw Monet's face again? And what if that baby she's carrying is yours? What would she be able to tell the baby about her father?"

"You and I both know the baby isn't mine. And when I think of Monet carrying that fool's baby, I feel even more strongly that she should've aborted the baby like I wanted her to," Marcus replied unyieldingly.

"You've never, not even once, allowed yourself to think that it could be your baby? Every doctor that you and Monet have seen over the years has told you that there is no medical reason that stopped her from conceiving. That would sure raise some doubt in my mind." Wade jogged Marcus's memory.

"No, that thought has never entered my mind. If she had gotten pregnant before the rape, or even two months afterward, then I would be the happiest man in the world. Dr. Armstrong pinpointed Monet's due date back to the rape. Now I'm just convinced that Monet is going to have trouble on her hands. What if that child is like Mad Dog?"

"Don't go there," Wade said. "We don't know Mad Dog's circumstances. For all we know, he could have come from a good family and drugs messed him up. We know firsthand the horrors that crack has perpetrated on our community. What we saw in there was the outcome of excessive drug use."

"I agree with you to a certain point. We don't know his story, but it doesn't matter; look at him now. I'll be glad when Monet has the baby, although I already know the outcome." Marcus nodded his head sorrowfully.

"You think you know the outcome, but only God knows that, and He surprises us at times when we least expect it." Wade nodded his head wisely.

"You're always throwing Christian nuggets at me, Wade. But

what would you do if Liz had been raped and was pregnant by her rapist? You've told me what I should do, but what would you do?"

"I don't think you're going to like my answer. But since you asked, I would accept the child and raise it as my own, because half of my Lizzie's DNA would be a part of that child. I would pray for strength to love the child as I have my own. Make no mistake, Marcus, everything happens for a reason. God never said this life would be easy, but knowing that I have my Father's strength to lean on and Lizzie's, I think I would be fine raising another man's child," he said honestly.

"That's easy for you to say because you're not in my predicament."

"You're right, I could say anything. But I think I'm a little further in my walk with God than you are. We've known each other for over twenty years, so if I say something, I mean it. I don't have to score brownie points with you, nor am I trying to influence your thinking. You've been adamant about your position from day one. You asked my opinion, and I gave it to you."

"You're right, Monet's pregnancy is driving me crazy," Marcus admitted, then he turned and looked out the window.

Wade continued driving, and they stopped only once to gas up the car. Marcus's cell phone beeped, and he winced when he saw the chief's number on the caller ID unit.

He spoke through his blue tooth device. "Hello, Chief. Yes, we had a little incident in Dwight. Everything is fine, and I'm okay." Marcus stopped talking and listened to Chief Davis. "You want to see me today? It can't wait until tomorrow? We're about an hour and a half from Chicago. Okay, I'll be there as soon as I can." He ended the call.

"I take it we're making a stop before we head home?" Wade inquired, as he glanced out the rearview mirror.

"No, I am. I'm going to drop you off at home. I have a bad

feeling about the chief calling me and asking me to come in. You have my back, don't you? That the situation that went down at the prison was beyond my control?" Marcus gazed pleadingly over at Wade.

"Sure I will," Wade reassured Marcus.

Silence filled the car as Wade drove to Chicago. Marcus chewed his lip when he was nervous, and he was gnawing on it like a squirrel with a nut. Marcus had a hunch that whatever the chief was going to tell him wasn't good.

Chapter 29

Aron was downstairs resting in his room in the basement, and Monet was upstairs lying on the chaise reading a book. She couldn't get comfortable when she had lain in bed. Her ankles had swollen slightly, so when she called her doctor, she suggested Monet stay off her feet. She had been experiencing contractions off and on most of the day, and she just attributed it to Braxton Hicks contractions. She knew that her body was preparing for the childbirth. Mitzi was curled up on the floor at the end of the bed.

Her due date of July 19th had come and gone. Her obstetrician had cautioned her that due dates were not a perfect science, that the baby could arrive two weeks early or two weeks late. Monet was now a week late. She looked at her suitcase lying against the wall near the closet. She had completed all her preparations for Faith. Now she just had to wait for the baby to arrive.

Monet felt jittery. She sensed a few hours ago that Marcus was in some kind of trouble, and the feeling kept niggling at her. She wanted to call him, but he'd stopped answering her phone calls a long time ago. She knew if she texted him with a 911 message, he would probably respond, but knew her feelings wouldn't qualify as an emergency to Marcus. Liz was working late at the hospital, so Monet couldn't call her. She guessed she just had to tough it out. But that didn't stop her from wondering if her husband was okay.

* * *

After Marcus dropped Wade off at home, he headed north to the police station. Twenty minutes later, he was sitting outside the chief's opened office door. He wasn't getting a good vibe about what the chief was going to say to him. Finally, the chief gestured for Marcus to come into his office.

Marcus went inside and sat on a chair. "Sir, you wanted to see me?" he asked.

"Yes. I got a call from Warden Jones at Dwight, and he told me what happened with Richardson. I knew I should not have given you permission to go there. What did you accomplish?" The chief was irate, Marcus could almost see smoke coming from his ears.

"I guess nothing. The prisoner just enforced what we already knew, that he's crazy." Marcus hung his head shamefully. Then he looked up and said, "I'm sorry, Chief, but it wasn't like I asked Richardson to attack me. The man isn't operating with a full deck. If I had remembered that I had arrested him in the past, I never would have gone to that prison and confronted him."

"In the past, a perp is someone that you never would have forgotten, and Smitty was remiss in not discovering that information sooner. Jones said that you froze up and Harrison saved your life. And because of your reaction, or the lack thereof, I'm ordering you to take a voluntary leave of absence from the job. You need time to get your head together. You were always too close to the situation, and now you need down time to get yourself together," Chief Davis informed Marcus, as he put a stack of papers into his in-basket.

"Sir, I don't feel that I need time off," Marcus said apprehensively. "I can't lose my job now. Why, it's all that I have." His voice broke up.

"Marcus, if you don't do this on a voluntary basis, then I'm

going to have to suspend you. You need help, and there are people in the department you can talk to, or you can find someone
on your own. I'm sorry. I'm doing this for your own good. You
will continue to draw your salary," Chief Davis said.

Marcus felt humiliated and even less than a man. He wondered how all this could be happening to him. Briefly he blamed
all his troubles on Monet, and then he remembered she was the
one who had been attacked. Then he thought of Mad Dog, and
wished he could've hurt him the way he had hurt Monet and
himself.

"How long is this leave suppose to last?" he finally asked Chief
Davis.

"I expect you to take off at least two months, and more if
needed." Chief Davis spoke with a finality that Marcus knew he
couldn't argue with.

Marcus stood up and asked, "Starting when?"

"Immediately. You can turn over your weapon now." The
chief held out his hand.

Marcus opened his jacket, removed his gun from the hol-
ster and the bullets from the weapon, and placed them in Chief
Davis's palm. Then he turned to exit the office.

"Marcus, trust me when I said what I'm doing is for your own
good. One day you'll look back on this day and thank me."

When pigs fly, he thought. "Sure, Chief, whatever you say.
My .38 is at the house. I'll turn it in tomorrow. That is, if that's
okay with you."

"That will be fine. Again, I'm sorry it came to this. You'll be
back on the job in no time."

Marcus nodded as he closed the door to the office. He was
furious. He had put in twenty years of service to the department,
and now he was suspended, no matter how much the chief tried
to sugar coat it. He started to go to his desk and decided not
to. Since he and Wade were partners, he didn't have to turn

over any information to him. He stalked out of the station and walked briskly to his car. A few officers spoke to him, but he didn't bother to acknowledge their presence.

Once he got inside his SUV, he hit the steering wheel in frustration a few times. Then he dropped his head in his hands. *How did my life come to this? I feel like I don't have anyone to turn to. Monet is off limits. Wade has been so patient with me, I don't feel like bothering him with my problems. I don't know what to do.*

His cell phone rang and home was displayed on the caller ID. He wondered if Wade had told Monet what happened already. *Jeez,* he thought, *I don't want to go home, if that's what you call it, and I can't bother Wade.*

Marcus closed his eyes and leaned his head against the back of the seat. He sat inertly for a few minutes. Then he sat erect and put the key in the ignition and started the car. He wasn't sure where he was going, but he figured wherever he went, it was better than going home.

He drove to Chatham. Marcus wasn't sure what drew him to the church. He wasn't even sure anyone would be there. It was Tuesday evening, and he knew there weren't any events scheduled at the Temple that night. He put on his left turn signal and pulled into the church parking lot.

The lot was empty except for one car, and Marcus knew that it was Reverend Wilcox's Cadillac. He debated with himself about what he should do, but he finally exited his SUV and walked to the front of the church plagued with doubts. He pulled the door handle and it was locked. He rang the bell, which went to the telephone system in Reverend Wilcox's office.

"Hello, who's there?" Reverend Wilcox asked.

"It's me, Marcus Caldwell," he said in a leaden voice.

Reverend Wilcox sounded the buzzer, Marcus pulled the door open, and walked inside to the reverend's office.

Reverend Wilcox was waiting at the door when he walked inside the church. She took one look at Marcus's face and knew that he was hurting. She held out her arms and he walked into them. She held him comfortingly for a few seconds, and then Marcus pulled away and looked at her hopelessly.

"Why don't you come into my office," Reverend Wilcox suggested. "We can talk in there."

Marcus followed her into the office her father had once occupied. She sat down and folded her hands on the desk. "What can I do for you, Marcus? What's wrong?"

"I feel like I'm losing it, Reverend Wilcox. I don't mean I'm suicidal or anything. My life has degenerated into a fiasco, and I seem to be powerless to do anything to change it."

She beamed benevolently at Marcus. "When you made the decision to come here this evening, that was the first step toward getting your house in order. Praise God for leading you here. Now tell me what's been going on with you."

Once he began speaking, he spilled his guts; Monet's pregnancy, how she disregarded his suggestion that she terminate the pregnancy, how he felt alienated on his job, his father-in-law moving into the house, and then to top things off, Monet's attacker being someone he had arrested, and who had raped her for revenge.

"I feel like things are escalating out of control, and I don't know what to do," he confessed sadly.

"First of all, I want to pray for you, son," Reverend Wilcox said. She rose from her chair, came and sat in the chair next to Marcus and took his hands in hers. They both bowed their heads and closed their eyes.

"Father above, I want to thank you for bringing Marcus to the Temple tonight. He may not know it, but this is the best place in the world for him to be: in your house, Lord. It is our spiritual home, where we can feel your grace and mercy, and believe with you, all things are possible. You give us strength when we need it, and we can lean on you when the going gets tough. And right now, Father, Marcus needs to release his burdens and lean on you. Let Marcus know that he is not alone, and you are available to him twenty-four hours a day. He just has to call, and you will answer. And Father, Marcus is calling, and I know you will grant him the peace that he seeks. These blessings I ask in Jesus' name. Amen."

"I can't give you the answers to the questions that you seek," Reverend Wilcox began, "but I can listen to you and give you advice, if that's what you want. Is that okay with you?"

Marcus nodded that it was as he lay his arms on the sides of the chair.

"I know the incident with Monet has hurt you badly. And the pain has cut to the quick. But she survived the attack, her wounds have healed, and your wife is a strong woman; one that most of us could aspire to be like. Legally, she could have terminated the pregnancy, but she has waited over half of her life for this moment, and she truly believes that the baby is yours, there is no doubt in her mind."

"I disagree. She just wanted a baby so badly that she would accept that child no matter how it was conceived," Marcus countered.

"You don't really believe that because you know your wife. You and Monet have always been attuned to each other's feelings. You've been with her since you were in high school. I think that even if she believed the baby was the result of the rape, she would still accept her child because that's her personality. Her livelihood has been one of nurturing babies. That would go against the grain for her to terminate the pregnancy. God is testing you, and the devil is trying to sneak in and steal your joy. I hope you don't let the devil win," Reverend Wilcox said. Marcus pondered her words. "Do you remember how Monet would come to the altar every Sunday because she needed a blessing, and how she dragged you to Jerusalem and Arkansas, praying to conceive a baby? And then she just stopped?"

Marcus nodded his head. "Yes, I remember. I thought she had given up hope of us having children and accepted it would be just the two of us."

"I also remember asking her about adoption, and she said you didn't want to go that route. She was hurt by your decision, but she respected your wishes, even if it meant depriving herself of what she wanted most in the world."

Marcus rubbed his eyes. He knew every word Reverend Wilcox spoke was true.

"Sometimes one partner has to be stronger than the other so their mate can lean on them. You were there for Monet after her attack, and there is no doubt in my mind that you were an integral part of her recovery. I know it wasn't easy, but you were there for her, and you comforted her, and why was that, Marcus?" Reverend Wilcox probed gently.

"Because I love her," Marcus said simply, and waves of love roared into his heart, emotions that he'd tried so hard to suppress for the past nine months. He dropped his head in his hands.

Reverend Wilcox nodded her head and whispered, "Help him, Lord. He needs you right now." She patted his back.

After Marcus collected himself, he said, "I failed my wife when she needed me most. I should have followed my first mind and picked her up from work like I started to. Had I done that, then the rape never would have happened."

"Marcus, you can't take that kind of burden upon yourself. Everything that happens to us in life is for a reason. Monet wasn't alone on that day because God was with her. She was hurt physically, but not permanently, and God, in His infinite wisdom, kept her here with us."

"That baby she's carrying is a permanent reminder of what she went through," Marcus remarked.

"If that is the case, then maybe that's what the Father wants you to do, raise that child to the best of you and Monet's ability."

"But why would God do that to us? We haven't hurt anyone. We attend church and try to lead good lives," he said.

"There are some things in life we may never understand, but maybe God has chosen you and Monet for those very reasons you mentioned. You're Christians, you go to church, follow God's teachings, and try to lead good lives, as you said. I know how you feel, Marcus. I went through the same doubts when my husband left me. I didn't think I could face another day, much less the gossip of the church. I had my father and brother to lean on, and they kept me sane. And out of all that heartache, I received my calling. So maybe I had to go through a trial to find myself in life. I imagine you're going through the same thing."

"I guess I've been so wrapped in my own feelings that I haven't considered anyone else's, and that was wrong of me," he confessed morosely.

"Life's journeys are made up of peaks and valleys, and sometimes that peak can be so sharp. But if we believe in God and know that He can help us, then that makes the going a little easier. Think of it as God providing a cushion."

"We probably should have had this talk a little sooner than today," Marcus said, clearly chagrined.

Reverend Wilcox said astutely, "I believe you came here when it was time. There is still time to talk to Monet and tell her everything you've been feeling, and I know she will comfort you just like you comforted her."

"I've been such a fool for the way I treated her," Marcus cried. "I hope I can make it up to her. But I don't know if I can be a good father to that child after what I saw of Monet's attacker today."

"You have more strength than you know, Marcus, and I don't mean the physical kind either. Don't try to do everything on your own. Pray for guidance, and I promise you God will deliver and help you."

"Thank you, Reverend Wilcox. I'm so glad God put it on my heart to come here tonight, and more importantly, that you were here to talk to me."

Reverend Wilcox beamed her beautiful smile at Marcus. "I've been staying at church a little later than usual the past couple of weeks. I knew emotions might become taut for either you or Monet as her due date approached. I wanted to make myself available to either one of you, whoever needed my assistance."

Reverend Wilcox reached for a pad on her desk and quickly began to write. When she was done, she looked at Marcus. "Sometimes we need something to focus on when we start to feel overwhelmed. Put this inside your wallet or someplace close by where you can access it quickly. I'm going to read them to you now. *"Oh Lord, you are my hiding place; You will protect me from trouble, and surround me with songs of deliverance."* That is taken from the book of Psalm 37:7. The next one is from the book of Ecclesiastes 7:14; *"When times are good be happy, but when times are bad, consider God has made one as well as the other."*

"And this one," Reverend Wilcox concluded, "is my favorite. *Trust in Him in all times, O People; pour out your hearts to Him, for God is our refuge.* That one is from the book of Psalms 62:8. Pray, Marcus, and trust in God. Give Him your burdens and trust that He won't fail you. I promise you that you'll feel better. Talk to Monet, open your heart to her and everything will be all right." She handed the paper to Marcus. He stood up and put it inside his wallet.

"Thank you, Reverend Wilcox. I promise I'm going to talk to Monet tomorrow. I hope she will forgive me."

There was a twinkle in Reverend Wilcox's eye. "Trust me when I say that I know she will. Go get your house in order, Marcus."

"I will," he promised earnestly as he held out his hand.

She clasped it firmly. "I will keep you and Monet in my prayers, and don't hesitate to call or come see me if you need to."

"I will, and Pastor, keep the prayers coming." Marcus turned to leave the office. "Do you need me to wait on you? I can stay here until you're ready to leave."

"No, that's okay. I'm going to be here a little while longer. You never know who may come by in need of prayer," Reverend Wilcox said.

"Okay, be careful," Marcus said as he walked out the door.

"I will, and the same to you." She waved good-bye to Marcus.

As he drove home, the ice that had encased his heart began to melt. He knew he still had a lot of atoning to do, especially to his wife. He now understood what Wade was trying to tell him earlier. Marcus wondered why sometimes people had to nearly lose everything before they realized what was most important to them. He could hardly wait to see and talk to Monet. Their conversation, like Monet's due date, was long overdue.

Chapter 30

When Marcus arrived home he found the house dark. Mitzi was asleep in her basket. He walked upstairs and Monet was asleep too. He went downstairs to the basement, and Aron, like his daughter, was asleep. After he showered and changed into his pajamas, Marcus let out the sofa bed and retired for the night. He took the piece of paper Reverend Wilcox had given him out of his wallet and read the words. He hadn't prayed in a long time, but that night he asked God to forgive him for being hardheaded, and to help him to find the right words to say to Monet tomorrow.

He glanced at the clock, and decided it was too late to call Wade. He added that to his to-do list for tomorrow. Then Marcus's stomach rumbled, and he realized that he hadn't eaten since earlier that day. He rose from the sofa and checked the mini refrigerator that he stored his food in. He discovered a cold carton of noodles that he'd bought a couple of days ago. He put it in the microwave. While his food was warming, he took a can of iced tea out of the fridge and placed it on the table. The microwave beeped, Marcus took the carton out of the oven and ate. After he disposed of the can and carton, he fell asleep promptly, drained by the day's events.

When the alarm clock sounded the next morning, Marcus turned it off and debated whether he should go into the station now or later. He decided to get up and go then, and when he returned he would talk to Monet and beg her forgiveness.

When he finished his morning ritual, he checked his other weapon to make sure it was unloaded, and placed it inside his briefcase. Marcus went upstairs and found Aron sitting at the table drinking coffee.

"Good morning," Aron said. "Could you drop me off at Duane's house? He and I are going to hang out today."

"You want to go there this early in the morning?" Marcus asked.

"Yes, we're going out to breakfast."

"Sure, I'll drop you off. " Marcus looked toward the stairs. "Is Monet up? Has she been downstairs yet?"

"She was down here earlier and said she didn't feel well, so she went back to bed. I asked her if she wanted me to stay here with her today. But she told me to go ahead and keep my plans with Duane." Aron stood up and took his white Panama straw hat off the coat rack and put it on his head.

"Let's head out." Marcus took his keys out of his pocket, and they left the house. He locked the door behind them.

Monet tried to get out of the bed to peek out the window. By the time she maneuvered her body out of the bed and waddled over to the window, Marcus's vehicle was no longer in view. She walked slowly back to the bed, and as she sat down, a pang sizzled through her body and caused her to lean forward and gasp.

"Well, okay then. Faith, are you trying to tell me that today is the day?" She smiled and patted her tummy, then picked up the remote off her nightstand and aimed it toward the television. Monet channel surfed for a few minutes.

She tried to get comfortable when another pain shot through her midsection as it tightened up. "Oh, I felt that one. I do believe that I'm in labor." Her body felt warm, and she dabbed at perspiration that had beaded on her brow.

Monet sat up upright in the bed and placed her legs on the side of the bed. She picked up her Bible and held it to her chest.

"Lord, you've blessed me so, and I hope I have done some things that are pleasing in your sight. I'm not a saint by any means, but I try to do the right thing most of time. Help Faith, and keep her safe as she transitions from one stage of life to another one. Help me to be a good mother, and I promise to raise her according to your Word. Lord, take care of me and give me strength to go through this labor . . . my labor of love. Most of all, Lord, continue to heal Marcus. He doesn't know that I know that he was in my room last night and kissed my forehead." She rubbed her back and massaged her abdomen.

Monet looked at the clock on the nightstand; her contractions were a little under twenty minutes apart. She knew that it wouldn't be long before it was time for her to go to the hospital.

She picked up her cell phone and called Liz, only to find out that she was in a meeting. Monet left her a voice mail message. She then called Wade and was routed to his voice mail too. She thought long and hard about calling Marcus, but decided to drive herself to the hospital if she couldn't find someone to drive her.

Finally, Monet called the hospital and informed the maternity ward that she was in labor and on her way there. The idea that she could call the paramedics or a cab to take her to the hospital flickered in and out of her mind. She decided to go downstairs and wait for Liz or Wade to call her back.

She stood up, took her purse off the dresser and toddled over to her suitcase. She picked it up, and remembered that she didn't have her cell phone, which she'd left on the bed. She slipped it in the pocket of her red smock top, which read *Mommy In The Making* with an arrow pointing toward her belly.

After inspecting the room one final time, Monet verified that she hadn't forgotten anything. After she left the bedroom, she peeped into the nursery. Then she headed down the stairs. She had almost reached the last few stairs when Mitzi ran to the bottom of the staircase and began barking. Monet's hand slipped off the banister, she dropped the suitcase in her other hand and slid down the stairs. She managed to fall backward instead of forward as her hands shielded her stomach.

Her head banged the wall, and the stabbing pain through her body made Monet feel as if she were a human pin cushion. She managed to remove her cell phone out of her pocket and press 911, as her water broke. When the operator answered the call, she moaned her name and address and asked for help. She leaned back against the banister and passed out. Her body slid slowly to the bottom step. Mitzi hopped up the steps and began licking Monet's face and alternately barking. It didn't take the paramedics long to arrive at her house.

Marcus had turned the corner onto his street when he noticed the ambulance parked in front of his house. He sped down the street and had barely put the car into park before hopping out of his car and jogging toward his residence.

The paramedics were about to break the door down when he stopped them. He shouted that he lived there and held up his keys. He ran to the staircase with the paramedics closely on his heels. Marcus nearly fainted when he saw Monet's lifeless body at the bottom of the stairs. He wanted to cradle her in his arms, but knew it was best not to move her.

"Sir, what hospital is your wife scheduled to give birth at?" one of the paramedics asked.

Marcus had never felt so low in his life. "I'm not sure, maybe St. Bernard Hospital. She's on staff there." His hands dangled helplessly at his side.

The two men looked at each other and shook their heads, as if to say, how could a husband not know where his wife was going to deliver their baby? One of the paramedics went outside to bring the stretcher in the house. The other one asked Marcus if Monet had a list of emergency numbers anywhere in the house.

He didn't want to leave Monet, but he ran into the kitchen and found Dr. Armstrong's number and the telephone number of the hospital on the refrigerator. He snatched it and ran back to the staircase where the paramedics were loading Monet's inert body onto the stretcher. He held her hand as the paramedics wheeled her out to the ambulance.

"Did you find anything?" the paramedic asked.

"Yes, her obstetrician is named Dr. Armstrong, and she's on staff at Northwestern Memorial Hospital." Marcus didn't have a clue whether the doctor was male or female.

The paramedic decided to take Monet to the nearest ho-spital; Advocate Christ Hospital located on Ninety-fifth Street in Oak Lawn, a suburb of Illinois, instead of Northwestern Memorial Hospital, which was located near the Chicago loop, because driving downtown would take too long.

One of the paramedics called Dr. Armstrong to notify her of what had taken place. The doctor promised to call Christ Hospital and fax Monet's medical records there so they would be available when Monet arrived at the hospital. Marcus climbed into the ambulance and rode with Monet and the paramedics to the hospital. Fear, like a playful puppy, nipped at the edges of his heart.

By the time the wailing ambulance pulled in front of the emergency room entrance, Monet began regaining consciousness. She looked at Marcus and said, "Uh-oh, I must really be in trouble for you to be here." Then a contraction rocked her body and her face crumpled from the pain.

The paramedics removed her gently from the vehicle and quickly wheeled her into the hospital. The staff had been alerted for Monet's arrival, and instructed the paramedics to wheel her to the second floor where the maternity ward was located.

Marcus went to the business office to start the paperwork. Before Monet left, she gave her husband a tremulous smile and whispered that she'd see him later.

She was quickly whisked into a birthing room and assisted by a nurse named Mrs. Murphy. After she had changed into a gown, Monet leaned back against the pillows and looked up to see a young woman, who looked all of eighteen years old, wearing blue scrubs enter the room. She walked to Monet's bedside and held out her hand.

"My name is Doctor Riddell, and I'll be filling in for your obstetrician today. How are you feeling, and how far apart are your contractions? When was the last time you timed them?" she asked.

"I'm okay." Monet nodded. "Before I fell at home they were about twenty minutes apart. They seemed to have slowed down somewhat."

The nurse handed Monet's chart to Dr. Riddell, who made notations inside of it. "I understand that you were unconscious for a while, and I'd like to examine you for that first, and then we'll see how the baby's doing." The doctor used an instrument that looked like a pen, which emitted light, and peered into Monet's eyes. She felt along the back of Monet's head. "You have a small goose egg there. Have you experienced any nausea or do you have a headache?"

"I don't feel nauseated, but I do have a mild headache, like a dull throb. It's not really bad," she responded.

"We'll keep an eye on that. Being in labor I don't think you're going to get much sleep, so we don't have to worry about you becoming sleepy and falling asleep. That's something we monitor for suspected concussion victims. Let me know if the headache worsens. Do you feel pain anywhere else from the fall or in your abdomen?"

"No," Monet said, and her eyes filled with tears, knowing that the situation could have been worse.

"I'm going to check the baby, and then Nurse Murphy will hook you up to a fetal monitor. Are you familiar with how that works?"

"Yes, I am. I'm a neo-natal nurse at St. Bernard's Hospital. Oh, did I mention my water broke while I was at home?" Monet said as she shifted her body in the bed, trying to get comfortable.

"Well, that's great then. Is this your first child?" Monet nodded yes. "The fax from your doctor is printing as we speak." Dr. Riddell put on latex gloves and raised Monet's gown and felt along her abdomen, all the while, asking her if she felt any pain. Monet replied that she didn't.

When Dr. Riddell finished her examination, she covered Monet's belly and told her, "All seems well. We'll monitor you and let nature take its course. I'll be in and out of here, and Nurse Murphy will be assisting me as your primary nurse. If you need assistance, press the button on the side of the bed."

"I will," Monet said. The doctor and nurse departed from the room. She closed her eyes. "Well, Lord, I guess Faith and I had a little scare earlier. We were wrapped in your loving arms, and no harm came to either of us. Thank you, Father, for blessing us. Marcus came home. I was so shocked to see him. I can't believe he's actually here in the hospital. After all the planning Liz and I did, You took control. I know Faith and I will be fine. Lord, I can't wait to see my baby's face."

The nurse returned to the room and stood at the foot of the bed. "Mrs. Caldwell, do you want an epidural or a pain killer? You doctor said it would be okay for us to administer one to you now if you'd like."

"The pain is tolerable for now. I didn't plan on taking any drugs. We'll see how I feel later as the labor progresses," she replied.

"That's fine. Don't hesitate to call if you need me." Nurse Murphy smiled at her patient. "I guess you're excited about being a mommy."

"Excited doesn't even begin to explain how I feel. I've waited for this moment for a long time. I'm sure you've noticed I'm not exactly a spring chicken." Monet's eyes sparkled with bliss.

"Events happen when they're supposed to according to the Master's plan. I wish you the best, and I'll be praying for you."

"Thank you," Monet said. She felt at ease by the older woman's words. Nurse Murphy was plump, had gray hair that was cut into a short haircut, and had a calming demeanor. Monet knew she was in good hands; another blessing.

Monet experienced a contraction, and she gasped. When it passed, she said, "That one was hard. I guess I can time them and see where I am."

"Don't forget you can also tell when a contraction is about to happen from the monitor." The nurse pointed at the machinery.

"You're right. I got so caught up about being in labor that I forgot about the equipment."

"If you change your mind about a painkiller, let me know." Nurse Murphy left the room, and Monet wondered where Marcus was. Did he plan to come upstairs and stay with her during labor, or had he called Liz?

Marcus put his insurance card back into his wallet and pondered if he should go up and see Monet or not. Despite his talk with Reverend Wilcox, he still didn't think Monet's baby was his offspring, and he didn't know how he would react when the baby was born. He decided to go outside and call Liz, Wade, Duane, Derek, and Aron. He walked out the glass door and pulled his cell phone out of his jacket pocket. He called Liz first and explained what happened.

"I'm glad you called me. Monet had called me earlier while I was in a meeting. I was on my way to Northwestern Memorial Hospital. I'll stay on the Drive since I'm near downtown, and I can hit the Dan Ryan from there. How is she doing?" Liz asked, as she signaled to move to the right lane.

"She's in a lot of pain. She fell down the stairs and hit her head. Liz, I thought I had lost her when I went inside the house and she was unconscious." Marcus's stomach knotted at the thought.

"The Lord took care of the situation, Marcus. She'll be fine. I know that in my heart. So are you going to take my place in the labor room?" she asked.

"Oh no, I'm not up for that. I really don't want to be here. I made sure she made it to the hospital, and I was thinking about going home," he explained.

"Marcus, please don't do that. Even if you can't go into the labor room with Monet, stay at the hospital. She'll feel so much better knowing that you're there," Liz pleaded.

Marcus became quiet. Then he said, "I guess I can do that. Hurry up, Liz. I know she needs you."

"I'll be there as soon as I can. Did you call Wade?"

Marcus said Wade was next on his list after he called Duane and Derek.

"Don't call Wade, I will. You call the twins and Mr. Reynolds, and I'll see you soon. Marcus, everything is going to be fine," she said.

"Thanks, Liz. I'll try to hold down the fort until you get here." Marcus told her good-bye, and then called Derek, but got his voice mail. When he called Duane, he said that he and his father would be at the hospital shortly. Marcus sighed with relief.

He had notified everyone he needed to, and now the waiting game would begin. He knew that Monet was strong enough to endure the labor by herself; he just hoped she would forgive him for not being there. He put an imaginary check mark on the growing list of things for which he needed to ask his wife's forgiveness.

He went back into the hospital and sat down in the waiting

area. He prayed Monet was faring well and nothing unforeseen happened to her or her child. *Lord, talk care of them*, he prayed over and over.

Chapter 31

Monet's contractions had diminished, and she was hoo-ked up to an IV with medication in it to strengthen her contractions. She dozed off, knowing that rest was needed for the hard labor that lay ahead. She dreamed of her mother, who was in the room with her, stroking her belly.

"Momma, you're here," she said joyously.

"You didn't think I'd leave my baby alone to have her baby, now did you?" Gayvelle smiled, and her dimple appeared in her left cheek. She hugged Monet's shoulders.

"Momma, so many things have happened to me, and still I've been blessed. First of all, Marcus left me. He still lives in our house, but he cut himself off from me. I almost couldn't bear it, but I knew I had to stay strong for my baby girl. Momma, her name is Faith Imani."

"I know, child," Gayvelle said as she stood next to Monet's bed. "I've been with you every step of the way. You and Faith will be just fine. The Lord has blessed you, and He will continue to keep you in His protection. I hope you've been talking to Faith and telling her about her unusual inheritance. I should have done that when I was pregnant with you, and I didn't." She sighed as she caressed her daughter's swollen midsection.

"Yes, Momma, I've been talking to her, singing to her, and trying to prepare her for what lies ahead. I love you, and I miss you so much. Thank for being here with me. Daddy's out of jail, and he's been staying with me. I love him, and he loves you and me. Did you know that?"

"Of course. Mothers know everything." Gayvelle winked at her daughter. "We had to wait for him to realize that. Don't be frightened little one, I'll be watching over you," she promised.

Monet whispered, "Momma." Then a contraction with the force of a Mack truck forced her awake." Her expression became staid. She sensed that Marcus wasn't going to share the childbirth experience with her, and she felt a momentary pang of sadness. Then she realized that she wasn't alone, God and her momma were with her, and if her intuition was correct, Liz should be at the hospital any minute.

As if on cue, Liz burst into the room energetically and walked over to Monet's bedside. "How are you feeling, honey? Marcus told me what happened. I can't leave you for a minute," she lovingly scolded. She was dressed in scrubs too.

"So what took you so long?" Monet mockingly rolled her eyes at her friend. "I thought I was going to have Faith by myself. What happened to all that support you talked about, girl?"

"You didn't tell me last night when I talked to you that you were having contractions, so I didn't know that my god baby was going to make her appearance today. How are you feeling? How far apart are your contractions, and have you been utilizing your breathing exercises?"

"Here comes another one." Monet began panting until the contraction passed. Her hair was matted against her head.

"Don't forget to take a deep cleansing breath when the contraction is over," Liz instructed, as she held tight to her friend's hand. Monet complied with her directive.

Dr. Riddell returned to the room. "How are we doing, Mother?"

"I think the contractions have sped up," Monet informed the doctor, after she relaxed against the pillows.

"I'll check. You had dilated five centimeters when you arrived here. Let's see where you are now."

Liz stepped away from the bed to give Monet and the doctor privacy. After the doctor finished the pelvic examination, she informed Monet, "You're almost nine centimeters. It won't be long now. Are you sure you don't want anything for the pain?"

Monet rocked back and forth as waves of pain rode her body. When she was able to talk, she told the doctor, "I'm good. I can do this without medication."

"Okay, I'll be back in a minute. You're aware the birth takes place in this room, so I'll send Nurse Murphy in to finish preparing the room." Monet nodded and Dr. Riddell left the room.

Liz walked back over to the bed. "Marcus is in the building. Do you want me to have him come up?"

"No, Lizzie, this is something I'll have to do on my own, along with you. I'm cool with it."

Liz smoothed back Monet's hair. "Okay, sister, let's do this." She looked at her watch and held Monet's hand. "We're almost there."

Nurse Murphy bustled about the room preparing for the birth and placing instruments on a silver tray near the end of the bed for the doctor. Monet's bed had been converted into a birthing table. The nurse pushed a stool across the room and positioned it at the bottom of the bed.

When Dr. Riddle returned to the room, Monet felt pain like she'd never endured before, and she wanted to push badly. Liz urged her to find her focal point and concentrate on it like they'd been instructed to do in Lamaze classes.

Nurse Murphy eased the stirrups up, and she and Liz helped Monet slide down to the edge of the table. Everyone was covered with gowns and masks, so only their eyes were showing.

"Okay, Monet, you can start pushing during the next contraction. The baby's heartbeat is steady, and I'm getting a good reading from the monitor. Okay, a contraction is coming, Monet. Go ahead and push," Dr. Riddell instructed, sitting on the stool.

"Another contraction is coming," Liz shouted elatedly. "Push, Monet!" she urged, and then winced because her hand felt like it was inside a vise from Monet squeezing it.

Monet's gown was damp. She looked tired and drained like she'd gone through a wringer. Perspiration coated her forehead, it was dripping, and her hair was matted to her head. As she pushed, the muscles from her neck bulged. She leaned against the pillows tiredly. Dr Riddell encouraged her to push again because the baby's head was crowning. Monet took a deep breath, reached deep within herself, and pushed with all her might.

Duane, Derek, and Aron were in the second floor waiting room, avidly awaiting word from Liz about the baby's arrival. Duane told Derek that he was glad he made it to the hospital in time.

Marcus and Wade were still on the first floor in the waiting room. Wade had talked Marcus out of leaving the hospital. Marcus had gotten out of his seat and paced the floor for what seemed like a thousand times. Finally he sat down in the seat next to Wade and tapped his foot on the tiled floor.

Wade leaned over to Marcus and said, "You know she's going to be fine, don't you?" It was almost comical to Wade to see his friend behaving like a nervous father-to-be. Wade felt good that Marcus was worried about his wife.

"Why is it taking so long?" Marcus complained. "You don't think anything happened to Monet, do you?"

"No, I don't think anything has happened to Monet. Childbirth is hard work, and babies seem to have a mind of their own as to when they're ready to face the world. Some of them take their time."

Marcus cut his eyes at Wade and his body quivered. His feet did another tap dance on the tiled floor.

"You know you could make this easy on yourself; we could go upstairs and see what's going on and not wait for Liz to call us. I don't think your folks are going to remember to come down here and give us the news. Liz will eventually. Still, it's going to take her awhile," Wade said.

"I feel like I've been here forever," Marcus commented. He drummed his fingers on the wooden arms on the chair.

"Why don't we go outside for a minute and get some air? Maybe by the time we return, there will be some news."

Marcus stood up and stretched his body. "That sounds good to me."

Wade rose from his seat and the two of them went outside.

"See how things worked out? You were so obstinate about how you wouldn't be at the hospital for the birth and here you are." Wade ribbed his friend.

"Yeah, yeah." Marcus held up his hands, shrugging off his friend's comment. He knew that Wade was going to have jokes.

They watched the cars pass by on Ninety-fifth Street. The temperature was mild, and the sun shone brightly from the azure sky. The wail from an oncoming ambulance could be heard in the distance, and soon the vehicle pulled up in front of the Emergency Room.

"You know that everything is going to work out just fine, don't you?" Wade asked, with a matter-of-fact tone in his voice.

"I don't know anything except I was suspended from active duty yesterday. I'm sure by now that you're aware of that. Then I go home this morning after turning in my gun to find Monet passed out on the stairs. So far this has been one of those days. Now, I'm here at the hospital waiting for the rapist's child to be born. What else could happen?" Marcus rubbed the area between his eyes.

"You've made it thus far by the grace of God. So count your blessings, Marc," Wade advised. "Trouble doesn't last always.

You'll look back on this day one day and see things differently," he promised.

"It won't be anytime soon," Marcus griped as he looked at his watch. "I guess we can go back inside."

They went back inside the hospital, and Wade suggested they go to the gift shop to purchase balloons and flowers for Monet. They walked down the hallway and took a left and walked inside the store. Wade picked up two balloons, a blue and green one with hearts and a baby lamb that had *Bundle Of Joy* written on it, and the other one was pink with bottles on it, and it read, *It's A Baby Girl*.

"Don't you think you're a bit premature with the girl balloon?" Marcus pointed at the Mylar balloon. "We don't know what Monet had yet."

"If Nay-Nay says that her baby is a girl, then I believe her," Wade answered steadfastly. "She's usually right about these things. Do you remember how she told Liz and me what sex our babies were, and she was right on the money?" Wade pulled out his wallet and handed the cashier his credit card.

Marcus's eyes roamed around the shop until they landed on a Blessed Baby Basket. Inside the basket, nestled in wrapping paper, was a teddy bear, a receiving blanket, bibs, a teething rings and lap pad. The items inside the basket were pink, blue and yellow, and the basket was encircled by a beautiful pink ribbon tied in a bow.

He knew Monet would love the basket, although she didn't need another item. The nursery was overflowing with gifts. He picked up the basket and swore he could smell the fresh scent of baby powder.

Wade smiled at Marcus as he held the basket clumsily in his hand. He knew God was melting his friend's heart, and that Marcus was returning to himself. "That looks nice. Are you thinking about buying that?"

Marcus put the basket in his other hand and paused indeci-
sively. "I guess so." He pulled out his credit card and told the
cashier, "I'd like a dozen red roses to go along with the basket."

Wade nodded his head. His cell phone vibrated in his jacket
pocket. He pulled the phone out and looked at the screen. "I got
a 411 from Liz. Monet has had the baby. Let's go upstairs and
see what's going on," he said.

Marcus took the basket from the cashier, and she told him
the flowers would be delivered to Monet's room shortly. "Sir,
what room should they be delivered to?"

"The patient's name is Monet Caldwell," he said.

"Okay, I can look her room number up on the computer,"
the cashier said as she began typing.

The men left the shop and weaved around bodies in the busy
hospital as they walked toward the elevator.

"What are you going to do, Marcus?" Wade asked, as he held
the balloons in his hand.

"Give me a few minutes, and then I'll be up," Marcus answered. His brow furrowed as he tried to control his emotions.

Wade patted Marcus on the shoulder with his free hand. "Okay,
but don't make me have to come looking for you." The elevator
door opened and Wade went inside.

Chapter 32

Wade hurried off the elevator on the second floor, walked down the hallway, and took a right turn. He stopped at the nurse's station and asked what room Monet was in. The nurse replied room 215, and gave him directions on which way to go.

Before he could turn the corner, he saw Liz walking toward him. She sped up her steps when she saw her husband.

"How is Monet doing? She had a girl like she said she would, didn't she?" Wade asked, as they walked toward Monet's room.

"Was there ever any doubt?" Liz asked. "Her name is Faith Imani, she weighed seven pounds and ten ounces, and she's twenty-two inches long. Mother and daughter are doing fine. Where's Marcus?" She looked behind her husband.

"I'm glad Monet didn't have any ill effects from the fall," Wade commented. "And Marcus said he'll be up later."

"I hope he will. If not, he's going to miss out," Liz said, beaming like she'd just given birth.

They walked inside the room to find Monet lying limply against the pillows, while her brothers and father admired the baby lying inside the crib sitting to the left of her bed.

Wade walked hastily to the crib, and baby Faith was as beautiful as he imagined she would be. Down gold hair covered her head, and she was fair skinned like the Reynoldses. She was lying on her side facing Monet's bed, and she yawned and opened her eyes. The orbs were hazel like her mother, grandfather, and uncle's eyes.

"She's a beauty," he murmured. "Marcus will have to fight the boys off.

"She looks just like Monet did when she was born," Aron said, with a lump in his throat. He knew how blessed he was to even be in the presence of his daughter, sons, and now, grand-daughter.

Wade walked over to Monet's bedside. "How are you feeling, Nay-Nay?" He took her hand and held it. "Good job."

"I'm tired, but a good tired. Thanks, Wade. It's a miracle. God is so good." She looked at the door. "Where's Marcus?"

"He's downstairs. He said he'll be up here shortly. The fact that he's even here is a miracle. I know he's going to come around, especially when he sees that little lady who looks so much like you," Wade said.

"I hope you're right." Monet smiled at Wade.

"You know, as much as she looks like you, I see Marcus in her. Faith has the shape of his eyes, nose, and she has thin lips just like his," Wade observed.

"I know," Monet agreed with Wade. "But that's not all. When Mr. Caldwell brings himself up here, I have something to show him."

"You did good, and God is so good," Wade said.

"Liz, would you bring my daughter here?" Monet asked. "Wow, it took me so long to be able to say those words. Thank you, Lord." She moved her body carefully and sat upright in the bed.

Liz took the baby from the crib, and holding the back of her head up, handed Faith to her mother. Duane pulled out his digital camera and took some pictures of mother and daughter.

A half an hour later, everyone decided to leave to give Monet time to get some rest. Liz put Faith back into the crib after her uncles, godparents, and grandfather took turns holding her.

A nurse's aide brought a couple of floral bouquets into the

room. Liz made a note of who had sent flowers so Monet could send thank-you notes.

"We'll be back later," Liz and Wade told Monet after they kissed her forehead. The Reynolds men promised to return later as well.

Monet looked at the dozen roses in a crystal vase. There wasn't a card with the flowers, but she knew they were from Marcus. He always bought her two dozen roses to celebrate an occasion. She looked at Faith again, and a smile as big as the Grand Canyon filled her face. She closed her eyes, "Father above, thank you for my greatest gift of all, Faith Imani Caldwell. Lord, you have answered my prayer, and I'm ever so grateful. I fell down the stairs this morning, and you protected me. You allowed me to have this baby without drugs, and both of us came through the labor like champs. I don't know what else to say except thank you, Father. I will take care of this child and raise her the way you would have me." She looked at her daughter one more time, then closed her eyes and went to sleep.

Thirty minutes later, Monet stirred. She looked up to see Marcus standing near the crib. He glanced at her and she feigned sleep. He walked over to the crib and just stared at the baby. Then he touched her tiny hand and Monet could hear him clearing his throat.

She opened her eyes and said to her husband, "Took you long enough."

He looked at her and smiled sheepishly. Then his gaze flew back to Faith.

"Don't be shy, pick her up," Monet urged.

"No, she's too little. I might drop her or something," he said.

"Marcus Caldwell, bring me that baby. You know I can't move well yet," Monet said seriously. Her heart was bursting with joy. God answered her prayers just like she knew He would.

Marcus carefully took Faith out of the crib. She opened her

eyes, and he swore that she smiled at him. He held a miniature version of Monet. His heart overflowed with love. He slowly walked the few steps to Monet's bed and handed her the baby.

He sat in the chair next to the bed. He wiped his brow and said, "Whew, I was scared I was going to drop her."

"Well, I wasn't," Monet quipped. "I knew you would do just fine."

"I guess I owe you an apology, Monet. I've been so wrong about so many things. It's a wonder God hasn't stopped me dead in my tracks." Marcus hung his head low.

"You were human and faced some difficult challenges. But none of that matters now," she said soothingly. She stroked Faith's face, and the baby looked up at her mother, blowing spit bubbles. Faith's tiny hands opened and closed.

"I should have been more understanding of what you were going through. All I can say is please forgive me. And if it takes the rest of my life, I promise to make it up to you; all the torture I put you through. When I look back on these past nine months, it's like I was in a daze, I acted mean and evil. I looked in the mirror at myself while I was shaving this morning, and I didn't like what I saw. You've shown me nothing but love the entire time we've been married, and I couldn't be there for you when you needed me because of my stupid pride. I'm so ashamed." Marcus's voice choked up.

"I never gave up on you, love, and I never will. We took vows that said we'd love each other through sickness and health, good times and bad. I will always love you, Marcus Caldwell, forever and a day."

"I'm so undeserving of your love." He pursed his lips together. "I messed up. Wade and Reverend Wilcox told me it didn't matter who fathered your child, because part of that child is you, and they were right. It took me a long time to see what they were talking about. I get it now. And when I visited the jail today—"

"Marcus," Monet interrupted him. "I know what happened. We can talk about that later. This is a happy, blessed occasion, and I just want to savor the moment." She shifted the baby from one arm to the other.

"No, let me finish. We can talk about what happened at Dwight later. I promise to love and care for Faith as if she were my own child. I swear to that from the bottom of my heart." He put his hand on his chest.

Monet smiled impishly at her husband, and moved over in the bed and laid Faith on top of the sheet. Then she pulled the booty off her tiny foot. "Look, Marcus," she said, as Faith's left foot danced in the air.

On the bottom of the baby's foot was a birthmark. Marcus looked at it and reached down and took off his shoe and sock from his left foot. He looked at the cherry colored mark on Faith's foot, and the matching one on his own foot. Marcus covered his eyes and sobbed guttural sobs that resonated through his body. Monet knew he had to cry and let it out so that the healing could begin.

He raised his tear streaked face and said to Monet, "Oh God, I asked you to kill our baby. Thank God, you didn't." He covered his face with his hands.

Monet patted the other side of her bed. "Come sit here," she said.

Marcus stood up, and his legs felt weak. He felt vanquished at the enormity of what he had asked Monet to do. He sat on the other side of the bed, and Monet picked up the baby and held her as Marcus's arm snaked around her shoulders.

"Do you see this little tiny mouth, nose, and the shape of her eyes? She may look like me, but those features scream Daddy. They are yours, love. God has never failed me yet, and when He told me I would have a child, I believed Him. I just had to wait for you to see the light." Monet winked at her husband. "We will be just fine. The two people I love most, after God, are in this room with me. We made it, Marcus, with God's help. Praise God, we made it."

Mother, father, and daughter sat in the bed huddled close to each other and savored the moment.

When Monet and Faith had fallen asleep, Marcus sat in the chair next to Monet's bed, looked upward, and said, "Thank you, God. Please forgive me for all my sins."

Epilogue

Two months later, at the conclusion of the morning service at the Temple, Monet, Marcus, Liz, and Wade stood at the altar as Reverend Wilcox christened Faith. The baby looked like a little princess clothed in her christening outfit. Aron, Duane, and Derek stood behind the parents and godparents as a show of love and support.

Aron was standing next to Derek. Father and son smiled at each other guardedly. They were working on mending their relationship. By the time Marcus and Monet brought Faith home from the hospital, Duane informed his twin that Aron was moving into their basement apartment. Duane explained that Monet and Marcus needed time to heal as husband and wife and bond with their newborn daughter. Derek knew his brother was correct and had no choice but to agree to his brother's demand that he allow their father to move into the twins' house. Aron and Derek returned their attention to the front of the church.

Reverend Wilcox prayed, "Father, we come today to give this child back to you. Help her parents stay strong and vigilant as they raise her in the turbulent world we inhabit. Lord, we give thanks for the miracle that is Faith Imani Caldwell. We dedicate her life to you. As the song goes, you made a way out of no way, Monet kept the faith, and in turn, she birthed Faith. Lord, her parents, godparents, grandfather, and uncles, along with our entire church, promise to raise this child in a Christian way that will be pleasing in your sight. Give her parents wisdom and plenty of patience." The church chuckled as Faith cooed loudly when Reverend Wilcox said plenty of patience.

Then Reverend Wilcox held the baby up toward the audience and said, "Church, I'd like to introduce you to our newest member of Jubilee Temple Baptist Church, little Miss Faith Imani Caldwell. Let the church say Amen."

The church stood and clapped, and yelled, "Amen!"

Reverend Wilcox handed Faith to her father, whose smile was so wide that one would have thought he'd won the lottery. Then Monet, Marcus, Liz, Wade, Aron, Duane, and Derek returned to their seats.

Monet heard a voice from above tell her, "*You're not done yet, my daughter. You will bear twins boys.*"

"Goodness gracious," she said aloud.

"What did you say? What's up?" Marcus asked her, as he put Faith on his shoulder.

"We'll talk later," Monet promised, as they stood for the benediction.

After reciting the benediction, the church members swarmed around Marcus and Monet as if they were celebrities. The sun beamed brightly through the stained glass windows, while well wishes rained down on baby Faith.

Monet's creed became; *Faith is the substance of things hoped for, the evidence of things not seen.* And for the remainder of her life, Monet urged people to never give up hope because for those who call on Him, God does answer prayer.

Discussion Questions

1. Monet has a talent her family called the gift; do you believe people have intuitive abilities?

2. How well would you say Marcus coped with his life changes under the circumstances?

3. Was Marcus justified in giving Monet an ultimatum to terminate the pregnancy?

4. Do you feel Monet could have been more understanding of Marcus's issues or were her responses valid?

5. Was Wade too preachy to Marcus? Should he have been less spiritual and more realistic toward his friend's plight?

6. Should police officers be allowed to investigate crimes against their families? Or are they too close to the situation?

7. Did Aron seem to be sincere about wanting forgiveness from his children and to be a part of their lives?

8. Should Monet's doctor have mentioned abortion as an option to Monet?

Discussion Questions

9. Which character did you relate to or enjoy the most?

10. Should Monet's mother have given her children the letters from their father sooner? Was she correct in determining the best time to give the letters to her children?

11. Which people were more supportive to Monet and Marcus during their dilemma?

12. Do you feel Marcus lost faith in God after the misfortunes that befell his family?

13. Is there anything else Monet could have done to persuade Marcus that he was Faith's father?

14. Who was your least favorite character?

15. Did you feel it creditable or disturbing that Marcus cried several times during the story in the face of adversity?

Urban Christian His Glory Book Club!

Established in January 2007, **UC His Glory Book Club** is another way to introduce **Urban Christian** and its authors. We are an online book club supporting Urban Christian authors by purchasing, reading, and providing written reviews of the authors' books. *UC His Glory Book Club* welcomes both men and women of the literary world who have a passion for reading Christian-based fiction.

UC His Glory Book Club is the brainchild of Joylynn Jossel, author and Executive Editor of Urban Christian and Kendra Norman-Bellamy, author and copy editor for Urban Christian. The book club will provide support, positive feedback, encouragement, and a forum whereby members can openly discuss and review the literary works of Urban Christian authors. In the future, we anticipate broadening our spectrum of services to include online author chats, author spotlights, interviews with your favorite Urban Christian author(s), special online groups for *UC His Glory Book Club* members, ability to post reviews on the website and amazon.com, membership ID cards, *UC His Glory* Yahoo! Group and much more.

Even though there will be no membership fees attached to becoming a member of *UC His Glory Book Club,* we do expect our members to be active, committed, and to follow the guidelines of the book club.

UC His Glory Book Club members pledge to:

• Follow the guidelines of *UC His Glory Book Club.*
• Provide input, opinions, and reviews that build up, rather than tear down.
• Commit to purchasing, reading, and discussing featured book(s) of the month.
• Respect the Christian beliefs of *UC His Glory Book Club.*
• Believe that Jesus is the Christ, Son of the Living God.

We look forward to the online fellowship.

Many Blessings to You!

Shelia E. Lipsey
President
UC His Glory Book Club

Visit the official Urban Christian His Glory Book Club website at **www.uchisglorybookclub.net